P R

RICH AND THE DEAD

"Refreshing and intelligent, *The Rich and the Dead* is a fine-tuned, fast-paced thriller by a new name in the game. Be careful taking this début book with you on the train. You just might miss your stop. Totally absorbing." —*New York Journal of Books*

"Spector's debut establishes an engaging, time-traveling heroine." —*Kirkus Reviews*

"Time travel, glitz, and a colorful cast of characters collide in what is surely the most inventive whodunit of the year!" —*New York Times* bestselling author Wendy Corsi Staub

"Exciting debut . . . well-crafted thriller." —*Publishers Weekly*

"The combination of mystery, evil, glamor, and light science fiction makes for an engrossing series debut." —*Booklist*

THE
BEAUTIFUL
AND THE
WICKED

A LILA DAY
NOVEL

Liv Spector

wm

WILLIAM MORROW
An Imprint of HarperCollinsPublishers

THE BEAUTIFUL AND THE WICKED. Copyright © 2014 by Alloy Entertainment, LLC. All rights reserved. Printed in the United States of America. No part of this book may be used or reproduced in any manner whatsoever without written permission except in the case of brief quotations embodied in critical articles and reviews. For information address HarperCollins Publishers, 195 Broadway, New York, NY 10007.

HarperCollins books may be purchased for educational, business, or sales promotional use. For information please e-mail the Special Markets Department at SPsales@harpercollins.com.

alloy**entertainment**

PRODUCED BY ALLOY ENTERTAINMENT, LLC
1700 BROADWAY, 4TH FLOOR, NEW YORK, NY 10019

Designed by Diahann Sturge

Library of Congress Cataloging-in-Publication Data has been applied for.

ISBN 978-0-06-225848-9

14 15 16 17 18   OV/RRD   10 9 8 7 6 5 4 3 2 1

For my sister

ACKNOWLEDGMENTS

AN ENORMOUS THANKS to Katie McGee, May Chen, and Joelle Hobeika, for their artful and indispensable editing, insight, guidance, and good cheer every step of the way.

I would also like to thank:

My father, for encouraging me to follow my passions.

My sister, for being my best friend from the moment I entered the world.

My mother, for continually opening my eyes to life's beauty, magic, and wildness.

My beloved friends David Aaron Bell, Sonia Verma, Jeff Oliver, Ayla Teitelbaum, Corey Kohn, and Sarah Browder. I feel so lucky to have you all in my life.

Anna Carey, CJ Hauser, Cristina Moracho, and Marie Bertino, whose brilliance and dedication to the craft of writing always leave me awestruck and inspired.

Tim Foy, a man who makes any old black-and-white day turn Technicolor. Thank you for making my life more magnificent than I could have imagined.

"Man is not what he thinks he is, he is what he hides."
—André Malraux

PROLOGUE

IT'S AN UNFORTUNATE fact of life that the more you have, the more you want. That's just how appetites work. Excess leads to insatiability. And whatever is true for humankind is writ large for the filthy rich. After all, it's not hard to see that the wealthy are ravenous.

Just listen closely to the idle chatter buzzing about the charity balls, the art-fair parties, and the gala benefits, which are the jet set's lifeblood. Beneath the casual flirting, the backstabbing, the grandstanding, and the posturing, what everyone is *really* talking about can be boiled down to one central question: who has more? Be it money, companies, sex, homes, horses, serenity, charity, love—whatever it is doesn't matter. Everything can be quantified. Everything can be bought.

And no one had more of everything than Jack Warren. He made sure of it.

A rags-to-riches Silicon Valley billionaire several times over, Jack was both envied and reviled. He'd been called a tech genius, a megalomaniac, a messiah, and a monster, depending on whom you asked. But, be he savior, Satan, or sadist, he was above all viciously competitive. Whatever he put his energies toward, he made sure *his* was the best in the world—no matter the cost.

This relentlessness wasn't always charming. He was known by everyone, but loved by very, very few. But Jack didn't mind the bad feelings—indeed, he thrived on them. To him, every new enemy was a mark of distinction, for he deeply believed that great men must have a great number of adversaries. And he didn't become the sixth richest man in the world by playing nice.

So, when the rumors began to circulate that Jack was turning his exacting attentions toward building a luxury yacht, everyone was anxious for details. How much would it cost? How big would it be? How could they get an invite? The two most interested parties were one Russian oligarch and a certain Middle Eastern emir who had spent the last decade waging a quiet two-man war over who could build the largest super-yacht imaginable. They weren't excited to find out that Jack was crashing their private skirmish.

But they had no reason to worry. Size didn't matter for Jack. That was a concern for men who were small of mind (and small in other departments, Jack would add with a wink). Let the Russian and the Saudi battle over whose behemoth was bigger. He was on a different quest—a quest for audacious beauty. It would take six years, $500 million, and hundreds of artisans, designers, builders, and craftsmen to make Jack Warren's dream a reality, but as always, he did what he set out to do. He built the most exquisite yacht the world had ever known: *The Rising Tide*.

In the early fall of 2008, the 423-foot yacht set off on its maiden voyage. With its interiors designed by Philippe Starck, accented with lavish Baccarat crystal tables, stingray-skin-upholstered walls, hand-stitched leather paneling, a helicopter pad, a swimming pool, a spa, and a three-thousand-square-foot master suite with a retractable moonroof for stargazing, it was the most luxurious thing anyone had ever seen.

But among all the endless speculation about the boat, what no one could have guessed was that this pinnacle of luxury would be the very site of Jack Warren's bloody murder. On a warm September night in 2008—during a celebration for Jack's fiftieth birthday—as his guests drank Dom Pérignon under a canopy of stars far out in the Caribbean Sea, Jack would finally meet a rival he couldn't best: death.

CHAPTER 1

LILA DAY WAS plunged out of darkness into a blinding, prismatic light. She shut her eyes against the glare. Wild flashes of color danced and darted behind her eyelids. A searing pain sliced through her fingers before she realized it was from the death grip she had on the arms of the leather chair beneath her. Her breath was shallow, struggling. Her lungs burned. A deafening whir ripped through her eardrums. She opened her eyes, trying to locate the source of the metallic screech. Everything erratically illuminated, then darkened. Her eyes darted around this strange space. It was an egg-shaped pod of sorts, about the height and width of an elevator.

Where am I? she wondered.

A small screen flickered to life before her blinking eyes, causing her nearly to jump out of her skin. The high-pitched noise suddenly stopped, replaced by a silence more frightening than the commotion that had preceded it. Now all she could hear was the sound of her own shallow breath.

A man with an angular face and light brown eyes came into view on the screen. Lila could tell he was looking directly at her. His face was serious, searching.

"Breathe, Lila," the man said. "Breathe."

Lila? Her own name sounded unfamiliar to her. The man looked worried, making Lila feel even more anxious.

A whoosh of air blew her long hair back. She looked up to see a large door opening outward, revealing a thin crack of golden light in the ceiling above her. The sudden change in pressure made her ears pop painfully.

"Lila?" the man said, studying her. "Are you okay?"

"I'm okay?" she croaked, realizing it was more of a question than an answer. Her own voice sounded strange.

The man turned away, talking to someone else offscreen. She strained to hear what they were saying, unable to make out a word.

Another man's face came into view, filling the entirety of the screen. He was much older than the first man, probably in his seventies. His broad shoulders were encased in a dark wool suit. Tufts of white hair peeked out from under a black chauffeur's cap, which was pulled low on his head.

"Your name is Lila Day," he said firmly. He had a crisp English accent. "You have returned from the year 1998. You are back in the year 2019. Do you understand me?"

She wondered if she was dreaming.

The man continued to speak calmly, as if he were gently waking her up from a hypnotic trance. "You are experiencing a brief period of readjustment. Focus on your breathing. Nod if you understand."

Lila nodded.

The small crack in the ceiling above her yawned wider as the giant door slowly opened like a single petal peeling apart from a flower bud. Cold air rushed to greet her. Her lungs drank it in. Goose bumps sprang up on her chilled skin. As the door lowered outward, down to the ground, she could see that her little cocoon sat in a much larger room, every inch of which was covered in gold foil. She leaned forward, hoping to see more, but a harness around her waist restrained her. When she craned her neck, she saw that the outside of the pod was constructed out of panels of highly polished green stone—jade or emerald, most likely. Her brain struggled to digest the incomprehensible reality of the scene.

Once the door opened completely, a metal staircase unfurled, giving her passage from the pod to the world outside. She undid the harness and started to stand up, eager to escape, but her legs were weak and buckled beneath her. She collapsed back into the chair.

The younger man came back on the screen. "Don't try to move," he said. "I'm coming to you." Then he disappeared.

Lila struggled to stand once more, but it was no use. She felt like a helpless rag doll.

Seconds later, the man she'd seen on the screen materialized before her, climbing up the stairs into the pod. Something about him instantly calmed her nerves. She had an innate understanding that he was there to help. The moment he put his hand on her shaking arm, his familiar touch unlocked something in her brain.

"Teddy?" she said, suddenly realizing who he was. The man looked at her. A flash of relief and excitement flickered across his face.

"You know who I am?" he asked cautiously.

Lila nodded. She saw the heaviness of his worry drop away as if he'd just shrugged off a cumbersome coat. He wrapped his arm around her back and hoisted her up. "You gave me quite a scare for a second," he said, with a relieved smile. She felt his warm breath on her face. She closed her eyes, taking in his now-familiar scent and touch.

With each step down the industrial steel staircase, Lila's memories began to unlock. What had felt foreign a mere second ago suddenly became familiar. Once again she remembered who she was, where she was, and what she was doing—though the truth of it all was still strange. She was Lila Day, in the home of her friend and patron, the billionaire Teddy Hawkins, returning from the past after hunting down a wanted killer.

As the disparate puzzle pieces of her story began to cohere into a recognizable self, Lila's brief moment of forgetting was forgotten.

Teddy placed her down in a straight-backed chair, in a room full of blinking and buzzing computers. The control room. She sat facing the jade geodesic dome from which she'd just emerged. It was a wonder to behold, Teddy's most brilliant creation—a machine that could travel through time. She closed her eyes, listening to the beep and click of all the machines surrounding her. She'd spent countless hours in this very room with Teddy and his right-hand man, Conrad, the distinguished gentleman in the chauffeur's cap she'd seen earlier onscreen. And it was Conrad who approached her now, putting a thermometer into her ear and clamping a pulse reader over the tip of her index finger.

"I hate to say it, but it seems the transient global amnesia is back," Teddy said to Conrad. Conrad nodded, prepping Lila for a few rounds of full-body scans and neuroimaging.

"Her vitals are weaker than I'd like," Conrad said.

"Don't fuss over me like a couple of mother hens. I'm fine," Lila slurred as she struggled to stay awake. She could barely keep her eyes open, and her head nodded to her chest. Conrad wrapped her up in a Mylar blanket, which crinkled as he tucked the silver sheet around the contours of her body.

"We need to bring your body temperature up," he said.

"I'm just going to close my eyes for one second," Lila murmured. She heard Teddy agree gently. "Of course. Rest."

Before the greedy hands of sleep pulled her down into the darkness, Lila raised her head and looked Teddy in the eye. "I got him. I know who the killer is," she managed.

"I wouldn't doubt it for a second," Teddy said with a comforting smile. But Lila could see from the way he was tensing his jaw that there was something else on his mind.

Slowly and with great physical effort, she wrestled a thumb drive from the depths of her jeans pocket, holding it out toward Teddy. "It's all here. All the evidence the police need." She tried to toss it to him, but couldn't summon any strength. The thumb drive slipped from her enervated hands and made a hollow clank as it fell to the floor.

"Great," Teddy said, bending down to scoop it up. "We'll go into it all soon enough. First, you should relax."

But before he had finished speaking, Lila was asleep.

WHEN SHE STARTLED awake, she saw she was no longer in the subterranean confines of Teddy's elaborate laboratory. She'd been moved to a chaise longue beneath a large umbrella in the shadow of Teddy's estate on La Gorce Island, the hyperexclusive, hyperprivate Miami Beach enclave. She could hear the waters of Biscayne Bay serenely lapping against the seawall just a couple hundred feet from where she lay. The high, midday sun bleached out the lush landscape surrounding her.

She sat up groggily, shielding her eyes and looking around the vast manicured estate. She was all alone. Then she heard the telltale splash of water coming from the direction of the pool. Of course, she thought with a smile, he's swimming. It was something Teddy could do in a seemingly endless loop, back and forth, for hours.

She walked along the soft grass to the edge of the long, slate-gray pool that bisected the villa's perfectly manicured lawn, pleased to feel that her strength had mostly returned. Teddy's lithe form cut through the water elegantly, but ferociously. She could tell from the intense effort and concentration of his movements that he was blowing off steam. A bit of concern crept into her thoughts. Something was wrong.

Once Teddy noticed Lila, he pulled up short, hauling himself out of the water effortlessly. Conrad appeared as if by magic, holding out a fresh, white robe.

"Thanks," Teddy said to Conrad with a nod, wrapping himself up in the terrycloth robe, which sported his initials monogrammed over the heart. Lila's gaze was absentmindedly focused on the two crescent-shaped indentations that Teddy's swim goggles left below his eyes. It took a moment before she realized those eyes were now staring directly at her.

"Lila?" Teddy said, waving his hand in front of her face. "Are you okay? You seem pretty out of it."

"I do?" she asked dreamily. Conrad and Teddy were giving her that concerned look again. "What?" she asked. "I'm fine. Totally fine. Just . . . yeah," she admitted. "Maybe a little out of it."

Teddy paused, giving her a sideways glance. It was the fifth time she'd traveled back from the past, and each go-round left her a bit more dazed than the last, but it wasn't a big deal. Nothing a few stiff drinks wouldn't cure.

"Let's sit," Teddy said, pointing to a cluster of furniture huddled beneath a saffron-colored cloth canopy. "We've got a lot of catching up to do."

"What's wrong?" she asked as they sat.

"Wrong?"

"I know you, Teddy. Something's on your mind. So you might as well spit it out." Lila paused, watching him carefully. "If you're worried about me, then don't be. I'm fine." But Lila's halfhearted reassurances did nothing. Teddy remained silent, preoccupied. She continued, "I got a little more knocked around coming back this time. No big deal. It's worth it, trust me. I'd suffer so much more to catch the Key West killer. I mean, that guy was sick beyond repair. A real—"

"Yes. Yes," he said, cutting her off. Lila felt a prickle of irritation. She hated being interrupted. "I had Conrad drop off your evidence at the police station for Detective Bellilo, just as we planned. I suspect they'll make an arrest within the next couple of days. You did excellent work, Lila. Excellent." He took a deep breath, like he was trying to build up his courage. "I'm just glad you're okay. And I know you need to rest, but I've got something to tell you. I don't think it can wait." He looked out to the ocean, his eyes following a kite surfer who was sailing twenty feet high in the cloudless azure skies.

"What is it?" Lila asked impatiently. Teddy usually wasn't one to shy away from difficult conversations.

"Something big happened when you were in the past." Teddy kept his eyes out on the ocean.

"How long was I gone?" Lila asked. She'd spent four weeks in 1998, but the present moved at a glacial pace compared to the time in the past. She had no idea how much of 2019 she'd missed.

"Not long. A little under two days. Forty-seven hours, thirty-eight minutes, and five seconds, to be precise."

Just then, Conrad arrived carrying a large silver serving tray loaded with countless treats. Lila saw lobster tails, a bowl of caviar chilled over crushed ice, cucumber sandwiches, and slices of mango. As always with Teddy, it was a magnificent spread, but she was desperate to know what he had to say. Food was the furthest thing from her mind.

"Wild Turkey for you," Conrad said to Lila, setting a crystal whiskey glass in front of her filled with one perfectly round ice cube submerged in her regular booze of choice.

"You're an angel, Conrad," Lila said, keeping her eyes on Teddy, who looked momentarily relieved by this brief interruption.

"And a gin martini for you, sir."

"Cheers, Conrad." Teddy immediately wrapped his fingers around the glass's elongated stem and threw half the drink back. He breathed a deep sigh, then nodded at Conrad, who wordlessly returned to the main house. Teddy leaned over and took Lila's hand in his, looking her squarely in the face. "I've got something to tell you, but I want you to promise me that you'll stay calm."

A nervous laugh burst from Lila's lips. How could she ever hope to stay calm when he was acting like this? "Just spit it out," she said, feeling her pulse begin to increase.

Teddy nodded. Then he downed the rest of his drink, still clearly stalling. "Enrique Herrera was found dead yesterday morning," he said slowly.

Lila suddenly grew cold, despite the fact that she was baking in the hot Miami sunshine. "What from?" Her voice was flat. Serious.

"Gunshot to the head."

"Why didn't you tell me earlier?" She scrambled to her feet. She didn't know where she was headed, but she had an overwhelming need to go . . . she'd figure out where in a second.

"When was I supposed to tell you? While you were *passed out*? Lila, a couple hours ago you didn't even know where you were. *Who* you were! I thought it would be better for you to catch your breath before you shot off again." He sighed. "I knew you'd react this way. Ready to leap before knowing where you'll land."

She shook her head. Teddy should know better than to try to control her. Avoiding his gaze, she focused on the ice under the untouched caviar, watching it as it slowly turned to water.

"What are the police saying?" she asked.

"That it's suicide. The maid found him in his bedroom with the back of his skull blown off and a smoking gun in his hand."

"Suicide! That's bullshit," she spat. She was growing angrier by the second. Her nerves were electric. "You and I both know he didn't kill himself."

"Let's not jump to conclusions, Lila. You don't know what happened." Teddy gave her a nervous look.

"I know *exactly* what happened. His wife killed him," she said defiantly.

"Elise Warren? You don't know that, Lila." He regarded her warily.

"Like hell I don't!"

Teddy and Lila had known each other for a little over a year, and in that time he'd seen how her obsessions could get the better of her. And there was nothing Lila was more obsessed with than Elise Warren.

Lila's mind was racing. She said, "She's done it before, Teddy. Twice. And she got away with it . . . twice. Two husbands dead. Are you trying to tell me she didn't off the third?" Lila had spent whatever spare time she had over the last ten years trying to prove that Elise Warren was guilty of murder in the first degree, and now, finally with Elise's latest husband dead on the ground missing half his skull, she had a shot at making a murder rap stick.

Teddy gave her a skeptical look. "This is exactly what I was worried out. I knew you'd think it was Elise. But sit down. Let's talk things through . . . together."

"Not a chance in hell. If Elise is guilty, and I can guarantee she is, she's already using her money and connections to dig her way out of this mess. And I've got to catch her before it's too late."

Before Teddy could say anything, Lila was already halfway across the lawn. She knew this was her chance for justice, and she had to take it. Finally.

Lila *knew* for certain Elise was guilty—because ten years ago, she'd offed her first husband, Jack Warren.

And Lila's sister had taken the blame.

CHAPTER 2

"I CAN'T TELL you much about the Herrera case, but I'll say it doesn't look good for Elise."

That was music to Lila's ears. She was on the phone with Mitch Kessler, an old buddy of hers from back when she worked homicide for the Miami PD.

"But officially they're still sticking to the suicide story?" Lila asked.

"Sure are. But from what I heard, it looks like there might've been some tampering with the crime scene. And all fingers point to Elise. Plus, the forensics report came in and there was zero gunpowder residue found on Herrera's hand. The whole thing stinks to high heaven."

Lila had to stop herself from laughing out loud. "Sounds pretty unlikely, right? That a guy can shoot himself without getting any gunpowder on his hand?" It couldn't get any better than this. It looked, finally, like Elise was going to get what was coming to her.

"Exactly. Anyway, she's here getting questioned now."

"I'm on my way."

Lila drove her silver Karmann Ghia toward the police headquarters as fast as she could. She turned west on a causeway that sliced low across the turquoise shimmering of Biscayne Bay, the warm winds swirling around her, making thick swaths of her long, black hair dance like marionettes held aloft by invisible strings.

"Listen," Kessler was saying, "just be sure to keep my name out of this. If anyone found out I was giving you information about the case, they'd have my ass."

"You've got my word," Lila said.

"Maybe you'll finally get her this time, Lila. I sure as hell hope you do."

Around the Miami Police Department, it was a well-known fact that Lila Day had it in for Elise Warren—and no one could really blame her.

ON SEPTEMBER 11, 2008, at 2:20 A.M., the captain of *The Rising Tide* radioed the U.S. Coast Guard from the middle of the Caribbean Sea, 154 nautical miles northeast of Cuba. He was calling for help. "Mayday, Mayday, Mayday. This is Captain Robert Nash on *The Rising Tide*. We are 23 degrees 10 minutes north. 79 degrees 21 minutes west. A passenger has been shot. Possibly fatally. And is now overboard. I repeat, Jack Warren has been shot and is overboard. Armed suspect still at large. This is *The Rising Tide*. We are requesting immediate assistance. Over."

Lila knew the recording by heart, as did most of the world thanks to the intense media coverage following Jack Warren's death. TV stations and radio programs would play the Mayday call in a seemingly never-ending loop. Over and over again, they'd play the captain's slow and shaky voice stuttering out those now infamous words. His every gasping breath serving as proof that he knew just how bad it was to have one of the world's most powerful men die on his watch.

An hour after the distress call was made, when the coast guard boarded the yacht, all that was left of Jack was a thick, viscous pool of his blood. Four bullet casings and a snub-nosed .38 were also recovered from the scene of the crime. The ship's captain confirmed that there were ten guests and fifteen crew on board when the yacht left Miami on the seventh of September, four days prior to the murder. When *The Rising Tide* was searched, everyone was accounted for. Except for Jack, of course—and Ava Day, a twenty-six-year-old landscape painter from Miami who just happened to be Jack's latest in a long series of mistresses.

The bloody event occurred during Jack's fiftieth birthday party. According to the police report, first responders noted that every person interviewed, be they passengers or crew, was either in a heavy state of intoxication or just sobering up from a heavy state of intoxication. Images from the crime scene showed a wild post-bacchanalian spectacle: booze bottles were littered all over the main deck, furniture was splintered, up-ended, or overturned, dirty mirrors with traces of cocaine were found in several guest cabins. And there were unsubstantiated rumors that several members of the crew had ingested LSD on the night of the murder. But despite the impaired states of everyone on board, their stories matched in several key areas: five people heard a man and woman arguing, followed by several gunshots. One passenger saw Jack's lifeless body fall overboard, hit the water, and sink down into the choppy seas on that moonless September night. And everyone verified that Ava Day, Jack's mistress, had been on board. The fact that Jack had invited his girlfriend on a cruise along with his wife and their only child was something police investigators chalked up to an eccentricity of the upper class.

"Rich people," they muttered, between interviews of the hungover or soon-to-be-hungover passengers. "They're not just like us."

Jack's wife, Elise, who the police report noted went from being cooperative to agitated during her interview, stated that she'd seen Ava flee the scene in a dinghy. "That whore murdered my husband!" she yelled. "With any luck she'll drown at sea!"

The police searched the waters for both Ava and Jack for days, but came up empty-handed. All that was found was the fifteen-foot inflatable boat, which Elise identified as Ava's escape vehicle. It was discovered capsized and drifting a couple miles offshore of a small Cuban fishing village. Ava was nowhere to be found, but forensics confirmed that her fingerprints were all over the interior of the boat.

After the prints found on the boat were linked to those found on the murder weapon, the commandant of the U.S. Coast Guard held a press conference naming Ava Day as the primary suspect in the murder of Jack Warren. "The suspect remains at large, but we will use every air and sea craft available to search for Ms. Ava Day. And our search for the remains of the victim, Jack Warren, is ongoing."

When Warren's body was never recovered, he was officially declared lost at sea.

The gory and sensational murder of the fifty-year-old tech titan by his lover shocked the world. Every news site and gossip rag was scrambling for details, desperate to know everything about this gun-wielding mistress who had murdered one of the world's Great Men. And as Ava was publicly vilified, picked apart, and condemned by public opinion, Jack was being canonized.

His good friend and golf buddy President George W. Bush released a statement: "The world lost one of its greatest visionaries today. A heartbreaking tragedy." The Beach Boys announced they were going to write an album-length opera-bio about Jack. And Sean P. Diddy Combs, who was a frequent guest on *The Rising Tide,* tweeted, "RIP to my homie Jack."

Jack's face graced the cover of every newspaper and magazine around the world. On cable news shows, talking heads pontificated somberly about how the loss of such a genius would negatively impact the development of global culture. Mourners left tokens of remembrance and flowers at the gates of the Silicone Valley campus of Jack's multitrillion-dollar company, Warren Software. It might seem strange that all this outpouring of sentiment was for a man uniformly believed to be an egomaniacal narcissist whose relentlessness and deep political conservatism often put him on the opposite side of the good guy. But nothing, it seemed, rehabilitated a toxic public image better than being murdered.

Lila and her mom found out about Jack's death when police came banging on her mom's door in the middle of night, looking for Ava. Lila was twenty then, and still living at home. The news that Ava was romantically involved with the world-famous Jack Warren came as a complete shock to both Lila and her mother. But no surprise touched the out-of-body bewilderment they felt when the police told them Ava was wanted for his murder. Slack-jawed and blindsided, the two women stood holding each other, pajama-clad and barefoot in their kitchen, weeping for Ava, as the police barged in, tossed things around, treated them roughly, accused them of lying, and threatened them with jail time for aiding a fugitive.

Lila never doubted her sister's innocence for one second.

How could the kindhearted, sensitive sister she knew be the violent and volatile temptress the police and newspapers were talking about? But the world had made up its mind. And leading the charge was Elise Warren, the former-model-turned-failed-TV-actress who took to the role of sad and vengeful widow like she'd been waiting to play it her whole life. The woman whom the tabloids had previously painted as an ambitious gold digger was transformed overnight into a beautiful victim of lust and betrayal. There was a sympathetic *Vanity Fair* profile, and continual TV appearances with Elise demanding the capture of Ava Day for the murder of her beloved soul mate. She even put up a $25 million reward for anyone who provided information leading to the capture of Ava. In Elise's hands, Jack's death became a three-ring circus, with her as the ringmaster. And with every maudlin and self-serving interview Elise gave calling for Ava's arrest, Lila hated the woman even more.

Amid the storm, Lila felt utterly helpless. And she hated that feeling. So a few months after her sister's disappearance, she enrolled in the Miami Police Academy, hoping that becoming a cop would be the best way to fight for her sister—to fight for every person unjustly accused of a crime.

As Lila worked her way up from a lowly beat cop to one of the most respected homicide detectives in all of Miami, she always kept tabs on Elise. She watched as Elise remarried the Austrian financier Helmut Stadtlander while police were still hunting for Ava. When Stadtlander tumbled down an alpine cliff to his death, on their *honeymoon,* Lila was sure that Elise would be charged with his murder. But nothing happened.

Now, with Elise's third husband, Enrique Herrera, suspiciously dead, things would surely be different. In a little over a decade, Elise had buried three husbands—and in the process, become one of the richest women in the world. But Lila was set on making sure that luck had finally run out for Elise.

BY THE TIME Lila got to the Miami police station, she was so anxious to see Elise in handcuffs that she practically bounded up the station stairs. The first to greet her was Sergeant Corey Kreps, as always. Forty years of police work under his belt and a weakness for Irish whiskey had left Kreps unfit for almost all law enforcement work, so the higher-ups stuck him behind the bulletproof glass of the station's front desk, where he could do little harm to himself or others.

"Hey, sweetheart," he called out to her. "Looking as gorgeous as ever."

"Same to you, Kreps."

"Oh, you know. I try to stay pretty for my suitors," he said as his rheumy eyes twinkled and his yellow-toothed smile shined brightly. "And what brings you down to this shit hole?"

"Got word that Elise Warren was going to make an appearance downtown." She grinned. "I couldn't resist seeing it in person."

"That's my Lila," Kreps said with a loud slap of his hand on his meaty thigh. "Still after the Warren broad, huh? Like a dog with a goddamn bone. But I've got bad news for you, hon. You just missed her."

"She's gone? Already?" Lila looked around the building's dingy lobby, but saw only the usual collection of small-time crooks and junkies, the hard-done-by folks getting squeezed between their shitty lives and the criminal justice system.

"Swear to God," Kreps said.

"Who did the questioning?"

Kreps flipped through the papers in front of him. "Looks like Detective Rafael Marana is the guy to talk to."

"Marana? Oh, Christ."

It was a well-known fact that Rafa Marana was one of the laziest, paint-by-numbers homicide detectives that the city of Miami had ever known. Having him as lead detective was nothing but bad news.

"Easy there, kid. Ever heard that you can't shoot the messenger?"

"Is Marana still here?" She needed to talk to him immediately. Too impatient to wait for Kreps's response, Lila rushed down the hall to the homicide department.

When she got to his office, she found Marana on the phone. The moment he laid eyes on her, he slowly shook his head, as if he couldn't believe a shitty day just got shittier. He put his hand over the receiver and whispered, "Not now."

His worn-out shoes were propped up on a corner of his old, steel desk, which was piled high with tiny mountains of files and yellowing papers, untouched for ages. By his feet, a bottle of Pepto-Bismol sat right next to his oversize "#1 Dad" coffee mug. Marana, Lila remembered, had no children. She walked over to him, ripped the phone away from his ear, and slammed it down.

"Goddamnit, Day!" Marana yelled. "That was an important call."

"Why'd you let her go?"

"It's none of your goddamn business, or did you forget you're not a cop anymore?"

"You forget you are one?" She slapped his feet off his desk. They fell to the floor with a heavy thud. "Where's Elise?"

Marana let out a titanic exhale. There was a lifetime of disappointments contained in that one gust of breath. "I knew it was only a matter of time before you came sniffing around here. As if getting a high-profile case isn't enough of a god-damn hassle. When I saw Elise was involved, I knew you'd be up my ass."

Marana leaned back in his chair and picked at a scab on his skull. He flicked the dried crust of skin to the ground and then sniffed at his fingers, deeply inhaling his scalpy scent. Lila felt a wave of revulsion crawl up her esophagus. "We ran into some problems," he said simply.

"Problems?"

Marana looked exhausted. Like everyone else on the force, he knew that Lila had some kind of vengeance thing for Elise because of what happened with her sister. But he clearly wasn't up for dealing with her wrath today.

"Tell me what happened," Lila asked, trying hard to swallow her anger.

"Some evidence has gone missing." He said it in a matter-of-fact way, as if it was the most natural thing in the world to misplace key evidence in a possible homicide case.

"What evidence?"

"The gun. It's gone. Okay? Gone. We've searched the evidence locker. We've searched the entire police station. Nothing. Nada. Zip." His words were coming at Lila rapid-fire, and his wide eyes were locked on hers. She noticed a little spittle had collected at the corners of his mouth. "Now I've got some fresh-out-of-law school A.D.A. chewing my ass out. And Elise's attorney is saying that she's going to bring a lawsuit against the city of Miami for fifty million bucks because we called her down to the station for questioning *and* lost key evidence. This case is only thirty-six hours old and it's already a colossal boil on my ass. So, the last thing that I need in this entire cocksucking day is to get any shit from you."

Marana fell into a strained silence. He was almost panting from the stress.

"Christ, take it easy," Lila said, sitting down in the metal folding chair opposite his desk. "I'm not going to bust your chops. Besides, it's not your fault."

Marana shot her a suspicious look. "You're right," he said cautiously. "It's not my fault." He sounded like he didn't believe it.

"It's simple. Elise probably offered one of your cops a shit-load of cash to destroy the evidence. End of story."

"Don't make accusations you can't back up, Lila."

"Then what do you think happened?"

"I don't know. I'm still trying to figure it out."

"Yeah, good luck with that." Lila stood up. There was no point wasting any more time. "Thanks for reminding me why I left the force, Rafa. Sometimes I miss this place, but it doesn't take much for me to remember it was never worth all the bullshit. I'll leave you to do what you're good at, which is absolutely nothing." She left his office, loudly slamming the door behind her.

She knew, right then and there, that as long as Rafa Marana was in charge of the case, there'd be no justice for Elise. She felt angry at herself for having any hope that the Miami PD could actually put the right person behind bars. In less than a day and a half, Elise had managed to sidestep a possible murder charge, and Lila knew that the corrupt and incompetent cops working the case wouldn't do anything about it. All they were worried about was how to protect their own sorry asses by not pissing off the powerful. It was really that simple.

As Lila left the station, the searing anger she felt began to be replaced by bewildered disappointment. Would Elise really get away with murder for a third time? It seemed, even with all the cards stacked against her, that justice was no match for her wealth and privilege. But Lila had been here before—up against the most powerful players in the city—and she'd come out on top.

In a flash, she knew exactly what she had to do. The only chance she'd have at putting Elise behind bars was if she did it herself. And there was only one man who could help her make that happen.

She picked up her phone and dialed the first person on speed dial. "Teddy, be at my place by six tonight. I want to talk about a new case. Okay? Got to run." Lila quickly hung up the phone. She knew getting Teddy on board with her plan would take a lot of coaxing, so she rushed home to begin preparing her pitch.

CHAPTER 3

LILA HEARD A knock on the front door. She glanced at the clock: 6:00 P.M. Teddy was right on time, as always. She pressed the space bar on her keyboard, pausing the video she'd been watching. Even with the moving images now frozen and Teddy waiting at the door, she found it impossible to look away from the computer screen.

The subject of her rapt attention was an old segment from a second-rate Miami news show. Recorded eleven years ago, back in September 2008, it was a puff piece about a very high profile superyacht docked at a hotel in downtown Miami. It was a Lifestyles of the Grotesquely Rich and Wildly Famous kind of thing that wasn't of any interest to anybody . . . except Lila, who'd played it so many times over the last ten years that she knew each and every frame by heart.

Her obsessive viewing wasn't just because the yacht being adoringly profiled was owned by none other than Jack Warren. It was mainly because this three-minute bit of throwaway TV contained the last recorded image of Ava, Lila's long-lost sister. Blink and you'd miss her. But Lila never did. Ava appeared for a few seconds on the very edge of the left side of the frame, just a pixelated blur in the deep background behind the cheerful reporter smiling brightly into the black-eyed Cyclops of the camera. But Lila could spot Ava anywhere. She knew the contours of her sister's face, her gait, the slight stoop of her shoulders better than she knew her own.

Lila had queued up the video because she planned on showing it to Teddy that night. But she'd been sucked into watching it once more. Then again. Then a third time, squinting at the screen, wanting, more than anything, to be there on the boat the night that Jack was murdered and Ava's life was destroyed. She wanted so desperately to be able to protect her older sister in the way that Ava had protected Lila for most of her early years, when their mom was too busy scrounging up a living to be at home with her two daughters.

Proving her sister's innocence was something Lila had dreamed about for a decade. And thanks to Teddy's time machine, she knew it was finally possible. But first, she'd have to make the case to Teddy, and she knew it wouldn't be easy. Tonight, she'd show him everything, starting with this video.

Lila's concentration was broken by yet another, now-impatient rap on the door. She tore herself away from her desk and walked to the foyer as the knocks grew faster and louder.

"Christ! Keep your dress on," Lila teased. "I'll be there in a second." She flung the front door open to find Teddy leaning against the doorjamb, tan and smiling with his light brown hair elegantly swept up and away from his handsome face. Outfitted in an expertly tailored cream linen suit, which hung perfectly off his long, lean body, he looked as if he'd stepped out of the pages of *The Great Gatsby*. A bottle of Veuve Clicquot in his arm provided the final touch.

"You're looking better," he said, gliding past her and entering the main room like he owned the place, which, in fact, he did. He handed her the champagne. The bottle was ice cold and perspiring in the humid Miami air. "Feeling up for a drink?"

"Champagne, Teddy? This isn't a celebration."

"I know," he said, shrugging off her serious tone, refusing to be chastened. "I can tell from your face that it's all business. But I figured, good news or bad, you could use a drink. I know I could." He headed straight for the wall of windows, which overlooked the cerulean expanse of the Atlantic Ocean, but were now covered by closed blinds.

He let out a tiny cluck of disapproval. "You know, Lila, people pay millions for this view, but every time I come by you have the windows covered like some shut-in vampire."

Lila bristled. Things were getting off to a bad start. She was ready to plead for a chance to save her sister and Teddy was fussing about the lighting.

He raised the blinds and pushed the windows open. The hot tropical sun poured into the apartment with a blinding ferocity, and the sounds of South Beach flooded in right after it. Car horns blared from the street below. Two lovers threw accusations at each other in a very public spat. House music pounded out of a convertible overburdened with large, booming speakers. In an instant, the pure essence of the Miami Beach boardwalk filled up the room. Teddy breathed it all in deeply, as if the sounds and smells of the street fortified his spirit.

"Much better," he said with a relieved exhale.

Lila lived in a penthouse apartment in one of the famous old Art Deco buildings that were once the pride of Miami Beach, but had mostly fallen into disrepair and out of fashion. Back in 2016, Teddy purchased this building on the corner of Ocean Avenue and Tenth Street when he found out a developer was going to tear it down and throw up yet another soulless, hastily built glass tower. Soon after, he'd offered Lila the penthouse for free. But she was uncomfortable with a favor that she couldn't reciprocate. They compromised. On the first of every month, she gave him money for the rent. Whenever Lila asked why he never once cashed any of her checks, he was always quick to change the subject. Teddy's generosity was something Lila had given up fighting.

Lila blinked rapidly as her eyes struggled to adjust to the sunlight. She retreated to the relative darkness of the kitchen to open the champagne. Maybe a drink was just what she needed, what they both needed.

She knew it would take an ironclad case to convince Teddy to let her go back in time to prove her sister's innocence. But she'd spent all afternoon practicing and knew exactly what she would say.

"Like I said on the phone, I've got a proposal for you." Lila walked back into the living room and handed Teddy a glass of champagne.

"Uh-huh," Teddy said. She detected a note of hesitancy in his tone. Taking a long, slow sip of champagne, he peered at Lila over the crystal rim of his glass with his eyebrows raised. She waited for him to speak. "Tell me, does this new case have anything to do with Elise Warren?"

"How'd you guess?" Lila asked with a sarcastic lilt in her voice.

Teddy shrugged his shoulders and walked onto the balcony, leaning out over the railing. Lila followed.

"Hear me out," Lila said.

"I don't need to. I already know what you're going to say. I knew it the very moment I heard about Herrera's suicide."

"Oh? Enlighten me," Lila said. "Tell me what I'm thinking. If you get it right, then you can add mind reader to your long list of unique skills." She curled into a large Adirondack chair painted robin's-egg blue and looked out onto the boardwalk. Her eyes fell on a bodybuilder wearing a stars-and-stripes string bikini flexing her muscles for a group of tourists who were happily taking her picture.

"You want to travel back in time to prove that Elise is guilty of killing Jack. And, more to the point, you want to prove your sister's innocence. Am I right?"

Lila wasn't surprised that Teddy had anticipated her plan. He had a knack for quickly sussing out people's motivations, but so did she. That's why they were such a good pair.

"And let me guess," Lila said. "You've got reservations."

"We're talking about your sister here, Lila. Working a case when you're *this* emotionally involved is too risky. And, honestly, it bothers me that you're asking."

"Bothers you?"

"After what happened on Star Island, you and I both swore to each other that we'd never take on a case when there was any chance that our feelings would blind us to the facts."

"You seem to forget that I *caught* the Star Island killer, Teddy."

"*You* seem to forget that you broke every goddamn rule there was, and you did it because you got wrapped up in the world you set out to infiltrate. The way you acted, it's a wonder you made it out alive."

Lila stared at him in disbelief. "Are you questioning my professionalism?"

"You bet your ass I am. But professionalism isn't your strong suit. Never has been. You're good at what you do because you *do* take things personally. You *do* become involved, which separates you from most detectives, who stopped giving a fuck a lifetime ago."

Teddy turned away from Lila. A tense silence hung in the air between them.

"You're proving my point. I'm the one to do it because I'm the only one who really cares." She kept her words simple and measured, being very careful to conceal any hint of the desperation she felt, even though she was on the verge of shaking Teddy by the shoulders until he capitulated.

"I didn't build a time machine just so you could get revenge on Elise Warren," Teddy said.

"I'm not after vengeance. I'm after justice. I thought you were, too."

Teddy had hit Lila right where it hurt, and she didn't want to hear it. With every case, she put all of herself on the line. That was what made her *good*. But it also made her hard to work with.

She'd been the youngest female homicide detective in the entire history of the Miami PD. And she was one of the most successful, too—until a two-year search for the Star Island killer got so personal that it ended with her forced resignation.

But what had been her undoing also became her salvation.

In 2018, Teddy, then a stranger, asked her to travel back in time to find the notorious killer who had eluded her for so long. At the time, she thought Teddy was completely insane. Time travel was nothing but science fiction. Then he proved to her that it was real and she said yes.

In the long, fraught months she'd spent in the past, hunting for the killer, she *did* break all the rules of time travel that she'd sworn to uphold. But then she caught the killer, and everything changed.

After she put one of the world's most notorious murderers behind bars, she had her brief fifteen minutes of fame. The mayor of Miami gave her keys to the city and the chief of police begged her to return to the force. But she'd never been a fan of the spotlight. When the world's attention moved on to other things, she felt nothing but a huge sense of relief.

Then there was the money. Lila had lived a life of barely scraping by for thirty years, but after she solved the case, Teddy had made sure she'd no longer be in need of anything. He moved her into a fabulous penthouse and let her select any car she wanted from the arsenal of luxury automobiles sitting untouched in his vast garage. Since he spent more annually on champagne than she made as a cop, she didn't feel too conflicted about being on his payroll. After all, she'd risked life and limb to catch the Star Island killer, a murderer whom Teddy was desperate to bring to justice. And she'd been solving cold cases with him ever since.

Now it was August of 2019—just a little over a year since she'd first traveled back in time, but it felt like a lifetime. It seemed as if her existence had been neatly divided into two parts: before time travel and after.

And now she was desperate to go back in time to solve the crime that made her become a cop in the first place. She couldn't let Teddy say no.

"Here," Lila said, standing up. "Come inside. I want to show you something."

She walked down the hall, with Teddy following closely behind, and stopped right outside her office door.

"I want you to know that I totally understand why you'd have reservations about sending me back to investigate Jack's death. But first I need you to hear me out." She opened the door to her office and they both stepped in.

"Jesus, Lila," Teddy gasped as he looked at the walls of Lila's tiny work space, every inch of which was covered in photos, maps, and evidence connected to Jack's murder. "How long have you been working on this?"

"Ten years," she said. "On and off."

"I can see that."

"No other case has ever meant more to me, Teddy. And I'm asking you to help me finally, once and for all, prove my sister's innocence."

As Teddy began to peruse some of the files stacked up on Lila's desk, she saw the stern look on his face begin to soften. "Okay," he said tentatively. "I'm not saying yes. I'm just saying I'll listen. I bet you have a plan, right?"

"Of course."

"I'm all ears, but first . . ." Teddy grabbed his cell phone and made a call. "Conrad. It seems Lady Day and I will be sequestered in her apartment for a good amount of time. Can you be a sport and bring us some dinner?" He paused. "Great. We'll keep it simple tonight. Just a few things from Nobu. The miso black cod, the lobster tempura, of course, a sashimi selection, and the king crab legs with wasabi glaze."

An amused smile momentarily flickered across Lila's otherwise serious face. Only Teddy would put this conversation on pause so that his manservant would pick up something with a wasabi glaze. She had to admit, she loved him for it.

Once he finished placing his order, he turned back to Lila. "Now you have my full attention."

"Sure you don't want to get some hand rolls or something?"

"Oh! I forgot you love those. And Conrad's probably already calling in the order! Just wait one second," he said as he scrambled to dial his cell phone.

"Jesus, Teddy. I was *kidding*."

He looked confused for a brief second, then he smiled. "That's good. A joke. And here I was worried that I'd be spending the evening with the humorless Lila Day. I'm glad the nice version has decided to come out to play."

It was then that Lila and Teddy settled in and began poring

over the piles of evidence connected to the Warren murder that Lila had spent the last ten years collecting.

She started with her point of entry into the world, her under-cover identity. Lila took down a picture she'd tacked up to her wall of a pretty young woman with short bleached blond hair, almond-shaped eyes, and full lips. She handed it to Teddy. "This is Nicky Collins, a member of the crew. Age twenty-eight in 2008. There's not much info on her. The data trail is really spotty. Doesn't have an extensive employment record, which probably means she did a lot of temporary, under-the-table work. Poor credit rating. She's got one credit card, a Visa, with an address in Shreveport, Loui-siana. Credit limit of only four hundred dollars. Back in 2005, she got picked up for possession of marijuana. She pleaded guilty and got her felony charge reduced to a misdemeanor. She served eight months at a minimum security prison, Gasden Correctional Facility. When she got out, she started working as a stewardess in high-end yachts. None of her applications make note of her arrest record, obviously. There's a Florida driver's license dated June 2004. Her passport was issued in August 2008, right after she was hired to work on *The Rising Tide*. It was the first passport she'd ever applied for. A staffing agency hired her for the job. I've got her application here," Lila said, tossing Teddy a photocopied piece of paper. "And an email that the staffing agency sent to the head stewardess, whose name is Edna Slaughter, right here."

Teddy studied the papers. "So this is the identity you're planning on assuming in order to gain access to the yacht?"

"Exactly."

"An ex-con. Sounds about right. And no one on the boat has ever met this Nicky Collins?"

"Never. She's a fresh hire. So, there shouldn't be any problem."

"But, look," Teddy said as he studied one of the papers.

"The agency sent a picture of her to the head stewardess for approval."

"True. But I think we look similar enough." Lila snatched Nicky's picture back from Teddy's hands and held it next to her face for his inspection. True, Lila was more beautiful than the woman in the picture, but they had similarly fine noses and wide mouths.

"I guess," Teddy said hesitantly. "But your hair will have to go."

"Won't be the first time."

"And how are you planning on bumping her off her gig?"

"You know me, Teddy. I'll read the situation once I get there. But, worst-case scenario, I'll offer her fifty grand to get lost. That's the kind of money it's hard to say no to."

Huddled together over reams and reams of evidence, Lila laid out her plan until the wee small hours of night, only pausing to gobble down artfully plated Japanese food served up by Conrad.

By 2 A.M. even the rowdy street noise from below had died down and Lila felt overcome with exhaustion as the stress from a long day finally got to her. She needed to go to bed, but first she had to show Teddy the video. She grabbed her laptop.

"The first few months after Jack's death were some of the darkest of my life," Lila said. "I couldn't believe that my sister was gone. All I wanted was to see her again and, with each passing day, I felt like there was less and less of a chance that she'd ever come out of hiding. And the way the press vilified her didn't help matters either. My certainty that she was innocent began to falter. I mean, she hadn't told me anything about Jack. I began to wonder if I knew her at all. Then I found this video."

Lila pressed play. Teddy watched it carefully, looking intently at the heavily made up TV reporter standing in the shadows of Jack's giant yacht.

"What am I looking at?" Teddy asked.

"It's coming up in a few seconds, at a minute and forty-three seconds. Watch the far left side of the screen."

When the video got to that moment, Lila hit pause and pointed. "That's my sister, right there," she said, tapping the screen.

Teddy squinted, seeing the fuzzy outlines of a woman with long blond hair wearing a canary-yellow dress. "This is the last video ever recorded of her. According to the testimonies given by witnesses, this is the day she boarded the boat. But the crew boarded the boat several days before."

"Okay," he said cautiously.

"She's beautiful, isn't she?" Lila said, staring at the screen.

She felt his eyes on her, watching her watch her sister.

"She's just a blur."

Lila felt an electric current of irritation run through her at Teddy's offhanded dismissal of something so precious to her. This quick video of her sister alive had given her so much comfort, but she couldn't exactly say why.

Teddy walked over to a wall that Lila had covered in nautical charts, mapping the course of *The Rising Tide* through its Caribbean tour. She could tell he was trying to figure out how to say something difficult. She felt her body tense in anticipation.

"I hate to say this, but . . ." He paused. "No matter what you prove, you may only be clearing Ava's name posthumously." Teddy cleared his throat. "I mean, the boat she used to escape was found capsized with traces of her blood and Jack's blood on it. And it's been, what, over ten years since she's disappeared? I don't mean to be too pessimistic, but maybe they never found her because she's . . . *gone*. And then what would be the point of all of this? You can't change the past, that's the rule. So Jack can't be saved, which means you'd be putting yourself in so much danger and through so much emotional agony to exonerate a woman who was lost a long time ago."

"She's alive, Teddy," Lila said, feeling a tightness grip her chest. "I know she is."

"How? The same way you know she's innocent despite every damn piece of evidence pointing to her guilt? Lila, all this," he said, gesturing around the room, "really concerns me. I think you're so mired in the details that you aren't asking yourself the tough questions."

"Trust me on this, Teddy."

"I don't think I can. I know you're not seeing things clearly."

"Maybe the real problem here is that you doubt everything too much. You don't know what it's like to believe in a person, to have faith in someone."

He shook his head, as if saddened by Lila's display of naïveté. "I have faith in *you,* Lila."

"Then let me do this."

She caught his gaze, but he quickly looked away. She could tell he wasn't convinced. Knowing she'd have to put all her cards on the table, she said, "There's one last thing I need to show you."

Lila left her office and walked to her bedroom without saying another word. The sky was a purplish black with a sliver of moon hanging low on the horizon. The sliding glass door was open, letting in the sound of crashing ocean waves and wind-rustled palm trees. Teddy silently followed her, standing in her doorway as Lila went into the bedroom closet. There was an intimacy in the act of entering her bedroom that gave him pause. She pushed her clothes out of the way and punched numbers into a wall safe she'd installed the first week she moved in. The safe's heavy metal door clicked open and Lila removed a small wooden chest, about the size of a shoe box.

Her fingers gripped the box carefully, as if its contents were explosive. She left the bedroom, setting the chest down on the dining room table.

"This is hard for me," Lila said. "I didn't even show these to my mom on her deathbed. So you've got to promise that what you're about to see stays between us and no one else."

"Of course," Teddy said quietly, matching Lila's solemn tone.

"Because if anyone finds out what I have here, I could be in big trouble."

"You can trust me, Lila. You know you can."

She slowly, ceremoniously, opened the box. Its contents were wrapped up in a pure-white muslin. As she unwound the cloth, Teddy saw she was holding a stack of small landscape paintings, each about the size of a paperback book. "This," Lila said in a whisper as she placed each painting on the table, "is how I know Ava is still alive."

Laying them out carefully in one long row, she pointed to one that showed sugarcane fields in the foreground and a large mountain range in the background. "This was the first one I received. It came in December 2008, only three months after she went into hiding, a few weeks after I turned twenty-one."

"It's magnificent," Teddy said. And it was.

Lila admired the painting with a small smile. "Ever since I was a little girl, Ava always painted me something for my birthday. And even in hiding, she kept doing it. Each painting is from a different place. This looks like Cuba. In 2009, I got this one that looks like coastal South America. The next year, Mount Kilimanjaro was painted in the far background. Then Greece. Then several from South Asia. This last one looks like she's back in South America. I've stared at each of them for countless hours, trying to decipher any code."

"Don't the stamps tell you where they're from?"

"Not always. One year the stamp on the package was from Argentina but the painting was clearly from somewhere in Africa. Two years ago, she sent me this painting of what looks like Thailand, but it was sent from Tanzania. What I do know is that she's circled the globe and back trying to outrun something she didn't do."

"Does she ever include a note? Telling you she's innocent?"

"Never. She'd know it would be too risky for her and for me. But I hoped I could find some answers in the paintings themselves. I even worked with an old forger I knew from my days back on the force. He helped me have all the canvases analyzed and the various pigments examined." She shrugged. "I thought I could find out where she purchased her materials, but that didn't go anywhere. It was all basic stuff, impossible to trace. Then I had each painting tested using infrared reflectography, which lets you actually see what's on the canvas underneath the paint, just in case she'd written me something. And that came up empty, too, except for the painting I got in 2018. It's this one." She picked it up. It was of a town square dominated by an old Spanish Colonial church. "The postage came from Quito, Peru, but, after spending months researching churches in this style, I finally discovered that this one is from San Cristóbal de las Casas in Chiapas, Mexico."

"And there was something written on the canvas?"

"Not written, but drawn. They uncovered a pencil sketch Ava had made on the surface of the canvas before she painted it. I've got a printout of the image here." She grabbed a folded sheet of paper from the bottom of the box and handed it to Teddy. It was a sketch of two children in swimsuits holding hands by the shore. Then Lila pointed to a framed photograph she had on her side table, of the exact same image from real life. "It's one of my favorite pictures. The one with the pigtails is me. It was taken Christmas Day in Key Largo. I was five, but I remember that day so vividly. Teddy," she said, turning toward him, her voice breaking, "I need my sister back. She's been on the run for so long. And I think what this pencil drawing means is that she's ready to come home. And I'm the only one who can make it safe for her to come out of hiding." She felt tears come to her eyes but blinked them back. She needed to appear strong, even though inside she worried that if Teddy didn't let her go back in time, she would crumble.

Teddy took Lila's hand and squeezed it. A look of understanding passed between the two friends. Then he picked up his phone, and even though it was after two in the morning, his faithful manservant picked up on the second ring. "Conrad, can you come join us? Lady Day is going on another trip and we need to make sure she's got all she needs. Passport. License. Cash. You know the drill."

Lila was beaming. "Do you mean it?"

"Yes," he said, then frowned. "But, Lila, promise me that this time you'll play by the rules. Keep your nose clean. No affairs. No drinking. Form no attachments. And, most importantly, *don't interfere with the past.*"

"I promise," Lila said quickly, careful not to say anything that might change his mind.

"And this time you've got to keep your promises," he warned her. Lila knew he was thinking of the Star Island murders, and how she'd tried to change fate. "Promise me you'll let Jack Warren die."

"I will." That was an easy promise to make. In this whole sad saga, the one thing that Lila never wanted to change was the moment when those four bullets were shot into Jack Warren's body. As far as she was concerned, the world was a better place without him.

CHAPTER 4

TWO DAYS LATER, wearing a white hazmat suit that covered her from head to toe, Lila climbed into Teddy's time-traveling contraption, ready to go back to 2008. Every detail had been ironed out, every move had been talked through, but the moment she strapped herself in and Teddy's face appeared on the screen before her eyes, she felt her nerves kick in.

Lila didn't know the first thing about how time travel worked, and frankly, she knew she never would. The science behind it was beyond her. But she did know there were dangers. She'd felt them firsthand as the physical toll of time travel wore on her with each and every trip. But as long as it got her where she wanted to go, it was worth it. This gift of traveling back in time to solve cold cases was worth every moment of panic and pain. It was what she imagined women felt like after they'd given birth—that all the excruciating agony of labor was instantly erased once it was over. The miracle of the reward trumped the cost.

And no case had ever mattered more to her than this one. At last, she'd prove to the world that her sister was innocent.

Conrad's disembodied voice came over the speakers. "We are approximately T-minus-ten from inflationary vacuum state."

She didn't have much time. Her heart began to race.

"Want to know my favorite Jack Warren joke?" Teddy asked, watching her from the control room. All her vitals were being intensely monitored, so he'd have seen that her pulse was racing.

"Not really." Lila wasn't in a joking mood. Whenever she was feeling overwhelmed or stressed, Teddy was quick to try to lighten the mood. It drove her crazy—even though, most of the time, his distractions worked.

"What's the difference between God and Jack Warren?" Teddy asked.

"What?"

"God doesn't think he's Jack Warren."

Lila smiled. She hadn't heard that one before. Then her mind shot off in so many different directions. Was she prepared? Would she finally be able to clear her sister's name? Or was Teddy right—was she too close to this case to have the perspective she needed?

"Lila?" Teddy called out, snapping her out of her ramble down second-guess lane. He and Conrad were both in the control room, peering at her on the screen just inches from her face.

"What?" she said.

"Everything okay?"

"Of course it is," she said somewhat defensively. She wrapped her hands around the briefcase on her lap, which was full of the supplies she always brought on a case: her gun; handcuffs; one hundred grand in cash; freshly forged documents, this time under the name Nicky Collins; and all her case info scanned and archived onto a thumb drive.

And, one thing extra. For this trip she'd decided to bring an object of sentimental value. In between the stacks of bills, she tucked the picture of her and her sister holding hands on the beach all those years ago. It wasn't a good idea to take along anything that connected Lila to her real life, and she knew that, which was why she didn't disclose the decision to Teddy. But she needed to keep that token of her sister close. She needed to remember why she was doing all this.

"Ready?" Conrad asked.

Lila took a deep, bracing breath. "I'm ready when you are," she said, though she didn't feel ready.

Though this was Lila's sixth go-round "slipping through the wormhole," as Teddy so cavalierly called it, the process never failed to put the fear of God into her.

The lights turned off inside the machine, but she could still hear Teddy's voice. "Good luck, Lila. See you on the other side."

"We are T-minus-two from inflationary vacuum state," Conrad said, sounding more like a computer than a man.

Almost instantly, the contraption began to violently shudder. Then came the deafening whir, preparing for what Lila thought of as "lift-off," though there was no lifting at all. Then, the last thing she heard was Teddy's voice booming into her ears, counting down her departure from this world out into the frightening unknown.

"Ten . . . nine . . . eight . . . seven . . ."

The first part was scary enough. Even a stoic like Lila would own up to that. But what came next was so much worse, simply because what came next was impossible to categorize, to name, to equate with anything that fit within the physical laws of the known world.

Suddenly a veil of blackness and silence enveloped her. It was a darkness so profound that it seemed as if no light had ever existed at all.

Her spatial awareness began to waver and distort. She felt tiny in a vast space and then gigantic in a shrinking space. Then her very body seemed to fall away until she was unable to differentiate between her own corporeal form and the hovering nothingness surrounding it, as if she had dissolved entirely.

The final phase, to Lila's mind, was the one she most dreaded. It was the endless plummeting. It reminded her of that brief but terrifying feeling of falling that sometimes tore her out of early sleep. But in time travel that feeling went on almost forever. She had once asked Teddy how long the process of time travel actually took, but he answered her only in riddles. "Somewhere between an instant and an eternity," he'd said, with his typical sly grin. Lila wasn't amused. She liked things black and white.

So here she was, once again falling between two parallel fields of time, quite convinced that this go-round would be her last, that she'd never make it out of this thing alive. And, once again, just at the very moment that she felt herself giving in to the fact that she was forever doomed, there was a surge of light and a breath-halting tug upward on her entire body, as if an invisible rip cord had been pulled to stop her free fall.

And then she found herself thrust back into the known world, spread flat, her back pressed against a cold cement floor. For a long, terrifying moment she had no idea who she was or where she was. She scrambled woozily to her feet, trying to force her mind and body to shake off the recent traumas. She needed to get her shit together, and fast.

With her heart pounding in her chest, her eyes darted around the strange space as she tried to fit the puzzle pieces together. But she was lost in the fog of the unknown until, after a few frantic minutes, the flood of adrenaline coursing through her body helped snap her out of her stupor. Then, like a momentarily forgotten name suddenly remembered, she instantly recognized her surroundings. The bare-bones, cinderblock room in which she was currently standing was in a North Miami storage building. She'd been there plenty of time before as it, bizarrely, served as the sole opening to Teddy's time-traveling portal. Even Teddy couldn't explain why this was the geographic location on the other end of his time warp. Lila didn't dwell on it. She was back in time, and that was all that mattered.

The first thing she did was immediately open the metal briefcase that sat at her feet, checking to make sure that the money, the gun, and her data had made the time leap with her. Relieved to see it all there, she rubbed her hand over the crisp dollar bills and the gun's elegant barrel, grabbed a solid steel padlock from beneath one of the $10,000 stacks of hundred-dollar bills, and took one look at the photo of her sister before clicking the briefcase closed. She peeled off the hazmat suit and headed out of the room, securing the padlock to the door and slipping one of the keys, which she had attached to a thin silver chain, around her neck. She tucked the other key above the doorframe of an adjacent storage unit. On Lila's first-ever time-travel trip, an unexpected lock on this very door had almost prevented her from returning to the present, coming close to stranding her in the past forever. Needless to say, she'd learned from that mistake.

Lila walked quickly down the narrow hall of the building. There was no sign of life except for the playing-card-size cockroach traps scattered here and there. She could hear sheets of rain barreling down upon the building's metal roof. Teddy had told her that a category-two tropical storm was moving up the coast of southern Florida, causing high winds and rain, but that it would clear in a couple hours.

Nothing makes predicting the weather easier than being from the future, Lila thought as she descended the stairs.

The Rising Tide's crew was scheduled to assemble on the boat at 5:00 P.M. on that very day, August 23. Teddy had programmed Lila to arrive back in 2008 on the twenty-third, but a few hours earlier, so she didn't have much time. She always cursed Teddy's ferocious strictness about how long she could spend in the past. It seemed that he never gave her long enough, but he claimed that every second she was back in time created an infinite number of ways that her presence could damage the known future. To limit the risks, he reduced her time in the past. It wasn't to Lila's liking, but it also wasn't in her control.

First things first, she needed to call a cab. Once she hit the ground floor, she entered the storage building's spare, fluorescent-lit office. The small room was dominated by a faux-wood counter, behind which a middle-aged man was napping. There was no sign of a pay phone, only a poor ficus tree busy shedding its few remaining dead leaves onto the gray linoleum floor. The rain beat against the windows, giving Lila the feeling of being in a giant car wash.

She nosily cleared her throat, hoping to wake the man who was now lightly snoring. He didn't move. As she got closer to the desk, she noticed that only half of his face had been shaved that day. The smell of mouthwash and cheap aftershave hung in the air. Probably a drinker, she thought.

"Hello?" she said. "Excuse me?"

Nothing.

Lila peered over the counter looking for a phone. The man's half-shaved chin was jutting up and his slack mouth was slightly open. He had a thin, almost wasted body, but his short-sleeved, button-down shirt was stretched tightly across his basketball-size stomach. A name tag with CHUCK hand-written in childlike block print sagged by his shirt pocket. Her eyes seized upon a pair of car keys sitting right in front of him attached to a big, gold Playboy Bunny key chain.

Without thinking, she went for the keys, but just before she could grab them, the man snorted awake. Lucky for her, she was able to withdraw her hand before he noticed anything.

"Welcome to U-Store-It, yer twenty-four-hour storage-needs expert. How may I assist you?" he said automatically, as if he were a talking doll and Lila had pulled his string.

"I need you to call me a cab, right away," she said, using the clipped and commanding tone that always overtook her in the company of slow-witted reprobates. It was a lingering habit from her years on the force.

"I'll be happy to call," he said, smiling. He had the syrupy accent of the deep, deep South and, Lila thought, a sweet dopey face. "But ain't likely you'll get anyone coming out here in this weather anytime soon."

"Possibly," she said as they both turned to look at the winds tossing the palm trees to and fro outside. "Still, I'd appreciate if you call."

"Chuck," he said.

"Sorry?"

"You'd appreciate it if I called you a cab. And I'd appreciate it if you called me 'Chuck' instead of bossing me around like some snotty-nosed lady."

"Okay," Lila said, silently congratulating herself for not throttling him on the spot. "Would you mind very much call-ing me a taxi, Chuck?"

"Sure thing." He picked up the phone and dialed the

number. He hung up and dialed it again, looking confused by the busy signal Lila could hear plain as day.

"Is the line busy, Chuck?"

"Reckon so."

"Can you please try another taxi service, then?"

"All right, but I gotta get the phone book first," he said, his neck craning around as his eyes searched the desk. There was a bluegrass cover of a song by Nirvana playing from a set of blown-out speakers installed above a vending machine. "I know I put it somewhere around here. But, gosh, I'm just not sure where it could be hiding."

As Lila watched Chuck paw around his desk drawers for the phone book, seconds slowed down to a crawl. There was no time for this.

"Can you look online?" she asked impatiently.

"Not sure that would be of help," he said, now with his head buried in a file cabinet. Lila let out an exasperated exhale that she hoped he heard. The world, she thought, could be broken down into two kinds of people: those that are helpful and those that are Chuck. Then she realized there was another option.

"How much would you want for your car out there?" she asked, nodding toward the ancient, red Pontiac sitting rusting in the otherwise empty parking lot.

"My car?"

Lila quietly popped open the briefcase that she was holding out of his sight and grabbed a stack of bills. She slapped it on the counter.

"Would ten grand work for you?"

Chuck's mouth dropped open. Lila thought it would be very safe to assume he'd never seen that much in cash before in his life. Before she got mixed up with Teddy Hawkins, Lila could have said the very same of herself. Now she threw stacks of hundreds around like they were nickels and dimes. "It'd . . . it'd a work for me," he stuttered, "but it'd a make a damn fool of you."

"Chuck, I'm sad to say that I've done plenty of things more foolish than this," she said as she reached down and grabbed the keys.

"Wait," he said, putting his palm over them right before she swooped down to scoop them up. "Those've got my house keys on them, too. Those ain't for sale."

"Of course," she said, standing impatiently as the man slowly worked each needed key off the tight key ring.

She anxiously stood there, dumbfounded, as she watched Chuck fumble through this as he probably fumbled through most things. The thought crossed her mind that if Teddy could invent a simple time machine that gave people back these lost moments of life he'd deserve the Nobel Peace Prize.

Soon enough, the transaction was settled and Lila found herself puttering south down a nearly empty, rain-soaked highway toward Miami Beach, in search of Nicky Collins.

CHAPTER 5

THE $10,000 DRIVE along the rain-ravaged streets of Miami took Lila exactly fifteen minutes and ended at the El Cordova Hotel, a run-down and shabby slice of old Miami on Collins Avenue just a few steps from the currently churned-up ocean. It was a favorite spot for midlevel con men, down-and-out gamblers, escorts aging out of desirability, and budget-minded tourists scrambling to remedy their bad choice of hotel.

She knew from the police files on the Warren murder that Nicky Collins told police she had checked into the El Cordova a little before 11:00 P.M. on August 22, but details about her whereabouts started and ended there. The only other information Lila knew was that just a few short hours from now, Nicky would board Jack's yacht, *The Rising Tide*. Lila didn't have that much time to bump Nicky out of the picture.

Lila pulled up to the hotel. She slipped the valet a hundred bucks to keep her car out front. She figured she'd have to tail Nicky sooner or later, and she needed her car ready when it was time. She entered the hotel's dingy lobby and went straight to the back, picking up the guest phone next to the empty concierge's desk. It was 10:45 in the morning.

"El Cordova, may I help you?"

"Can you connect me to the room of Nicky Collins?"

"One moment, please."

After two rings, a woman picked up. Lila was relieved that Nicky was still in her hotel room. "Hello . . . Hello?" Her voice was deep and croaky, a smoker's voice, as if she'd been awakened out of a profound sleep. Lila stayed silent, listening intently.

"Who's this?" Nicky said after a long pause. "Hello?" The paranoia in her voice was almost palpable.

Lila put on a phony southern accent and gave a fake name, saying she was calling from the staffing agency that hired her for *The Rising Tide*.

"Okay?" Nicky said, sounding confused.

"You'll need to be at the marina by noon, not five P.M. as previously instructed." Lila needed Nicky up and out of her hotel room, so she decided to set a little fire under her ass.

"Are you fucking kidding me? That's impossible."

"I'm just passing on the instructions. Have a good day!"

Just as Lila was about to hang up, she heard Nicky mutter, "Fuck me." Then the line went dead. Now that Nicky thought she had to be on the yacht in a little more than one hour, Lila knew she'd come down in the next handful of minutes. She grabbed a seat in one of the cheaply upholstered lobby armchairs, sure to select the one that had the best view of the elevators.

As she waited, a tingle of excitement overcame her. She was never happier than when she was working a case. And here she was, back in 2008, after slipping through the creases of time, about to come face-to-face with the woman whose identity she'd soon assume. This was life at its most invigorating.

Five minutes later, she snapped to attention when the elevator doors opened and Nicky stepped out. The first thing that struck Lila was how ghastly she looked. Her eyes were ringed with puffy, dark circles and her complexion was both pale and flushed, like she'd just been on a booze and drug bender and didn't have time to pull herself together. She was dressed in oversize blue jeans that were barely held up by her thin, boyish hips, and despite the terrible rain, heat, and humidity, she wore a slim-fitting black leather jacket. As it was on her passport picture, her hair was bleached blond and cut very short into a pixie haircut, though the dark roots were severely pronounced.

Nicky had an unlit cigarette dangling inelegantly from her lips and a blue duffel bag in her hand. She quickly cut across the lobby, exiting the hotel through the revolving door, lighting her cigarette as the door spun around her. Lila, careful to keep off Nicky's radar, waited until she was outside before getting up to follow her. Nicky handed the valet a ticket for her car, all the while taking deep, satisfied drags, as if she hadn't smoked in weeks.

With a nod to the valet, who winked back, Lila hopped into the old rusted Pontiac, observing Nicky the whole time. As she stood waiting for her car under the hotel's awning, Nicky seemed very jumpy. Her hands were constantly fidgeting, so much so that she accidentally dropped her cigarette on the pavement two times. And her eyes kept darting around, looking for what, Lila couldn't guess. But with her mannerisms and her strung-out looks, it was a safe bet that Nicky was dipping into some pretty heavy drugs—probably meth or crack from the looks of her.

After Lila had watched Nicky twitch and scratch and smoke two cigarettes down to the filter, the valet finally pulled a 5-series black BMW up to the curb. Lila was shocked to see Nicky climb into the driver's side seat. Lila knew that a young, strung-out woman with an entry-level job on a boat could never afford an $80,000 car. Maybe her stint in prison for drug possession was only the tip of the iceberg when it came to Nicky's misdeeds.

Lila spent the next hour tailing Nicky in the pouring rain as she drove around Miami, gathering the gear and supplies she'd need before setting sail. All throughout these errands, she made a mental note that Nicky had not once let go of her grip on that large blue duffel bag. There was the trip to the pharmacy to pick up deodorant, sunscreen, toothpaste, tampons, and a couple prescriptions, which Lila wasn't quick enough to ID. Walmart for socks, underwear, and a couple paperback books. In a 7-Eleven, she bought two prepaid disposable cell phones, four cartons of Marlboro Lights, and several cans of Red Bull.

"Not so into the healthy lifestyle, are you, Nicky?" Lila said to herself as she sat in the idling Pontiac. She looked at the time. It was getting close to noon, which meant she needed to settle on a concrete plan to get Nicky to give up her spot on the yacht.

As she watched Nicky walk her quick, nervous walk across the 7-Eleven parking lot to her car, she decided that she'd need to go with her fallback plan—offer Nicky fifty grand to get lost, so Lila could assume her identity and board *The Rising Tide*. The plan had its holes, for sure. It could leave too many loose ends, especially once Jack's murder took place and the police got involved. Once the murder made international news, the real Nicky Collins might come out of the woodwork and tell the press or, even worse, the police that a strange woman had paid to be on the yacht in her place. That was a complication Lila would much rather avoid. But if it was the only option open to her, Lila would take it and deal with the consequences.

Just as Teddy had said, the rain finally began to let up a little before noon as Lila tailed Nicky down the South Dixie Highway.

The black BMW got off at the Kendall exit, heading into the mostly Colombian section of town. When Nicky pulled up in front of a small, aluminum-sided house with a black El Dorado in the driveway, Lila couldn't believe her good luck.

"No shit," she muttered as she pulled her own car over, a few houses down. She watched Nicky grab the duffel bag and enter the house through the side door without bothering to knock. Clearly, she was expected.

Grabbing her gun from the metal briefcase, Lila got out of the car and swiftly ran down the street toward the humble ranch house she knew so well. In 2009, a few months after this very moment, Detective Lila Day would take part in a raid on this house. The police would seize 33.17 kilos of cocaine, 10.09 kilos of heroin, and enough weapons and ammunition to take down a small city—all of it belonging to the extremely dangerous and powerful Colombian Cali cartel. It would be one of the most heralded moments of Lila's already stellar police career.

"What are you mixed up in, Nicky?" Lila wondered as she made her way to the back of the house. She quickly ducked next to a window; then with her gun drawn, peeked inside. There she saw the man she recognized as Fernando Henao, a foot soldier for the Cali cartel, standing in the kitchen with Nicky. Two duffel bags sat on the table between them. Lila ducked back down. She went around, looking in all the windows, careful not to be detected.

She couldn't believe her luck. Just when she was worrying about how to get rid of Nicky, the perfect out presented itself to her. It was so good it should've been wrapped in a red, shiny bow. Once Lila confirmed that Fernando and Nicky were in the house alone, she knew just what to do.

She kicked in the side door to the kitchen. "Freeze! Police!" she shouted, trying to hide the delight on her face.

Fernando lunged for his gun as Nicky reflexively crouched under the table. Lila aimed and fired right where Fernando's hand was reaching, making him jump back. Nicky's scream came out from underneath the table.

"Hands on your head!" Lila shouted, but Fernando didn't move. "I said *now!*" she yelled, pointing her gun right in his face.

Lila bent down to see Nicky shivering under the table. "Nicky, you can come out from under there," she said, consciously sweetening her tone. "Here," she said, reaching the hand that didn't have the gun out to her, "let me help you up."

Nicky took Lila's hand, eyeing her cautiously. She had no idea why this stranger with a gun was being so nice. Once she got to her feet, Lila said, "Nicky, is this the man you've identified to police as Fernando Henao?"

"What?" Nicky said, her eyes wide with confusion, her breath coming in rapid gulps. "What are you talking about?"

"Cut the shit, Nicky," Lila said, instantly switching her mode from sweet to stern. "You reported to me that a drug deal was going down today between you and Fernando Henao at approximately noon."

"What?" Nicky stood there slowly blinking as what was happening started to sink in. She looked from Lila to Fernando and back again. "No. No. NO! I didn't say shit, I swear." She was shaking her head no as tears sprang to her eyes. She knew as well as Lila that if the Cali cartel had even a tiny suspicion that she was a snitch, she'd be dead within the hour. "Fernando," Nicky said, rushing up to him. "You believe me, right? I didn't tell the cops nothing."

But Fernando wouldn't look at her. *"Puta,"* he said, spitting in Nicky's direction as he kept his gaze trained on Lila's gun.

"Backup will be here in five minutes," Lila lied as she checked her watch. "Fernando, get on your knees." But he didn't move. His face was locked in a defiant grimace. "Now!" Lila said as she shot one bullet into the floor right in front of his feet. Cursing loudly in Spanish, he fell to the floor.

"Put your hands behind your back and lie flat on your stomach." This time he quickly acquiesced. "Nicky, grab that duct tape over there by the sink."

"I'm not doing fuck all for you," Nicky said. Her face had drained of all color, her body was visibly shaking.

"Cooperate or you won't get that deal we talked about," Lila said, giving her a conspiratorial grin.

"I've never seen you in my life!" She crouched down to the floor, putting her face close to Fernando's. "You hear that, Fernando, I've never seen this bitch before in my life."

He slowly, calmly, turned his face away from hers.

"Just do what I say," Lila said. "Now, wrap his wrists and feet up in the tape. And, Fernando, if you so much as move a hair on your head, I'll shoot you dead, and that's a promise."

Nicky's hands were shaking so hard that it took a few minutes to steady herself enough to hog-tie Fernando. But after she'd wrapped the tape several times around his wrists and his ankles, Lila said, "That's good enough. Now grab both bags and let's get out of here."

"I'm not going anywhere with you," Nicky said.

Lila pointed the gun at her head. "Do it. Now. You don't have much time."

Nicky dropped her head and her defiant posture sank into a defeated slouch. She slunk to the table and threw both duffel bags over her narrow shoulders.

"Fernando, don't you fucking move," Lila warned. "This

place will be swarming with cops in two minutes, and if they see you've moved an inch, they have orders to shoot first, ask questions later."

"Whatever," he said. "You two bitches will be dead and buried before the day is over. No doubt about that."

"Not likely," Lila said as she hustled Nicky out of the house and then down the street.

When they got to Lila's rusted, dented Pontiac, Nicky's suspicions were confirmed. "This ain't a cop car. You want to show me that badge of yours?"

"Just get in." Lila was growing impatient. She had to dispense with Nicky and be in her place on the yacht in a little under five hours. All Nicky's protestations and foot dragging weren't making life easier for either of them.

As they drove north up the South Dixie Highway, back to Miami, Nicky continually oscillated between scowling and pleading for her life. One second she'd be cursing Lila, the next she'd be weeping, begging for her freedom. "I can't go to jail again," she cried.

"What were you going to do with those drugs?"

"If you don't know, I ain't telling you a damn thing," she said, feeling brazen. But then a moment later, her defiance was replaced by despair. "But what does it matter anyway? It's all over. If Fernando thinks I'm a rat, I'm done." She looked out of the car window, slowly shaking her head. "That bullshit you pulled today made me a dead woman. Simple as that."

Lila's conscience twisted inside of her. She really had put Nicky in a bad situation, but what choice did she have? Her sister's freedom depended on it. "Is someone on Jack Warren's boat expecting those drugs?" she asked. She weaved in and out of traffic along the highway, always keeping Nicky in her sights.

Nicky arched one eyebrow and shot Lila a suspicious look. "How the fuck do you know about my gig on the boat?"

"Just answer the question." Lila had to know what she was walking into. If someone had hired Nicky to be a drug runner or a smuggler, she needed to know.

"Why should I help you with anything?" Nicky asked.

"Because you don't have any other options. And I'm going to save your life."

"And how do you plan on doing that?"

"Answer the question! Are you smuggling for someone on the boat?"

Nicky paused, giving Lila a good once-over as if she was weighing her options. Then she looked out the window, a forlorn mood settling over her. "Nope. I don't work for nobody but myself. Planned on doing some dealing wherever we were docked."

"That many kilos of coke is a lot of weight to move for one woman."

"That's the thing about rich people on vacation. They've got loads of money and no idea where to buy drugs. Trust me, the demand is there. It's the whole reason I started working on these fucking yachts in the first place."

"And no one on the ship has ever met you before?" Lila pressed.

"Why the hell do you care?"

"What I wouldn't give for just one straight answer," Lila said aloud to herself.

"No," Nicky said, staring straight ahead at the road. "I've never met anyone on the yacht before. Okay? Are we done with the questions?"

They drove along in silence for another few minutes, until Lila pulled the car up to PortMiami, where a large cargo ship was being loaded with shipping containers.

"Why the fuck are we stopping here?" Nicky said. "Shouldn't you be taking me to the police station? I knew you were a lying bitch. I'm going to sue your ass so fast. If you so much as—"

"Do you ever shut the hell up?" Lila said as she pulled handcuffs out of her briefcase, clicking one to Nicky's thin wrist and the other to the car's steering wheel. She grabbed two $10,000 stacks out of one of the duffel bags and opened the car door.

"That's not your money to take," Nicky growled.

"Just stay here. Don't move."

"Fuck you."

"Fuck you, too," Lila said. As she was getting out of the car, she turned to Nicky, "And if you don't know I'm your only hope right now, then you're dumber than you look." She slammed the door shut and began to walk toward a dockworker who was supervising the loading of the ship. Right before she approached the man, she heard three short, loud honks from behind her. She turned to see Nicky sitting in the car, giving her the finger.

"What an idiot," Lila muttered under her breath, returning Nicky's gesture in kind.

Lila knew that any longshoreman worth his salt would play ball with her if she flashed enough money around. Sure enough, in just two minutes, the dockworker took the twenty grand she was offering, promising he'd keep Nicky safe. Then she walked back to the car.

"Feel like taking a trip?" Lila said as she opened the passenger door, leaning over Nicky as she removed the handcuffs.

"What are you talking about?"

"See that ship there? It's headed to Qingdao, China, and it's leaving in half an hour."

"China?" Nicky said slowly, as if she'd never heard the word before.

"That's right. But it stops in New Orleans, and Japan, and Vietnam, and plenty of other places along the way." Lila handed Nicky the duffel of drug money. "How much is in there?"

"A hundred grand. Or I should say it *was* a hundred grand before you dipped your sticky fingers into my pile," Nicky answered, pressing the bag tightly to her chest.

"Take it and go somewhere far away and start a new life."

"In China? What am I going to do in China? I don't speak Asian!" Nicky protested as a steady flow of tears began to stream down her face.

When Lila concocted this whole plan, she hadn't really thought through how it would impact Nicky. But looking at this strung-out and confused young woman weeping, on the brink of the unknown, she felt terrible.

"Listen," she said softly as she put a firm, reassuring hand on Nicky's shoulder. "The life you had here wasn't going anywhere good. Now you have a chance to make a fresh start. The world is yours for the taking." Her attempt at a pep talk made her internally cringe. She was no Oprah, that's for sure.

And Nicky seemed to agree. The more Lila talked, the harder she cried.

"Plus," Lila said. "The truth is, if you stay here, they'll kill you."

"Thanks to you!" Nicky shouted. Her drawn face was now red, mascara pooled around her puffy eyes.

"Listen, I'm sorry, okay. But this was something I had to do."

"Whatever."

"But, there's one more thing I need before you go," Lila said somewhat sheepishly.

Nicky shot her a bewildered look. This strange woman had, in the course of an hour, totally obliterated her life, and that, seemingly, wasn't enough. "Are you seriously asking me for a favor?"

"I'm not *asking* for anything," Lila said, going back into tough-cop mode. She couldn't let this profoundly messed up woman get the better of her. She was here for her sister. She had to remember that. She reached into Nicky's pockets and fished out her cell phone. "I'm going to have to take this."

"Fuck you do!" Nicky said, trying to grab it back. But Lila slapped her grasping hands away.

Lila said, "Just one more thing."

"What?" Nicky scowled.

"Smile for the camera." Lila pointed Nicky's phone at Nicky and took a picture.

When the shutter noise sounded, Nicky gave Lila a confused look. "What the fuck is that for?"

"A little keepsake of our time together," Lila said. "Now get on the boat, Nicky. It's your only choice." She got into the Pontiac and began to drive away, watching Nicky in her rearview mirror. At first, she didn't move. Then, right before Lila exited the port, she looked back to see Nicky slowly running to the boat, the duffel bag slung over her shoulder.

CHAPTER 6

As SHE DROVE the rusted Pontiac along the streets of down-town Miami, Lila's conscience started nagging at her. She pictured Nicky, marooned on a freighter headed to the middle of nowhere, crammed between the looming towers of cargo, her pale, oval face stained with running rivulets of black mascara as seamen wolfishly eyed her and her big bag of money with hungry, sideways glances.

Then again, she got the sense that Nicky was nobody's victim.

Nicky had just been in the wrong place at the wrong time, and got swept up in something that was bigger than she was. Lila knew how that felt, and she knew that it sucked. But considering Nicky was transporting a hundred grand of cocaine, she was probably street savvy enough to take care of herself, or so Lila hoped.

There was no point feeling bad about things. She had a job to do, and if that required her to disrupt the lives of a few people along the way, then so be it.

Nicky's cell phone vibrated, startling Lila. The caller ID was blocked, but Lila picked it up anyway. No time like the present to start being someone else. She took a deep breath and answered the phone.

"Hello," she said, trying to keep her voice flat and affectless like Nicky's.

"Nicky Collins?" It was a man's voice.

"Speaking."

"This is Second Officer Asher Lydon calling from *Rising Tide*."

Asher Lydon. From what Lila could glean from the police report, Asher was an interesting character. Now twenty-eight years old, he'd started working for the Warren family almost six years ago—months after he suffered a career-ending injury when he hit a reef headfirst during a Big Wave World Tour, back when he was pro surfer. He'd always worked on Jack's yachts, but in his police interview he said that Jack had repeatedly promised to bring him into the Warren Software fold. ("He said I'd be great in sales," Asher told the police.) Whether that was true or not was impossible to say. No one else had corroborated Asher's story.

"Oh, hi."

"Hey there," he said in a breezy, sexy voice. "Just calling to tell you that everyone's got to report to the ship by five P.M. this afternoon."

"Great. Thanks."

"And don't be late. The chief stewardess has a real stick up her ass. Trust me, you don't want to start off on the wrong foot."

"Thanks for the warning. I'll be sure to be on time."

"No worries," he said. "Oh, and we're at the Miami Beach Marina, in case no one told you."

"Sounds good," Lila said as the palm trees and the big-box stores lining Biscayne Boulevard flew by her car window. "What slip?"

"Don't worry," Asher said with an amused chuckle. "I don't think you'll have any trouble finding the boat."

"Right," Lila said. "Of course. See you then."

"Looking forward to it."

Lila hung up the phone, not knowing if she'd played that right. She was going undercover as an experienced stewardess, yet she knew absolutely nothing about yachts except that they were big boats full of really rich people. But she'd pick things up quickly. She didn't really have any other choice. And how hard could it be?

It was already a few minutes after 2:00 P.M. Anxious to get everything done, she pushed the Pontiac as fast as it could go, causing the car's rusty metal body to vibrate violently. She cursed herself for not taking Nicky's BMW. She had so much to do, so little time, and zero patience for rundown cars.

So, first things first, she dumped the Pontiac. She had just forced a drug smuggler to hog-tie a Colombian psychopath with very flimsy duct tape and left them both alive to tell the tale. There was a good chance that the cartel member had had an opportunity to ID the shit box she was now so cavalierly driving around the streets of Miami. She didn't want to run the risk of getting into a firefight with pissed-off members of the Cali cartel looking to get their drugs and money back, so she took the car through a car wash to get rid of any of her or Nicky's prints on its exterior, making sure to get wipes for the inside as well.

Then she made her way to the Aventura Mall. There were plenty of things she needed before boarding the yacht, and she figured she'd be able to get everything at this vast megamall. Once she was in its endless parking lot, she carefully wiped the car's interior and grabbed the metal briefcase with the money and her gun.

For a brief moment, she stood staring at the coke-filled

duffel bag, weighing her options. Nicky had said that she was going to sell it herself. If that was true, then it would be better for Lila to ditch the coke with the car. But if Nicky was lying, as Lila's instincts warned her that she was, then she should take the drugs along with her. Lila knew that carrying that amount of class-A narcotics made her incredibly vulnerable. If she was searched, she'd be up on federal trafficking charges with a mandatory minimum sentence of ten years—and if she got herself thrown in prison, she'd never make it back to 2019. It would put an end to her entire existence, and probably fuck with the space-time continuum that Teddy was always going on about.

But if someone on that yacht was expecting those drugs, and Nicky Collins couldn't deliver, Lila's cover would be blown, and any chance she had at solving her sister's murder would be lost. She couldn't take that chance. Deciding to keep the coke with her, she grabbed the duffel bag and bid the car adieu, knowing it would sit in this lot for many days before the city eventually impounded it. Just another abandoned piece of rust baking away in the South Florida sun.

With the metal briefcase in her hand and the cocaine-stuffed bag flung over her shoulder, Lila walked into the antiseptically cheerful megamall. In a little over an hour, she bought all the supplies she needed for the yacht. A laptop for research and reviewing evidence, underwear, a swimsuit, shoes, sunglasses, a few simple items of clothing, and toiletries. She even found ammunition for her handgun at one of the sporting-goods stores.

Lila crammed all her goodies into a tiny, mirrored department-store dressing room and carefully packed her new purchases in an olive-green army-navy bag. The bricks of coke and the cash went on the bottom. Her clothes on top of that. She bought a waterproof case for her gun, which she tucked underneath the small mountain of her bras and underwear. She slid the metal briefcase under the bench in the changing room, leaving it empty and open just to avoid the inevitable bomb scare.

Then came the question about her appearance. She looked into the full-length mirror as the hum of the fluorescent lights buzzed above her. Standing there, barefoot, wearing only a simple white cotton bra and underwear, she regarded herself closely. She was five feet nine inches, a couple inches taller than Nicky.

Lila grabbed the purloined cell phone and looked at the picture she'd just taken of a very pissed-off Nicky. She felt a little twinge of pity as she studied the young woman's face, but mostly she was worried. In truth, she may have overestimated how much she and Nicky looked like each other. They were both white and around the same age. Nicky's eyes were hooded and brown, whereas Lila's were much bigger and hazel. They both had prominent cheekbones and large mouths, but the difference in their noses was problematic. Even though Nicky hadn't met anyone on the yacht, it was safe to assume that they had copies of her documentation—that was standard protocol. That meant it was crucial for Lila to come as close as humanly possible to resembling the rather ragged-looking woman in the picture.

Lila's only hope to pass as Nicky hinged on successfully copying her haircut. She was in need of a salon, and on the mall's first floor, next to a frozen-yogurt stand, she found one. She walked right in.

"Can I help you, hon?" asked the hairdresser closest to the door. She had heavy foundation and teased hair the color of cherry Kool-Aid.

"I need a quick cut and color."

"Sure thing. Sit right over here," the hairdresser said, pointing to the adjacent chair with the pink teasing comb she was using to diligently back-comb the hair of her aged customer into exactly the same style as her own. "I'll be with you in a couple minutes. I'm just putting the final touches on Ruth-Anne here."

Lila settled into the chair, carefully placing her oversize duffel bag at her feet. And true to her word, the hairdresser was hovering over her in two minutes flat. She introduced herself as Siggy, and then immediately began raking her fingers through Lila's long, dark hair.

"What a treat," Siggy said. "I never get pretty young things like you in here. And this mane of yours is out of this world."

But the woman's excitement soured the moment Lila showed her what she wanted.

"You want me to make you look like this poor weeping girl?" Siggy studied the cell-phone picture of Nicky. She was aghast. "Chop it off and bleach it to holy hell? I will do no such thing."

"I'm going away and I need something quick and easy that I don't have to think about," Lila said, annoyed that she had to explain herself to this woman.

"Then I'll put it in cornrows or something." She gave Lila an encouraging nod and smile. There was a smudge of fuchsia lipstick on her teeth. "I'll give you a real Bo Derek look. That'll do the trick."

Lila shook her head no while fighting the urge to jump out of the chair and find another, more agreeable salon. But she knew she didn't have the time. She needed to cajole Siggy, so she plastered a forced smile to her face. "I totally hear you. But I need this done and I need it done quickly. Can you do this for me?"

The two women looked straight forward into the mirror, staring into each other's eyes, their mutual fake grins stretched tight. It was a game of makeover chicken, but Lila wouldn't be the one to give in.

"Fine," Siggy conceded, exhaling in defeat. "I'll do it, but I won't like it."

"Thank you. That's all I ask."

Siggy's mournful sighs and whimpers could be heard throughout the salon as large chunks of Lila's hair floated down into piles on the linoleum floor. After sixty minutes, Siggy was done.

"If anyone asks you who did your hair, feel free to forget my name," she said, her disgust with her work preventing her from making eye contact with Lila.

Lila thought the hundred-dollar tip she was leaving would help ease Siggy's suffering, but the hairdresser just shrugged her shoulders as she slid the bill into her bra. "I guess girls your age don't want to be pretty anymore. It's a real shame."

"Don't worry," Lila said as she picked up her duffel bag loaded with cash, cocaine, and ammunition. "Most girls aren't like me."

"God, I hope so," Siggy said as she started sweeping up the remnants of the old Lila Day.

CHAPTER 7

BY THE TIME the cab dropped Lila off at the entrance to the Miami Beach Marina, it was already five minutes past five o'clock. She was late, just as she'd been warned not to be. As she rushed under the white-and-turquoise gates toward the walkways floating atop the churned-up azure waters, she immediately spotted *The Rising Tide*. True to Asher's word, Jack Warren's yacht was impossible to miss. Moored at the farthest end of dock, the boat was a behemoth, dwarfing everything that fell in its oversize shadow.

At over four hundred feet, it was as long as ten double-decker buses placed nose to tail. Though it wasn't the largest superyacht in the world, it certainly was nothing to sneeze at. As Lila approached the yacht, she spotted a man standing on the dock shouting up to several uniformed crew who were scurrying around frantically. She knew from having studied photos of all the crew and passengers that it was Asher. In fact, she recognized everybody she saw on and around the giant boat. And then there was *The Rising Tide* itself—seeing it for the first time in real life felt surreal, like she was stepping into a movie she'd watched a thousand times.

"Goddamnit, Pedro," Asher yelled to a slight boy dangling

from a rope just above one of the yacht's four decks. Pedro had a giant bucket in one hand and a sponge in the other. A miserable look was locked on to the boy's face as he attempted to wash the many windows of the sleek yacht's exterior.

Asher continued to bark orders. "I told you to handle this yesterday. Now there's no time."

Lila could only see Asher from behind. He had a perfect back—broad along the shoulders, descending down into a narrow waist, each muscle beautifully delineated. He had sun-bleached hair that he wore long; and his skin, which was deeply tanned caramel color, was almost entirely exposed, except for the long surfer shorts that hung low on his narrow hips.

"Excuse me," she said to his muscular back as she approached.

"What?" he barked, spinning around sharply to show his annoyance at being disturbed during such a busy moment. But the instant he saw a beautiful woman standing in front of him, his stern face transformed into a wide smile, revealing a row of dazzling white teeth. Lila could always spot a so-called ladies' man. And this guy was definitely a member of that ever-preening, ever-attentive tribe.

"I'm sorry," he said with a playful lilt to his voice, studying her intently with his ice-blue eyes. He had a smattering of light freckles on the bridge of his nose and full, womanly lips. "How may I help you?"

"I'm Nicky Collins. The new stewardess."

"Ah, yes." His grin turned slightly devilish. "Don't you mean the second stewardess?"

"Right," Lila said. "Of course." She felt a wave of heat rise to her face. The world she was about to enter was as hierarchical and regimented as the military, and she'd just gotten her rank wrong. She'd have to be more careful.

"Not that I care," he said apologetically, seeing the flash of embarrassment on her face. "It's just that the chief stewardess does. She runs a tight ship, let me tell you. Anyway," he said, sticking out his hand toward her, "I'm Asher Lydon, the *second* officer. Pleasure to finally meet you in person." He shook her hand firmly, keeping hold of it for a beat or two longer than required. They'd known each other for ten seconds, and he was already signaling his interest.

"And speaking of the chief stewardess," Asher continued. "She was just here a second ago, asking about you. None too pleased, if I can give you a little warning."

"Perfect." Lila sighed as she switched her giant bag from her left to her right shoulder. It was getting heavier by the second, and its straps were digging painfully into her skin.

"One thing about starting off on the wrong foot," he said as he went to grab Lila's bag, "is you can only go up from there. Right?"

"Let's hope so."

As he slung her bag over his bare shoulder, she noticed he was wearing a Rolex Deepsea watch. Surf shorts and a $10,000 watch. That kind of getup told Lila a lot about Asher. He was a man who liked the finer things in life, but didn't like working too hard to get them—the type of guy who wouldn't mind being bought for the right price.

"Wow," Lila said. "Nice watch. Where'd you get it?"

"A friend gave it to me," he answered obliquely.

"I could use friends like that."

"Don't worry. On this boat, those are the only type of friends you'll make."

Just as Lila had suspected, Asher was more than happy to use his looks and charm to cajole his way into the good life.

"Follow me," he said as they walked up a sturdy gangway to

board the yacht's grand back deck. "I'll show you where you're staying so you can change into your uniform."

Lila was beyond grateful that Asher was being so helpful. It did a lot to quell the nervousness she always felt on her first day undercover.

They walked onto the main level of the yacht, through a swarm of activity as everyone readied for a long voyage. Lila soaked the whole scene up. If she didn't already know Jack Warren was notorious for his limitless appetite for opulence, she'd have figured it out within a minute aboard *The Rising Tide*. There were cases upon cases of Ace of Spades Armand de Brignac champagne being loaded belowdeck. At $6,000 a case, she figured there was probably a hundred grand alone in the bubbly. And it didn't stop there. Crates of wines—all super-Tuscans and Burgundy grands crus—were being handled with the extreme care that their value necessitated. There were tins of Ossetra caviar, boxes of gorgeous fruits and vegetables, macaroons from Ladurée, and goodies from Dean & DeLuca all being stowed away in the lower deck. It was a spread befitting a sultan, a king, or someone who thought he was God.

"It's mayhem now, so I'll give you the grand tour later. Right now I'll bring you into the bowels of the ship, where us lowly crew are stashed."

She followed him down a narrow staircase into the crew quarters. The moment they traveled from the open expanse of the aft deck to the cramped confines of the lower deck, she began to feel claustrophobic. A wave of nausea and dizziness overcame her as the ground swayed and shifted beneath her feet.

"Are we rocking?" Lila said, feeling out of control as she tried to steady herself against a wall as the boat slightly pitched to the left.

Asher looked back at her and laughed. "You're kidding, right?"

She was seasick and the boat hadn't even left the dock. This was going to be tougher than she imagined. She laughed it off. "Of course I'm kidding," Lila replied, trying to stand still and straight though her head was swimming. "It just takes me a while to get my sea legs is all."

"Right," Asher said, with a wink. "And when that fails, I've got some seasickness tablets for you. Just ask if you need any."

"I'm sure that won't be necessary," she said, though she feared the exact opposite would be true.

"Whatever you say," he said.

They walked a couple more feet down the narrow hall, then Asher opened a small door. "And here you are. Home sweet home." Lila looked into the cabin. It was a windowless box, much smaller than a prison cell, about the width of a double bed, and painted bright white. Two sleeping cots were bolted to the wall with storage drawers under the bottom bunk. "You'll be in here with the third stew, Sam Bennett. Everyone's on the main deck right now, where you should be. So hurry up, get changed, and join us up there."

Lila knew all about Sam, or Samantha, from the police report. Age twenty-three, from Belle Glade, Florida. A high school dropout who won enough rinky-dink Florida beauty pageants to want more from life than the poverty and ugliness she saw around her. She'd been working the luxe yacht circuit since she turned nineteen.

"Great," Lila said. "I'll be up in a second."

"Listen," Asher said, stepping too close to Lila for comfort, given that she was on the verge of blacking out. She could feel the heat of his skin and smell his coconut tanning oil. "I don't know if you know this, but just a few days ago, Jack Warren, the guy who owns this ship, fired absolutely every single member of his old crew with only a few exceptions. I am," he said proudly, "one of those exceptions. So, I know this guy and I know what a hard-ass he is."

Lila wasn't sure what point Asher was trying to make, but she wanted him to hurry up with it. She felt like she was quickly losing her battle with a claustrophobic meltdown.

"I'm telling you this because you seem like a nice person. And you were late today, which means you already didn't listen to me once. So listen to me now. Be ready to work really hard and try not to draw too much attention to yourself. Smile and be a good girl. Got it? Your uniform should be in one of the drawers. Throw it on, and see you in a couple minutes, okay?"

Lila nodded. She wished she were upstairs, drinking in deep breaths of sea air.

Dropping his professional facade, Asher relaxed into a boyish smile. "Okay. I'll leave you to it, then." He dropped the duffel bag on the floor, where it landed with a heavy thud. "Christ, what did you pack? Gold bricks?"

A nervous laugh dribbled out of Lila's mouth, which she had stretched into a fake smile. She was quite sure that the panic in her eyes was impossible to miss.

Just as Asher turned to go, and Lila was lurching forward to shut the door behind him, he turned back around. "Remember, we work like bitches, but we're paid like kings!"

Lila gave him a feeble thumbs-up. This was going to be harder than she thought. Then he was gone.

"Fuuuuck," she quietly exhaled once she was alone. This wasn't a bedroom so much as a Japanese nap pod. *And* she had to share it with someone else. Lila slid open the left side of drawers to see all of Sam's stuff neatly folded. Then she opened the right-side drawers. They were empty, save for three clean and pressed uniforms and one small black dress, which were all folded perfectly. She checked the size. Of course Nicky must have told someone her measurements so that the clothes fit. Lucky for Lila, they were all in her size, a two. In the back of the drawer were a couple pairs of white canvas sneakers, one size smaller than her feet, but she'd have to make do.

She quickly shed her clothes and put on the uniform: a starched white, sleeveless, button-down shirt, a crisp white A-line miniskirt that barely covered her ass, and a navy-blue silk handkerchief with white polka dots that Lila tied around her neck.

Now she turned to unpacking her stuff. She locked the cabin door and dumped the contents of her duffel bag onto the floor. Unlike her roommate, Sam, with all of her pastel-colored clothes, lacy underwear, and tiny bikinis folded into neat piles, Lila's belongings could have her thrown in jail for a decade. She had an abundance of totally damning contraband and absolutely no place to hide it.

She ripped the bottom mattress off its frame, sending sheets and pillows sailing through the air. Her first thought was to stuff everything into the mattress itself. But she didn't have a knife to slice into its heavy fabric. Shit, she thought. She was on the brink of a panic attack as motion sickness and claustrophobia collided into one big neurological clusterfuck in her brain.

There was a loud knock on the door.

"Miss Collins?" a posh British voice inquired.

Lila froze. The extent to which she was completely screwed struck her, only momentarily, as very funny. She wondered if this was something she and Teddy could laugh about once she was safely back in 2019.

There was another, louder knock on the door. "Miss Collins. This is the chief stewardess. We are waiting for you on the main deck."

"Just a second," Lila cried cheerfully, her voice calling out with a singsongy lilt that she hoped didn't betray her growing alarm. Behind the door was Edna Slaughter, age fifty-three, from Bristol, England. She'd been Elise Warren's maid, protector, confidante, and scratching post since 1999 and stayed on with Elise after Jack's death, after her second husband's death, and even after her third husband's death. Lila would bet that no one on the planet, not any of her three husbands, not her child or even her psychiatrist, knew Elise Warren better than Edna Slaughter.

Lila began to frantically arrange the $10,000 stacks of hundred-dollar bills side by side with wrapped-up bricks of cocaine atop the mattress frame. She grabbed the gun, released the magazine clip, then put the pistol at the foot of her bed and the cartridge in a drawer. Even though she knew that it would take only a quick second for someone to discover this paltry hiding spot, it was the only solution available to her at this desperate moment, and it would be a temporary one. She reassured herself that she'd find something better once she got a sense of the giant yacht's layout.

Trying to hoist the unwieldy mattress back onto the frame felt like wrestling an alligator into a shoe box. Just as she got it into the proper position, she accidentally knocked the lamp to the floor. The subsequent metallic clang and crash reignited the knocking.

"Miss Collins. Open the door this instant!"

"I'm just changing! One moment!"

Finally, she got the bed on the frame. True, it sat a bit high, but it was less obvious than she feared.

She ran to the door and flung it open. She was short of breath and covered in a light mist of panic sweat. From the look of horror on the face of the woman standing in the hall-way, Lila guessed that she appeared fairly deranged.

"I'm Chief Stewardess Edna Slaughter and you are off to a ter-ribly poor start," the woman said in her English upper-class accent with its deep rich tones and overly enunciated syllables, as if she was permanently enrolled in an elocution class. From her profile, Lila knew Edna was from a strictly working-class background, so that accent was as phony as Lila's subservient attitude. Lila reached out to shake Edna's hand but the woman failed to return the ges-ture. Instead she slightly raised her chin and turned her gaze away in apparent disgust. Lila let her hand drop.

"My God," the chief stewardess said, looking into Lila's room in horror, "what happened here?"

Lila inhaled sharply, worried that, in her haste, she'd left money or drugs on the floor. But as she turned, she was relieved to see that it was just littered with sheets, an overturned lamp, pillows, clothes, and underwear absolutely everywhere.

"I was just in the middle of unpacking, Mrs. Slaughter. Or should I call you Edna?"

The woman's eyes widened. "It is most surely Chief Stew-ardess Mrs. Slaughter to you."

"Well, that's a mouthful," Lila said, desperately trying (and totally failing) to lighten the mood. Mrs. Slaughter was a rather tall woman—taller than Lila, who was quite tall herself. She wore her light brown hair short and heavily layered around her long face, reminiscent of Camilla Parker Bowles. As she looked Lila up and down, Lila could feel her eyes lingering on all that was wanting—the messy hair, the untucked shirt, the untied shoelaces, the handkerchief improperly knotted.

"Listen here," Mrs. Slaughter said, her voice cold. "If you think you can be flippant with me, you have another thing coming. Now, you will do exactly what I say, exactly when I say it, with zero hesitation, cheek, sulk, or moods. Do we understand each other?"

Lila nodded in agreement, trying to suppress a smirk. Who was this third-rate tyrant chastising her like a naughty little schoolgirl?

"First thing, clean this mess up, and then report to the galley in five minutes. Remember, we are still docked and there are a hundred girls just as dumb and pretty as you walking around this marina looking for work. Keep in mind that you are easily replaceable."

The two women regarded each other silently. Lila nodded.

"Five minutes, then. No later," Mrs. Slaughter said between tightly pursed lips.

"No later," Lila repeated. "Of course."

Once Mrs. Slaughter left, Lila righted the mess she had made as fast as humanly possible, placing her computer and her ever-important thumb drive underneath her bras and swimsuits. Then she left to find the galley. As she walked down the carpeted hall, she realized she had absolutely no idea where she was headed, but once she climbed the stairs from the lower deck to the main deck, she was ecstatic to once again be outside with the sea and sky and away from the claustrophobic rat's maze of the crew's quarters.

Spotting another member of the crew washing down the deck, Lila approached him. Her legs were still unsteady.

"Excuse me?"

The man turned with the hose in this hand. He was a squat, red-haired fellow, with meat paws for hands and powerful, stocky limbs. His freckled skin was a deep reddish brown, as if it had been repeatedly sunburned into permanent defeat. He looked at her silently. His inquisitive green eyes were as bright as emeralds. Like everyone else she'd met so far on the boat, she knew him from the police report. His name was Hamish Rankin, but everyone called him Mudge. His Scottish brogue had been so thick during his interview with police that she had to listen to it three times to understand everything he'd said.

"Hi, I'm new to the boat," she began.

"We're all new," he said in a heavy Scottish accent. "Name's Mudge. Lead deckhand." He extended his giant hand with its thick, short fingers. Lila shook it. She had never felt calluses so profound.

"Pleasure to meet you," she said. "I'm Nicky. Second stewardess. And I'm also late. Would you happen to know where the galley is?"

He gave her a perplexed look, then burst into laughter. "Oh, that's a good one. Next you'll be asking me where's the ocean?"

Lila just stood there blankly. Seeing her serious face, Mudge quickly pulled himself out of his swell of merriment. "You mean you're serious?"

Lila nodded.

"No ship I've ever seen has a galley anywhere but below-deck," he said. "But that don't mean I know it all." There was a sheepishness in his voice. Lila could tell he was trying to be kind and she was grateful for his momentary generosity. "It's back where you came from," Mudge said, pointing to the staircase that led to the lower level.

With a thanks and a sigh, Lila returned to her subterranean dungeon and hightailed it to the galley, where she found an ever-frowning Mrs. Slaughter along with a sunny blonde and a tiny, beady-eyed man in an impeccably white and starched chef's coat. The chef was using long tweezers to carefully place crystallized lilac flowers on a tray of elaborate pastries.

Lila had a hard time explaining to Mrs. Slaughter why it had taken her eight minutes to get to the galley as opposed to the five minutes the head stewardess had allotted. It was imperative that Lila pass as someone who had at least a bit of a clue about life on a yacht, otherwise she knew she'd be out on her ass.

The blonde leaned in to Lila. "Hiya," she whispered. "I'm Sam." With her tanned, long-legged, bubbly radiance and sweet southern accent, Sam was the absolute platonic ideal of an all-American beauty.

"I'm Nicky, your new roommate," Lila said with a smile.

"If you can call that a room," Sam said.

A serious and straight-backed Mrs. Slaughter cleared her throat loudly, annoyed at the two whispering stewardesses. "You'll have plenty of time to get to know each other, I assure you. Now it's time to get to work. In less than twenty-four hours, Jack Warren and one hundred VIPs will board this ship expecting nothing less than utter perfection. And that's something, given the current state of affairs," she said, looking directly at Lila, "that frightens me. I need not tell you that most of the crew is new to this boat, and to its owner, so we must be flawless. Of course, we are greatly honored to have the Michelin-starred chef François Vatel aboard." Mrs. Slaughter turned toward the chef, acknowledging him with a ladylike smattering of applause, to which the chef just snorted in response and returned to his painstaking work.

"The French," Mrs. Slaughter silently mouthed, with a roll of her eyes and a shake of her head. "Chef Vatel and his sous chef will be hard at work preparing for tomorrow, and so will we. I have precisely detailed the tasks that need to get done and the exact time each job must be finished and ready for my personal inspection."

Mrs. Slaughter handed both Sam and Lila a clipboard. Lila glanced at the endless list of tasks: iron linen sheets, make beds in all ten guest suites, scrub toilets, polish all brass knobs and door runners, restock clean towels, etc, etc, etc. She bit back a groan as she set off to work.

For more than six hours, she scrubbed, polished, folded, and ironed every inch of *The Rising Tide* until her knees ached, her back throbbed, her hands began to cramp in protest, and her fingertips were red and puckered from hours in soapy water. Each and every move she made was icily observed and monitored by the ever-present Mrs. Slaughter. Whenever Lila looked up from the task at hand, there she stood, with straight back and chin thrust up, staring down on Lila with overwhelming disapproval.

"Miss Collins," she'd ask in a voice full of disdain, "aren't you familiar with how to iron and fold a fitted sheet?" "Miss Collins, I hope you aren't planning on using Windex to clean the mahogany." "Miss Collins, are you sure you've scrubbed a toilet before?" And on, and on, and on, and on.

As Lila moved about the yacht, she took in all of its grandeur and elegance—even if she was seeing most of it while scrubbing the floor on her hands and knees. There was the glass-encased whirlpool on the top sun deck that Lila had to make streak-free; a white-tiled spa (which, she noted, was four times the size of her quarters) that she had to scrub vigorously so that it sparkled enough for Mrs. Slaughter's specifications; a special-order copper bathtub in the master cabin's en suite bathroom that needed to be polished; a ten-person screening room that had to be vacuumed and each of the plush leather theater seats gently wiped down.

Lila swept the helicopter pad. She laundered and stacked the towels for the yacht's vast workout room, cleaned its floor-to-ceiling mirror, vacuumed under its barbaric-looking Pilates equipment, and sprayed down all the yoga mats. Then there was making the baking-soda-and-water preparation to clean the walls of the red cedar, eight-person sauna.

And that was only in the first couple hours of work.

But she had to admit, the yacht was one exquisite piece of work, even if it was a total bitch to clean. No expense had been spared, no luxury denied. Each choice was the absolute best and most elegant example of its kind. Lila had plenty of experience living among the most indulgent billionaires imaginable, and she knew that money didn't just buy the fine things in life. It also bought flashy, garish, over-the-top displays of hideous grandeur. But *The Rising Tide* was nothing like that. It was perfection, classic and exquisite. It was as close to a work of art as a boat could get.

By midnight, when Mrs. Slaughter tersely said, "That'll do for now," Lila was beyond relieved to call it a day. She was so profoundly vanquished that returning to her little coffin tucked into a nook of the lower deck sounded like heaven. Lucky for her, her claustrophobia and seasickness were no match for her profound fatigue. But the moment she entered the room, a jolt of energy shot through her as she saw Sam, her bunkmate, stretched sleepily out on the bottom bunk, unaware that she was a thin mattress above a treasure trove of drugs and money.

"Hiya, Nicky. Long day, huh?" Sam chirped. Glowing with vibrant good health, she seemed untouched by the day's endless labors.

Lila just nodded in agreement. She wasn't sure what to say. Did Sam really not feel the lumps and bumps of the contraband beneath her? How could Lila get her off that bed?

"Who knew old Slaughterhouse could be such a horrific shrew?" Sam asked. "I've never been bossed around so much in my whole fucking life."

Again, Lila nodded. Sam shot her a perplexed look.

"Is something wrong? Or is speaking just not your thing?" Sam asked with a teasing smile.

"It's only that . . ." Lila paused, looking at Sam's cheerful, inquisitive face. She bet that Sam was the prettiest and most popular girl in her run-down town. Most likely she believed the whole world was about ten times kinder than it actually was, a naïveté shared only by the beautiful and the dumb. "I'm afraid of heights," Lila lied. "Could I sleep on the bottom bunk?"

Sam, dressed only in a tank top and ruffled pink cotton underwear, bounced right off the bed like a spring. "Oh, totally!" She clambered up to the top bunk, which was so close to the room's low ceiling that sitting up was impossible.

"Thanks. I really appreciate it," Lila said, shedding her soiled uniform and throwing on a camouflage T-shirt in size XXL, which she was horrified to discover had a deer caught in a rifle scope on its front. She'd been in such a rush at the sporting-goods store in the mall when she grabbed it that she hadn't noticed what was on it, which was something she now deeply regretted.

"Nice duds," Sam laughed. "Now I know why we're bunking together."

"Why?" Lila asked.

"Because we're both a couple of rednecks."

"Just don't tell the chief stewardess. I don't want to give her yet another reason to hate me," Lila said as she lay back on her bed. Never had lying horizontally felt so good. "Hey, thanks again for switching bunks with me."

"Actually," she heard Sam say quietly as she closed her eyes, "I picked the bottom bunk because it *was* so lumpy. I thought you'd be more comfortable up here. But if you prefer the bottom bunk, then all the better. If you change your mind, let me know. I'm easy. The main thing about me is I don't want any drama. I always get along with everyone, except this one time . . ."

While listening to the sweet nattering of her bunkmate as the yacht slowly swayed side to side, Lila felt her eyelids grow heavy. She blinked a few times before she fell into a profound sleep within seconds.

That night, as the boat rocked Lila like a baby in a cradle, she was visited by her sister in a vibrant, Technicolor dream. In the upside-down world that her sleeping mind created, Lila found herself back in her childhood home, which was floating in the middle of a vast lake. She and her sister were on its main floor as ice-cold water began pouring into the house from the windows and under the doors. As Lila rushed about with a bucket trying to keep their home from sinking, Ava was focused on protecting her paintings from the deluge, clutching them to her chest as the water rapidly rose around her. Lila, angry that Ava wasn't helping bail out the house, grabbed the paintings from her hands. Then she looked at them, seeing, with horror, that every canvas was covered in violent black brushstrokes with bloodred slashes through the middle, a sight so frightening that it ripped her out of sleep.

She sat up, hitting her skull on the bunk above her. "Crap," she said under her breath, rubbing her head and wincing. The panic she felt in her nightmare still clung to her as she tried, in the pure blackness of her windowless room, to shake off the haunting image of Ava getting swallowed up by the water. But, as the sounds of Sam's whistling snore sailed down from above and she felt the ship gently rock below her, Lila managed to calm herself enough to lie back down, close her eyes, and let her painful dream drift out of her memory.

BEING A STEWARDESS on a superyacht had its downside, as Lila learned bright and early the following morning at her 5:30 wake-up call. But her job also had a great number of potential advantages. If the previous day was at all standard, she would have access to almost every imaginable corner of the ship, including the guest rooms and, hopefully, Jack Warren's massive master suite on the fourth deck.

The very essence of her job was to be invisible until she was needed, and then to promptly recede into the background once her duties were done. Nothing could have suited her mission more. She was there to prove that Elise Warren had killed her husband on the night of his fiftieth birthday, and to gather enough evidence so that she could, once and for all, clear her sister's name. A lot of snooping would be involved, and she was in the perfect position to do it.

Though she was desperate to stash the drugs and the money in a safe hiding spot, she knew that moving either now would be premature. Once the crew and the guests were settled in and Lila had a better sense of what went where, she'd be able to find a location where the contraband wouldn't be discovered. Until then, she'd just hope and pray no one looked under her mattress. But really, she figured, no one cleans the room of the cleaning ladies, right?

Lila threw on a robe, grabbed her toiletry bag, and sleepily padded down the narrow hallway to the crew bathroom. Just as she was about to turn the door's handle, the door flew open and out popped a very bright and chipper Sam.

"Morning, sunshine!" Sam said, a little too ebulliently for Lila this early in the morning. Sam stood before her, with her flaxen hair, the pale vibrancy of corn silk, twisted up in large Velcro rollers, her makeup perfectly applied, and her lips, painted a deep coral, stretched into a smile.

"Morning," Lila grumbled as she slipped past Sam into the tiny doll-size bathroom.

Once Lila was dressed and presentable, she made her way to the crew mess, where Sam was happily chattering away with an exhausted-looking Mudge, who was bent over a cup of coffee and failing to acknowledge her sunshiny existence.

The mess was a cozy spot, with a few portholes that allowed Lila a glimpse of the outside world, not that there was any sun at that ungodly hour. She nodded to Pedro the deckhand, who was slumped down in one of the two banquettes. She poured herself a cup of coffee and slid a piece of bread into the toaster. Just as the caffeine was beginning to help her feel like a normal human being, Mrs. Slaughter marched in and ruined the whole thing.

"Ready to work?" she said to Lila and Sam. Sam jumped to her feet so quickly that Lila thought she was seconds away from saluting.

"Can I finish making this toast?" Lila said.

Mrs. Slaughter glared at her. "You most certainly can*not*! Eating happens on your own time. It's six A.M. now. Mr. Warren and his guests will be arriving in mere hours, and there are countless things to do before then. We simply must get started."

Lila did as she was told. No cheek. No sulk. No moods. No breakfast.

WHEN JACK WARREN glided onto the boat at a quarter to 4:00 P.M., along with his wife, Elise, and their twenty-year-old daughter, Josie, a perfectly appointed yacht awaited them. Only minutes before the owners boarded, there was total frenzy throughout the boat as the fifteen crew members dashed around putting the final touches on everything. But now, in place of the chaos, all was pristine order and calm. Nothing was out of place. Everything was just as it should be. That was the thing about having a $500 million boat that cost $250,000 a week to maintain—the price tag gave you the right to expect absolute perfection.

Lila didn't see the family board, because she was busy hiding her contraband while the rest of the crew ran around like chickens with their heads cut off. Earlier that afternoon, when she was bringing lunch to some of the engineers in the gigantic all-white engine room, she'd spotted the perfect place to stash her stuff—a lifeboat. She figured that no one would use a lifeboat unless circumstances were so terrible that they wouldn't care the least if they found bricks of cocaine underneath their life vests. So, careful to stay unnoticed, Lila went to her cabin, stuffed the drugs and money in the duffel bag, crept to the lifeboat, and quickly hid all of it in a small compartment at the bow.

Feeling an incredible sense of relief, she resumed her current duty of placing flower arrangements throughout the three-thousand-square-foot sprawling master suite, which had its own private deck stretching out above the sea and a retractable moonroof. She placed five vases full of cherry blossoms, fanning high above a gorgeous cluster of pale yellow garden roses and pink peonies, around the room in the exact locations that the chief stewardess had specified.

Just as she was about to leave, a chauffeur burdened with

several pieces of Louis Vuitton luggage entered. She gave him a cordial nod, and was about to return to the main deck when she heard Jack Warren's booming voice coming down the hall. After a decade spent learning as much about him as was possible, it felt like a voice she knew intimately.

"I won't hear it. This is a goddamn disgrace," Jack barked, his growl getting louder and louder as he drew closer to Lila with every step.

"Just shut up, Jack," a woman hissed. Elise Warren.

Lila froze. She was feet away from the man who would supposedly die by her sister's hands and the woman who used all her wealth and privilege to destroy Ava's life, and her first instinct was to hide. Then another horrified thought dawned on her. What if he recognizes me? What if my sister showed him pictures of our family?

But as they came closer, she knew she had no choice but to face him. Jack and Elise entered the master suite with an icy tension hovering between them. He was taller in real life than Lila thought he'd be, with rich caramel-colored hair that was graying around the temples, a long, aquiline nose, and a neatly manicured beard. He wasn't what Lila would consider handsome, but he had a strong presence, and exuded the power of a man accustomed to getting his way. His wife, on the other hand, was gorgeous, no question about it. A former model whose failed acting career had peaked with her role as "Dead Call Girl" in a *Law & Order* episode, Elise was five ten, with willowy limbs and shoulder-length dark brown hair. Her side-swept bangs expertly framed her perfectly symmetrical face.

Lila stood by the doorway, holding her breath. It suddenly dawned on her as she watched Jack and Elise go about their business in the suite—she on the balcony, he on the computer, each ignoring the other—that she was in the same room with Jack *and* Elise Warren and they hadn't once looked at her. In fact, neither of them had so much as acknowledged her existence. That was one thing Lila had learned about rich people: they were experts in not seeing the help. To them, she was as good as invisible.

And she was determined to take full advantage of it.

Just as Lila was about to leave the room, Josie Warren, Jack and Elise's twenty-year-old daughter, barged in. She was wearing jean shorts, a string of Tibetan prayer beads around her neck, and nothing else.

"Jesus Christ." Jack gasped when he saw her. "Cover yourself!"

"Way to reinforce the patriarchy, Dad," Josie snarled.

"The patriarchy? I can see your goddamn tits!" Jack said, covering his eyes with his hands as he rushed into the bathroom and slammed the door behind him.

"Really, darling," Elise said to her daughter. "I know how you enjoy torturing your father, but remember what I told you. If you don't behave, no semester in Bali. Got it?"

"Whatever," Josie said, with a practiced pout, as she sprawled out, half-naked, on her parents' bed.

Josie had inherited the long leanness of her mother's catwalk-ready body but, unfortunately for her, she didn't get her mom's show-stopping face. That prominent proboscis and weak chin sulking underneath a curtain of long, highlighted hair was one hundred percent from Jack Warren's gene pool.

Lila stood there, momentarily absorbed in the particular brand of gilded misery that was the Warren family life. Quite remarkably, none of the subjects of her careful study took any notice of her. They continued to ignore each other and her. So, as the unseen specter she was, she slipped out of the hornet's nest relieved to find herself unscathed.

CHAPTER 8

THAT AFTERNOON THE crew of *The Rising Tide* was in full, frenetic swing putting the finishing touches in place for Jack Warren's lavish birthday bash, which was set to begin at dusk. This one spectacular evening had required months of planning and preparation and millions of dollars to pull off. Every minute detail had to meet the exacting standards of Jack and Elise Warren. Each member of the crew was given intricate instructions outlining such specifics as how the polished ebony floors needed to be "shiny" but not "glossy" and how the pale pink peonies had to be the color of a ballet slipper, not darker nor lighter.

Jack and Elise knew they had a reputation to uphold. After all, Jack's parties were the stuff of legend. It was, unsurprisingly, the most eagerly anticipated event of the social season. With its A-list celebrity invitees, a performance from the pop star du jour, and only the best food and wine known to man served in abundance, receiving an invite to one of his parties was akin to joining the world's most exclusive club: a universe solely inhabited by wealth, beauty, and celebrity. Music moguls mixed with stars of the art world while models and actresses flirted with the titans of Hollywood and Wall Street.

For the previous ten years, Jack had held his birthday party on his famed Antiguan estate, built on the grounds of an old sugar plantation. But for his fiftieth birthday, he wanted to do something special, something totally over-the-top. So he built himself a $500 million yacht—which may seem like a very indulgent birthday present to give oneself, but with a net worth of over $30 billion, Jack buying *The Rising Tide* was roughly the equivalent of a millionaire buying himself a used Chevy Nova.

Such was the magnitude of Jack's fortune.

But tonight's party, rumored to cost about five million, was just the beginning of the birthday festivities—an amuse-bouche of sorts to kick off Jack's celebratory fortnight. In order to truly honor the half-century he'd spent becoming the legend he was, Jack decided one party wasn't enough. Following tonight's blowout bash to celebrate himself and show off his latest and greatest yacht to all the big wigs, movie stars, and models that were lucky enough to be his friends, Jack would set sail on a luxurious island-hopping cruise for a couple of weeks, culminating with an intimate celebration of his actual birthday on September tenth, while sailing on the warm waters of the Caribbean Sea.

Such was the magnitude of Jack's megalomania.

The guests were set to arrive at 7:00 P.M., so Lila was startled when she felt the leviathan of a yacht pull away from the marina when it was a little after four in the afternoon.

"Are we moving?" she asked Sam, who was helping her make the bed in one of ship's grandest rooms.

"It feels like we are," Sam replied nonchalantly.

They were preparing one of the staterooms for the surprise musical guest that evening: the notorious Allegra Opal, a pop star who'd recently been released from a psychiatric institute following a very public nervous breakdown. The crew had been instructed to never look her directly in the eyes.

Lila got a whiff of coconut tanning oil, so she knew Asher must be close. She caught a glimpse of him walking down the hallway and called after him.

"Hey, Asher. Why's the boat leaving the dock before the guests arrive?"

"Pleb control," Asher said with his typical offhand smugness. He was, once again, wearing nothing but his Rolex and surf shorts. "It's the best way to stop the uninvited from getting on board. Plus, a yacht really isn't a *real* yacht unless you need a boat to get to it."

"Always important to separate the haves from the have-yachts," Lila said to Sam with a roll of her eyes.

"Funny," Asher said without a smile or a laugh. "Ladies," he said, by way of goodbye. Then gave them both a suggestive wink and went off on his way.

"I call dibs on him," Sam blurted out, which made Lila laugh, thinking she was joking. When Sam shot her a hurt look, she backtracked.

"Oh, sorry, Sam. I mean, he's all yours."

"He's not now, but he will be," Sam said. "Oh, yes. He will be mine." Then she broke into a faux Bond villain cackle that made both women break into genuine laughter as they got back to work.

The boat stopped about three hundred feet from the marina and moored just off the southern tip of South Beach. Lila looked out the stateroom window to see that several small boats had encircled the vessel. Each was filled with paparazzi, their long-range zoom lenses trained on *The Rising Tide*.

Sam stood up to look at the boats now swarming like mosquitoes. She rushed out on the deck. "Hello, there!" she shouted, waving her arms. "Wanna take my picture?" She arched her back and stuck out her breasts in a suggestive pose, but the paparazzi weren't biting. They wanted actual stars, not stewardesses with stars in their eyes.

Sam sullenly returned to the room. "They'll want pictures of me one day. I can tell you that much."

An hour later, after Lila was done preparing for the party, the chief stewardess surveyed all of her work.

"An additional fifteen cater waiters will also be working the party to help serve food and drinks. But," she warned, "it's *your* responsibility to make sure everything runs according to *my* standards. Do you understand?" Lila nodded obediently, knowing that no one could possibly match Edna Slaughter's standards.

"You've got to change," Mrs. Slaughter ordered, keeping her eyes down, studying the list she had in her hand.

"I apologize, Chief Stewardess Mrs. Slaughter," Lila said deferentially, sure to use the woman's full name as instructed. "I *will* change. I won't let you down." She worried she was groveling.

Mrs. Slaughter, with her chin still tucked down, turned her icy blue gaze to Lila. "I didn't mean change like that, though don't think your incompetence hasn't been duly noted." A little twisted smirk puckered her lips. "I mean you have to change your clothes for the party."

Lila felt her face flush beet red in embarrassment. "Oh," she mumbled.

"Your dress for tonight's event is in your cabin, along with a picture of how you need to style your hair and makeup. The yacht will be full of VIPs and nothing can be left to chance."

By the time Lila returned to her tiny cabin, Sam was already there, dressed and applying the finishing touches to her perfectly applied makeup. Lila wondered how her bunkmate was always a few steps ahead of her.

"Jesus," she said when she laid eyes on her. "Is that what we're supposed to wear?" Sam was in a long, flamingo-pink satin halter-top dress with a very high slit up the side. Her lips were painted a deep bloodred, her eyelids were lined with a delicately flicked cat eye, and a yellow orchid was pinned into her hair.

Sam's eyes widened. "What? Do I look bad?"

"No. On the contrary. You look magnificent, but you look like sex on a plate."

"Then I look just right," Sam said with a coy smile and a sultry wag of her shapely hips. "Maybe I'll meet my future husband tonight," she said, studying herself in their cabin's tiny mirror. "And wouldn't *he* be a lucky bastard."

"Well, he'll be a bastard, at least," Lila teased.

As the sun began to set, throngs of people crowded the marina, hoping to catch a glimpse of the celebrities, heiresses, fashion icons, and CEOs as they boarded the speedboat shuttles bound for Warren's decadent yacht, which sat glittering just beyond the spectators' grasp.

Upon boarding, the first thing partygoers discovered was that on Jack's boat, there were absolutely no shoes allowed. This was an extremely unpopular rule for many of the guests. Why bother spending $800 on shoes that you weren't allowed to wear? But those accustomed to the strictures of yacht etiquette, which held that street shoes must be taken off before boarding, just kicked off their heels or loafers and headed straight into the party. After all, everyone's hair was already ruined from the speedboat ride. Why not abandon decorum and give in to the reigning mood of opulent debauchery?

It was Lila's job to hand out flutes of champagne to arriving guests and then to collect their shoes, no matter how much they protested. After she tore the women away from their heels, she'd slip each pair into a purple velvet sack with a golden rope closure and give the women a ticket number to claim them at the end of the night, though Lila saw many of the guests absentmindedly drop their tickets as the party progressed. Mrs. Slaughter had said that lost shoes were a constant source of stress, so it was Lila's job to monitor the endless pairs of Louboutins, Blahniks, Jimmy Choos, Roger Viviers, Guccis, Tom Fords, and Pradas that were slipped off the perfectly pedicured feet of the privileged.

With bare feet and champagne in hand, the guests then climbed a flight of stairs and journeyed to the yacht's main deck, which had been transformed to resemble a magical Japanese garden. Paper lanterns gave off a warm, pinkish glow and the long branches of cherry blossoms were woven together into a romantic canopy. The fifty-foot pool on the yacht's third level was filled with lotus flowers; there, two Cirque du Soleil acrobats, costumed in nothing but mermaid tails, shimmied and undulated like exquisite sea nymphs.

From the galley on the lower level, Chef Vatel sent up tray after tray of delicate and delicious canapés served with flutes of Ace of Spades and Cristal. But the real coup of the evening was the presence on board of the legendary octogenarian sushi master Kazuo Murai. It was well known that Jack Warren was a consummate, bordering-on-obsessive Japanophile. So Elise Warren's gift to the husband who had everything was hiring Kazuo Murai to cook for his birthday. Persuading this aged and taciturn genius to leave his Michelin-three-star, closet-size Tokyo restaurant to spend a couple of days preparing his unrivaled food for Jack's party wasn't easy. It took months of delicate courting and plenty of bowing and scraping—not something Elise was fond of doing. The cost of this extravagance was a measly $325,000, not including the round-trip, first-class airfare for Kazuo and his two sons.

As Lila greeted the partygoers, she was on the lookout for the guests she knew would be joining the Warrens for a two-week, island-hopping adventure in the Caribbean. Namely: Senator Baines and his wife, Charity; the Brazilian power couple Thiago and Esperanza Campos; the artist Daniel Poe; the financier Paul Mason; and Warren Software's CFO, Seth Liss.

The Florida senator and his wife were the first of the core group to arrive. Though most of the party guests were dressed in the flowing linens and silks that an "Island chic" dress code requires, the Baineses' look was pure, unadulterated Beltway. The senator had a magnificent mane of thick, pure-white hair, which was combed back and away from his wide forehead. He was wearing a dark blue suit, white shirt, and red tie. There was a flag pin on his lapel, and Lila noticed his gold cuff links boasted the seal of the U.S. Senate. His wife wore a Republican-red sleeveless dress that accentuated her perfectly toned arms and fine-boned form. In keeping with her husband's regal mane, Charity's hair was swept up into a bleached, teased, and shellacked chignon that not even hurricane winds could shake.

When Lila offered the senator a glass of champagne, he shot her a suspicious look. "Is that liquor there American made?" he asked. His voice was deep, slow, and southern, as if each syllable had to be pushed out of his mouth through a vat of thick molasses.

"I believe it's French, sir," she replied deferentially. Though all she could think was, Is this freedom fries guy for real?

"Well, I don't drink my enemy's swill," he said as his face hardened into a menacing glare.

"I'm sorry, sir."

He then threw his head back, letting out a giant guffaw.

"Lighten up, little lady. I'm just yanking your chain." He grabbed the flute out of Lila's hand and drained it in a single gulp.

"My husband, the gentleman," Charity said with mock exasperation. She whispered to Lila, "Do I *really* have to take off these shoes? I'm barely five foot without them. I'll wind up trampled and it'll be your fault."

"Now, honey, hand them over," Clarence Baines said to his wife. "You know Jack's rules are Jack's rules."

"Well, I'll follow his rules only until the election," she said with a smile as she gave up her red satin Valentino heels. "And after you're reelected, I'll won't take off my heels for anybody."

"Hear, hear!" the senator exclaimed as he took his wife's hand and escorted her to the main deck.

For the next twenty minutes, Lila greeted an endless stream of mostly older men with giggling and doe-eyed twenty-year-olds on their arms. She was beginning to lose focus as they all started to blend together. But she snapped out of her daze when Esperanza and Thiago Campos arrived. Though Lila believed that no one had more to gain from the death of Jack Warren than his wife, she was very interested in this mysterious couple from São Paulo, Brazil, who would both be aboard the yacht on the fateful night of Jack's murder, a mere two weeks from this very moment.

Thiago had met Jack Warren in 1976, when they were both freshmen at Harvard, and had been part of Warren's inner circle ever since. He came from a prominent Brazilian family that was chock-full of politicians, army generals, and industrialists. His father, General Humberto Campos, played a leading role in the 1964 coup that put a brutal right-wing military dictatorship in power. The connection benefited the family's coffers but damaged the family name.

A bon vivant who was a known fixture on the international

social scene, Thiago made the best-dressed list of countless magazines out of Paris, New York, and Milan. He always brushed off these accolades as "mere trivialities," but anyone who knew him understood that he was a man of great vanity about his clothes and his looks—both of which were always impeccable. He was also vain about his new wife, Esperanza—a woman of such profound beauty and poise that she was considered a muse to many of the best and brightest in the art and fashion worlds.

Though she was only twenty-three years old, Lucien Freud and Francesco Clemente had already painted her. She modeled for Patrick Demarchelier and Karl Lagerfeld. And she was a fairly accomplished painter in her own right. Almost thirty years her husband's junior, Esperanza came from the same circle of privilege in São Paulo. Ten months before this very moment, they had met at a wedding in Capri, and four weeks later, Thiago proposed to her on a ski lift in Gstaad. They'd been inseparable ever since.

Boarding the yacht with a casual grace, Thiago wore a white linen shirt unbuttoned to his sternum and a slim-fitting white suit. Esperanza had long, straight black hair that fell around her thin shoulders and large, soulful dark brown eyes. A pale lavender floor-length dress with a plunging neckline and a hip-high slit showcased her lithe body. They were locked in conversation when they boarded the yacht and continued speaking in Portuguese as they grabbed champagne and kicked off their shoes. Neither acknowledged Lila's existence.

A few minutes later, Paul Mason and Daniel Poe climbed onto the yacht together, surrounded by a gaggle of underage Russian models. They also would be on *The Rising Tide* the night of Jack Warren's murder, so Lila was familiar with their backgrounds. Paul Mason, age fifty-one, was a lawyer and a legendary investment banker, famous for brokering some of the biggest merger-and-acquisition deals of the last decade. He and Jack had been friends and colleagues for years after Paul was the lead banker in charge of Warren Software's IPO, which made them both very rich men.

Daniel Poe, age thirty-eight, was a superstar of the art world, famous as much for his bad-boy persona and his insatiable drug habit as for his over-the-top, multimillion-dollar art installations. Like Jack, he was a working-class boy done good. Today, he was the most successful living artist in the world, worth about $100 million, with every new piece breathlessly covered by all the leading art critics.

On the surface, Paul Mason and Daniel Poe couldn't have seemed more different. Where Mason was preppy incarnate, with his slicked-back hair, Nantucket-red pants, Sperry Top-Siders, and custom-made shirt, Poe had the rich-artist look down to a T. He reminded Lila of Keith Richards in the seventies, before he started looking like a deranged pirate. He was disheveled and emaciated, but still wore leather pants that easily cost five grand. He had thick, black, square-framed glasses, a black leather jacket, and a skull ring with diamond eyes on his left hand. Lila reckoned that Paul and Daniel's odd-couple friendship was based on their shared love of money, beautiful girls, and getting their way.

"Aren't you a lovely thing," Paul said to Lila as she was bending over to help one of the young models off with her heels. She could feel his eyes burrow down the front of her dress. Lila instantly shot back up.

"I expect nothing less from Jack," Poe said, with a dreamy-eyed slur. "He always surrounds himself with the most beautiful women. Doesn't he?" He grabbed Lila's hand and gently kissed it. His skin felt cold and clammy despite the heat. From his tiny, pinprick pupils and the slack, rag-doll heaviness of his arms and head, Lila guessed he was on heroin, or some other opiate.

"What's your name, gorgeous?" Daniel said to Lila as he grabbed the tiny ass of the model who was closest to him.

"Nicky Collins, sir," Lila said.

"Will you be with us the whole trip?" Paul asked.

"Yes, sir."

"Delightful. Absolutely delightful," Daniel said, giving her a wolfish look. "Then we'll have all the time in the world to get to know each other."

Lila wanted to punch this perv in the throat, but she controlled herself. She needed to stay on the boat, and even if that meant putting up with the creepy advances of Daniel Poe, she'd do it. For Ava, she'd do anything.

"Of course, sir," she responded, giving both Paul and Daniel a demure nod. The men walked with their harem into the boisterous party.

Once the majority of the guests were on board, Mrs. Slaughter informed her that she could leave her shoe duty to help Sam and the rest of the crew with service. But Lila found out quickly that she wasn't much of a waitress. Carrying those heavy silver trays laden with food and drink as she navigated around the tipsy and mingling revelers was more difficult than she expected. Her arms were shaking from the strain.

And then, out of the corner of her eye, she saw her sister far across the room.

Lila felt her heart jump into her throat. She hadn't laid eyes on Ava in more than ten years. And here she was now. A gaggle of dancing models moved right in front of Lila, obscuring her view. She dodged them with the ease of a running back and cut quickly across the room toward Ava. How her sister could have boarded the boat without her noticing was something she didn't even question. Then Lila saw her again from behind, walking toward the side deck all by herself. It was unmistakably her—the long, flowing strawberry-blond hair, the pale, almost alabaster skin. Lila, burdened with the tray, hurried after the woman who was quickly weaving through the crowds.

She wanted to shout out her sister's name, but she knew she couldn't. After all, how would the conversation go? "Hi, I'm your sister from the future. I've traveled through space and time in order to save your life." This was an instance where the truth was stranger than fiction.

"Miss?" Lila called out, deepening her voice so that her sister wouldn't recognize it. But her sister didn't hear her. She kept walking quickly with Lila not far behind. Lila's pulse was pounding in her skull as she finally got within reach. She removed one hand from the tray so she could stretch out her arm to grab her sister. She tried to say something else, but when she opened her mouth, nothing came out. The magnitude of the moment had robbed her of her voice. Mute and terrified, she brushed her fingertips up against her sister's bare shoulders. But the moment she touched her, she knew it wasn't Ava.

She instantly withdrew her hand as if she'd just been scorched. The strawberry blonde whipped around to see who had touched her. Lila's heart sank. She didn't even closely resemble Ava. Feeling light-headed and short of breath, like she'd just seen a ghost, Lila thrust her tray out toward the confused woman, who didn't understand why a breathless server was chasing her down.

"Champagne?" she panted, trying to pull herself together.

The woman grabbed a glass, gave Lila a little frown, and then went on her merry way. Disheartened, Lila quickly turned around and . . . disaster. Upon reversing her direction, she collided with a dark-haired man who she hadn't realized was standing directly behind her. She lost control of the tray and glass upon glass of champagne precariously teetered before—no, no, no, Lila said in her mind—the whole thing loudly crashed to the ground in an ear-shattering explosion of smashed crystal. The very revealing, slightly diaphanous dress that she'd been forced to wear to the party was now dripping wet and totally see-through. Lila held the unwieldy silver tray over herself, hoping to cover up her now very visible breasts. She shifted uncomfortably, hearing hundreds of dollars' worth of premiere champagne squish around in her one-size-too-small high heels.

"Are you okay?" she heard a voice ask. She turned to see the very familiar face of someone who was also soaked to the bone in champagne. He was the one she'd bumped into.

"Ben Reynolds," Lila said, without thinking. She recognized him instantly from her research. Thirty-two years old and a lifelong sailor, he was the first officer of *The Rising Tide,* and from what he and the other crew members were to say in their police interviews, he was the closest to Jack of any of the yacht's employees.

"I'm sorry," he said, looking confused. "Do we know each other?"

"No, it's just. I . . ." Lila was tongue-tied. Though she'd seen plenty of pictures of Ben, his inquiring, kind eyes staring intently into hers worked some kind of black magic on her, rendering her speechless.

But before she could get a complete sentence out, Mrs. Slaughter came storming toward her, a tablecloth in her hand. Was it possible that Lila saw actual steam coming out of her ears?

"Take this," Mrs. Slaughter hissed between her clenched teeth, grabbing Lila by the shoulder and moving her to a quiet corner of the deck. She tore the tray out of Lila's hands and gave her the tablecloth. "Cover yourself."

As Lila wrapped the stiff cotton around her now-see-through dress, she whispered, "Sorry," to Ben.

"Edna," Ben said. In the thirty-six hours Lila had spent suffering under the thumb of the chief stewardess, she'd never heard anyone use her first name. It struck her as some kind of blasphemy, the oral equivalent of looking directly into the sun.

"Yes, Ben," Mrs. Slaughter said, keeping her back to him. Despite her polite tone, her extreme annoyance was clear.

He looked at Lila and gave her a warm, reassuring smile. "This was totally, one hundred percent my fault," he said. "I ran into . . . um . . ."

"Nicky," Lila answered. He was ruggedly handsome, with long, curly, dark hair, heavy brows, and light brown eyes. She felt something close to mesmerized as she stood, wet and humiliated, looking into those long-lashed eyes of his.

"Right, Nicky. I ran right into Nicky here and knocked over all these glasses. So, don't blame her."

Mrs. Slaughter straightened her back and turned to look at Ben. "I don't tell you what direction to steer the ship," she said. "Do I, Mr. Reynolds? Nor do I give you my thoughts about the route you've chosen. Correct?"

"Nope, you sure don't," he replied with a frown as the combination of being soaking wet and scolded quickly stripped away his good mood.

"Then refrain from telling me how to do my job, please, and thank you."

Ben nodded. Lila found it somewhat reassuring that even this strapping man seemed rather terrified of Mrs. Slaughter. At least she wasn't the only one.

"I'll leave you to it, then," Ben said. "But remember, *I'm* the oaf who caused this. Nicky, nice to meet you. And apologies.

Hopefully next time we run into each other, I won't make such a god-awful mess. Now, if you'll excuse me, I've got to go to my cabin and slip into something less"—he paused, holding up his wet arms and looking down at his dripping shirt—"soggy."

Ben and Lila exchanged a smile before he quickly marched across the deck and took the staircase to the lower level.

Lila was still smiling when Mrs. Slaughter turned back to her. "What are you grinning about?" the older woman sneered. "Oh, Ben, of course. You two are peas in a pod. Neither of you knows the value of respect. You should be aware of the fact that I will discuss this matter with Captain Nash. This subordination will not stand."

"Please," Lila begged. "I know we got off to a bad start, but I promise that I won't let you down again." She absolutely could not get fired. If she was forced to leave the yacht, then the whole mission would be botched.

"A promise, then a blunder, then a grovel. That seems to be your flavor of ineptitude and I'm quite fed up with it," Mrs. Slaughter said. "But I'm too short staffed to lose you tonight. So pull yourself together. Go to your room, change, and then go to the galley. Mr. Liss needs his dinner brought to his room, which is stateroom three on the third deck. Think you can handle that?"

"Yes, Chief Stewardess Mrs. Slaughter." Lila stood there, not sure what to do to please this impossible-to-please woman.

"Well, stop standing there staring at me like an idiot. Go do as I say. Then come back here directly."

"Yes, ma'am," Lila said as she hurried across the deck to go to the crew quarters.

She changed into her regular all-white uniform, then went to the galley to pick up Liss's food, excited that she'd finally be face-to-face with the chief financial officer of Warren Software—Jack's second-in-command. She'd kept an eye out for him all night, but now realized that he must've boarded the boat sometime during the day—probably when she was doing one of her hundred menial tasks.

Jack and Seth were polar opposites. Where Jack was famous for his A-list celebrity friends and million-dollar toys, his CFO disdained the spotlight and abhorred excess. Even though this fifty-eight-year-old numbers whiz from Wisconsin was a multimillionaire, he lived like a pauper. "I keep my nose as clean as my spreadsheets," he told *Forbes* in a profile that detailed how "the frugal millionaire" brought a tuna fish sandwich to work every day, drove an Acura sedan, and lived in the same three-bedroom house he bought for $325 grand when he first moved to Silicon Valley back in the 1980s. Though Liss's disdain for Jack's way of doing things was a well known fact among business-world insiders, Liss had never publicly challenged Jack's authority.

When Lila entered the galley to pick up Liss's meal, she encountered a snarling Chef Vatel.

"He's a philistine," the chef said, his thick French accent full of disgust as he pushed the tray toward Lila. "A well-done hamburger with Miracle Whip and this hideous plastic cheese on top. They don't pay me enough to prepare this travesty." He paused as his outrage bubbled up out of him. "I am an artist!"

Lila just shrugged her shoulders at the chef, grabbed the tray, and left. She had enough to worry about.

As she walked down the hall toward Liss's room, she heard a voice loudly speaking what sounded like Mandarin. When she knocked on the door, the voice abruptly stopped. Then Liss shouted, "Enter!"

Lila walked into his room. With a cell phone pressed to his ear, he waved her in and resumed barking Mandarin into the phone.

He had the second largest stateroom on the yacht, with elegantly curved walls covered in exotic stingray skin. The furniture was constructed out of brass and hand-stitched leather. The stateroom came with its own en suite bathroom and a large office with a spacious balcony overlooking the water. It was a room fit for a king, a luxury that would have astounded even the one percent of the one percent, but Seth Liss looked far from happy. He gestured toward Lila, pointing to where she could put the tray on the desk, which was heaped with manila file folders, several bound presentations, and his laptop, open to a very complicated-looking spreadsheet. She cleared a little space on the desk, placed his dinner down, and turned to leave. But Liss waved his hand at her to get her attention, then, putting his palm over the cell phone, whispered, "Stay one minute."

She froze in place, watching Liss. He was a hulking bear of a man, six five and around 350 pounds, with a bloodless complexion peppered with rosacea on his jowly cheeks. His small mouth seemed permanently downturned and he was seriously balding, which he tried to conceal by brushing his reddish hair up from the bottom into one of the shoddiest comb-overs Lila had ever seen. He was the complete opposite of all the beautiful, well-groomed, charming people who were feting his business partner just down the hall.

After a few minutes, he got off the phone. Without acknowledging Lila, he sat down at his desk and began shoveling the hamburger into his mouth. Lila wasn't sure what to do. "Does this asshole realize I'm still standing here?" she said to herself silently.

"I haven't forgotten about you," Liss said, as if he could read her mind. He kept his eyes on his food as he talked to her. "Just give me one goddamned second. Or is your time more valuable than mine?" As he was barking at her, a piece of hamburger bun dropped from his open mouth. He quickly picked it up and popped it back in.

"No, sir," Lila said, averting her eyes. She stood in the middle of the room listening to the smacking, scarfing, and swallowing as one of America's richest men inhaled his dinner. She'd been a patrol cop and a homicide detective. She'd gone undercover, assuming identifies that ran the gamut from socialite heiress to down-and-out junkie, but never had she been so relentlessly bossed around and shat upon as she had in this job.

"See that over there?" the CFO asked, brushing crumbs off his pants then pointing to a large pile of clothes by the closet. "All that needs to be pressed and laundered, then hung in the closet. And, see all of these?" He gestured to the many empty cans of diet chocolate fudge soda strewn about his room. "Remove them. And make sure the fridge is restocked."

"Yes, sir."

"I shouldn't be the one telling you what to do, should I? You should just see these things and do them, shouldn't you?"

"Yes, sir." She bent down to retrieve the two cans that were closest to her.

"Don't do it now!" he barked, causing Lila to jump back up and drop one of the cans.

"Sir?"

"Do it when I'm not in the room."

"Will you be joining the party?"

"Honestly, I'd rather chew glass," he said. "This is Jack's boondoggle, not mine. I'm only on this fucking boat to remind His Lordship that we've got a company to run, which is something he likes to forget. Though tonight I finally figured it out. It's simple. Jack just got into the wrong business. Considering how much he loves spending time with all these assholes, I'd say his real calling should've been proctology." He smirked at Lila, taking great pleasure in his joke, which was so stiffly delivered that Lila figured he'd told it hundreds of times before. Her forced smile drained the delight from his pale, waxy face. He turned his back to her, picking up his cell. "Remove this tray and get out of here. The day is only starting in Beijing and I've got work to do."

And the night was only getting started on the main deck. The guests had progressed from champagne and *toro nigiri* to shots of Patrón and undulating on the dance floor to the bass-heavy, auto-tuned, lip-synching pop star Allegra Opal, who had just stumbled onto the stage, happy to toss herself around to the beat in order to collect a million-dollar payday. As the young wives, girlfriends, and mistresses danced, their older companions stayed on the sidelines, happy to watch the parade of young flesh while chomping on their Montecristo cigars and sipping their cognacs.

While Lila, Sam, and the army of cater waiters made sure everyone's drinks were refreshed and the tables were cleared, Lila kept an eye out for her sister. But there was no sign of Ava. Lila was both disappointed and thankful. She really wanted to see her, but she didn't want to think of her sister associating with these jackals.

As Lila walked around the party handing out shots of high-end tequila, she saw, smack in the middle of the dance floor, the biggest jackal of them all. The man of the hour, Jack Warren. He was impossible to miss. With his shirt undone down to his belly button, his suit jacket off, and a gloss of sweat covering his beaming face, he looked like he was having the absolute time of his life. He had a bottle of Cristal in one hand and the ass of a sumptuous brunette in the other.

Watching Jack murmur something into the girl's ear as she giggled and squirmed in his arms, Lila was shocked at his lack of discretion. But she wasn't at all surprised to see, across the deck, Elise Warren staring directly at her husband, her hands balled up into tight little fists, with an unmistakable glare of hatred burning in her eyes.

CHAPTER 9

IN THE DUSTY-ROSE-COLORED light of early morning, a few party stragglers stumbled down the walkway of *The Rising Tide* just as the sun was beginning to peek its golden head from beneath the ocean's blue horizon. The party hadn't completely wound down until 5:00 A.M. Lila and Sam had been on hand until the wee hours of the morning and then cleaned up after the guests had left, so when their 6:30 A.M. wake-up call rang out, they'd been able to squeeze in only about five minutes of rest.

"You shower first," Sam groaned from the top bunk. "If I have to get up right now, I'm pretty sure I'll die."

Through a haze of exhaustion, Lila showered, dressed, grabbed some coffee from the mess, and headed up to the main deck. There was a pretty good chance that Mrs. Slaughter had complained about her to the captain sometime yesterday, so she had to be on her very best behavior today. She'd start by being the first of the crew up and ready to work.

The yacht, which had been party central just two hours prior, was now as quiet as a church. Lila was sure that profound and debilitating hangovers were blooming in the heads of most of the sleeping guests at that very moment.

She was on her way to the dining room, careful not to disturb anyone who was slumbering. As she walked along the side deck, she saw a lone figure descend the staircase from the master suite level. It was Elise Warren with an Hermès head scarf tied under her chin and enormous sunglasses obscuring most of her face. Lila ducked out of sight, waited a few seconds, and then turned around to see Elise exit the yacht and climb into a chauffeured Cadillac Escalade that was waiting for her at the foot of the dock.

"Where are you off to so early?" Lila whispered, wishing she could hop off the yacht to tail the woman. But she knew it would cost her her job, and thus cost her everything. So, she did what she had to do, which was set the table for breakfast.

According to a rigid protocol, meals on *The Rising Tide* were served in the dining room at precisely 9:00 A.M., 1:00 P.M., and 8:00 P.M., and each meal required silver table service. Jack Warren made it clear that all guests on board were expected to eat with him if he was going to be in attendance.

Lila smoothed a French linen tablecloth over the large table. She set ten plates down, saying everybody's name silently to herself, "The birthday boy, Jack Warren. The spoiled brat, Josie. Mr. Charm himself, Seth Liss. The best-looking-couple-of-the-year award to Thiago and Esperanza Campos. Moneybags Paul Mason. The Right Dishonorable Clarence and Charity Baines. The not-so-*enfant* (but very) *terrible* Daniel Poe. And, last but not least, the murderess, Elise Warren." Had there, she wondered as she set each plate down, ever been such a despicable bunch of scoundrels all joined together at sea?

Next went the crystal water glasses, then the fragile and fussy porcelain coffee cups, with their tiny little handles that had to be pointed in the same direction, which then had to be set upon fine, gold-rimmed saucers. She removed the Gucci flatware from its black-lacquered chest and laid the forks, knives, and spoons out on the table, careful that everything was in the proper spot.

Just as she was struggling to fold the white linen napkins into shapes that seemed one hundred times more complicated than an origami swan, Ben walked by the dining room wearing his sailor whites and, upon seeing Lila, headed in to say hello.

"Wow, look at you in your officer's uniform," Lila said with a smile.

"I'm not soaked to the bone like last time you saw me."

"Big improvement," Lila said, stepping back to take him all in.

He playfully struck a pose. "My mom always told me I clean up nicely. Listen," he said, his face turning serious, "I hope you didn't catch too much shit from Edna last night."

"There was too much shit coming my way to catch."

"Sounds terrible."

"You can say that again. Now I'm bracing myself for round two."

"Round two?"

"She said she was going to talk to the captain about what a mess I've been. I'm preparing myself for the worst."

"I'm sure it'll be fine," he said distractedly. He kept glancing at the table.

"Is something wrong?" Lila asked, scanning the table herself to try to see what he was seeing.

"It's nothing really," Ben said as he went over to the flatware chest. "But it'll cost you your job, trust me on that one."

"Oh, God. What did I do now?"

"It's just that, to be quite honest, I've never seen a table this poorly set in my life." He let out a sweet, astonished laugh. "It's like you were *intentionally* trying to do it all wrong."

"Do you know how to fix it?" Lila asked frantically.

"Of course."

In a flash, Ben set to work. Putting one spoon above the plate and the other down next to the knives. He grabbed a ruler from the top drawer of the dining room's sideboard and used it to make sure the flatware was precisely aligned and spaced. Lila cringed each and every time Ben corrected her many mistakes, but despite her humiliation, she was impressed by his grace, know-how, and swiftness.

After ten minutes, he had transformed the table into a piece of perfection. "There," he said as he closed up the flatware chest and returned the ruler to its rightful place, "that's better."

"How on earth did you learn that?" Lila asked. "I thought the rule of the ship was the women did the inside jobs and the men did the outside jobs."

"Yeah, usually that's the way it goes, as absurdly out-of-date as it sounds. But not in my case. You're looking at the very well trained son of a former chief stewardess."

"Really?"

Ben nodded proudly. "My dad was the chief engineer and my mom was the chief stew on a bunch of different charter yachts. When I was a kid I'd help my mom set tables, clean up, do laundry, and help my dad with all the maintenance of the engine, the plumbing, the a/c. You name it and I've done it."

"So, you must know these boats inside and out."

"I wish! But every year there's always some new mind-blowing innovation. I feel like I'm constantly scrambling to keep up." Ben sighed, "And, to be honest, that's kind of why yachts aren't my favorite thing. It's too much about the latest trend or whose is bigger or better. I mean, just look around. This boat is *crazy*."

"Totally," Lila said, happy that she'd found someone on the ship who wasn't totally mesmerized by Jack's ostentatiousness.

"Don't get me wrong. I love that I make my living on a boat. It's just sailing's *my* thing. It's so much better. It's about being out in the ocean, working with the elements, enjoying the silence. On a yacht, I feel like I'm on a floating luxury hotel."

"Absolutely," Lila said, immediately becoming aware that she was agreeing *just a little too emphatically* and staring *just a little too hard* at the handsome first officer. She switched her gaze to the floor.

"But it pays the bills. And it's mostly great. Although I'm pretty sure that half the people who own yachts don't even like being out on the water."

He was handsome, humble, and funny. Lila had to be careful with this one. "What about the Warrens?" she asked, trying not to look at his perfect lips.

"They're the opposite. Well, at least Jack is. I think Elise would rather be anywhere else, but Jack lives for the water. It's the only reason I work for him, actually. But he and I've got bigger plans than just this." His eyes suddenly brightened.

"Plans?"

"The America's Cup. We're going to win it in 2010, I'm totally convinced. Jack is, too. Actually, we're working on some incredible new designs for a boat that I think just might give us the edge we need against the Australian team." Suddenly Ben stopped speaking and shook his head. "Christ, I'm sorry, Nicky. Once I get started about it, I ramble on until I've bored absolutely everybody to tears. Forgive me." He leaned in close to Lila, lowering his voice to a conspiratorial whisper. "What I really want to know is how *you* managed to get a job on one of the most exclusive yachts in the world with, as far as I can tell, almost no experience. What's your secret? Sleeping with the boss?"

Lila's brief moment of relaxation instantly evaporated.

Ben must have seen her tense up. "Relax," he said as he put a reassuring hand on her shoulder. "Sleeping your way to the top is an age-old secret to success. I wouldn't be anywhere without it."

When Lila shot him a bewildered look, he broke out into uproarious laughter. "Oh, please forgive me, Nicky. I have a bad habit of teasing pretty girls. I just can't help it."

"The truth is . . . I do have experience. It's just my last boat did things differently."

"Of course," Ben said sweetly, trying to reassure her that he meant no harm. "I was only kidding."

He was a good guy, Lila knew that. But it was worrisome that he'd spotted her lack of experience instantly. She felt like he had something on her, which made her vulnerable. And being vulnerable to anyone, even a nice guy like Ben, wasn't an option. Just then, Mrs. Slaughter walked by, shaking her head at both Lila and Ben, for what infringement Lila was not sure.

Mrs. Slaughter entered the dining room, looked at the table, and gave Lila a curt nod of approval. "Ben, please leave Miss Collins to her duties. Breakfast will commence at nine A.M. and there is much to do before then. I'm sure you have your own business to attend to?"

"Always a pleasure, Edna. Nicky," Ben said, before retreating to the yacht's bridge.

Mrs. Slaughter straightened her already stick-straight back and haughtily stuck her chin out, the way she always did when she found someone or something annoying. Then she turned back to Lila. "And where is Miss Bennett?"

"She's in the laundry room, pressing some of Mr. Liss's shirts," Lila lied. For all she knew, Sam might still be in bed.

"But I was just in the laundry room and Miss Bennett was not there."

"Then maybe she's . . ." As Lila was trying to come up with some excuse, Sam herself, as bright as the morning sun, came running down the hall, carrying an antique milk-glass vase dripping with gorgeous pale pastel flowers.

"Morning, Mrs. Slaughter," she said cheerily. "Just grabbing flowers for the breakfast table."

"Fine," Mrs. Slaughter said quietly. She seemed almost disappointed to have nothing to complain about. Then she came alive again. She had spotted a mistake. "There are ten settings on the table. It should be only nine, as Mrs. Warren will not be joining us for breakfast. Now, I trust I can leave you ladies to serve breakfast."

Both Lila and Sam nodded. And with a stern look, Mrs. Slaughter went belowdeck.

"Did old Slaughterhouse notice I was late?" Sam asked.

"Not really. You arrived a minute or so after she did."

"Thank goodness," Sam sighed in relief. "The last thing I need is her up my ass. But I couldn't drag myself out of bed this morning for the life of me. It's all Asher's fault. Next time, remind me to stay away from him. That boy is nothing but trouble. A really *hot* slice of trouble."

BY 9:15, THE guests of *The Rising Tide* were quietly sitting down to breakfast. Most were shaking off the excesses of the previous night, barely able to touch the food that sat before them. Esperanza Campos, looking perfect in white linen pants and a slim-cut white tank top, quietly sipped hot lemon water. Her dapper husband read the *New York Times* business section while picking at an egg-white omelet. Josie, wearing a string bikini top and an Indian skirt, sucked down a carrot-and-beet juice while looking like she was so bored that she just might die in that very spot. Daniel Poe was standing on the deck off the dining room, chain-smoking hand-rolled cigarettes while drinking black coffee. Paul Mason was letting his eggs Florentine go cold as he checked his stocks on his iPhone. At the head of the table was Jack Warren, who was eating his typical Japanese-style breakfast of gyokuro tea, miso soup, rice, and steamed fish. At the opposite end of the table was Seth Liss, bent over his meal of scrambled eggs, extra-crispy bacon, and white bread lightly toasted and covered in a thin layer of margarine.

When Lila was forced to go down to the galley to ask Chef Vatel for the ketchup Liss wanted for his eggs, she momentarily thought the apoplectic cook was going to gouge her eyes out. But she didn't know what was worse, not giving Liss what he wanted or pissing off Chef Vatel. She opted for the latter. Next time, she'd find the ketchup herself.

As she circled the table, refreshing everyone's juice and coffee, she carefully listened to the small talk.

After slurping down his miso soup, Jack leaned back in his chair and surveyed his guests. "Who's up for a sail today?" he asked. "The folks at Perini Navi have given me a day with one of their newest boats. They want me to take it for a test drive. Give them some notes."

Liss, who had been crouched over his breakfast plate, sat straight up with a bewildered look on his face. "Jack," he said sternly, as if warning him to be careful, "what's this about a sail?"

"I just told you," Jack said in a belittling tone. "I'm testing out a new boat. Depending on how the winds are, we're going to aim for the Keys. You're welcome to come with us, Seth.

There's always room for you no matter how many Tater Tots you shove in your face."

Liss shot him a withering look, paused, and then banged his fists on the table, causing his coffee cup to clatter in its saucer.

"We've got a call with the shareholders at noon, Jack," he said. His voice was loud, but its tone was measured. He was trying to keep his rage under control.

"Oh, you don't need me for that," Jack said, stretching back as if he hadn't a care in the world, which just made his CFO more angry.

"You're right, Jack." Liss stood up and threw his napkin down on the table. Everyone else was silent, neither moving nor, it seemed, even breathing in this awkward moment. But Lila was riveted. "*I* don't need *you* for shit. The stockholders on the other hand, *your* stockholders, are under the false impression that you still have some interest in the company that affords you all these fucking luxuries that you seem so fond of."

As Liss spoke Jack's eyes narrowed and his jaw tensed.

"I'm CEO and chairman of the goddamned board," Jack yelled. "You can't speak to me like this in front of my guests, on *my* boat! Or are you forgetting that you work for *me*?"

"I won't be for much longer," Liss spat as he stormed out of the room.

After a couple minutes of strained silence, Paul Mason was the first to speak. "Jack, I'd love to go sailing with you, buddy. We all would. But I think Liss may be right. The shareholders need to hear from you. We can postpone the sail for another time."

Paul's gentle coaxing didn't work. Jack wasn't going to budge. "And let Liss think he can throw a tantrum and get his way? No fucking chance. And don't you go siding with him. Show some fucking loyalty," Jack said, pointing his finger in Paul's face. "I've saved *your* ass more times than I can count.

Plus, I can't think of anything worse than spending this beautiful day talking to a bunch of hysterical shareholders. It's like I'm supposed to treat every dip in the stock price like the goddamn sky is falling. I just can't do it anymore. No more groveling. No more hand-holding. It isn't worth it."

"Yeah," Josie snorted. "Like you've got anything to complain about. You know there are, like, actual people out there that work just as hard as you do, but don't even have any food to eat. Like a couple billion of them, Dad. Do you ever think about that?" She stared at her father with a defiance that was palpably lacking in confidence. Her father returned her look with a patronizing smile.

"Please forgive my daughter, everyone. She's going through a Marxist phase at the moment."

"Shut up, Dad."

"The funny thing is, I'm paying sixty grand a year to a college that's turning her into a fucking socialist. That's a high price for such disloyalty, don't you think? Her mother and I are hoping it'll pass as quickly as that unfortunate Hare Krishna period she went through . . . When was that again, honey?" he asked his daughter, looking like he could barely suppress the laughter on his lips. "Though you did look adorable in those little peach robes."

Josie's lips curled into a snarl. "You can't just . . . Don't think I care . . ." she sputtered, desperate to put her father in his place. But language failed her. Instead, she stood up and screamed, "Pig!" before rushing out of the room. Jack broke out into a rueful laugh. But his jaw was still clenched.

"Just another lovely breakfast," he said. There was a defeated tone in his voice. He looked around at the few people still left at the table, but no one met his gaze. Everyone kept their eyes down, trying, and failing, to come up with something to say.

CHAPTER 10

WITH HER FATHER somewhere in the middle of Biscayne Bay trying out a new multimillion-dollar toy and her mother mysteriously roaming around Miami, Josie, the only child and heiress to the great Warren fortune, decided to spend her afternoon sunbathing topless by the yacht's pool while reading Jean-Paul Sartre's *Being and Nothingness*, probably hoping to scandalize and/or titillate anyone who was lucky enough to get a good look at her.

She was a real piece of work. But as Lila watched Josie out on the deck, her lip-gloss-laden lips moving slowly as she read, her smooth brow slightly furrowing above her red, heart-shaped sunglasses as her mind attempted to penetrate the almost impenetrable text, she felt a great amount of something close to sympathy for the girl. She was spoiled rotten, self-righteous, and ridiculous—but given her parents, how could it be any other way? Could anyone in the entire world become a good, upstanding citizen with Elise and Jack Warren as their mother and father?

Lila knew that despite Josie's obvious contempt for her parents, she would crumble without them. Actually, she'd already seen it happen. After Jack's murder, it wasn't long before

Josie completely disappeared from the society in which she was raised. No one knew where she'd gone. Some said she was living in Marrakech, others said she'd permanently relocated to a remote castle in Scotland where she was raising sheep, while another story circulated that she'd joined a paramilitary wing of the Church of Scientology. There were more rumors concerning her whereabouts than about the questionable sexuality of certain Hollywood superstars.

It seemed like without something to push against, Josie didn't have any way to define herself. Where her mother bloomed in the very public role of the bereaved, vengeful widow, Josie rejected any media attention. In the one interview she gave during the ten years following her father's murder, besides demanding that the reporter not disclose her location, she claimed that she'd cut all ties with her mother. Lila strongly believed that Josie's self-imposed exile was because she knew that her mother had murdered her father.

Which was precisely why Lila was very interested in the sun-bathing heiress, that sunny afternoon off the coast of Miami.

With everyone else off the boat—except Seth Liss, who was busy with back-to-back conference calls—Lila focused on getting what she could out of Josie. The heiress had to know *something* about her father's infidelities or her mother's state of mind. But befriending the twenty-year-old socialite-turned-socialist posed a challenge. It had been made abundantly clear to Lila that she was not an equal of the guests on the boat. She was their inferior, their servant, nothing more than an invisible hand that cleaned and served. She was not to have opinions, needs, or, given how few hours she was allowed to rest, a proper night's sleep. And if asked a question, she was expected to smile demurely, answer, and quickly shuffle back into her hidden corner.

But there were exceptions. Somehow Ben and Asher seemed to be exempt from this upstairs-downstairs divide. Ben, at that very moment, was out sailing with Jack, Paul, Thiago, Esperanza, the senator and his wife, and Daniel Poe. Granted, Ben was probably the one doing the heavy lifting on the sail, but he was clearly higher in the pecking order than Lila. She'd never seen him grovel, and at Jack's party last night, he was a guest, not a server.

And then there was Asher.

His role was that of the good-time guy on the yacht, the man responsible for making sure everyone was having fun. A deep-sea diver, surfer, certified personal trainer, and self-declared "dude" and "party animal," with looks that made both young and old women swoon, Asher was the perfect man for the job. But today, out on the deck with Josie, as he blended her a steady stream of piña coladas, he seemed much more reserved than usual. As he busied himself behind the bar, he kept his eyes mostly on his work of cutting up limes and polishing the barware. Every once in a while Lila saw that he would let his eyes drift toward the mostly naked Josie stretched out before him.

And Josie was paying him no mind, though Lila could tell she was enjoying his watching her.

While the strange psychosexual drama between Asher and Josie played out, the crew moved around busily, like squirrels readying for winter. The deckhands were washing, polishing, and shining every inch of the gigantic yacht, in the constant battle between man and the corroding effects of salt water. And Lila and Sam, having finally finished cleaning the staterooms and en suite bathrooms, were stocking the pool area with freshly laundered Frette towels. When Lila bent down to remove the empty piña colada glasses sitting on Josie's copy of *Being and Nothingness,* Josie gave her a smile.

"Don't work too hard, Nina," she said. "Your name is Nina, isn't it?"

"It's Nicky, miss."

"Oh, that's right. I'm sorry, Nicky. You should join me here. The weather is too perfect to waste it working. I mean, look around. It's totally gorgeous. And I'm dying of boredom."

"But you've got Asher here to keep you company."

"Oh, him," Josie said as she turned over on her stomach. "He's no fun at all."

Lila looked at the two of them. They were both acting bizarrely. Maybe, it dawned on her, they were sleeping together and trying to hide it? She couldn't be sure, but something was definitely going on. As she walked away from the pool area, she ran into Sam by the stairs.

"Do you think there's anything happening between Josie and Asher?" Lila asked in a whisper.

"Happening? Like, what, are they fucking?" Sam asked.

Lila nodded.

"Definitely not," Sam said with more assurance than Lila thought was warranted, but after all, Sam had apparently hooked up with Asher. She had her reasons to be blind to what she didn't want to see. "He's been working for the Warrens for the last five years. She's more like a kid sister to him. Why? Did you see something?"

"Not at all," Lila said carefully. Sam was clearly jealous. "Just forget I said anything." Happy to change the subject, she said, "Hey, I know Slaughterhouse told you to take Liss his lunch, but let me do it."

"Are you serious?" Sam asked. "Because if you are, that would be amazing. Have you heard him today? He's been yelling on the phone like a madman. I think I may have heard furniture breaking."

Liss's fight with Jack this morning had Lila's wheels turning. She had known there were tensions between the two, but she'd had no idea how bad it was. It was clear that Liss wanted Jack's job.

The real question was, after years of suffering Jack's derision and abuse, would Liss consider *killing* for the top spot at the company?

"I'll take him his lunch. Don't worry," Lila said. "But if I don't make it out alive, I hope you feel bad about it for the rest of your life."

"Highly doubtful." Sam flashed a relieved smile.

When Lila entered the galley, she once again found a scowling Chef Vatel holding a plate out for her.

"I come from Paris to sit in some American backwater cooking chicken fingers for this fucking oaf? I don't think so."

"Just think of the paycheck, Chef," Lila said as she quickly grabbed the tray and walked away. One furious man per day was enough for her. "That's what the rest of us are doing."

The moment she stepped into the hallway on the third deck, she could hear Liss. His authoritative and bullying voice was impossible to ignore. Her hands gripped the tray as she listened.

"Yes, Urs, the Q3 numbers aren't where we want them to be. That's a given. We haven't had the most robust quarter, but that's because of necessary expenses related to our sector-wide expansion. We've still got work to do. The Justice Department needs to approve our acquisition of Peregrine Software. That'll be forthcoming. We're currently working closely with Senator Clarence Baines, who's head of the Senate Judiciary Committee overseeing this matter."

So, that's why Clarence Baines was receiving the five-star treatment, Lila thought. Jack entertains him on his fancy boat and introduces him to the types of people who write big checks for his upcoming reelection campaign. In exchange, Baines pushes the Peregrine acquisition through the Justice Department. Classic quid pro quo.

"No, we won't get nailed on it. We do things different here in America. Business and government can work together."

Lila politely rapped on Liss's door.

"Come in," he bellowed.

She slipped into his room, trying to be as quiet as possible, but her foot loudly crunched down on something. She had just flattened an empty can of diet chocolate fudge soda. Liss, who was back to yelling into his phone, shot her a look of death. He covered the receiver with his hand and hissed, "I'm on an important fucking call. Put the fucking tray down. And close the fucking door behind you on your way out."

He continued talking on his phone as Lila crossed the room to deliver his lunch. "Yes, I'm with you. Jack should've been on this call. If you put up bad quarterly numbers and the CEO isn't there to reassure investors, then people start to buck. They put their money elsewhere. Jack knows all this, but he just doesn't goddamn *care*. And between you and me, I've fucking had it with him. I didn't sign up to be the dark cloud to some middle-aged baby who thinks life is just an endless stream of perfect tits, drinks with Bono, and sailing his fucking boat."

After Lila delivered the tray, she slowed down her pace, picking up dirty clothes and discarded plates in order to hear more of the conversation. Then she felt something hit her in the head. She looked down and saw a half-eaten and heavily buttered dinner roll at her feet. Liss had thrown it at her. She looked up at him, seeing only fury in his eyes.

"Get. The. Fuck. Out," he silently mouthed to her, careful

to overenunciate each word so she understood him. Knowing her time was up, she quickly exited the room, closing the door behind her. But she lingered in the hallway, pressing her ear against the door. She needed to hear the rest of this conversation.

Liss continued, "Several board members have come to me directly, including you, Urs, to talk about the Jack situation. So, I'll be sending out an internal memo to all the members of the board that outlines my concerns with how Warren Software is being run and addresses ways in which I propose to fix these problems. It'll be in your in-box later this afternoon. They say that different times call for different leaders, and this is one of those times. Needless to say, all of this dialogue must not include Jack."

It sounded to Lila like Seth was trying to stage a corporate coup d'état. And he was trying to get the board of directors on his side, starting with whoever this Urs guy was. Lila knew that after Jack's death, Liss had been named interim CEO of Warren Software, and then confirmed as the permanent CEO fourteen months later. Plenty of people had killed for less.

Lila needed two things. First, she had to get her hands on the secret memo Liss was going to send to the board of directors. Second, she needed to find out more about Urs. She headed down to the lower level, anxious to get started on these new leads. But just as she was about to head into her room, she heard the chief stewardess call her.

"Nicky, just where in bloody hell do you think you're going?"

"I just needed to—"

Edna cut her off. "You just needed to fetch Ms. Warren some lunch. That's what you just needed to do."

"Yes, ma'am," Lila said. Then she began her forced march up to the main deck to see what vegan delicacy Josie wanted for lunch. But the girl wasn't by the pool. And there was no sign of Asher either. When she asked Sam, who was busy steaming some of Elise's Dior blouses, where Josie was, she just shrugged and said, "I am not that spoiled slut's keeper," before resuming her work.

Lila made a quick sweep of the yacht, checking the dining room, Josie's stateroom, the den, the TV room, the spa, the gym, and then headed up to the sun deck, at the very tippy top of the boat. And that's where she saw a topless Josie sitting back in the hot tub with her eyes closed, holding a large red bong.

Lila cleared her throat, but Josie didn't open her eyes. Then she said, "Ms. Warren. I'm checking if you need anything for lunch."

Josie nearly jumped out of her skin at the sound of Lila's voice. She looked around nervously. She dropped the bong in the roiling water and climbed out of the tub like a guilty puppy caught eating a shoe.

Dripping wet, she wrapped a towel around herself. Her bloodshot eyes were darting around the boat as she shivered ever so slightly, despite the heat. All the way up at the top of the giant yacht, with a worried look on her face and her tiny arms pressed at her sides to keep the towel on tight, she looked a lot younger than her twenty years.

"Sorry to disturb you, Ms. Warren."

"What are you doing here?"

"Can I get you anything for lunch?" Lila asked again.

"Oh, lunch?" Josie said, as if she'd never heard the word before. "Lunch. Yes! Yes, you're right. I'm actually really hungry." She lunged at Lila and locked her in a very wet embrace. "Thank you so much. Lunch, exactly."

"What would you like me to bring you?" Lila asked, trying to suppress a smile.

"Oh, my God. I could *never* decide. I'll, like, follow you down to the kitchen and just see what's there, okay?" the girl asked.

After they made their way to the galley, Josie prowled around peering in the refrigerators and pantries, wearing nothing but the bottom half of her skimpy string bikini. Upon seeing her, Chef Vatel fled the scene faster than you could say *"Merde!"* His sous chef, who was a lot more interested in the presence of a half-naked heiress in the kitchen, had to be dragged out by the muttering chef, who had been around long enough to know that when trouble comes in the door, you get out as fast as possible.

A voracious vegan is a hard customer to please, but after she located some coconut-milk ice cream, a jar of pickles, and hummus with pita, Josie stood at the counter, gulping it all down. "Okay," Lila said. "Now that you're settled, I've got to go." She had a lot more important things to do than watch Josie cram food into her stoned face.

"Noooo," Josie pleaded. "You have to stay with me. I can't be here by myself." She paused, giving Lila a long, concerned look. "You aren't going to tell my parents about the pot, are you?" She paused to devour an entire pickle. "Oh. My. God. That's soooo good." She looked at Lila again. "I mean, hear me out, it's not for my sake. I don't give a good fuck. It's Asher that I worry about. I got the pot from him and I don't want him to get in any hot water."

"My lips are sealed."

"Oh, goody!" Josie squealed. "I knew you were a keeper. But can I ask you something?"

"Sure," Lila said hesitantly, interested to see where this was going.

"Why are you working on this dumb yacht?"

"It's a job, I guess."

"But doesn't it make you sick? All the wealth. All the bullshit. I mean don't *we* make you sick?"

"Seems pretty nice to me."

An exasperated groan erupted from Josie's mouth. "No one gets it. Okay, like, I grew up around this wealth, so it's all I've known. But ever since I started at Wesleyan, I've seen a totally different side of life. A nonrich side, and it is sooo much better. It's like people only see what they want to see. They see the boats and the clothes and the planes and the jewels."

"Well, those things are hard *not* to see."

Josie continued talking. "But what no one seems to see is how miserable all this stuff makes people."

"Like your parents?" Lila asked, though she immediately regretted the question, worried she had pushed too far. She knew saying the wrong thing on the yacht was much more dangerous than setting the breakfast table incorrectly. She was in a world full of unspoken rules, and breaking even the smallest one could cost her the entire mission.

Luckily, Josie was happy to talk shit about her parents. "Yes! Exactly! *Just* like them. My parents are the two most miserable people I've ever met. I mean, first off, my dad can barely stand my mom. If you really watch him, you'll notice he almost never looks or speaks to her. It took me years to realize it! And today's a perfect example: he's off on some new boat with everyone *except* my mom."

"And you."

"Yeah, me, too. But that was my choice. If he was actually nice to my mom even once, I think we'd all die of shock."

"And where exactly is your mom today?" Lila was hoping the least Josie could do was shed some light on the mysterious disappearance of her number one suspect.

"Where do you think? A bit of shopping followed by yet another trip to Dr. Menzin's office for some fine tuning."

"Dr. Menzin?"

"He's only *the* premiere plastic surgeon of South Beach. For my twenty-first birthday, I'm thinking of having my nose and my chin done. Don't you think? It's like, thanks for the DNA, Dad! I mean, my mom's a famous model and I look like my goddamn father. As if life wasn't already disappointing enough."

Lila remained silent. There was no right way to answer.

"But," Josie continued as she shoveled some hummus into her mouth, "I don't know why *she* even bothers. It's not like my dad notices. When it comes to him, she might as well be invisible. I mean, what does he care if her she's got new cheek implants or whatever? I can't understand why they stay together."

"Maybe it's for you?" Lila offered, not believing it at all, but despite herself, she felt bad for Josie.

"Ha. Highly unlikely. They're too selfish for that. I think my mom wants to turn the marriage around. And my dad tries just as hard to be as far away from her as possible. The fact that they're locked on this boat together for weeks will be interesting. It'll be a miracle if they both make it out alive." Lila noticed that Josie had a large dollop of hummus hanging at the corner of her cheek.

"*Alive?* Really?"

A big snorting laugh burst out of Josie. "Omigod, no. Haven't you ever heard of, like, hyperbole?" she asked, clearly proud to use one of her SAT words. "I was *exaggerating*, you know?"

Just then the sound of an enormous crash rained down upon them from overhead followed by a riot of shouting voices.

"What the hell?" Josie said as she turned her bloodshot eyes up to the ceiling.

"Wait here. I'll go see what's happening." Lila practically leaped out the door, pleased to finally have a reason to extract herself from this less than illuminating conversation. Josie shrugged and began searching the fridge for more food.

The cacophony continued as Lila walked up to the main deck, where she found several men in brown polyester delivery uniforms standing around a giant wooden crate gesticulating wildly while yelling over each other. The crate was about eight feet long with its "This End Up" arrow very much pointing down. The men were arguing about the best way to right it.

"Excuse me," Lila said. The men ignored her as two of them crouched at one end of the box and, with great strain, began to lift it up. "Can I help with something?" She tried once more, but no one looked at her. Frustrated, she hollered, "STOP! Can someone *please* tell me what's going on?"

The men were finally silenced. A squat, muscular guy with a heavy, dark unibrow turned to Lila. "Yeah. Sorry about all the noise. We got a package here for, um . . ." He paused to check his paperwork. "For Daniel Poe. He around?"

"No, but I can sign for it."

"Sure. Whatever works for you." It was clear he wanted to be rid of this delivery as soon as possible. "But be careful. It's heavy. You sure you don't want my guys to put it somewhere?"

"It'll be fine. Thanks."

Now that the business at hand was done, the deliveryman seemed to instantly relax. "Pretty classy boat you got here," he said as he took in the undeniable excess and grandeur of *The Rising Tide*. "How much would one of these set you back?"

Lila said, "Around five hundred million bucks."

Each of the delivery men let out a howl or whistle of some kind.

"Yeah," Lila said, "exactly."

As they were leaving, she saw a black Cadillac Escalade pull up to the end of the dock. After several minutes of idling, the driver got out to escort a very wobbly Elise Warren back to the yacht. Lila saw Mrs. Slaughter rush up from the lower level to greet her,

But before the chief stewardess left the yacht, she turned back to Lila. "Listen to me," she said with great solemnity. "Straightaway go and get four ounces of tequila on the rocks, with a good squeeze of lime, ten ice-cold cucumber slices, and grab a packet of gauze from the first-aid kit and go soak it in the chamomile tea that I left in the galley fridge. Can you remember all that?"

Lila nodded.

"Fine. Do it now. Bring everything to Mrs. Warren's room and make sure not to uncover any of the mirrors or open up any of the curtains. Do precisely as I say. Now go!"

And off Lila went to gather this small collection of items for the teetering mistress of the ship. A clink of ice cubes in the glass, a squeeze of lime, four ounces of tequila precisely measured, cucumbers—cold and cut in a variety of thicknesses—and the gauze soaked in the chamomile concoction chilling in the fridge. With everything arranged artfully on a lacquered serving tray, Lila made her way to Elise Warren's room.

When she opened the door to the master suite, she saw Mrs. Slaughter struggling to help Elise take off her jacket. The enormous room's blackout curtains were drawn, and all mirrored surfaces were covered with silk scarves, giving the place a dark, cavelike feel. There were two large humidifiers by the bed pouring water vapor into the air.

Elise Warren, still wearing large sunglasses and a now slightly askew silk head scarf, was muttering loudly and incoherently as Mrs. Slaughter tried to keep her upright.

"Nicky," Edna said sharply. "I need your assistance."

Lila rushed to her side. "You hold her here, right under the armpits, to keep her steady while I get her ready for bed."

Doing as she was told, Lila slipped her hands under the little bolero jacket that Elise was wearing over the Oscar de la

Renta dress that Lila had pressed yesterday. Elise's skinny arms hung limply at her sides. Lila could feel her rib cage through the dress's thin fabric.

"Good," Mrs. Slaughter said, now standing behind Elise, "hold her just like that."

Though Elise was a hundred pounds max, Lila had to struggle to keep her deadweight upright. She looked into the woman's face. Her eyes, of course, were hidden behind dark lenses, but her mouth was hanging slightly open.

"What's wrong with her?" Lila whispered to Mrs. Slaughter, who shot her a stern look and said nothing.

Together they managed to get the tiny jacket off, and then Mrs. Slaughter unzipped the dress, which fell stiffly to the floor as Elise woozily swayed above it. They laid her down on her bed, and when Mrs. Slaughter removed the head scarf and sunglasses, Lila was barely able to suppress a gasp. The swollen, red, and raw-faced woman that lay before them was no closer to the beautiful Elise Warren than a steak is to a cow.

Careful to stay silent, Lila watched as Mrs. Slaughter expertly wrung out the gauze, then placed it on Elise's face and applied two cucumber slices to the swollen slits hiding her eyes. She took several bottles of prescription pills out of Elise's Céline handbag and set them on the bedside table. She opened the one labeled *OxyContin,* and propping her mistress's head up in the crook of her arm, she placed the pill on her tongue and then coaxed Elise to swallow it down with a tiny sip of water.

After Lila got over the surprise of seeing Elise Warren in such a debilitated condition, she was even more shocked by the tender care Mrs. Slaughter exhibited. Had she not been there to witness it, she could have never guessed that this hard-hearted hard-ass of a boss could offer such a sweet and maternal touch.

This went above and beyond the duty of a chief stewardess. This was an act of love.

When Lila and the chief stewardess finally left the darkened bedroom, Lila could tell that Mrs. Slaughter was incredibly upset.

"Barbarians," she whispered to herself bitterly. "Butchers. Why a woman like Elise Warren thinks she has to do *that* to herself, I'll never understand." Lila couldn't be sure, but she thought Mrs. Slaughter might have actual tears in her eyes. "Well, it's not a world I want to have any part in, I'll say that much."

"You really care about her, don't you?" Lila asked, looking thoughtfully at Mrs. Slaughter.

To Lila's dismay, that brief glance, that small reach for a connection with her boss, pushed things one step too far. She watched as Mrs. Slaughter returned to her steely self. The iron curtain that she kept over her heart had once again been lowered.

"That's quite enough of all of that, Miss Collins. Thinking we are on familiar terms would be a mistake."

"I understand."

"I should hope you do. Now, in exactly two hours you must come back here with fresh gauze, more cucumber, and another drink. But this time, in addition, bring her some warm bone-marrow broth. I'd do it myself, but my presence has been requested elsewhere by Mr. Warren," she said with a curl to her lips, as if saying Jack's name left a bad taste in her mouth.

As instructed, exactly two hours later, Lila entered the dark and silent room with a tray stocked with new supplies.

Elise was half-propped up in bed. She wore dark sunglasses over her bandaged face, making her look like the Invisible Man.

"Edna," she called, her voice slurred by pills. "Is that you?"

"No, Mrs. Warren. It's Nicky. Mrs. Slaughter asked me to bring you some things."

"Oh, Edna." Elise sighed, then emitted a teary whimper. "I'm in so much pain. Can you give me another pill?"

"It's Nicky, and yes. Do you know what pill you need to take?" Lila looked at the various bottles on the side table. OxyContin. Percocet. Zoloft. Senokot. Valium. Neurontin. Klonopin.

"Where's Jack?"

"He's still out sailing."

"Yes, of course. Always without me. Now, about that pill." She tried to sit up farther, but even the simplest shift seemed to result in a great jolt of pain. A miserable groan escaped her lips. "Can you give me two Percocet, Edna? My angel." She held out her hand toward Lila, who obediently tapped two ten-milligram pills into her shaking hand.

"That's my girl," Elise said. "Always on my side, right, Edna? Mr. Warren's got nobody as good as you, does he? He doesn't have anything that he didn't buy. And soon he won't have anything at all. Right, Edna? Now, here, help me with these pills, will you, dear?"

"What do you mean, 'he won't have anything'? Is something going to happen to your husband?" Lila asked. She was hoping that, in her drugged state, Elise would be out of it enough to confess to the crime. It wouldn't be enough to convict her of the murder when Lila returned to 2019, but it would be a damn fine place to start. "Elise?" she said, but there was no answer. "Elise?" Lila lightly shoved the woman's shoulder, trying to revive her, but the drugs had taken hold of her body. She was dead to the world.

Lila sat there for quite a while, staring at the pathetic shell that was Elise Warren. She felt alternating waves of pity and bottomless contempt for the woman she blamed for her sister's ruined life.

CHAPTER 11

AFTER JACK MADE a brief speech and went through the tradition of breaking a champagne bottle across the bow for the dozen or so members of the press in attendance, *The Rising Tide* set sail on its maiden voyage, at sunset on August 26, 2008. Their first stop would be the Exuma Cays, a little-known archipelago in the Bahamas where Paul Mason had a small thirty-acre private island. The three-hundred-mile journey would take the grand yacht about twenty hours in total. They were set to arrive sometime the following evening.

As Lila watched the glittering cityscape of Miami recede into the distance, she couldn't help but feel overcome by a sense of melancholy. There had been no sign of Ava. She knew it was better if her sister wasn't on the boat because it allowed Lila to do her job freely without worrying about Ava recognizing her. But in truth, Lila longed to be close to her sister once more. Even if she had to conceal her identity to do it, she was desperate to see her sister's face, and see that smile of hers, which never seemed to fade, even in the worst of times.

But Lila wouldn't have to wait much longer. In just twelve short days, the yacht would return to Miami, and Ava would board *The Rising Tide*, which didn't leave Lila much time. Luckily for her, now that the core group of passengers and all the crew were stuck together on this giant yacht, she'd have an easier time tracking everyone. But she knew she needed to be extremely cautious. Getting caught, even for the tiniest slipup, could cost her everything.

That night, the guests sat down to a light meal of charred octopus and Pinot Noir in the open-air dining room on the main deck. Being at sea, with the brisk ocean breezes swirling around them, seemed to greatly lift the spirits of both the crew and the passengers, at least for a moment. It seemed there was a collective exhale throughout the entire yacht.

With everyone out of their rooms and seated around the table, Lila knew that now was the perfect time to grab that secret memo off Liss's computer. After she and Sam had finished serving, she told her fellow stewardess that she'd bring some more wine up from the cellar on the lower level. That bought her some time. Instead, she ran up to the third deck, headed as quickly as discretion allowed toward Liss's stateroom. Once she reached his door, she looked around to make sure no one had followed her, then snuck into his room.

It was filthy and smelled of cold french fries. There were clothes all over the floor and stacks upon stacks of financial documents on every flat surface. She grabbed a few of Liss's dirty shirts with one hand while she looked for his laptop. If someone walked in on her, she'd at least be able to say she was there to get his dirty laundry.

After a few minutes of frantic searching, Lila finally found his laptop in the bathroom leaning against a cabinet adjacent to the toilet—meaning the last time he was on his computer, he was on the can.

"Charming," she said as she picked up his computer, closed the bathroom door, lowered the toilet seat, and sat down.

The first place Lila went was his email. If Liss sent the presentation to all the board members, she'd be able to find it in his "sent" folder. His email was password protected, but in her present world, in 2019, even a toddler could crack a password this rudimentary. Still, every second that passed put her in more danger, and she knew it.

Then, finally, she was in his email. And there it was: a PowerPoint presentation saved as *Project King Charles*. With her heart racing, she plugged her thumb drive into the computer and copied the file, along with several others that might or might not be useful. The handful of seconds that she waited while the information was transferred to her drive felt like the longest moments of her life.

Then she heard the door to Liss's room open. She froze, moving only her eyes to locate where she could hide. Unfortunately for Lila, the bathroom presented few options. The shower stall was glass and the sink cabinet was too small. Without pausing to think, she pulled the thumb drive out of Liss's laptop, and taking a few wide strides on tiptoe across the tiled floor, she threw herself into the giant marble bathtub.

She lay in it, pressing her body as far down as she could, trying to quiet her panicked breathing while she listened to the sound of footsteps in the bedroom. The anxiety in that moment was further sharpened with the fear of fumbling the most important case of her life. What if this one misstep ended her quest to clear Ava's name?

The bathroom door opened. Lila stopped breathing entirely. Then she heard Edna's voice. "What a cretin," she muttered to herself. "Just thinks none of us have anything better to do than clean up after him."

Lila's heart was pounding so hard that she was convinced Edna could hear it. Then she heard the sound of Edna snapping Liss's laptop shut and walking back into the bedroom. A couple of minutes later, Edna was gone.

Lila, still feeling the flood of adrenaline pumping through her body, gingerly climbed out of the tub, and noticed the fresh flowers and clean towels that Edna had just dropped off. There were more fresh flowers next to the bed, which had been turned down, along with a little box of Teuscher's Champagne Truffles set on his just-fluffed pillows.

As she left Liss's room, she finally exhaled, knowing that calls don't come much closer than that.

By the time she got back to the dining room, the guests were starting on dessert.

"Jesus Christ," Sam said, looking at Lila's disheveled appearance. "It looks like you just got chased by a tiger."

"Did anyone notice I was missing?"

"I think they're all too drunk to notice," Sam answered. "They've plowed through all the booze. Where's the wine?"

"The wine?" Lila gave Sam a confused look, then she remembered. She had said she was going to the cellar. "I couldn't find the bottles I was looking for."

"Okay," Sam said, smirking. Then she leaned in and whispered, "I think someone might've left for a quickie."

"What?"

"You've got all the telltale signs! The flushed cheeks, the mussed-up hair, the lame excuse. Just tell me, who was it with? Mudge? Ben?"

"Oh, stop," Lila said, with a shake of her head. "You don't know what you're talking about."

"Don't worry." Sam grinned. "I'll get it out of you soon enough!"

AFTER DINNER, THE guests gathered by the pool, drinking themselves blind, while Lila, her heart rate finally settled after the scare in Liss's room, longed to be back in her cabin. All she could think about was what could be in Liss's files. By the time the guests were drunkenly poured into bed, and Sam and Lila had cleaned up, it was 2:15 in the morning.

Back in their tiny prison, Lila sat cross-legged on the bed and pulled out her computer to review the files. Sam was off God knows where, probably with Asher. Lila was thankful for the solitude as she opened the files titled *Project King Charles*.

A quick search online told her that Charles I was the king of England who was executed in 1649, and that his death brought an end to the rule of the monarchy. A pretty pointed name for a presentation outlining how to oust Jack from the company he'd founded. Lila began reviewing the presentation, which began with two charts linking Warren Software's waning market share and declining stock price to Jack's dwindling participation in the company's day-to-day operations. This was Liss's call to action to murder the king of Warren Software. Kill the tyrant to save the union.

As she made her way down the list of recipients who were sent this presentation, she saw Warren's board of directors, along with the name Urs Hunziker, the person Liss had been speaking with on the phone. Lila had never heard the name before, but a quick search told her that he was a Swiss banker, head of the wealth management division of a small private bank in Geneva, which had been the underwriter for a number of Warren Software's recent acquisitions.

But among the fifteen people who received this poison pill of a document, Lila was most surprised to see the names "Paul Mason" and "Thiago Campos." Two of Jack's best friends and closet advisers were in on a cabal to overthrow him. They were swimming in mighty dangerous waters.

About forty-five minutes later, as Lila was reviewing some of the company's financials, Sam finally returned. She entered the room smelling of booze and sex, and in the mood to talk. Lila didn't mind. Her brain needed a break. There was so much information to digest and she needed time to let the pieces all fall into place.

"I know it sounds dumb or conceited or whatever, but I always thought I'd be famous. It was just something I believed about myself," Sam said quietly, drunkenly, as Lila stared up into the dark. "I grew up in bum-fuck nowhere Florida, where everything was cheap and small and dingy. I hated my hometown like you can't believe. For as long as I can remember, I wanted out. I tried everything I could think of to get discovered. I did beauty pageants. I got a few small-time modeling jobs where I'd have to do my own hair and makeup. I'd take the bus, even when I was little, to Miami for any open audition I heard about. I got head shots and some crappy agent that didn't do shit. But soon enough I'd spent all the money I had, plus some I didn't have, and I was right back where I started, stuck in hicksville living in my mom's double-wide with no cable and a busted swamp cooler."

The ocean was calm that late August evening, and their cabin rocked gently as the yacht headed south. Lila's seasickness and feelings of claustrophobia had mostly subsided by day three on the boat, but she was far from comfortable. If she even allowed her mind to drift toward any tiny thoughts about how confined she was on this boat, a claustrophobic panic would overtake her. Her trick to avoid the anxiety, when she felt it coming, was to focus her mind on the only thing that mattered: Ava.

"It's so tough out in the real world," Sam continued, her

Florida accent deepening the more freely she talked. "In school I was treated like some kind of royalty. I didn't get good grades or anything, not by a long shot, but I was always popular. Prom queen dating the quarterback. You know, that whole thing. And I'm not bragging about it. Trust me. I know enough to understand that it's not much to brag about."

Lila didn't doubt Sam in the least. Her beauty was indisputable. She had an effortless, healthy, blond gorgeousness that Lila knew was both a blessing and a burden. Lila understood quite well that beauty wasn't always a woman's quickest way to happiness or to power. She figured Sam had learned the same lesson, though neither of them said as much out loud. Few subjects garnered less sympathy than the burden of beauty.

"But it didn't take me long to figure out that I wasn't one in a million. I was just like everyone else. Moments like that can change a person, harden a person, you know?" Sam paused. "When I was a kid there was this amazing carnival that used to come to our town, full of lights and games and rides. It had this fun-house room that was all mirrors. You'd walk in and all you'd see was yourself reflected thousands of times over and over and over. I don't know why, but it terrified me. My mom said the first time I went, I just broke down into tears, that she had to carry me out. I think I was five or six. Anyway, that's how I felt every time I went to an audition, like I'd just walked into that mirrored room surrounded by thousands of versions just of myself. That's when I decided to call it quits."

"Is that when you started working on boats?" Lila asked.

"Uh-huh. A couple years ago, I met this girl at one of my auditions. She'd just come off a four-week trip to Anguilla where she was third stew. She said she'd made, like, five grand in a month, without having to pay any living expenses. Told me that pretty girls could always get a spot on a boat as long as they were willing to work hard and follow orders. I figured I could do that. I was broke, as always, so that kind of money sounded like the answer to all my prayers. She told me to just show up very early at the Miami Marina and walk around saying I was free to work. I got jobs right away. That led to a few steady gigs on charter yachts, then I landed this assignment, which is a dream come true."

"Is it?" Lila asked. She was surprised to hear that someone thought of scrubbing toilets and ironing linens, all of it under the eagle eye of Edna "Slaughterhouse," as a "dream come true."

"Of course!" Sam said emphatically. "Every day we work in the most glamorous world imaginable for some of the most wealthy and powerful people alive. How can you not find that exciting? I mean it's not perfect. I do things I never thought I'd do in a million years."

"Like collecting Seth Liss's chocolate fudge soda cans and hand washing Josie Warren's organic cotton thongs?" Lila asked, which made Sam laugh.

"Yeah, that and other things," Sam said quietly. Was she hinting at deeds darker than the ones listed in the job description? Lila wondered. Who exactly had she been with tonight?

"But I just keep my mind on the big picture," Sam concluded, in an artificially cheerful tone. "Whenever I'm down, I think of myself as Cinderella and the other women, like Josie and Elise, as my evil stepsisters. I'm beautiful and deserving and they're the cruel, jealous hags with all the money. One day they'll get theirs and I'll get my prince."

Lila had never heard anything quite as deluded as that, but she kept her mouth shut. If this childish fantasy allowed Sam to get through these grueling days, then who was she to disabuse the young woman of her dreams?

"You're right," Lila lied. "That's a good way of looking at things." There was a long moment of silence as she got up the nerve to ask her bunkmate something rather personal. "Sam, mind if I ask you a rather direct question?"

"Of course not!"

"Were you with somebody tonight?"

"What do you think?" Sam replied, her voice turning rather flat and cold.

"I think you were, but I'm wondering who it was."

"I'll tell you. It's not like I'm embarrassed about it or anything," she said defensively. "I was with Jack. I went to his room to see if he needed anything before I went to bed, and it just happened."

"Oh . . ." Lila said, quite surprised. She had guessed it was Asher.

"Like you've never slept with one of the guests before?" Sam asked, obviously indignant about the surprise in Lila's voice. "I mean, you'd be the first. I don't know one stewardess who hasn't."

Clearly it was a well-known fact that the pretty girls hired to work on the boat were also supposed to be available for the men who wanted them. Lila wasn't going to play that game, not for the world.

"I'm not judging you, Sam. I'd never do that."

"You better not. Plus, Jack's not that bad. I mean, yeah, he's an asshole, but he's pretty nice once you get him alone. And he's loaded. Maybe he'll give me a really big tip at the end of the trip," Sam said, yawning loudly, filling the tiny chamber of their room with her boozy breath.

"Maybe," Lila said, gripped by a sadness for Sam—a sweet, somewhat empty-headed young woman who dreamed of being a star, but was now happy enough with making a few extra bucks with the occasional bout of high-seas prostitution.

Lila waited for Sam to say something, but when she heard her breath begin to deepen, she knew that she'd fallen asleep. But Lila's restless mind made sleep impossible even though her body was beyond tired.

More than anything, Lila felt angry over what this corrupt world did to people. To be around Jack was to risk being used, exploited, and discarded. That's what would happen to Sam and that's what would soon happen to her sister. Who knew someone so rich could cheapen people so much.

She thought of Ava. Poor Ava. When her sister fell in love, she fell hard. And now she'd fallen in love with a married man who sport-fucked stewardesses on his superyacht. Nothing could've been worse than that. It was clear that Jack didn't care about Ava, about his wife, about Sam, about anyone . . . except himself. Even the knowledge of his impending murder didn't stop Lila from absolutely hating Jack Warren with all her heart.

This case was the first time she felt absolutely no desire to save the victim.

She not only wanted to let Jack Warren die, she'd love to do him in herself. He certainly deserved it.

CHAPTER 12

LILA AWOKE EARLY the next morning feeling exhausted and overwhelmed, memories of her sister mixed with visions of Elise's swollen, tearstained face and Liss's spreadsheets all swirling around in her head. Dragging herself through her early-morning routine was excruciating, but the moment she walked into the fresh, open air, she was taken aback by the beauty surrounding her. The sunrise at sea was breathtaking. The sun peeking up along the horizon glowed a deep, almost mystical orange, turning the clouds a vibrant purple and the ocean a deep cerulean blue. There wasn't a bit of land or any sign of human life in sight. Lila paused to let the profound perfection of the scene wash over her. She deeply inhaled the balmy, salty air. For the first time in her life, she understood why someone would crave the feeling of being out at sea.

"Miss Collins, don't just stand there," Lila heard Mrs. Slaughter call out as she climbed the stairs from the galley, putting a quick end to her momentary reverie. "We've got too much work to do for daydreaming."

"Yes, ma'am," Lila said, flashing back on last night with a shudder. She'd come so close to getting caught by Slaughter. Her escape was a lucky break, but a good detective never counted on luck.

"First things first," Mrs. Slaughter said crisply. She never seemed happier than when she was giving orders. "Mrs. Warren needs to be brought a cup of consommé and hot lemon water, right now. Chef Vatel is putting together a tray for her at this very moment. Fetch that, bring it to the master suite, and provide any assistance needed with her morning medication."

"Isn't it too early?" Lila asked.

"It's much too early for you to ask foolish questions," Edna said. "Not that I need to explain my orders to you, but Mrs. Warren must take her pills at set intervals, one of which is at six A.M. And she can't take her pills on an empty stomach, hence the broth. Now that I've satisfied your imbecilic curiosity, will you do as I say?"

"Of course," Lila said with a hateful little smile.

Mrs. Slaughter, in return, gave Lila her usual glower, which was an irritatingly effective combination of patronizing and withering. Then she briskly walked away.

But with her overlord no longer watching, Lila grabbed a couple more minutes to, once again, let the absolute magnificence of her surroundings overwhelm her. There she was, a solitary woman in the middle of the endless ocean, breathing in all the abundant beauty for just one sweet moment—then she headed down to the galley to begin her day of subservience.

Hurrying down the hall, her arms straining to carry the heavy silver serving tray full of Mrs. Warren's liquid diet, Lila turned the corner—and ran straight into Ben Reynolds. It felt like she was always crashing into him. The dishes clattered around upon impact, but she managed to hold on to the tray and prevent everything from smashing to the floor.

"Nicky!" Ben said in a loud whisper. "What are you doing here?"

His eyes searched the hall nervously and then peered at Lila, trying to read what she was thinking. He seemed flustered.

Lila nodded at the tray she was holding. She could hear snoring coming from the room, so she quietly said, "I'm bringing this to Mrs. Warren."

"Oh, right. Of course," Ben mumbled.

"What are you doing up here?" she asked, confused about why Ben was wandering around outside the master suite. The captain and the first and second officers were never on this floor of the yacht.

"Oh, Jack wanted me to . . ." Ben paused. His eyes darted around as his mind searched for some excuse. " . . . to give him an update about our arrival time."

It was obvious that he was lying. Lila had spent her entire career dealing with hustlers, sociopaths, and murderers that someone so bad at hiding the truth struck her as kind of endearing. "This early? Isn't Jack still asleep?"

"Nope. Not at all. Well, I should be off. Okay? I'll see you soon," he said, in a rush of nervousness.

He headed toward Jack's room. After waiting a few, Lila crept behind him. She peeked around a corner to watch as Ben paused momentarily at Jack's door. He looked side to side to see if anyone was watching him, then continued down the hall.

What was Ben so anxious to conceal? She needed to keep an eye on him. But first she needed to drop off this tray. She entered Elise Warren's pitch-black room, hearing only her muffled snores. The room smelled like dying lilies—overwhelmingly sweet and floral, tinged with something rotten. As she put the tray down on the bedside table, Elise began to stir.

"Edna, is that you?"

"No, ma'am, it's Nicky," Lila said.

Hearing that, Elise let out a groan. "Oh, it's *you*," she sneered in disgust. "Here, turn on this light."

With the room barely illuminated by the lamp on the bedside table, Lila could see that the swelling on Elise's face had gone down considerably, and there was no longer any sign of the terrible redness. Her beautiful face, the face that created such hatred in Lila, was almost back to normal.

"Do you need any help with your morning pills, Mrs. Warren?"

"No, thank you," Elise said sharply. "I'm well practiced at swallowing. But I bet you do a lot more of it than I do." Her taunting eyes narrowed into little slits as she glared at Lila.

"Excuse me?"

"My husband only wants women who swallow. I myself never got used to it. But that doesn't matter anymore, does it? Now he gets little whores like you to do my dirty work."

Lila's mouth dropped open as she stared at Elise, whose twisted little smile contorted her silicone-enhanced lips. The brief feeling of pity that she had felt for the woman completely evaporated. This wasn't some poor, pathetic creature who was ignored by her husband. She was a poisonous bitch who had to be brought to justice. Lila took this moment as just one more reminder to keep a clear focus on why she was on that yacht. She was there to make Elise pay. She was there for her sister, Ava.

"That will be all, dear," Elise said as she took a dainty sip of her hot lemon water, keeping her narrowed eyes on Lila the whole time.

AT PRECISELY NINE, breakfast was served in the dining room. It would be several more hours until the boat reached land, and there was a bit of cabin fever brewing in the air. As Lila and Sam

were serving the guests, Seth Liss was bent over his laptop looking at more spreadsheets, shoveling Tater Tots into his mouth,
Paul Mason was reading *Cigar Aficionado* as his poached eggs
grew cold, Josie was picking at some vegan glop called "chia
pudding" while damaging her eardrums with bass-heavy music
on her iPod, the newlyweds Thiago and Esperanza were sitting
close and whispering inaudible words to each other, and Daniel
Poe was drinking a beer shandy and smoking a joint the size
of a child's finger on the balcony off the dining room. To date,
Lila hadn't seen him actually eat anything. Clarence Baines
was on the phone with the head of his reelection committee,
going over the latest polls while his wife circled items in the
Neiman Marcus catalog.

It was, all things considered, a pretty peaceful scene. Until
Jack Warren came into the room screaming.

"You goddamn son of a bitch! You fucking, backstabbing
bastard!" he boomed, his bulging eyes trained on Seth Liss.
His face was beet red with rage. Despite Jack's terrifying state,
Liss looked totally calm, like he'd been expecting, maybe even
looking forward to, this outburst.

"You didn't think to tell me about this? You wanted me to
just find out on my own? You made me look like a fucking
fool," Jack ranted.

Liss slowly closed his laptop and straightened up. Even
though there was a spot of ketchup from his Tater Tots on
the right-side corner of his mouth, he looked almost dignified
compared to the apoplectic Jack.

"What do you want me to do? Read you the minutes of
your company's meetings? I'm not your goddamn secretary,
Jack," the CFO said. "Listen, if you want to know what's going
on, maybe you should've just been on the call. But *you* wanted

to go *sailing*. So that was your choice, not mine. It was also your choice not to even ask me how the call went."

"You didn't think I'd care that the shareholders and the board scheduled a vote to halve my executive compensation? Are you kidding me? I *am* this company. And now the people I've handpicked to help me run it want me to make less?"

"You made two hundred million dollars last year."

"I earned every fucking cent!" Jack's eyes were almost popping out of his head.

"It's obscene. You're getting rich while the company's stock price is stagnating," Liss said. "The board knows it's not good for the bottom line. It's that simple."

"It's not the board. It's you. I can see your greasy fingerprints all over this whole fucking thing."

"You're making no sense. I had no hand in this. Your shareholders don't believe in you anymore, and that's your own doing. This is just a case of the chickens coming home to roost."

Jack lunged toward Liss, but Thiago jumped up and put himself between the two. "Settle down, Jack. You can't blame Seth for this. The shareholders are trying to get your attention. That's all this is. And, see, it worked."

"Yeah," Paul Mason said, not looking up from his cigar magazine. "Not being on that call was a boneheaded move."

"Especially given the numbers from the last few quarters," Thiago said. "You know as well as anyone in this room that if the numbers are down, the shareholders will want your head. You've got to remember you have *responsibilities*." Thiago hit the last word really hard, emphasizing it by simultaneously putting his hands on Jack's heaving shoulders. Lila saw a flicker of something unspoken pass between the two men.

"I take care of my responsibilities," Jack said, shrugging off

Thiago's hands. "I've made everyone in this room rich, and I won't stand for one second of disrespect or betrayal from any of you." He walked over to the table and picked up a Tater Tot from Liss's plate. "Especially, you," he said to his CFO as he pinged the golden bite of potato off his head; it landed on Liss's shirt, leaving a large ketchup smear. "I will not let you hijack my legacy!" he screamed. Then, before he walked away, he took a Japanese vase from the table and smashed it to pieces on the floor.

"What a goddamned animal," Paul said.

"I'm just glad everyone's seeing what I've known for years. He's a menace to us and to the company," Liss said, giving Paul and Thiago a knowing look. Lila knew that whatever was brewing between them, they were all in on it together, and Jack was now the one on the outside.

"And he's got a conveniently short-term memory," Thiago continued as he pushed the shards of the vase into a little pile with the toe of his Ferragamo slipper. "Without my family's money, Jack Warren would be nothing. And he has the nerve to tell me that *he* made *me* rich? That's something I will not stand for." He looked to his wife, Esperanza, who gave him a decisive nod, letting him know that they were of one mind.

Esperanza then said something quietly to her husband in Portuguese, and though Lila's Portuguese was pretty rusty, she thought she said, "Some things are very dangerous to forget."

As Lila looked from face to face around that dining room table, she didn't see one person who had anything but contempt for Jack Warren.

CHAPTER 13

FROM THE MOMENT *The Rising Tide* came within eyeshot of Paul Mason's private island, which was the crown jewel on a long necklace of tiny islands off the coast of the Bahamas, the welcoming party erupted.

Paul called out to all the guests on the ship to join him on the deck. Lila, Sam, and Asher, curious to know what was going on, went along with them. There wasn't another island for miles and miles, and the remoteness of the location, with its lack of light pollution, transformed the night's sky into a shimmering, electric, pointillist painting. Every inch of the heavens was dripping with an infinite number of stars.

Just across the dark ocean waters, like a fantastical mirage, stood Paul's island mansion—a low-lying collection of glass, steel, and palm-frond buildings tucked into a jungle so verdant and wild that it seemed as if it was on the verge of engulfing this tiny bit of civilization. There was a riotous bonfire raging on the pure-white sand of the beach, its errant flames licking the black skies around it. This grandeur was framed by gigantic palm trees, all breathtakingly lit up from below.

"Welcome," Paul said, with a beaming smile and his voice full of gravitas, "to paradise." He dramatically stretched out his arms with his palms facing up to the sky, like a magician who'd just pulled off an impressive trick. There was a high-pitched whiz of something moving through the air that got everyone's eyes searching upward, and then, with a crack, an explosion of fireworks illuminated the sky. Gold. Red. Green. Concentric circles of light danced across the black sky, accompanied by silver streaks of man-made shooting stars racing, booming, dancing, fleeting, falling. It was quite an accomplishment. Everyone ooh'd and aah'd. There are few people harder to impress than a crowd of constantly aggrieved billionaires, but Paul managed to do it. The glorious fireworks display was as awesome as he had intended. Pleased with himself, he looked happily at everyone's delighted faces—everyone with the exception of Jack Warren, whose features were set in a bitter scowl.

As the thunderous sounds of the fireworks waned, music came pouring across the waters. It was reggae, the music of the tropics, of joy, and of relaxation. Two large speedboats raced out toward the yacht, which had just dropped its mighty anchor in the deep waters.

Josie, wearing a breezy Isabel Marant minidress, clapped her hands in delight.

"Everyone off," Paul yelled as he scooted people into the speedboats now idling by the yacht's rear. They all piled in: Thiago, Esperanza, Elise, Jack, Josie, Seth, Clarence, Charity, Paul, and Daniel. Even Ben hopped aboard.

"Do you think we can go?" Sam whispered to Lila as both women stood watching the giddy guests on the cusp of a fabulous night.

"You both certainly cannot," Edna said from behind them. Of course she was listening, Lila thought. Even Big Brother wasn't this intrusive.

"But—" Sam whined.

"But nothing. This is a party for the guests of this boat. You are not a guest, you are a *stewardess,*" Edna said, in a slow and clear voice, as if she was speaking to a dim-witted child.

"Then why does Ben get to go?" Sam asked. Her eyes, full of longing, were glued to the speedboat that was taking Ben and the others to the island.

"He's been invited by Mr. Mason. Our captain was also invited, but Captain Nash declined." Edna's eyes narrowed. "Remember, no cheek, sulk, or moods. There's plenty to do on board. All the guest cabins need to be cleaned. The sheets need to be laundered and pressed. The silver needs a good polishing. Shall I go on?"

"No, Chief Stewardess," Sam and Lila said in unison.

"The guests will reboard the yacht in less than twenty-four hours, so we don't have much time. Sam, why don't you begin with scrubbing the toilets? And, Lila, you get started with the bed linens. That ought to help remind you girls about who you are on this ship."

With a forlorn look over her shoulder at the carnival of delights just out of her grasp, Sam slunk down belowdeck to get her cleaning supplies, a sadsack Cinderella still waiting for her fairy godmother.

Lila, on the other hand, was happy to be away from the pulse and push of the party. Though she wouldn't have considered herself a fan of housework before she went undercover, now she realized there was no better way to scour the yacht looking for clues. With every tuck of a sheet and fold of a towel, she hunted for evidence to finally prove her sister's innocence.

As she went from room to room, carrying out her duties both as a maid and as a detective, she went through a laundry list of what she knew so far. Elise still remained her number one suspect. That much was certain. Every day, as Lila watched Jack serve up steady doses of betrayal, humiliation, scorn, and neglect to his wife, she grew more and more convinced that Elise was the killer. Even if Elise had been a stable and good woman, which she most definitely was not, such circumstances could turn her murderous. Not to mention the billions of dollars that would become hers the moment her monster of a husband was dead. No one else had more to gain, and less to lose, than Elise.

But there were questions Lila couldn't ignore. Elise Warren seemed incapable of doing almost anything, much less committing a murder, by herself. She was practically drowning in a soup of booze and pills. Did she really have the fortitude to put a bullet in her husband and then frame Ava for the whole thing? However, Elise could get someone else to do her dirty work for her—Edna, maybe. It was obvious that the chief stewardess would take a bullet for her precious mistress.

Then there was Seth Liss. He and Jack clearly detested each other. Liss had already started going through the corporate channels to remove Jack as head of the company, with the full consent of the board, Paul, and Thiago. But that could take ages, and Liss knew perfectly well that a well-publicized shake-up in the leadership of the company would greatly damage its reputation and profit margins. On the other hand, if Liss got Jack out of the way quickly, like say, with four bullets to the chest, then he wouldn't have to wait to assume the reins of leadership.

The biggest surprise for Lila was Thiago Campos. From all her research over the last decade, she thought she knew a fair amount about the man. But there was something between Jack and Thiago this morning over breakfast that she couldn't put her finger on, something loaded. Thiago had said Jack had "responsibilities," and he meant more than just running Warren Software – that much was clear. Now Lila needed to figure out a way to decode the message Thiago was sending to Jack.

All of these thoughts were spinning through her mind as she devoted hours to combing through all of the staterooms. She searched every drawer, examined the tops and bottoms and insides of every cabinet, opened makeup bags, purses, prodded the insides of every shoe, and lifted up every mattress, knowing eventually she'd find something hidden or in plain sight that would point her to Jack's killer.

But it was in Jack's room that she found a real treasure. There, atop his unmade bed, was a laptop that she'd never seen before. He must normally keep it locked away in his desk drawer. Her pulse quickened. She closed the door behind her and opened the computer, pulling up his email. She was surprised to see that Jack had a dozen or so messages from Urs Hunziker, the Swiss banker who was counseling Seth on how to handle Jack.

Lila opened one of the emails. Just as she began to read, Edna Slaughter walked in. Lila slammed the laptop closed and leaped off the bed so fast that the chief stewardess didn't see her on Jack's computer. All Lila had seen in her quick scan of the correspondence were the words "King Charles" and "betray" and "Liss."

"I've got this room, Chief Stewardess Mrs. Slaughter," Lila said to Edna as she began to take the pillowcases off the pillows.

"I have repeatedly told you that Mr. and Mrs. Warren have requested that *only I* service their rooms."

Lila stood there silently, desperate to return to her search of Jack's computer but, once again, Edna would be a giant roadblock. Not only was there the constant threat of being fired, which would completely and disastrously derail her mission, but having every move and moment strictly monitored made gathering facts and evidence next to impossible. The worst part was, there was absolutely nothing she could do to stop it.

"I'm sorry. I'll leave you to it," Lila said in the most deferential tone she could conjure, but really she wanted to tell Edna to shove it where the sun don't shine.

"Yes, you will," Edna said. "I'll finish up here. You go to the laundry room. There's a load of linen sheets that need to be pressed."

And with a nod, Lila left Jack's room. She was annoyed, but that didn't stop her brain from buzzing. Could it be possible that instead of Liss playing Jack, Jack was playing Liss? If Urs had told Jack about Project King Charles, then how much did Jack know? And was he aware that his two closest friends and advisers were on Liss's side? Or, *were* they?

These were the questions she ran through her head as she was stuck doing the laundry until midnight. She was getting so wound up that she didn't hear Sam calling her name until she felt Sam's breath on her neck.

"Nicky!" Sam cried directly in her ear, scaring Lila half to death. "Didn't you hear me? I've called your name like a thousand times."

"Sorry," Lila said as she folded her last bedsheet. "My mind was on other things." Like when was Ava going to board the yacht? Or, what bad blood was brewing between Thiago and Jack? Or, was Seth willing to murder his boss to become CEO? And according to the police report, there would be four gunshots the night Jack died. But, except for her own revolver, Lila hadn't yet seen a gun on the ship. Where was it?

Sam gave her a relaxed smile. Lila could smell beer on her breath. "A bunch of us are having a little party of our own in the galley. Ready to come join us?"

"Actually," Lila said, "I'm really beat. I think I'll go back to the room and lie down."

"Don't be so lame," Sam said with a roll of her eyes. "Is it just because Ben won't be there?"

This caught Lila off guard. "What? Ben?"

"You can tell me!" Sam begged. "Come on, I'm not stupid. I've seen how you two look at each other. And I don't blame either of you. You're both freakin' hot! You'd have such gorgeous babies. It'd be insane."

"Oh, Sam, please," Lila said with an embarrassed grin. Yet as she walked back to her room alone, she couldn't stop her thoughts from drifting to Ben. A little heat did exist between them. It wasn't something she'd admit to out loud but it was impossible to deny. But so what? She'd learned her lesson the hard way. Getting mixed up with anyone in the past was never going to happen again.

Lila returned to her tiny coffin of a room, grabbed her laptop from the drawer underneath her bunk, and unearthed the thumb drive, which she'd stuffed into the toe of one of her canvas boat shoes. Since she'd gone undercover on *The Rising Tide,* she hadn't had more than a few minutes alone to herself, so this moment of quiet solitude felt like a luxury. Her bunkmate was away, it wasn't too late, Mrs. Slaughter was nowhere in sight, and she had a bit of time alone to devote to the case.

Tonight, she wanted to review all her information on Thiago Campos. Lila knew Thiago was from the Brazilian elite, and that he and Jack were old friends from Harvard. She knew that Jack dropped out of college to focus on his company and Thiago went on to graduate in 1980. But what Thiago had said that very morning was news to Lila. She had no idea that his family's money had been used to start Jack's software company. Because of the Camposes' role in supporting the brutal Brazilian dictatorship, all Thiago's family money could be perceived as dirty. If Jack never publicly acknowledged that his friend from São Paulo had provided him with the seed capital he needed to finance his company, maybe it was to avoid any unsavory connections surfacing between Warren Software and the South American torturers and kleptocrats who ran Brazil for twenty years.

And if the Campos family gave Warren Software its funding, then to what extent were they still invested? From the intensity of Thiago's concern this morning, Lila would guess that his family fortune was deeply tied to Jack.

Lila decided to analyze Warren Software's public records to see if she could figure out how big a stake the Campos family held in the company. But she quickly realized the search wouldn't be easy. Like most investors looking to stay anonymous, Lila knew that the Campos name could be kept hidden through numerous shell companies. Just as she was about to dig deeper into Warren's SEC filings, there was a knock on the door. Lila quickly closed up her computer and returned the thumb drive to the tip of her shoe. She opened the door to find Ben smiling at her from the hallway.

"Sam sent me to bring you to the party," he said, grabbing both of Lila's hands and pulling her out of her room. He had a tipsy glaze to his eye, and his hair and clothes smelled like wood smoke from Paul Mason's bonfire.

"I should change," Lila said. Her hair was in a messy ponytail, and she was dressed in cutoff jeans and a threadbare tank top.

"Please," Ben said. "Don't change a thing. It's just us crew. I mean, we've seen you in your little stewardess uniform. It can't get any worse than that, right?"

Lila playfully punched his arm, and he grabbed her hand, dragging her down to the crew's mess, where she heard soca music playing above the sound of boisterous conversation. When they entered, their arrival was cheered by one and all.

A very drunk Sam was dancing with Mudge, who had his cal-lused hands on her hips as they awkwardly swayed to and fro. Pedro, the nineteen-year-old deckhand, was drinking from a red plastic cup while tending to the music on the stereo. Asher, the most devoted partier of the crew, was nowhere to be seen.

Lila was surprised to spot the elusive Captain Nash sitting in the corner drinking whiskey. He was a weathered-looking man, with skin that spoke of a lifetime of sun and salty air. He had a thick, silver beard and dark, prominent brows that sat heavily over his stern eyes. He didn't look like a guy who smiled very much. Since she'd been on the boat, she'd never seen him socialize with the crew or with the guests. Mostly he just stuck to his captain's quarters and the bridge. Even now, as fun and merriment swirled around him, he sat there solemnly, keeping his eyes trained on Lila.

"Why is he staring at me?" Lila whispered to Ben, who had just returned from grabbing her a drink.

"Aren't you used to men looking at you?"

"Not quite like that," she said as she returned Nash's con-centrated stare with a curious, questioning look of her own. "He's looking at me like I owe him money or something."

"Don't worry. I think that's just what his face looks like," Ben said, trying to reassure her.

She gave Nash a small wave, but he sat unmoved. Lila, uneasy under his gaze, faced away from him.

"So," she said to Ben, "why are you here on the yacht when you could be sipping champagne with the rich and fabulous?"

"Oh, you know. It all gets pretty tiresome, right? When people have so much of everything, nothing seems to mean anything to them. Do you know what I mean?"

"More than you know." In her undercover work hunting for the Star Island killer, Lila had assumed the identity of one of these multimillionaires and she'd learned that the most essential part of fitting in with the glitterati was to never act impressed by all the extraordinary things money could buy.

Ben continued, "Daniel Poe was the only one who wasn't boring me to tears. He put on quite a show tonight, stripping off all his clothes and dancing around the fire shouting, 'The natives are restless. The natives are restless.' It was definitely worth the price of admission."

"I would've liked to have seen that."

"Trust me, you wouldn't. But the real pain in the ass was Jack. Everyone was having a good time, some more than others, except him. He bit my head off a few times over absolutely nothing. Sometimes I think I played this all wrong."

"Played what wrong?" Lila asked. It seemed as if Jack's mood might have been contagious because, despite this being his second party of the night, Ben was agitated.

"Oh, you know, Jack's always said that I'm his man. That I'm the one who'll get him the America's Cup. *That's* why I'm here. The *only* reason I'm here." Ben sighed. "Then he goes and treats me like I'm just some fly he can swat away when he's feeling shitty."

"It seems like that's Jack's way. I wouldn't worry too much about it," Lila said with total conviction. Soon enough, Jack would be dead and Ben would be without the sponsor he needed to race in the America's Cup, so why worry? But that's one of the things that time travel had taught Lila; the empty platitude about not sweating the small stuff wasn't just another tired old cliché. It was profound and true.

"You're right. It's just hard with Jack. It's like he's only in control when he makes everyone else feel out of control."

"Yes!" Lila said, nodding her head, pleased with Ben's insight. "You're right. He's a control freak who likes operating in chaos."

"Not a pretty picture." Ben sighed.

"Not at all." Lila looked back to see that Captain Nash had disappeared, and that Mudge had Sam pressed up against the kitchen counter with his tongue down her throat.

"But I can't complain. I'm in a tropical paradise having a drink with you. Life ain't so bad," Ben said, looking down at Lila with a warm smile. She leaned into him despite herself, and he put his arm around her shoulder.

She turned her face toward his, about to say something, but when she noticed that his lips were inches away from hers, she forgot what it was. Then things became quiet as he leaned a fraction closer. Suddenly she pulled away, backing up and shaking her head as if she'd just awoken from a spell.

"I didn't mean to . . ." Ben started to apologize, but then he fell silent. He grabbed Lila's hand. "Why don't I walk you to your room?"

"Not tonight," she said. She knew there was no point in putting either of them through an awkward moment in front of Lila's door. She'd made up her mind to keep things strictly friendly with Ben. It was better for everyone.

As she headed toward her room, silently congratulating herself for having the strength to walk away from a gorgeous and interested man, Lila saw Asher's door open slightly, and a very disheveled Josie Warren slip out into the hallway. She was still wearing the dress she was in earlier, but now its halter top was twisted and the skirt was rumpled, as was her hair. It was clear that she and Asher had just had a rather vigorous romp in his cabin.

When Josie spotted Lila, the young heiress didn't bat an eye. She just slunk by, wearing a devilish grin on her face, with the telltale scent of Asher's coconut oil trailing behind her.

CHAPTER 14

EVERYONE RETURNED TO the yacht the following evening and waved a fond farewell to their opulent stopover at Parrot Cay. The next destination on their island-hopping extravaganza would be Turks and Caicos, one of the Caribbean's most star-studded, luxurious hot spots.

The time off the boat seemed to do each of the guests a world of good. That night, as they gathered around the dining table for a dinner of raw oysters and roasted bone marrow with sea urchin, there was a lightness of mood and a quickness to smile that took Lila by surprise. After all, just two days ago, everyone had been at one another's throats.

Even Jack seemed to be in a good mood. He flopped down at the head of the table with a satisfied sigh, picked up his mouth-blown lead crystal wineglass that Lila had just filled with vintage Barolo, and made a toast. "Paul, we've been friends and business associates for the last two decades and I know what a good and generous man you can be. But the hospitality you extended over the last two days to me, my family, and my guests was unparalleled. I'm sure I speak for everyone when I say thank you."

A chorus of thanks was accompanied by the sound of expensive crystal glasses clinking in a friendly "cheers." Paul Mason beamed at the group, drinking in their attention and adulation. His cheerful cheeks were as pink as his Bermuda shorts.

But while all the guests were joyful and relaxed, Daniel Poe seemed giddy. He was looking quite grand and ridiculous that night—part Elton John, part Batman villain. Despite the late-August Caribbean heat, he was wearing a three-piece paisley suit and a little bowler hat perched high atop his head, set at a jaunty angle. His eyes were largely obscured by his thick, square black eyeglass frames, and a large, crooked-toothed smile was spread across his thin face. He was shivering ever so slightly. His fingers, several of which were heavy with silver-and-diamond skull rings, drummed excitedly on the table. He hadn't touched his food, but gulped the $500 per bottle wine down as if it were lager. Lila couldn't even begin to guess what combination of drugs he was on.

"I feel inspired right now. So inspired," Poe said in his throaty, working-class English accent. "I've been overwhelmed by the beauty of things. I see, for the first time, the divine beauty of the mystery and the unity of all of us here together." He slowly stood up from his seat and wobbled slightly as he found his feet.

Everyone else looked at one another nervously.

"Are the natives restless again?" Josie asked, with a roll of her eyes.

"Good Christ, my man," Jack said amicably. "What are you on?"

"My usual recipe for success," Poe said. "Plus an extra dash of lysergic acid."

"What the hell is that?" Jack asked, bewildered.

"It's LSD, Dad," Josie said, giggling into her napkin.

Jack shook his head. He watched Daniel Poe begin to slowly

bend his long, emaciated limbs with a newfound joy, as if he'd never before inhabited his body. "I'll never understand the artistic temperament," Jack said with a fatherly frown. "And I count myself a lucky man for that."

"Don't be such a square," Josie said dismissively. "Everyone drops acid at Wesleyan. It's, like, the only way to see beyond our lies."

"Oh, shut up, Josie," Elise said as she drained her glass of wine.

"Yeah," Paul Mason said, with a playful mockery. "Just a lifetime of dropping acid and you, too, can sell your paintings for five million a pop. I wish someone told me *that* recipe for success at Yale."

"I think I should excuse myself," said an unsmiling Clarence Baines, brusquely getting up from the table. "Mrs. Baines and I will go to our room now. Jack, please have one of your girls serve us our dinner there. Elise, excuse us."

"Please, Clarence," Elise said. "You mustn't go." Elise disliked when people made a spectacle of themselves, hence Daniel Poe's very public acid trip was not appreciated. But she wouldn't stand for Baines jumping ship on dinner. That was just bad manners.

"You know my position on drugs, Jack," Baines said to his friend. "I know that you keep, let's call it, *eclectic* company, but I won't break bread with someone who holds all my values in contempt."

"Please, don't go because of me," Poe said dreamily. "I'm feeling kingly, gallant, magical, electric." He began to bounce on the tips of his toes like a Southern Baptist preacher on the verge of speaking in tongues. "I fall on my sword for you, Senator Baines. I will be happy to leave you fine folks to your dinner."

"That's mighty gentlemanly of you, son," Clarence Baines said as he and his wife returned to their seats and Daniel Poe exited the dining room with a curious backward slinking motion.

But just before he was out of sight completely, he bounded back toward the table. "That's it!" he exclaimed. "I know just what I'll do. I have a surprise for you all. At the exact stroke of midnight tonight, I'd like you all to join me on the main deck. I will unveil the masterpiece I have created in honor of our great host's fiftieth birthday. I just can't keep it under wraps a moment longer. Until then!" Poe said with a deep bow, and sprinted down the hall.

Three hours later, everyone congregated on the main deck, ready for the great viewing that would hopefully meet all Daniel Poe's psychedelic desires. A six-foot statue stood in the middle of the floor, covered in a red silk sheet. It was the very special sculpture Poe made in Jack's honor, which had been delivered to the yacht days earlier and been stashed since then until the final moment of its great unveiling.

Poe had asked that Sam and Lila have champagne ready for everyone, so as people filed in, the two stewardesses handed out flutes of Veuve Clicquot. He'd also asked that they wear black masks over their eyes and nothing else, but to that request, they sweetly said no. It was a rare treat when Sam and Lila could refuse a guest's request. They both quietly cherished the moment.

"Gather round, children of light," Poe said, waving everyone toward him. In honor of this grand unveiling, he had changed from his paisley suit into one of Elise Warren's floor-length, low-cut Bob Mackie sequined gowns, which showed off his pale skin, dark chest hair, and jutting collarbone. Lila saw that his pupils were extremely dilated, which confirmed what she already knew. He was having some pretty profound hallucinations.

"Daniel," Elise said flatly. "You're wearing my dress."

He looked at her, confused. Then, peering down at himself, he understood what he'd done and began to laugh. "Yes, darling. Apologies for not asking, but I needed to shine tonight and nothing in my closet did the trick."

"I think you look ravishing," Josie said, taking pleasure in seeing her mom unhappy.

"Thank you, my little lamb." Poe began to light a very large smudge stick, which he waved in the air as he danced around the still-cloaked statue. "I must purify the aura of this space. I must welcome in birth and death. Creation and destruction." The hallucinating art star circled the statue over and over again. Jack and Paul looked at each other in total exhaustion. Clarence Baines, needless to say, had declined Poe's invitation, but his wife, who fancied herself an experienced and sophisticated art connoisseur (though no one else would have agreed), was paying rapt attention to this whole bizarre performance. Thiago and Esperanza looked on with a combination of mild curiosity and boredom. They were part of a very arty aristo-boho jet-set group that would consider the spectacle of a raving man in a $5,000 evening gown part of just another typical night.

"It's getting late," Jack said to Poe, hoping to hurry him along. More than anything, Jack seemed anxious to see what the artist had created.

"Oh, yes. Of course," Daniel murmured, as if getting pulled out of a trance. He stopped his circling and blinked at everyone on the deck as if seeing them for the first time. He steadied himself and stood squarely next to the statue. "This moment means a lot to me. Not only does this work celebrate my dear patron Jack Warren, but it is the culmination of my twenty years as an artist. And," he said as he pulled the sheet off the statue, "here it is."

Lila heard someone gasp, but after that there was nothing but a very uncomfortable silence. Standing before them, with a red silk sheet pooled at its base, was a six-foot-long and one-foot-wide golden penis, with a stream of ejaculate made out of diamonds shooting out from the top.

Josie began to snort and giggle. Elise stared blankly at the penis while holding her champagne glass toward Lila for a refill. Paul Mason was frozen, with his eyes on Jack, waiting for a cue from him on how to react. Thiago and Esperanza smiled slyly at each other, knowing that this would be a story they'd be dining out on for years to come. The artist didn't look at his patron or the other guests. He was staring reverentially at his creation, running his hand up and down the cool, golden shaft.

Charity Baines, the only one brave enough, or dumb enough, to speak, said, "Well, how interesting." She was following the rule that all good southern girls are taught by their mothers: when you don't like something, just say it's interesting.

What Daniel Poe didn't see, but what everyone else did, was that Jack Warren was extremely unhappy. Livid, in fact. He tossed his champagne down his throat and then smashed the empty flute to the deck. The violent crash finally ripped Poe's attention away from the giant gold phallus.

"How dare you!" Jack shouted, almost shaking with rage. His hands were clenched into fists and the veins in his forehead popped out. "Do you think I'm a fool?"

"What?" Poe said, totally confused.

"I give you ten million dollars to make something in honor of my birthday and you give me this?"

"You don't like it?" Poe asked innocently. He looked lovingly at the statue, confused as to how anyone could fail to adore and admire such a thing.

"No, you fucking idiot. I love it. I think it's wonderful that, in my honor, and with my millions, you've made a big gold dildo with diamond cum. Yes, that's just what I was dreaming of."

"Are you being serious?" Poe asked. His face was contorted

from his extreme state of confusion. He was obviously way too high to comprehend sarcasm.

"Fuck me," Jack exploded with frustration. "No, Daniel. No, I'm *not* being fucking serious."

"Oh, no! You don't understand. Please let me explain." Poe, bewildered, hallucinating, shuffled toward Jack. The ball gown made it impossible for him to take anything but tiny little steps. He was in no state to calm a pissed-off billionaire. Lila really felt for the guy. He launched into a nervous spiel about how this statue harkened back to the Roman fertility god Priapus and was intended as a celebration of Jack's masculinity, virility, wealth, and status. But Jack wasn't having it.

"I know what you're *really* saying," Jack said. "You're saying you think I'm a dick. A giant, gilded dick! Well, I won't be insulted on my own fucking boat by some drug addict who calls himself an artist."

Jack rushed toward the statue, placed his hands on it, and with all his strength, pushed it over until it crashed to the floor.

"Noooooo!" Poe screamed. "You'll ruin it!"

"Paul! Thiago! Get over here now! I want you to help me lift this thing." The two men joined Jack. When he was in this kind of rage, no one would refuse him anything lest he bite their heads off. With Thiago holding the tip of the penis, Paul on the shaft, and Jack on the base, they all groaned as they tried to lift it up, but it was too heavy.

"Sam!" Jack shouted at the terrified stewardess. "Go get Ben, Asher, and Pedro. Fast."

Within a minute there were six men hoisting the statue, while Poe began to whimper and wail. "Please, Jack. Don't destroy it." Then he became enraged. "No!" he shouted over and over again with more and more anger cracking his voice. "I'll give you all your money back. Just don't do this."

But there was no reasoning with Jack. He ordered all the men, groaning under the weight of the statue, to walk to the railing and throw it into the ocean. Poe's screams were too loud for Jack to hear the satisfying splash of it hitting the water.

"That will teach you," Jack said, jabbing a finger in Poe's face, "not to ever, ever fuck with me."

Poe ran to the side of the boat, bending over the railing to see where his beloved masterpiece had gone as he howled in despair.

Needless to say, the good mood that existed over dinner had evaporated completely. Lila looked around at all the blank faces and the champagne flute smashed into shards by the large dent in the deck left by the toppled statue. It was a disaster. Everyone seemed afraid to breathe out of fear of Jack's wrath. Only Thiago, who had managed to somehow surreptitiously wrench the diamond arc of semen off the statue before assisting in tossing it into its watery grave, was smiling.

Within a couple minutes all the guests had returned to their cabins, even Daniel. But that wasn't the end of the drama. Throughout the night, there were crashes, slashes, screams, pounding, and a steady stream of cursing coming out of Poe's cabin. Smash went the flat screen. Crash went the mirrors. Slash went the pillows. And on and on. An entire rock band couldn't inflict the damage he did to his room that night.

Around 3:00 A.M., Lila and Sam finally were able to return to their tiny, underwater closet and stretch out on their bunk beds. But even though she was bone-tired, Lila couldn't fall asleep. A thought kept tugging at her mind. She kept seeing Daniel Poe's anguished, tear-soaked face. He had seemed utterly destroyed. It was like Jack had thrown Poe's *child* into the vast, churning ocean.

What if Poe's anger turned deadly? The man was unstable enough that it was a distinct possibility that he could be Jack's killer. Her profound exhaustion, mixed with the realization that there might be yet one *more* person with a motive to kill Jack, made Lila feel lower than low.

"Can't sleep?" Sam asked in the complete darkness of their cabin.

"Nope. My mind's going a hundred miles a minute."

"You have no idea," Sam said with a groan. "I'm beyond fucked at this moment."

"What's wrong?" Lila asked.

"Well, after all that golden-dick bullshit went down, I checked on Mr. Warren to see if I could get him anything . . ."

"Oh, Sam," Lila said, knowing what was coming.

"What? I can't help it if what he *wanted* was a blow job. I mean, I was thinking he might need a drink, but I guess he was looking for something stronger. Anyway, right in the middle of the whole thing, guess who walks in?"

"Who?"

"Who else but Chief Stewardess Edna Slaughterhouse! Big Brother herself."

"No!" Lila had to admit that that really was rotten luck, but at least Elise hadn't been the one walking in on her husband getting blown by the maid. Neither of them would've made it out alive.

"You know that spiteful bitch will make me pay for it," Sam spat.

"You think she'll kick you off the yacht?"

"I'm worried that she'll make my life such a living hell that I'll *wish* she kicked me off the yacht."

"Let's hope not," Lila said. Listening to Sam's troubles took her mind off her own long enough that she was able to close her eyes, and gain a few brief hours' respite from this ship of fools.

THE NEXT MORNING over breakfast, no one dared mention the goings-on of the previous night. Then again, people had other things on their minds besides the giant golden cock gathering barnacles somewhere on the floor of the Caribbean Sea.

Clarence Baines was grumbling about some weak polling numbers that had come out that morning, and put him ten points behind his challenger in the Republican primaries. "He's burying me, Jack," Clarence said. "I gotta go after him. I need a whole new TV campaign, but you know that means more money."

But Jack wasn't biting. He didn't even look up from his miso soup at the worried senator. Everyone around the table seemed to know what Clarence was too obtuse to realize, that this was not the morning to be pestering Jack Warren for more donations. Their host was still seething. Hell hath no fury like a billionaire mocked.

Baines wasn't the only one who got bad news that morning. Paul Mason had received word that a major institutional investor was running scared at the current shakiness of the financial system and had backed out of underwriting a major M&A deal Paul was handling, meaning he'd lose tens of millions of dollars. Lila heard it all when he was barking into his cell at the breakfast table before everyone else sat down.

"I'm stuck on this goddamn boat having to hand-hold a fucking baby, meanwhile everything's about to go to hell. That's just fucking great," Paul said as he repeatedly jabbed a halved grapefruit with a tiny serrated knife. "Yeah, I'd leave, but if Jack pulls out, too, then the whole thing is done. Kaput."

Despite the tense silence, Clarence just wouldn't let up. "What about you, Paul? You're a king on Wall Street. Can you help me raise some dough? Otherwise my goose is cooked."

Just when Paul was about to tell Clarence that begging for money before a man had a chance to digest his breakfast was strictly verboten, the now-disgraced and extremely strung out Daniel Poe stormed into the dining room.

"You fucking bastards! You goddamn, bourgeois, philistine, fucking bastards!" he screamed. All he was wearing was a pair of stained silk pajama bottoms that hung so low beneath his pointy hipbones that you could begin to see the dark swell of his pubic hair. There was a long red cut on his forearm that was slightly bleeding.

"You aren't welcome here," Jack said, in a low, stern voice, keeping his angry eyes trained on his breakfast.

"Like I give a fucking toss," Poe said. "I'm not following your rules anymore."

The smell of booze, cigarette smoke, and vomit emanated from him. It had clearly been a very rough night for Daniel Poe.

"I'm only here because I want to look into the eye of my betrayer," Poe said to Jack, pointing his long ring finger in his direction. "Insulting me as an artist is one thing, you bastard. But sabotaging my entire fucking career is another goddamn thing entirely."

"What do you mean, Daniel?" Elise asked, to which her husband shot her a withering look. Lila felt like this might've been the very first time she'd seen Jack even so much as lay eyes on his wife. Elise returned his look with a deadly scowl of her own.

"I just got off the phone with my gallery," Poe snarled. "It seems that your sick, fucking husband has been slandering me to everyone who'll listen. I just found out that two major commissions have already been canceled. And all those dumb fucks at the Guggenheim are meeting this afternoon to discuss if they still want to go forward with an already-confirmed retrospective of my goddamn fucking work."

Jack finally looked up at Daniel, giving him a playful wink. "Wasn't me, pal. But can't say I'm too sad to hear the news."

"That's fucking it," Poe said as he started to rush toward Jack, but he tripped over his own feet, crashing into Thiago.

"Easy," Thiago said, putting his hands out to break Poe's fall. "Get a hold of yourself."

Poe leaned around Thiago and spit right in Jack's face. Jack jumped up out of his seat and lunged toward the artist. "Get off my goddamn boat, you freak!" he screamed. Now Paul was forced to join the melee, restraining the enraged billionaire.

Lila pressed herself against the wall to avoid coming into contact with any errant fists or bodily fluids. As the madness swirled around her, she observed all the women still sitting at the table. Josie looked delighted, like she was watching an exciting wrestling match. Esperanza appeared bored, as always. Charity had a worried glint in her eye. But it was Elise who really took Lila by surprise. She sat there utterly serene, with the first real smile Lila had ever seen on her face, as if nothing could give her more pleasure than seeing her husband angry and humiliated, with another man's spit dripping down his cheek.

CHAPTER 15

WHEN THE SUPERYACHT docked on a tiny island in Turks and Caicos, Daniel Poe was the first one to stumble off in a state of drunken, drugged mania, vowing to burn everything Jack Warren owned to the ground. As she watched him leave a tsunami of vengeful promises in his wake, Lila was certain: Poe was now a suspect. Yet with his magnificently destructive drug habit, she thought he seemed just as likely to kill himself as murder Jack.

But she couldn't keep tabs on him anyway, now that he was leaving, which was itself a cause of great consternation for Lila. After all, she knew for certain that Poe was on the yacht at the time of Jack's murder. He'd given his account of the night to police just like all the others. But here he was, storming off and highly unlikely to return, considering the bad feelings shared by everybody.

Would he, eventually, return to the yacht? Or, she worried, was there another explanation? As much as she hated to admit it, it was possible that Lila had caused a rupture in the space-time continuum, and inadvertently created an alternate reality. What if Lila's very presence, no matter how unobtrusive she attempted to be, had been disruptive enough to change the past and somehow send Daniel Poe off the boat? Did that mean that the 2008 she thought she knew no longer existed?

Another time-travel mindfuck, she thought, shaking her head as she watched Poe piss on the side of the yacht before taking his final exit. Nothing she could do about it now.

The Daniel Poe incident had left everyone kind of shell-shocked. Once he was off the boat, people retreated to their private corners to recover. Sam and Lila were quietly having their breakfast in the galley with Asher and Ben as the remaining guests prepared to leave the yacht for the day. Mrs. Slaughter walked into the kitchen, looking very pleased with herself, which Sam and Lila knew meant only trouble. Immediately, they were on edge.

"Ladies, there's been a change of plans. Nicky, I've got some good news." At that, Sam and Lila gave each other a questioning look out of the corners of their eyes. Mrs. Slaughter wasn't what anyone would call a bringer of good tidings. Edna continued, "I'm going to give you the day off to enjoy Turks and Caicos."

"Really?" Lila asked warily. She was wondering if this was some kind of terrible trick. Her first impulse was to jump up out of her seat and rush off the boat so she could find and trail Daniel Poe.

"Absolutely," Edna replied. Then she turned to Sam. "That means you'll have to do all of Nicky's work, plus your own today. And you should probably start in Mr. Poe's old room. But, just a warning," she said as a smile spread across her face, "it seems he defecated and vomited several times in his stateroom, so be prepared."

Sam audibly groaned. "Of course he did," she said with pure beleaguered exasperation.

Mrs. Slaughter turned back to Lila, "Nicky, be back on the

yacht by four P.M. at the latest." Then, looking quite pleased with herself at a job well done, Edna left the room.

"Sucks to be you," Asher said to a pouting Sam. As he stood there relaxed and cheerful, smelling of coconut oil and wearing only his Rolex and surf shorts, it was clear that Asher Lydon was not a man capable of profound empathy.

"Shut up, Asher," Sam said, giving him a flirty slap on his muscled shoulder.

"It doesn't seem fair," Ben said.

"That's for sure," Lila agreed, trying to look sympathetically at Sam while her mind was focused on her next move. She thought about where she'd look for Poe first. She'd start with the bars.

"Well . . ." Sam sighed. "That ugly bitch is a goddamn revenge specialist. And I knew she was going to zing me, I just didn't know how or when."

"Why?" Asher asked. "What'd you do?"

"Oh, nothing," Sam said, avoiding Ben and Asher's eyes by looking down at the ground. Lila kept her mouth shut.

"I guess I better get started," Sam said as she downed her cup of coffee. "Oh, lucky me! I'm in Turks and Caicos, just living the dream! I think I'll wear rubber gloves on top of my rubber gloves. God only knows what diseases that freak has."

When she left the room, Asher sat down to watch TV, and Ben turned to Lila. "If you don't have any plans today, you can tag along with me if you'd like." He looked at her hopefully.

"Actually, I was thinking I'd spend the day in town." When she said this, Ben's face fell with disappointment. "But . . . what are you going to do?" she asked, despite herself.

"Remember when I told you the new boat Jack's building for the America's Cup?"

"Sure," Lila said, already losing interest. She finally had

an opportunity to do some good legwork on her case and she couldn't afford to waste a second of it.

"Well, this is the island where the boat is being built, so Jack and I are going to check out how construction is going and review some new design ideas."

"You and Jack?" Lila perked up immediately. If Jack was going, she'd go in a second.

Ben nodded and continued, "Jack's so excited about it. It's really something to see. You should come along."

"I'm game," Lila said.

They made plans to meet on the dock in fifteen minutes. Lila hustled to get ready. She knew this was an invaluable opportunity to spend some one-on-one time with Jack. Before this, the only time she'd been around him was when she was serving him meals, which wasn't an environment conducive to finding out much of anything about him except how rare he liked his steak.

But when she walked down the gangway to meet Jack and Ben, only Ben was standing there waiting for her.

"Where's Jack?"

"Oh, he decided to do something else. I think he was able to get on a golf course he wanted to check out. He told me I could handle the boat stuff on my own, which is true," Ben said, somewhat proudly. "I mean, this boat's as much mine as it is his. He'll look over the blueprints tonight."

Lila noticed that Ben talked about Jack as if they were equals. It was a dangerous thing to forget one's place in this land of haves and have-nots, and Lila guessed that Ben's tenuous position between both worlds might cause him trouble somewhere down the line.

Ben wrapped his arm around Lila's shoulders. "It's better this way, right? Now it's just the two of us."

"Great," Lila said with a weak smile. She was trying to mask her disappointment. Her chance to spend some real time with Jack was gone and so was her other plan to trail Poe. Now she was stuck looking at ships with Ben. But, she thought, trying to look on the bright side, it could be worse. Ben was close to Jack, and seeing this boat still might reveal something. If she'd learned anything about working a case, it was that you never knew where you would find the key that unlocked the whole mystery.

Still, she had reservations about spending time alone with Ben. She had fallen in love once while undercover, and it led to the most profound heartbreak she'd ever experienced outside of the death of her mother and the loss of her sister. This time, she was going to keep her distance.

It had been five whole days since Lila set foot on land, and the moment she walked on the marina's wooden dock, she felt both relieved to be ashore and terribly discombobulated. It seemed that the tumult of the ocean waters had, amazingly enough, become the new normal for her body. The ground swayed beneath her feet causing her to stumble slightly and fall sideways into Ben.

"I think you may have a slight case of land sickness," Ben said pulling her close so that she wouldn't lose her footing again.

"I've got what?" she said. She felt light-headed, making it hard to take everything in.

"Land sickness. Do you feel unsteady, like you're rocking a little?" Lila nodded.

"It just means that your body has become used to being at sea. It's no big deal, happens to all of us. I'll make sure you're okay."

They walked toward a rental stand for scooters, which was set up under a cluster of coconut palms next to a riotous bush of eye-popping purple bougainvillea. Ben selected a mint-green

Vespa, threw a helmet at Lila, and both of them climbed on, Lila in back, Ben in front.

"Hold on to me," Ben said. Lila hesitated, not wanting to cross into the physical intimacy of wrapping her arms around him, but she had no choice. She slipped her bare arms under his and lightly pressed herself into his strong back, feeling the muscled contours of his chest with her hands. The heat she felt off his body was as dizzying as her land sickness. Not giving in to this temptation might be harder than Lila thought.

They sped through the narrow streets of Provo, hugging the road that curved along the island's endless oceanfront. Lila placed her cheek against Ben's back and watched the white sands and turquoise waters whiz by. She saw osprey and pelicans dive into the Caribbean waters for fish as the kite surfers competed for their share of the sky, flying high into the air on their colorful sails. They drove past grand, pastel-colored resorts with their acres of clipped green lawns and perfectly manicured palm trees behind tall, wrought-iron gates. Then they zipped through local neighborhoods made up of rows of tiny run-down shacks constructed out of weather-beaten wood slats and corrugated steel. Ben dodged errant roosters, one meandering cow, a group of uniformed schoolchildren, and an elderly British couple wearing matching Princess Cruises T-shirts. The air smelled like the salty ocean, burning trash, and jasmine flowers warming under the hot sun.

After about a twenty-minute ride, they pulled into a small parking lot in front of a hangar-size building. A small sign that read DAEDALUS BUILDERS swayed above the glass door. As Lila and Ben walked into the cavernous shop, a short black man with a trim, white beard and a powder-blue suit quickly came over to greet them. Ben embraced the man warmly.

"Good to see you, son," the man said to Ben in a thick West Indian accent.

"Nicky, I'd like to introduce you to Kingston S. Duxbury, one of the true geniuses working today in boat design."

Kingston tried to suppress a smile of pride, but didn't quite manage it. His face relaxed into a wide grin as he clasped both of his hands around Lila's hand. "How do you do?" he said, with a small, chivalrous bow.

"Nicky here is working on Mr. Warren's yacht with me. I thought I'd let her tag along." Ben gave Lila a playful nudge before turning back to Kingston. "So, do you have those new sketches for me? Jack's anxious to see them."

While Kingston brought Ben into his office on the other side of the building, Lila wandered around the workshop, watching a dozen or so men in hard hats laboring over a large black carbon structure that looked like an alien bird wing. Careful to keep to the periphery of the workshop, Lila meandered to the other side of the room to check out some framed pictures on the far wall. There were six dusty photos dating back all the way to 1989— each with Jack Warren, Kingston S. Duxbury, and various sailing crews triumphantly posed in front of a series of racing yachts that became bigger and sleeker over the years. In every photo, Jack held a shiny trophy aloft, his face in a state of beatific joyousness. This happy, smiling man seemed to be a different person entirely from the controlling jerk Lila knew from the yacht. Maybe the only thing that made Jack Warren truly happy was sailing. Or maybe it was the winning that he enjoyed even more.

A few minutes later, Ben and Kingston emerged from the back with Ben carrying a poster tube stuffed with blueprints. As he walked toward Lila, he ran his hand delicately along the black carbon wing propped up a couple feet off the ground.

"Kingston, my man, you've outdone yourself this time."

"What is it?" Lila asked when the men joined her.

"It's a sail, if you can believe it," Kingston said with pride. Lila didn't understand. She'd seen sails before, but this looked more like an airplane wing.

"I know," Ben said, seeing the confusion on Lila's face. "It seems crazy, right? It's not like any sail made before. It was Jack's idea, actually. He thought that if Kingston could create a carbon-fiber mainsail, it would make us the fastest boat on water. We'll soon see if he's right. Win or die trying. Huh, Kingston?"

"Exactly," the boat builder replied.

Kingston then gave Ben a full tour of the new construction while Lila tagged along, wondering where Jack's passion for yachting fit into her case. She knew that it put Jack in hot water with Liss, Paul, Thiago, and his shareholders for choosing boats over running his company. But did winning the America's Cup really mean more to Jack than the business he'd built into one of the most successful software companies of all time?

After a warm good-bye, Ben and Lila were back on the Vespa heading to the boat. "We've got a couple hours before you're supposed to be back. And I know this fantastic place that's a few minutes from here. Right on the water. Amazing food. Great drinks. Any interest in getting lunch?" Ben asked Lila as he maneuvered the scooter down a dirt road lined with locustberry shrubs and sea-grape trees.

"Perfect," Lila said. The prospect of getting a drink and digging her toes into some of this perfect white sand was impossible to pass up. Plus, she rationalized, there was a chance that Daniel Poe could be there. It was a small island and the number of tourist bars wasn't large enough to make such a possibility out of the question.

A few minutes later, Ben parked the scooter at a wooden archway that was painted white with bright pink lettering spelling out DA CONCH SHACK.

"This is one of my favorite places in the world," Ben said as he led her down a white sand pathway out into one of the sweetest restaurants she'd ever seen. The kitchen and bar were housed in tiny open-air buildings fitted with turquoise shutters and shingled roofs. White-and-yellow picnic tables were arranged in the sand, all sheltered by palm trees. Lila saw a pyramid of discarded conch shells piled up by the rum bar, which was her first stop. She ordered two rum punches and brought them over to Ben, who was busy ordering everything off the menu.

"Two conch fritters. One conch salad. A plate of curry shrimp. Jerk chicken wings. And a side of plantains," Ben said, almost drooling.

"Think you ordered enough food?" Lila said as she handed Ben his rum punch.

"I know. It's too much. But I never get here as much as I'd like. And their conch is mind-blowing. Trust me."

As they sat down with their feast, Lila quickly realized that Ben was totally right. The conch was divine and so was the setting. It was the first time since she'd gone undercover that she felt even remotely relaxed and at ease.

"God, it's so nice to be away from the boat," Lila said, as she took the first sip of her second rum punch.

"Tell me about it," Ben said as he stretched out his long legs and dug his bare feet into the soft sand.

After a long moment of contented silence, Lila asked, "You're pretty close to the Warrens, right?"

"Sure, I guess." He shrugged, keeping his eyes out on the ocean.

"Is every trip this . . . colorful?"

"What do you mean?"

"Are you kidding? The screaming, the smashing of glasses, the golden phallus tossed overboard? It's insane. I feel like we're all part of some psychological experiment where a bunch of people who hate each other are forced to spend time together in a totally isolated environment." Lila felt relieved to actually say out loud how surreal and ludicrous this whole trip had been.

Ben laughed and nodded in agreement. "You know, I'm so used to the madness that I don't even notice it as much anymore. And you're the one who bears the brunt of it. I'm up on the bridge with the captain, so I don't have to deal with it as much. You're down in the trenches."

"Let me tell you," Lila said, "it isn't pretty. I feel like an hour doesn't pass without some major problem."

"Yeah, Jack has a bad habit of always bringing out the worst in others."

"So I've noticed." Lila leaned forward. If her hopes of spending the day with Jack or trailing Poe were a bust, at least Ben might be able to give her some background information that she couldn't read in a file. "You've been working for the Warrens for how long?"

"Let me see, I started out as a deckhand for them back in the summer of 1999." Ben's eyes grew wide. "Christ, that's almost ten years. Oh, God." He took a dramatic sip of his rum punch. "Now I'm going to have a midlife crisis. I've spent a decade of my life trapped at sea with the Warrens."

"Have Jack and Elise always been so . . . ?"

"Miserable? No. Not at all. I never would've stuck around for so long if that was the case. Actually, it used to be the opposite. Elise was always Jack's fiercest defender. But somewhere along the line it changed."

"Why?"

"I don't know." Ben looked away, out toward the ocean. "He fucks around. Everyone knows that. I can't imagine she doesn't. I've walked in on him getting blown by stewardesses more than once . . . way more than once, really, which is to say he's not very discreet. It's sad. They're certainly not passing the boat test, that's for sure."

"The boat test?"

"My dad always told me that being on a boat brings out the best and worst in people. It's like salt in food, it just intensifies everything. But I'm not sure if he's right. I mean, you look more intensely beautiful now than you did on the boat. Who knew that was possible?" Ben laughed and slapped his hand to his forehead. "Oh, Christ. Did that sound as cheesy to you as it did to me?"

"Just a little," Lila said.

"Sorry. I can't help it. Having you here in one of my favorite spots is making me a happy man." He reached toward her, running his hand down her arm, but she pulled away.

"Ben, please."

"Sorry," he said, quickly apologizing, but his hand was now holding on around her wrist. He didn't want to let go.

"No, *I'm* sorry. I mean, I'm flattered. Really I am. And in another time and place I wouldn't hesitate. But right now I think it's best to keep things strictly professional."

Ben slowly nodded. Lila could tell he was disappointed, even though he was trying to hide it.

"Well, you may be able to refuse *me*," he said playfully. "But can you refuse getting another order of these conch fritters?" He popped the last fried golden bite into his mouth and, with one flash of his warm, toothy smile, all the tension between them instantly evaporated. She laughed in delight. Everything was fine once more. He jumped up for more food, and she went to order another round of drinks.

THEY ARRIVED BACK at the yacht around four. As Lila climbed onto the boat, she felt lighter and happier than she had in weeks, and also slightly tipsy. But the moment she saw Sam's face, a wave of guilt crested over her. Sam looked exhausted. It was very clear that the day of handling both of their workloads had kicked her ass.

"I'm so tired of sweeping up the hideous messes left behind by hideous people," Sam said. She, who was usually made up to perfection with glossy hair and expertly applied makeup, looked as bedraggled as she said she felt. Her hair was a collection of clumps and frizzes, her hands were red and raw from too much scrubbing, and her shoulders hung forward in defeat. It looked like this swamp-rat Cinderella had given up hope that her prince would come. Lila told her to go rest in their cabin for the remainder of the day. Jack and his guests were having dinner on the island that night, so Lila could handle the remaining evening's chores by herself.

By nine that night, the guests had returned—the men beaming from their day on the golf course and their evening at the bar, and the women glowing as well after countless steams, massages, wraps, and exfoliations. Lila felt a flicker of envy as she watched the group saunter onto the perfectly appointed yacht. She knew that they never once considered all the hard work behind every dust-free surface, every neatly folded towel, every perfectly executed meal, every smiling nod that masked the deep well of resentment bubbling up underneath it.

By 9:30, everyone had changed into their evening attire

and gathered by the pool, where they were drinking Asher's face-numbing, tequila-heavy margaritas under the canopy of stars. As Lila served drinks and listened to the mindless small talk floating on the air like so many fireflies, things seemed momentarily as calm as the warm Caribbean Sea lapping at the yacht. But Lila had come to realize that such respite from drama wouldn't last for long before the next clash of the titanic egos. And she was right.

An hour later, just as Lila was serving the third round of drinks, the yacht pulled up anchor, heading south to their next port of call: Anguilla. By then, only a few people remained scattered around the pool. Josie, as bored as always around a bunch of adults, had snuck off to her room with a bottle of coconut rum tucked under her arm. Clarence and Charity Baines, as very practiced WASP drinkers with livers of steel, gulped down a steady stream of cocktails while playing a cutthroat game of gin rummy. After a quick and perfunctory gin and tonic with the others, Seth Liss had returned to his room for a conference call about the Peregrine Software acquisition, which he announced loudly in Jack's direction, hoping he'd guilt the CEO into joining. But Jack was busy flirting outrageously with Esperanza Campos, and quickly swept the young Brazilian bride away from the group to show her his newest acquisition, the two-person submarine he kept in the yacht's internal dock. Thiago, who'd been watching Jack and Esperanza like a hawk, left shortly after them to make sure his old friend didn't pull anything. Asher went on an ice run, but never came back, leaving Lila all alone and forced to serve Elise Warren tumbler after tumbler of straight tequila on the rocks with a squeeze of lime.

A few minutes later—as Lila picked up dirty glasses and emptied ashtrays of half-smoked Montecristos, and Clarence cheered triumphantly at a particularly successful hand of gin rummy while Elise drank herself into a semicomatose state—there was a single, solitary scream. Then, all of the sudden, they heard a huge ruckus of voices coming from somewhere on the yacht.

"Do you hear something?" Elise slurred as she stood up slowly, swaying drunkenly.

"Do I ever!" Clarence laughed. "Sounds like a fox got into the henhouse." The senator winked at his wife, who shushed her tipsy husband.

"How dare he!" Elise said as she began walking toward the melee. "I told him to keep his hands off Esperanza," she muttered, assuming that what she was hearing were the consequences of Jack making a pass at Thiago's wife.

But Elise Warren was wrong. What she found, with Lila tagging close behind, was Jack Warren in a total fit of rage, at the door of his daughter's room. His face was bright red, and he was pacing back and forth in front of her door, screaming so loudly and so quickly that it took Lila a second to understand what he was saying.

"You fucking tramp!" he screamed. "How could you?"

"*Jack!*" Elise yelled, the way an owner yells at a dog who's shitting on the carpet. She still had a tumbler full of tequila in her hand, which was now trembling. "What's going on?"

Without turning to look at his wife, Jack spat, "Just your precious daughter fucking the help."

And then he stepped aside, and Lila saw what had made Jack so angry: Asher Lydon in his daughter's bed. Josie and Asher were sitting naked on the bed, with only a thin sheet covering both of them. Josie's face was pale as tears ran down her cheeks. Asher looked embarrassed as he searched the floor trying to locate his shorts. It was clear what had happened. Jack walked in on a member of the crew having his way with his one and only daughter.

Within a couple minutes the scene had a large audience: Jack, Elise, Lila, Clarence, Thiago, and Esperanza were all witnesses to the scandal. "I'm going to leave," Asher said, standing up while still clutching the sheet. Asher kept his eyes to the ground and wrapped the sheet, which Josie was trying to grab back, around his narrow hips—leaving Josie shivering, weeping, and naked on the bed as her father looked away in disgust. Then Josie leaped up toward her closet and threw an orange silk robe around her thin body.

"Get the fuck out of here, now, or I'll throw your ass overboard this very second," Jack growled as he leaned aggressively toward Asher, who quickly retreated. Then Jack swiveled around and looked at all the people staring at him. "And what the fuck do you idiots think you're gawking at? This is a private family matter!"

Lila stood there with the others, frozen, staring straight into Jack's bulging eyes as she smelled his boozy breath pour out of him. She looked at Josie, who was now in the fetal position on her bed, weeping like a little girl.

"Didn't you hear me!?" Jack screamed. "Get the fuck out of here!"

As Lila hightailed it away from the latest Warren-family meltdown, a frantic Edna Slaughter swept past her on her way to rescue her beloved mistress, Elise. Before Lila went back to the lower level, she turned to see Edna, the stewardess in shining armor, standing protectively by Elise, with her arm around the drunken woman's shoulders.

The only thing Lila could hear as she turned back around was Josie wailing. "But I love him, Dad. I *love* him!"

CHAPTER 16

THE NEWS THAT Josie and Asher had been caught in bed together swept through the yacht like wildfire. As Lila finished up with her chores for the night, she could hear every guest and every crew member dissecting the gossip in gleeful whispers like a bunch of teenage girls at a slumber party. Given Asher's reputation as a ladies' man and Josie's obvious flirtations with the shirtless and well-oiled second officer, the only thing that most people found surprising was that Jack was surprised at all.

But Lila soon found out that Jack wasn't the only one who hadn't seen it coming.

"That rotten son of a bitch," Sam said, with her jaw tightly clenched. Lila was taken aback by the vehemence of her bunkmate's reaction. She'd been so wrapped up in how this latest development changed her theories about who killed Jack that she'd momentarily forgotten that Sam was sleeping with Asher.

"I mean, I had my suspicions," Sam said, blinking back tears. "But he told me I was crazy. That he'd never be with that 'spoiled princess,'" she repeated, using air quotes. "He said she wasn't even pretty, which she isn't!"

"Does he know you're sleeping with Jack?" Lila asked sheepishly. Sam always seemed very prickly when it came to her re-lationship with the boss.

"Of course not!" Sam said, as if she'd never heard anyone ask anything quite so obtuse.

"But then can't you call it even and just forget about it?"

"Are you kidding? Anyway, it's over now. He'll be kicked off the boat in the morning and then I'll never see him again," Sam said, throwing her face into her pillow.

Lila searched her mind for something to say, but found nothing. She had a hard time conjuring up any real sympathy for Sam. After all, the chance that two promiscuous, preening, attention whores like Asher and Sam had any chance of build-ing a real relationship was nil. And after witnessing such a dra-matic display between Josie and Jack, Lila didn't have it in her to pretend that she cared about Sam's momentary heartbreak. Most of Sam's feelings resembled a summer storm—dramatic but brief, and over almost as soon as they started.

Standing there listening to Sam's muffled weeping, Lila was relieved to hear a knock on the door. She was even happier to discover that it was Ben who was doing the knocking.

"Hey," he said with a sweet smile. He was wearing worn-in jeans and a gray V-neck T-shirt, and his dark, curly hair was going every which way. Lila thought he looked absolutely deli-cious. Just what she needed. "I take it you heard the news?" he asked.

"I didn't just hear the news. I was there," Lila said. "I saw the whole thing."

"Was it everything I'd imagine?"

"It was . . ." She faltered in the attempt to describe what she'd seen. "It was quite a sight. My favorite part was buck-naked Asher stealing Josie's bedsheet. He left her totally nude and weeping in front of her own father while he ran out of there like someone on fire."

Ben cringed. "That's Asher for you, all class."

"Can you guys please shut up!?" Sam yelled. "I don't want to hear about it!"

"Sorry, Sam," Ben said, giving Lila a confused face. "I'm hanging out in the mess with Asher. Just wanted to know if you'd join us."

"That would be great," Lila quickly responded. Of course Lila wanted to talk to Asher. He'd just been humiliated and fired. Lila needed to find out how he was feeling. Angry? Bitter? Mad enough to seek violent retribution?

"Asher? Have you talked to him?" Sam said, peeling her face off her pillow. "How is he?"

Ben saw Sam's red, weepy face and shot Lila another questioning look, to which Lila just shook her head. "He's been better. Captain Nash told him he's fired. He'll be leaving the yacht as soon as we dock tomorrow."

"Has he said anything about me?" Sam asked.

"Um," Ben said, rubbing the back of his neck with the palm of his hand. It was obvious he didn't know how to respond. "He's pretty drunk and upset, Sam. I doubt if he's thinking too much about anyone but himself."

"Well, that's nothing new!" Sam said. "Don't tell him I asked about him, okay?" She flung herself back down on the bed, once again burying her head in the pillow.

"Sure," Ben said. "Um, anyway, you both should join us for a drink. I think everyone could use one or two or twenty right about now."

"I'll pass," Sam muttered into her pillow.

"I'm in," Lila said as she left her bunkmate to cry by her lonesome.

"What the hell's with Sam?" Ben asked Lila once they were alone in the hallway.

"What do you think?"

"Oh," he said, the realization hitting him. "Sam and Asher. I should've guessed. It's like *Real World: Yacht Edition* or something. Feels like everyone is sleeping with everyone else."

"So I'm beginning to notice."

Way before they walked into the mess, they could hear Asher's voice.

"I should warn you," Ben said, "this won't be a pretty scene."

"Don't worry about me," said Lila. "I can handle it."

But Asher was much more out of control than Lila had expected. The laid-back surfer she'd come to know had all but disappeared. What had replaced him was a very angry, drunk, and aggrieved young man who was feeling mighty vengeful at that particular moment in time.

He was sitting in one of the booths, surrounded by Pedro, Mudge, and Captain Nash. All four of them were drinking straight from a bottle of thirty-year-old Scotch that Lila happened to know cost Jack Warren about three grand. She figured Asher had grabbed it from the case Jack kept in the galley. Just one more way he could say "fuck you" to his former boss.

"We're going to miss you," Mudge said in his thick brogue as he put his arm around Asher's still-bare shoulders. Even at his worst, Asher refused the comforts of clothing.

"The fuck you are," Asher said. "You jokers aren't going to miss me one goddamn second."

"Easy there," Captain Nash said.

"And fuck you," Asher said, jabbing a finger in the captain's face. "You coulda stood up for me, but you didn't do shit."

"The boss walked in on you screwing his precious daughter. You're beyond saving," Nash said, with a dismissive scowl.

"Who says I can't fuck his daughter? It's not like he doesn't fuck everything in sight. I'm sure you've fucked him, haven't you?" Asher said, looking directly at Lila.

An uneasy feeling overcame Lila as she looked into Asher's eyes, which were narrowed into two furious slits, glaring at her. This was a totally different side to him than she'd ever seen. He looked as if he'd rip anyone apart who got in his way. Including her. Including Nash. Including Jack.

"Watch it, Asher," Ben said. "Nicky's got nothing to do with this."

"That's what you think," Asher said. Ben stepped toward his friend and Asher scrambled out of the booth, climbing over Mudge and Pedro. But Lila grabbed Ben's arm to hold him back.

"Just let it go," Lila whispered. She didn't want Ben to fight her battles for her. She was more than happy to fight them herself.

Pacing the room, Asher ripped the Scotch bottle out of Pedro's hand and took a very long swig. "Don't think he's got the better of me." A nasty smile slowly spread across Asher's drunken face. "I've got plans for him."

"Oh, yeah?" Nash asked, shaking his head.

"Yeah," Asher replied defiantly. "He acts like no one can get to him. But I can."

"You better give that cock of yours a rest and let your head do some of the thinking," Nash said.

Lila wanted to see just how much of Asher's attitude was bluster and how much of it was real. She needed to test him. "Really? You think *you* can get to Jack Warren?" she asked, observing him steadily.

"What did you say, you dumb bitch?" Asher spat. "Are you questioning me?" He took another swig. His face was slack, his body was covered with perspiration, and his eyes were red with rage.

"Know what I think?" Lila asked. "I think you're full of shit." She wanted to get a rise out of him. She needed to know how quick-tempered he was.

Asher lunged toward Lila, but she ducked out of the way. He was drunk and slow, easy to avoid.

"Nicky!" Ben said. "What're you doing?"

Asher tripped into a chair, causing him to drop the bottle, which smashed on the ground. As he steadied himself, he turned toward Lila. Then a nasty, dismissive laugh erupted out of Asher's mouth. "You don't know me," he said to Lila.

"You're right. But I do know that you don't have the balls to stand up to Warren." She paused and looked closely at Asher.

Everyone in the room went quiet.

"Fuck you. You don't know shit!" Asher said, moving again toward Lila, but this time she didn't jump out of his way. She faced him calmly, feeling his hot, whiskey breath in her face. It was then that she knew he wasn't just full of shit. She felt the pulse of violence running through his veins. This was a man who was capable of killing.

"Whoa! Whoa!" Mudge said, waving his hands. "Simmer the hell down, the both of you."

Ben grabbed Lila by the arm. "I'm getting you out of here."

"I'm fine," Lila said, ripping her arm out of Ben's grasp. She was pissed off now and didn't feel like backing down.

"The hell you are."

He put both of his hands on her shoulders and steered her into the hallway. Only when they were far enough away from the mess to no longer hear Asher's taunts did Ben say something. "What the fuck was that about?"

"I don't have a lot of patience for that macho show-off shit."

"But the way you got in his face. It was crazy. I mean, what were you thinking?" Ben stepped back and gave Lila a thorough once-over.

Lila gave a little laugh. "Wouldn't you like to know?"

"You know I would," Ben said. But all Lila could think about was Asher. Could he be Jack's killer? But Ben had other things on his mind. "Do you want to cool off upstairs on the main deck?"

Lila knew what Ben was getting at. He was inviting her to take a moonlight stroll, which would lead her somewhere that she didn't want to go.

"I think I'll just turn in. I've had enough excitement for one night," she said.

Romance was not on her mind. She was too focused on Asher. He was threatening, out of control, and looking for an outlet for his rage. Plus, he'd said he wanted Jack dead, and Lila knew that went beyond drunken ranting. He was truly dangerous.

Then, just as her mind was working through these thoughts, she felt Ben put his arm around her waist. He twirled her toward him and gently backed her up against the hallway wall. His touch was so unexpected that she practically jumped out of her skin. But before she could say anything, he pressed his lips against hers. She pulled her head away in protest, but only momentarily. She didn't know if it was the taste of his mouth, the feel of his body against hers, or just the madness of the moment, but she turned back toward him and kissed him greedily, with a hunger she could no longer deny.

It didn't last long.

Lila heard someone clear their throat. She turned to see Josie leaning up against Asher's door, watching them, a half-empty bottle of coconut rum in her hand. Her eyes were ringed with smeared black mascara and her face was swollen from crying.

"Oh, hey, Josie," Ben said, pulling away from Lila as he wiped his mouth.

"Sorry to interrupt," Josie said in a flat tone.

"It's not what it looks like," Lila said.

"Whatever," Josie said as she went into Asher's room and slammed the door behind her.

The brief wave of passion that had just swept Lila away instantly retreated, leaving her feeling like an idiot who couldn't control herself even when she most needed to. She knew she had to put an end to this immediately. Her focus needed to be on the case, and only the case. She looked up at Ben who was beaming down at her.

His smile evaporated when he saw Lila's concern. "Oh, don't worry. She won't say anything."

"That's not what I'm worried about," Lila said.

"Come on. A little hallway kiss is good for you," Ben said playfully. "Anyway, how am I supposed to keep my hands off you?" he said as he took her face in his hand. "You're utterly magnificent."

He leaned in to kiss her again, but she pulled away, for real this time. "It's late. And I've got to go to bed."

"All right," he said, stepping away from her. "Have it your way. I'll head to my little room. But you can't stop me from wishing you were with me."

Lila didn't let herself smile at what he said until she knew she was out of his sight. She didn't want to give him any encouragement.

With Sam in a deep sleep on the top bunk, Lila was about to quietly change for bed when she heard Asher and Josie's voices down the hall. Wanting to know what they were talking about,

Lila slipped back out of her room and tiptoed toward Asher's door, which was slightly ajar. She peeked in through the crack.

She saw Josie sitting on Asher's single bed surrounded by small piles of pills—red, black, white, purple—a veritable rainbow of psychopharmaceuticals, which Josie was counting and transferring into little sandwich bags while Asher paced around.

"He wouldn't do it, Josie. Trust me. You're his only kid," Asher said. It seemed like he was trying to calm Josie down, but Lila could tell just how angry he still was from his tone and the way he was manically walking up and down his tiny room.

"Ash, I hate him so much," Josie cried, burying her head into her hands, her long hair falling over her face like a curtain. "I wish he'd just die." She threw her body down on the bed, upsetting the carefully arranged pills.

"Hey, watch it!" Asher said, bending down to pick up the large white pills that had fallen to the floor. Lila knew they were OxyContins. "Listen, your old man will get what's coming to him. That's a guarantee."

"He said he's going to cut me off completely!"

"I'm not going to let that happen."

"You can't do shit. And my mom won't stop him. She's just some collagen-injected zombie who does whatever he says."

"Okay. I know we can figure this out. I just need to sober up." He slapped himself in the face hard a few times. Then he plucked a pumpkin-orange Adderall off the bed, popped it into his mouth, and chased it down with a swig of coconut rum.

"How fast do you think your dad can change his will?" Asher asked. Lila wasn't surprised that Asher's focus seemed to be on the money, but Josie was.

"Why do you care about the will?" Josie asked, pushing herself up out of her miserable little curled position.

"Baby, listen. You don't know what life without money is like. I do. Trust me. If we can keep you on your dad's payroll, it'll be better for everyone."

"But I can't take his money if I'm with you! How many times do I have to say it?" she sobbed. "I chose *you* over his money."

"This is what we'll do," Asher said, completely ignoring Josie. The amphetamines had begun to trick his mind into some kind of faux clarity. "We've got to call your dad's bluff. Show him that he can't boss us around. He wants me off the boat and he wants you to come crawling back to him. But fuck him. Right? So we'll get off together in Anguilla."

"Then what?" Josie asked.

"Then we do what we've talked about."

"Do you think we have to?"

"It's the only way you'll be free, baby. The only way." He walked over to her, lifting up her chin with his hand and kissing her deeply. "I know what I'm doing," he said.

"Don't you have *any* money?"

"No, baby. I told you. Nash said your dad won't pay me shit. But I'm going to take what's mine. I always do."

"You could sell your Rolex," Josie whispered tentatively.

Asher slapped his hand to his wrist, covering up the watch as if Josie was about to snatch it off his body. "No way!" he said. "You know how special this is to me. If you understood me at all, you'd never ask that. God, maybe we should rethink this whole thing."

"No, please!" Josie desperately pleaded. Now that Josie had been cut off from her family, she was terrified to lose the only thing she had left: Asher. "I'm sorry I asked. I'm sorry. I should've known better." Josie's groveling made Lila feel sick in her stomach.

"You should have," Asher sniffed in a patronizing tone. "Not all of us have grown up getting whatever we want. I had to work for this," Asher said, pointing to his watch. "You haven't had to work for anything."

"You're right," Josie said as her shoulders slumped and her head hung limply on her chest, as if she were trying to make her tiny body look even smaller.

"Your inheritance. That's the most important thing. We've got to do whatever it takes. Then you'll finally be free," Asher said. He was so obviously manipulating Josie, but she couldn't see it.

"My dad says I can't live without him? Well, fine." There was a small catch in Josie's voice as she spoke, but she swallowed it quickly and replaced it with steel. "We'll show him. Won't we, baby?"

"Of course we will," Asher said, reaching for her. "Of course we will. Now stand up." Asher's voice changed from consoling to controlling. Josie, quick to obey, got up from the bed as a few errant pills tumbled to the floor. She went to wrap her arms around Asher, but he leaned away. "No," he said coldly. "Turn around."

"Not tonight, Ash. I don't—"

"Turn around," he said loudly, interrupting her.

She obeyed. Lila wasn't sure what was going on, but one thing was clear, Asher was totally in control.

"Put your hands up against the wall," he said.

"I'm tired. Can't you just hold me tonight?" Josie asked quietly.

"Do it."

Lila thought she heard small whimpering sounds from Josie as she placed her hands against Asher's cabin wall. She stood there looking down at the floor as if she was about to get frisked by a cop. Asher opened the drawer to a side table and took out a silk tie. He went behind Josie, pushing his weight against her as he greedily ran his hands over her body, between her slightly parted legs, up her waist, then down over her breasts. He whispered something into her ear that Lila couldn't hear.

Asher used the tie to wrap one wrist and then the other, binding them tightly together above Josie's head. As he tied a final knot, Josie winced in pain, which just made him tie the knot even tighter. He lifted her dress up, putting the bottom of it over her head like a mask. Then he slid her underwear down around her ankles. Josie had started to shake ever so slightly as Asher stood back, observing her before he took a couple of long swigs of rum. The moment Asher began to disrobe, Lila turned away and went back to her room with a sick feeling in her stomach.

No point in sticking around for what was next. She'd seen enough for one day.

CHAPTER 17

THE NIGHT OF Jack Warren's murder was just ten days away, and for the first time in the entire decade she'd spent thinking about this case, Lila no longer believed Elise Warren was the primary suspect. She was now convinced that Jack's daughter and her lover were his killers.

As Lila tried and failed to fall asleep that August night while the yacht sailed south to Anguilla, she went through the details of what she knew about Josie. On the surface, Josie seemed about as likely to commit murder as the Dalai Lama. Vegan, existentialist Josie with her peasant blouses and her power-to-the-people politics didn't even faintly resemble someone who could murder her father and then frame someone else for the crime. But when Lila factored in Asher, the scenario changed radically.

Asher wanted money and Josie wanted Asher. It was that simple. And the only thing that stood in the way of their getting what they wanted was Jack Warren. Lila thought about Patty Hearst. If that nineteen-year-old socialite could be kidnapped and brainwashed into robbing banks for the "revolution," then twenty-year-old Josie Warren could be manipulated into killing the controlling father from whom she'd been longing to escape. Just chalk it up to the things we do for love.

Plus, there was something chilling about the scene Lila had just witnessed between Josie and Asher. He had been domineering and sadistic, nothing like the laid-back persona he presented to the world. And strong-willed and free-spirited Josie totally disappeared in Asher's presence, transforming into a desperate-to-please weakling willing to do whatever he wished.

Lila knew that light S&M wasn't a precursor to murder, but the dynamic between the two of them was undeniably volatile and toxic. It all amounted to one giant red flag waving around in Lila's restless mind.

For the remainder of the night, Lila kept a close eye on Asher's door by periodically sneaking out into the hallway. But every time she checked, it was closed and the lights stayed off. It seemed that all the sex, drugs, and scheming had finally worn Josie and Asher out—for now.

THE NEXT MORNING, none of the guests could talk of anything else over breakfast.

"We've known each other for a long time, Jack," Thiago said as he took small and elegant sips from a Wedgwood china coffee cup. "Longer than anyone else here, including your beautiful wife. And I've never seen you overreact as badly as last night. And over such a small indiscretion. I'd venture to guess that everyone at this table has known the joy of feasting on forbidden fruit? Yes? Including you, my friend."

Thiago looked around, but the only one who met his eye was Jack, who had a treacherous snarl on his face.

"Stay out of it, Thiago," Jack warned. "You of *all people* have no right to tell me how to treat and protect my family." The two men held each other's gaze. Lila, as she poured more green tea into Jack's cup, once again wondered what was going on between these two men. Was it about money? Or something more?

"I'm only offering my humble advice," Thiago said. He reached for his wife Esperanza's hand. "Young women need to be treated with great kindness and understanding. Not control and anger."

"And I'll say it again. Stay out of it."

"It'll all blow over," Clarence Baines said as he chewed his eggs noisily.

"What do you think, Elise?" Charity Baines asked, reaching out her little hand, with its pink nails and large diamond ring, toward Elise, who had been sitting silently at the head of the table, her meager breakfast untouched.

Elise began to speak, but Jack jumped in before she could say anything. "I'll tell you what *she* thinks," he said. "*She* thinks I'm driving Josie away. But mark my words, that girl will come running back the moment she gets a taste of the real world. This one here," he said, jabbing a fork at his wife, "wants to coddle her like a baby. And I'll tell you what that does. It creates a spoiled, insipid brat who wants to run off with the help. So, I'm done listening to *her*," Jack concluded with disgust. "I've got to instill some real values in my daughter before it's too late."

"Hear, hear!" Clarence Baines said. "It's never too late to teach our children the important lessons of personal responsibility. I've had my own children read the great Stoic philosophers since they were little tykes. I think it was Marcus Aurelius who once wrote, 'The first rule is—' "

"Clarence?" Jack interrupted.

"Yes, Jack?"

"I think I speak for everyone at the table when I say, put a fucking sock in it, will you?"

THE YACHT ARRIVED in Anguilla a little after noon. As the crew scrambled to dock the behemoth and the passengers gathered on the main deck, anxious to get on dry land, Josie and Asher, absent all morning, finally made an appearance. Holding each other's hand, they solemnly walked past everyone without saying a word.

Josie had made herself up to look like a hippie bride. She was wearing a long, white maxidress with a plunging neckline. Her hair was braided and pinned up elaborately. A wreath of flowers encircled the top of her head. Lila had never seen two people supposedly in love look so incredibly unhappy.

As they were about to walk down the gangway, Josie turned to her father, who was standing silently watching them.

"I want to read you all something before I go," Josie said, unfolding a piece of paper she had been holding tightly in her fist. She spoke like someone who was onstage in front of a large crowd for the first time—stiff and serious, with fear evident in every tight-chested breath. "This is a poem from Rumi that I'd like to share with you."

"You've got to be fucking kidding me," Jack said, with a disgusted roll of his eyes.

But her father's words only made her more defiant. Josie read, "*Let the lover be disgraceful, crazy, absentminded. Someone sober will worry about things going badly. Let the lover be.*" Her face was grave, as if she'd just shared a piece of deep wisdom with this group of hard-hearted adults. She folded the paper back up, then took her lover's hand. Asher looked anxious to go. He pulled Josie toward the dock, but she wouldn't budge. She was having a profound moment of defiance and she wouldn't let anyone cut it short. "Let me be, Dad," Josie said as she descended the gangway.

"With pleasure," Jack yelled out to his daughter, who kept walking away.

Lila had no idea where Josie and Asher were going. She was desperate to follow them, but leaving the yacht was an impossibility. She had a long list of tasks to complete and her own personal overlord constantly hovering around to make sure everything was done just right.

Only crew were on the yacht that day. Jack and Ben were meeting Caleb Johnson, an experienced helmsman whom they were interviewing as a potential addition to their America's Cup team. The plan was to go out together for a long sail. They brought Thiago, Esperanza, Clarence, and Paul Mason along for the ride. Having zero interest in racing around the Caribbean on an uncomfortable sailboat, Elise and Charity decided to take a chartered speedboat over to St. Martin, the French-Dutch Virgin Island only a fifteen-minute ride away, for some very expensive retail therapy. After all, Elise did have to find some way, aside from her usual diet of alcohol and sedatives, to cope with the fact that her only child had just run off with a muscled sailor with dollar signs in his eyes.

One of Lila's tasks that day, the only one that she was actually looking forward to, was clearing out Asher's room. If she couldn't tail him, then she hoped that having unfettered access to the things he'd left behind would give her some sort of insight into the man that had Josie Warren wrapped around his coconut-scented finger.

At first, she found nothing, just a lone white sock at the back of the closet and a jump rope left dangling on a hook. Because

Asher's room was identical to the minuscule one she shared with Sam, a thorough search took only a couple minutes. After she came up with next to nothing, Lila rechecked every surface of the room. As she was running her hand inside the three dresser drawers under the bed, she felt something taped to the top side of the middle drawer. When she pulled it carefully off, she saw it was a thumb drive.

Her heart jumped. Finally, something! Praying there was useful information on it, Lila rushed down the hall to her room, shut the door behind her, and grabbed her laptop. And there she sat, hunched over the computer, opening the first folder and then click, click, clicking her way through image after image . . . all of Josie. The digital pictures went back four years, which meant that Josie and Asher had been involved for much longer than anyone had ever suspected.

There were three folders in total. The first one contained pictures that Josie had taken of herself either with her phone or with her computer. The earliest photo was dated September 21, 2004, and showed a baby-faced Josie shyly posing, her eyes down, a smattering of teenage acne visible on her forehead, her shirt bashfully pulled aside to show a hint of her nipple. But as the months and years progressed, and as Josie grew up and got bolder, the pictures became much more graphic in nature. Nothing was left to the imagination.

The next folder was filled with hundreds of pictures that Asher took of him and Josie together. These started in 2005. None were sweet pictures of lovers smiling for the camera. On the contrary, they all felt dark and humiliating, showing Asher sexually dominating the young heiress. One had Josie on her knees, her wrists bound, Asher's hand at the back of her head, forcing himself into her mouth. Another showed Asher taking

Josie from behind while he shoved her face to the floor. It was clear that Josie knew these very private moments were being documented, but Asher was the one in control.

The last folder was by far the most jarring. It contained fifteen videos, all about thirty minutes long, of Asher and Josie having sex, a lot of it involving bondage, some including other people. In one, Josie and Asher took turns snorting coke off the body of a naked woman. Any randomly selected ten seconds of these hours and hours of videos would result in a media firestorm and a huge family scandal.

As Lila perused what felt like the digital diary of a twenty-first-century Marquis de Sade, her conviction that Asher and Josie were behind Jack's murder grew stronger. There was only one reason for Asher to methodically categorize four years of these pictures and videos on a thumb drive that he left behind on Jack Warren's yacht. He *wanted* it to be discovered. He wanted the Warrens to know that he held information that could destroy them. Lila knew that Asher's next step would be to extort Jack for money. And if the Warrens didn't pay, which Lila figured they wouldn't, Asher would understand that the only way to get the money he was after was by killing Jack.

Lila stored Asher's thumb drive in her drawer. He had clearly planned on Jack and Elise Warren discovering this little treasure trove of sexually explicit images and videos. But for now, Lila decided to keep this information to herself.

The sailing contingent returned a little after sunset, all sunburned and windblown. Jack seemed electrified by his day out on the water. Per Edna's instructions, Lila was waiting for them with flutes of Dom Pérignon. As everyone talked about how lovely the day had been, no one so much as mentioned Josie's or Asher's names. Jack talked at length about how the helmsman had turned out to be everything he'd wanted him to be, plus some. Despite, or because of, his daughter's absence, Jack Warren seemed in better spirits than Lila had ever seen him since Miami.

Elise was another story entirely. When the boat that she and Charity chartered pulled up to the yacht, all anyone could see was a laughably large number of high-end shopping bags: Hermès, Louis Vuitton, Céline, Gucci, Saint Laurent, and Chanel. It was safe to say that each woman had spent more money in one day than Lila made all year as a homicide detective. But the retail therapy didn't seem to have the mood-bolstering effect Elise had wanted. She stepped onto the yacht as the hired hands carrying her many, many purchases trailed behind her, looking as sour and tight-jawed as she had before.

"Has anyone heard from Josie?" she asked the group. But everyone shook their heads and said nothing. Jack, as usual, ignored his wife. "I'll be in my room. You there," she said, snapping at Lila. "I'll need a vodka martini with a twist brought to the master suite immediately."

"I'm sure she's fine," Esperanza said to Elise before she retreated to her room. "You shouldn't worry too much. She's just a young girl having some fun."

A look of absolute disgust crawled onto Elise's face as she stared at the gorgeous Brazilian, standing there with her young, flawless, caramel-colored skin and her long, black, curly hair, made wild from the salt air and the wind. Despite Elise's scowl, Esperanza kept smiling at her.

"You're not a mother, are you?" Elise asked Esperanza.

"Not yet," Esperanza said with a shrug, giving her husband a sly wink.

"Then you don't know what the hell you're talking about."

The encouraging smile that Esperanza had on her face was instantly wiped off. "I was only trying to help," she said.

"Well, don't," Elise responded coldly as she left the group to be alone with her martini and her misery.

"Now that Josie's out of my hair," Jack said jovially, "all I need is for someone to run away with my *wife*. Then I'd really be a happy man. Say, Ben, are you up for it?" Jack asked, throwing his arm around the shoulders of his first officer. Seeing that Ben and the rest of the group were made uncomfortable by his joke, Jack said, "Oh, hey, Ben. Don't worry. I'm only kidding. I wouldn't wish that bitch on my worst enemy."

"Now, Jack, really," Liss said with a frown, once again gravely disappointed at how badly his CEO continued to act.

"Shut up, Seth. You can try to control me out in the world, but here on my boat among my friends I can say whatever the fuck I want."

Despite the note of sourness in the air, Jack stayed upbeat. Declaring that he wanted a late-night dinner, he had Chef Vatel cook up an impromptu feast of watermelon salad, grilled calamari, chilled lobster tail, and tuna ceviche, which was served poolside. Glass upon glass of perfectly chilled Montrachet was gulped down as Seth, Clarence, and Jack debated the pros and cons of outsourcing manufacturing while a bikini-clad Esperanza stretched, slithered, and floated in the pool, ravenously watched by her husband who had Charity Baines chattering in his ear about her excitement over the purchase of a new electric-blue crocodile-skin Birkin bag. Jack couldn't keep his eyes off Esperanza as well, which was something that Thiago was only too quick to notice.

"I was so lucky to get it," Charity was saying. "I only realized how expensive it was after I bought it." She brought her voice down to a whisper. "It was thirty-three thousand euros, which sounded fine to me. But then I realized only after I'd left the store how much that is in American dollars. Around forty-five thousand. I mean, I don't mind. It's not about the money. It's the perception. If anyone in Washington spots me with this bag, I'll be skewered by the press. I mean, something like that could cost Clarence the reelection. It's so awful. Whenever I'm home, I'm forced to dress in Ann Taylor suits and carry around Coach bags like some kind of secretary."

Lila eavesdropped while Thiago kept nodding and smiling, though she figured the Brazilian had no idea what this politician's wife was blathering on about. He watched his beautiful wife, who was performing some sort of Esther Williams–esque routine for his benefit, only occasionally looking away to glare at Jack.

No one seemed to take notice when the police sirens disrupted the serene tropical silence, drowning out the gentle sound of the Caribbean waters lapping up against the side of the yacht. As the sirens grew closer, it became impossible to hear Esperanza splashing in the illuminated turquoise pool, or the sound of ice clinking in glasses, or the sound of Charity Baines yammering on excitedly about the lining of her new handbag.

No one really paid attention until two uniformed policemen began walking up the gangway to the yacht's main deck. Then everyone stood up the moment they all saw the same thing—a weeping and frightened Josie, in handcuffs, being dragged onto the boat between the two officers from the Royal Virgin Islands police force.

"What the hell?" Jack asked, looking around for Paul and Thiago, his two most trusted advisers. Both men jumped to their feet with confused looks on their faces. No one knew what was going on.

"Daddy!" Josie cried when she got up to the main deck, staring desperately at the father, who, just hours before, she'd completely denounced.

"Is there a Jack Warren on this ship?" asked one of the police officers in a heavy Virgin Islands accent. Both cops wore white short-sleeve button-down shirts, police hats, and long shorts accented with two red stripes along the outside of the leg. Lila's mind was racing. She had no idea what was going on. All she knew was there were no records of arrest in Josie's files. This made no sense. Had she somehow messed with the past, again? And where was Asher?

"I'm Jack Warren," Jack said, stepping forward. His voice was deep and powerful and his presence was commanding, making it clear that nobody could push him around.

"Do you know this woman?" the other officer asked.

"Yes, of course. She's my daughter."

"I'm so sorry, Daddy," Josie wept. Her head was hanging down, but her eyes were trained on her father. Lila could see that Josie was silently pleading for his help and forgiveness.

"We picked her up selling drugs to tourists at a beach bar."

"You what!" Jack exclaimed, totally flabbergasted. "That's not possible."

Paul Mason stepped forward. "Officers, I'm the Warren-family attorney. What exactly are the charges?"

"Drug trafficking."

"That's ridiculous!" Jack barked.

"On what grounds?" Paul inquired, putting his hand on Jack's shoulders, signaling his friend to calm down.

"We apprehended this young woman and found she was in possession of a large number of prescription pharmaceuticals with the intent to sell them. Once we had her in our custody she said her family was on the big yacht down in West End Bay, so we came here to verify her story."

"That's fine, Officers," Paul said. "Why don't we go somewhere where we can talk this through privately?"

The cops looked at each other. One nodded to the other, who then said, "Fine. Please lead the way."

Paul Mason brought the officers into the yacht's interior, down the hall, to a small office next to the dining room. Jack followed. Josie, still handcuffed, was left behind. The moment the cops were out of sight, she collapsed into tears.

Esperanza, the guest closest to her age, sat down by her feet and tried to soothe Josie by gently rubbing her leg.

"Good Christ, little missy," Charity Baines said. "What on earth did you get yourself into?"

Before Lila could hear Josie's response, she left the main deck, following the procession down the hall. She wanted to find out what Jack and Paul were up to. But when she walked by the office door, it was firmly closed. She went through the dining room and down the exterior walkway to look through the window. Though the blinds were lowered, the slats were angled in a way that allowed Lila to see a bit of the room if she crouched down. All she could see were four pairs of legs standing in the office. Then she saw Paul Mason go to the desk and remove a large, green steel box, which he set down on the table. Jack walked over to the box and put his thumb on the fingerprint lock. The box opened and Lila watched his hands remove two bundles of bills, both with the mustard-colored $10,000 band wrapped around them. Each officer grabbed a stack, and then all four men exited the room.

Lila sprang up from her crouched position outside the window and hustled back to the main deck. When she arrived, she saw the officers taking the handcuffs off Josie and then swiftly leaving the boat, with a nod to Jack Warren. That was probably the quickest money those two corrupt bastards had ever made, Lila thought to herself. Though she'd never taken a bribe herself, she'd been offered plenty of times; every cop had. And she knew how strong the pull was to take the easy buck, especially when a police officer's pay was so shitty and the rewards were so few. But she still passed judgment on the cops who took bribes. How could she not? They were the source of so much ill, not just for civilians, but for all cops in general. How could there be any faith in the system or any possibility of justice when anyone who was rich enough could buy a "get out of jail" card so easily?

Once the cops had left, Jack Warren dropped his intimidating billionaire routine and became what he really was at that very moment—a very pissed-off father. He walked over to Josie, who was slumped down in a chair with her head buried in her arms as the rest of the guests silently huddled around her.

"Josie!" Jack yelled at his daughter, who didn't move.

Josie did nothing but begin to weep at a louder volume. Esperanza grabbed her hand, trying to soothe her.

"Esperanza," Jack said sternly, "I'll take it from here."

Esperanza scrambled to join Thiago, but Josie still didn't move. Jack grabbed the top of her thin arm and hoisted her up to her feet. "Josie, I'm talking to you," he yelled, but she just flopped back down into the chair. Jack hovered over her like a drone ready to strike. "Just tell me one damn thing. Where's Asher? Huh? Where's your goddamn Prince Charming?"

"I don't know," Josie whimpered.

"I'll tell you where he is. He's probably on top of some drunk tourist right about now," Jack said. "I told you he was no good."

"Easy there, son," Clarence Baines said to Jack. A southern gentleman to the core, Baines liked to keep things civilized, even at the worst of times.

Charity walked over to Josie, "Now, honey, tell your father what you told us. I'm sure he'll understand."

Josie slowly looked up at her father. She sniffed and wiped the slick of tears from her cheeks. "We didn't have any money."

"Figures! I pay my crew top dollar. And that vulture has the gall to claim he's penniless? It's just unbelievable! And this is the man my only daughter chooses?!" Jack yelled, but the rest of the group shushed him and encouraged Josie to go on.

"So, um, we decided, I mean Asher decided, that we should get Mom's pills and sell them at some tourist spots so we could get money. He told me if we got enough, we could sail to St. Croix and get married." Her voice caught in her throat for a moment. She had begun to shake. "He found a couple who wanted some Oxy, and he sent me over to give them the pills and get the money. But then the cops grabbed me. And when I looked up," Josie said with a deep, profound sob, "Asher was gone. I called out to him, and nothing. He disappeared." She went back into the fetal position. Then she whimpered, "I'm so sorry, Dad. I should've listened to you. I'm so sorry." She began sobbing. "He didn't ever love me, did he? Did he just want money the whole time?"

The iron fist in Jack relaxed as he hovered over his daughter. He patted her head in a gesture that struck Lila as both condescending and comforting at once. "There, there," he said to Josie. "Daddy's here. Daddy's here."

Josie desperately flung her arms around her father, as if he were a life raft and she were drowning. Jack was clearly pleased to, once again, be the man in control as everyone else fell to pieces around him. He had reasserted his dominance and Josie was back in the fold, freshly chastised and weaker than ever.

Lila watched the whole scene with a sick feeling growing inside her. She tried to think through every angle. Maybe Josie was putting on an act to make sure her father kept her in the will until Asher somehow got back on the boat, and they both murdered Jack. But that seemed far-fetched. As she watched father and daughter, with their matching prominent noses and weak chins, sitting closely together, Lila's gut told her that Josie's emotions were real.

And the chance that Josie and Asher were the killers was minuscule. Lila tried to stay calm as she realized that her latest theory had been shattered into a thousand jagged pieces and she was back to square one. She was running out of time.

CHAPTER 18

ON THE EIGHTH day of *The Rising Tide*'s Caribbean tour, the grand yacht sailed across ocean waters as blue and iridescent as a peacock. They were a day away from St. Barts, their next glamorous destination. But it seemed the charms of the trip had grown thin. Without any land in sight, and sick of one another's company, the passengers slipped into the doldrums, dragging themselves listlessly around the yacht, no longer aware of its unparalleled beauty and luxury. After countless scandals, betrayals, and bad behavior, everyone had gone to their separate corners for a much-needed breather. And a quiet routine replaced all of the dramatics, which was good for Lila. It allowed her the time and head space to focus on the investigation.

Her eyes remained trained on Seth Liss and his machinations to climb to the top of Warren Software. She was monitoring Liss's correspondence by hacking into his computer every day. As a result, Lila knew that Seth had convinced the board of directors to hold a vote to oust Jack as CEO. The vote was scheduled for mid-September, once the yacht's voyage was complete. Liss's progress with his coup seemed to soften his seething anger into a lesser state of persistent grumpiness.

Lila was still unable to confirm if Jack knew about his CFO's treachery. Jack himself was impossible to read on the matter. And when Lila finally got another opportunity to scour Jack's computer for any contact with Urs Hunziker, she found that all Urs's emails had been totally wiped clean off Jack's hard drive.

Things with Josie had also stabilized. After her public abandonment and humiliation, she spent her time lying low, sitting quietly by the pool (always with her bikini top on), reading books by Deepak Chopra, meditating in her room, and listening to mournful Fiona Apple albums on repeat. But in the meantime, the dynamic between her and her father had changed greatly. The Asher imbroglio resulted in the two of them becoming closer than ever. Jack, it seemed, had felt Josie learned her lesson, and Josie was happy to be safe within the comforting confines of her father's wealth and all the security it brought.

Lila was most interested in how the renewed affection between father and daughter impacted Elise. Feeling that her daughter had now defected to the enemy camp, Elise further retreated into her world of pills and bitterness. Lila started once again to think that her first theory was her best one—that Elise was the one who was going to pull the trigger.

Lila observed the push and pull of all the complicated relationships as she and Sam served breakfast that crystal-clear morning. It was September 5, 2008. In three days, Ava would be aboard the ship. Two days after that, Jack would be murdered.

She had to figure things out, and fast.

"Did you see this article about Daniel in the *New York Times*?" Charity Baines asked the group as she held out her iPad, almost knocking over the empty glass that once housed her second mimosa of the morning. It was only 9:30 and she was already drunk, but such was being stuck in the doldrums.

Jack, who was busy slurping up his morning miso soup, looked up at her. "No, what does it say?"

"Well, frankly, darling," Charity said, "I don't think you'll like it."

"If I cared about the opinions of those hacks at the *Times,* I don't think I'd be where I am today, would I? Now spit it out."

"To be brief," Charity said, obviously relishing the fact that for the first time, everyone around the table was waiting to hear her talk, "it says that Daniel is a genius and you're a . . ." She paused, and consulted the article on the screen. "Well, it says here, you're a 'destroyer of avant-garde culture,'" she read aloud with great pleasure.

"Let me see that," Jack said, grabbing the iPad out of Charity's hand.

In a mocking voice, Jack read, *"'Like John D. Rockefeller before him, who famously ordered the removal of the extraordinary mural he had commissioned from the late, great Diego Rivera, tech billionaire Jack Warren is the latest power-mad tycoon to commit art slaughter by destroying the brilliant work Warren himself had commissioned from the art provocateur Daniel Poe.'"*

Jack handed back the iPad to Charity. "That's the biggest bunch of bullshit I've ever heard. Aside from that imbecile comparing me to John D. Rockefeller, like it's a bad thing."

Charity went on, "It says that ever since your little row with Daniel, he's never been a hotter commodity. It's just great news. I'm quite relieved, actually. I never did say anything about it, but do you all remember when Daniel stormed in here yelling about how his commissions were canceled?"

"Duh. That's not something anyone could forget," Josie said with a roll of her eyes. Despite her new role as daddy's docile little girl, the young heiress was acting, more or less, like a total brat toward everyone else on the yacht.

"Remember, Jack," Charity continued, anxious to not lose her moment in the spotlight. "Daniel thought it was you who told people about the statue being thrown overboard? Well, actually, it was me. Sorry about that," she said with a high-pitched, nervous giggle. "I told my art-dealer friend Franz and then he, the incorrigible gossip that he is, spilled the beans to everyone in his Rolodex. But I was mortified when Daniel said his commissions had been canceled. But now, see, it was good in the long run. Daniel's never been hotter." She sat back with her head held high, looking extremely pleased with herself.

"It was you who blabbed?" Jack said, outraged. "Then why'd you let me take his shit?"

"The man was on drugs!" Charity exclaimed like she was some kind of modern-day Scarlett O'Hara and not the battle-scarred Beltway veteran she was. "I was too frightened of him to speak!"

"Oh, don't play the scared Southern belle act while I'm around," her husband said. "I won't buy it and I won't let anyone else buy it either. You didn't say anything because you wanted to get away with it."

"Then why am I admitting to it now?" Charity asked.

"Simple. Because now that Daniel's fine, it doesn't matter," Clarence answered.

"Oh, phooey. What do you know?" Charity said, with a dismissive wave of her hand.

"Actually," Paul Mason said as he read the article, "it doesn't seem like Daniel is fine at all. It says here that no one has seen or heard from him in days. All this information is just from his gallery."

"He could be dead in a ditch somewhere," Elise observed, with a small smile. She'd never been a fan of Daniel Poe.

"Oh, Mother. Stop being so fucking macabre all the time," Josie said, really drawing out every syllable in "macabre."

"It's nice to have you back, Josie," Jack said, happy to have someone else be cruel to his wife. Lila had never witnessed such a toxic marriage.

Just as breakfast was winding down and Lila was clearing the plates, Ben walked in. A pulse of excitement shot through her when she saw his face, but she suppressed her smile. She hadn't spent any time alone with Ben since they shared that kiss in the hallway, and that was fine by her.

"Nicky, the captain asked to speak with you," Ben said, keeping things strictly professional in tone. Many of the guests were still in the dining room.

Lila was surprised. She couldn't think of one reason the captain would have to speak with her. "Did he say what it was about?"

Ben shook his head and shrugged his shoulders. "Nope. Just told me to come get you and bring you up to the bridge." Lila could see from the look in his eyes that Ben was just as curious as Lila about what exactly was going on. After making sure that Sam could handle clearing away the remainder of the breakfast dishes by herself, Lila followed Ben up to the bridge.

There was a stiff silence between the two of them. Ben, it seemed to Lila, was in a sour mood, which was something she'd never seen him in before.

"Anything wrong?" Lila asked, hearing the awkwardness in her own voice. There was a part of her that was worried he was mad at her, which was something she didn't want either him or her to feel for the other.

"It's nothing. But . . ." Ben paused.

"But what?"

"I got some shitty news today is all. Jack told me that the helmsman we sailed with the other day is joining our team."

"What's wrong with that?"

"*I'm* the helmsman for Jack's boat," Ben said, his voice full of hurt and indignation. "I had no idea I was spending the whole day sailing with my replacement. But of course Jack didn't tell me what he was planning. He never misses an opportunity to let me twist in the wind. To be honest, I'm fucking furious about it."

Before Lila could ask any more questions, they walked into the bridge, where Bobby Nash was sitting by himself in a large leather captain's chair. He was in front of five large flat screens flashing ever-changing information on the yacht's course, the topography of the ocean's surface, and other bits of data that Lila couldn't fathom. It was a gorgeous space, part spaceship control room, part luxury automobile. It reminded her of the ornate beauty of Teddy's time machine.

The bridge sat up at the highest point of the ship looking over the bow. The wall that Nash faced was all windows, slanted at a forty-five-degree angle, from which Lila could see an endless expanse of ocean, almost perfectly matching the cloudless robin's-egg-blue sky. It was breathtaking.

She turned toward the opposite wall, overlooking the aft deck at the back of the yacht. From there, she had a perfect vantage point of the small corner on the second deck where, soon enough, Jack Warren would be murdered.

Without looking up from the middle screen in front of him, Captain Nash spoke to Ben. "Leave us."

Ben and Lila exchanged glances. Neither knew what was going on. Lila shrugged and Ben quickly grabbed her hand, giving it a reassuring squeeze before he left the room.

Once Ben was gone, Nash got up from his seat and walked over to Lila. She'd never been this close to the captain before, and for the first time, she noticed the auburn strands streaked throughout his silver beard.

He stood a few inches away from her, too close for her comfort. His round potbelly was a deep inhale away from touching her own stomach. His small blue eyes fixed on her. "You've got something of mine."

Perplexed, Lila stood there wondering what on earth he could be talking about. "Did you request something from the kitchen? If so, I apologize, but I didn't get that order." Lila gave him a demure smile, but his face remained stony.

"Don't play games with me." His thick Boston accent was almost comical to Lila, but the captain's grim countenance let her know that nothing funny was going on. "Where is it?" He leaned closer to her, trying to intimidate her. Little did he know she could kick his ass in under a minute. She wasn't afraid.

Lila took a couple steps away from the captain, putting her hands up in the air as a sign of surrender. "Listen, Captain. I'm in the dark here." But then, in a flash, she knew just what he was talking about—the drugs. A question that had been nagging at her since she boarded the yacht was finally answered. The cocaine had all been for Captain Nash. But Lila kept her face neutral. Playing dumb seemed her best defense.

"I was told you'd be bringing me something. And now that we're about to get to St. Barts, I need it." She saw that there were beads of perspiration on his brow. He was on edge.

She remained silent. So, Nicky had lied to her after all, but Lila had expected as much. There was no way one person could move that much product on her own just selling to tourists. Lila was glad she knew enough to bring the drugs with her.

He came toward her and whispered directly into her ear, "If you even *think* of holding out on me, I'll slit your throat so fast you won't know what hit you."

The pure violence of his threat startled Lila, but she could handle it.

"Oh, *now* I know what you're talking about," she said, with an empty-headed nod.

"Yeah, light dawns over Marblehead. Finally. Now do you fucking remember?"

She nodded, looking at the captain's ferocious face. If ever she'd seen a man look like he was capable of murder, it was this man standing right in front of her. Nash hadn't even been on her radar as a possible suspect.

Lila looked at him closely, which made him grow even testier.

"Well, don't just stand there with your thumb up your ass. Go get it and bring it to me . . . NOW. I've got everyone out of my hair for the next thirty minutes, so you've got to hustle."

"Okay," Lila said as she continued to watch Nash with an intense curiosity. The captain was mixed up in some high-level shady business. It couldn't be with any members of the Cali cartel, she knew that much. Because if Nicky was a runner between Nash and the cartel, the Colombians would've told Nash that she was a snitch, and someone would've tried to kill Lila before the boat even set sail. She needed to find out what drug cartel Nash ran with.

"Why are you still standing there?" the captain said angrily. He reached out to her, grabbing the front of her shirt and pulling her toward him. "Let me make one thing crystal clear. I'm a man who doesn't like to be fucked with and I don't like to be kept waiting. So, move," he said, shoving her in the direction of the door.

She ran down several flights of stairs. She dashed by Sam, who was carefully dusting the Matisse collages and Picasso pencil drawings hanging in the hallway on the upper deck. She whooshed by Pedro and Mudge, who were scrubbing the floors of the main deck. She went all the way down to the lower level, grabbed the duffel bag from her room, then headed to the lifeboat in the engine room where she'd stashed the drugs.

She threw the duffel bag down on the ground, then carefully removed the wrapped packages of cocaine. She was just about to pile everything into the duffel when she heard Ben's voice.

"Nicky?"

She nearly jumped out of her skin, but she tried to hide any sign of panic. How had she not heard him come into the engine room after her?

"Oh, hi, Ben," she said as casually as she could even though she was currently holding a wrapped-up package of cocaine in her hand. She'd been caught. There was no denying it. So she decided to keep on doing what she was doing, hoping he wouldn't have any idea what was going on. The gun and the money that were still stashed down in the tender were another problem for another day.

"What the hell are you doing?" he asked, walking toward her.

"Nothing. Just grabbing something."

"I'm not an idiot, Nicky. I know what *that* is. I just can't believe you're mixed up in it."

"If you're not a part of it, then how do you even know what I'm doing?" Lila heard herself. She sounded defensive and ridiculous, but Ben had caught her red-handed. She didn't know what else to do.

"I told you, I grew up on boats. And guess what? People smuggle shit on boats. It's not that complicated. I've been at sea long enough to know what a kilo of coke looks like. This," he said, scooping up one of the packages, "is what it looks like." Then he slammed it back to the ground.

"This isn't me," Lila said to Ben. "I'm just helping someone out."

"This isn't you?" Ben spit back. He couldn't even look her in the eye. "Who are you anyway? I checked up on Nicky Collins, turns out she has a shit ton of experience on yachts. Not green like you are, or are at least pretending to be."

"Ben, please. Let me explain." But then her mind went blank. She could only stare at him. After all, what could she possibly say to him to make him understand? The truth about who she was and what she was doing was something that no one on this yacht could ever, ever know.

"Is Nicky Collins even your real name?"

She paused, feeling her heart thump quickly in her chest. "Yes," she lied.

"You know what? It doesn't matter. Nothing you say matters anymore." He turned and marched up the stairs to the main hallway of the lower level. Before he went through the door, he turned back to Lila, who still stood dumbly, with stacks of cocaine piled around her feet. "Just stay away from me. I've worked my whole life to be where I am. And I won't risk you putting any of it in jeopardy."

Once he had gone, Lila exhaled. "Fuuuuuck," she said as she bent over, stuffing the drugs in the bag. She knew she'd be pushing it with Nash if she took too much time delivering the coke. As she hustled back up to the bridge, feeling the wrapped bricks of drugs bump around in the bag, she realized what a tricky position she'd found herself in. What Ben knew could be detrimental to her completing her mission. He'd discovered she wasn't Nicky Collins. And worst of all, he knew she had stashed drugs on board, which not only meant she'd get thrown off the boat; it also meant possible jail time, which could result in her being forever stuck in the past.

The question was, what could she do next? She could do

what Ben wanted—stay far away from him and pray that he wouldn't say a word. But that was too passive a plan for the likes of Lila.

As she climbed her way to the bridge, she decided it might be better to pull Ben closer, if he'd let her. He had feelings for her, or at least he used to. Maybe her best bet was to play on those feelings. If she could seduce him and get him on her side, she might be safer than letting him go without a fight.

"Here you go, Captain," Lila said, dropping the heavy bag at Nash's feet.

"About fucking time." Nash scowled as he quickly crouched down to inspect the contents. When he found everything in place, Lila saw a wave of relief wash over him. He stood up and flung the bag over his shoulder. "You're lucky everything is square because I can't tell you what a fucking pain you've been," he said, shaking his head. "Edna demanded that you be let go more times than I can count. And I had to save your incompetent ass every step of the way."

Lila thought back to all the times she'd been worried about losing her job. Now she knew why she'd been allowed to stay. It was all thanks to Captain Bobby Nash, her silver-bearded, drug-running fairy godmother.

"So now what?" Lila asked.

"So now, nothing. This never happened. I'll do what I do and you'll work until the end of this trip and then you're free to go back to wherever you came from. Don't say a word to anyone, or you're dead. Got it?"

"Got it," Lila said as she started to think about her next move. Whether this hundred grand of cocaine was connected to Jack's murder was something she'd have to figure out, and fast.

CHAPTER 19

IT WAS 5:22 A.M., and Lila's alarm was due to go off in just a few minutes, but she was already awake. Despite her profound physical and emotional exhaustion, sleep had been an impossibility.

With Jack Warren's death mere days away, there were so many loose ends and so many potential suspects that her mind couldn't slow down. She stared out into the blinding darkness of her cabin as she mentally sorted through everyone on the boat for what must have been the hundredth time that night, cataloging their motives for murder. Bobby Nash was only the latest to join the list of suspects, all of whom were potentially able—and willing—to gun Jack down. Seth. Daniel Poe. Josie and Asher. And of course, Elise.

In an attempt to center herself and focus her thinking, Lila had spent the last hour or so with the childhood picture of her and her sister, which she'd smuggled from 2019, pressed against her heart. Even though it was too dark in her cabin to actually look at it, holding it flat against her body gave her a strange kind of comfort. Thoughts of that sweet, sunshiny day so very long ago floated into her mind. She remembered Ava had just lost her front tooth, and both girls were excited about what the tooth fairy would bring that night. Ava, with her strawberry-blond hair braided in a long, thick plait that reached to her midback, showed Lila which seashells were the most beautiful and how to hunt for sand dollars. Both sisters spent the day collecting all the exquisite bounty from the sea, and presenting their riches to their mom, who flashed them a heart-swelling smile.

But even this treasured memory had failed to soothe Lila's mind. Lying there in her bunk bed, listening to the rise and fall of Sam's breathing, she felt defeated and anxious. It seemed like *everyone* was a suspect.

The other big question that kept nagging and nagging at Lila throughout the silent darkness of the night was the most important question of all: what did her sister have to do with any of this? With every passing day and with every port of call checked off the list, Lila was counting down the days until she'd see Ava. Sweet Ava, her cherished sister. Lila still couldn't even wrap her mind around the fact that Ava's life was in any way intertwined with these damaged people.

But, amid all these puzzles, one thing was certain: time was running out. And Lila would have to work even harder, be even more vigilant, and risk everything if she was going to make sure that the innocent were exonerated and the guilty were punished.

THREE HOURS LATER, as Lila was busy serving breakfast, the guests' table was buzzing. Soon they'd be docking in Port de Gustavia, at the marina of choice for all superyachts visiting St. Barts. The women were the most excited because Esperanza Campos had arranged for them to visit the world-renowned psychic Lady Kitty, who had a devoted following among the jet set.

"Supposedly Lady Kitty told Jennifer Aniston that Brad would leave her!" Josie said with unbridled glee. "And the CIA is using her to help them find Osama bin Laden. But no luck there, right?"

Lila smiled to herself as she refilled everyone's coffee cup. She could tell these women a decade's worth of predictions, all of which would come true—because she'd lived through them. But nobody would believe her. And anyway, her knowledge wasn't for sale.

Mostly Lila was happy that the women would be off the yacht and out of her hair, as would the men, who planned to spend the day scuba diving with sharks at the bottom of the sea. Even Seth Liss had put business away for this one day to experience these glorious and deadly creatures up close. If only one of the sharks would have the insight and wisdom to gobble every one of these nasty characters up, Lila thought, then it would save her a lot of trouble.

Minutes after the yacht was safely moored in the azure paradise of St. Barts, the guests filed down the gangplank one by one, excited for the adventures set before them. As Lila carefully watched them pair off into groups and wind their way through the French island's main harbor of Port de Gustavia, she took in the overwhelming beauty and opulence of the place. Flanked on three sides by verdant mountains dotted with terra-cotta-roofed villas, the port was dripping with superyachts full of Russian billionaires, hip-hop impresarios, Greek shipping magnates, and the supermodels who loved them. It was a landscape of oiled skin, string bikinis, Ace of Spades champagne, Montecristo cigars, thick gold chains, and diamond rings. Everyone within eyeshot was either very, very rich or very, very beautiful or maybe, for the very, very lucky, they were both. It was Caribbean exclusiveness and opulence in its most concentrated form. There was no mistaking the fact that this very elite port on this very elite island was the wealthiest place Lila had ever seen in her life—and given her other undercover missions, that was really saying something.

Standing on the main deck, Lila watched as Jack Warren led the men across the marina to board a speedboat that would take them diving, while the women, led by Esperanza, climbed into a black Cadillac Escalade for their highly anticipated day with Lady Kitty. As Lila watched a couple of surgically enhanced, bikini-clad women standing on the dock in front of *The Rising Tide,* posing coquettishly for pictures that would be hitting Facebook within minutes, out of the corner of her eye, she saw Captain Nash descending the gangplank. He was carrying her blue duffel bag, which meant he was carrying the drugs. Lila knew, then and there, that she had to follow him.

But before she could do so, she'd have to disguise herself. After all, blending into the background of this playground for the very rich and very famous would be impossible if she was wearing her white stewardess uniform. As quickly as she could, she ran down the hall to Josie's room, taking off her uniform as soon as she closed the door behind her. In a matter of a few frantic seconds, Lila threw on a Fendi string bikini, tightly wrapped one of Josie's many sarongs low around her hips, put a pair of enormous black Hermès sunglasses on her face, Marc Jacobs flip-flops on her feet, and a wide-brimmed straw hat on her head. She threw her uniform, bra, and underwear under the bed, knowing that she'd be back at the boat hours before Josie and the gang returned.

In a matter of thirty seconds, Lila had transformed herself from a servant girl into a carbon copy of almost every other young and beautiful woman decorating the streets of St. Barts.

With her disguise in place, she blasted out of Josie's room and hurried out to the main deck. Her prayers were twice answered when she didn't run into any other member of the crew *and* caught sight of Captain Nash, whom she spotted turning onto the main oceanfront drag of Gustavia.

Lila hurried forward, lagging fifty feet behind Nash to avoid being spotted. The mingling and flirty crowd enveloped them both almost instantly. It was clear that Nash knew where he was going. He walked purposefully through the center of town, past the entwined couples drinking white wine in open-air cafés and the luxury boutiques housed in charming white clapboard buildings, even failing to notice that he marched right by the Hollywood starlet wearing a strapless terrycloth romper whose gigantic Céline bag dwarfed her tiny, underfed body.

Nash ducked down a narrow alleyway, climbed up a steep set of stone stairs, then turned left and momentarily disappeared from Lila's view. She followed him up the stairs just in time to spy him turning past a mint-green stucco building with wooden shutters the color of a ripe papaya. Lila slowly walked by the colorful house and its adjacent alley, catching sight of Nash standing about a hundred feet or so away from her, in front of a small shack behind the green house. She doubled back and leaned up against the mint house, her shoulder pressed against the outer wall's farthest edge, furtively peeking down the alley. She saw Nash put the blue duffel bag on the ground as a disembodied arm picked it up and dropped a red bag in its place. After Nash picked up the red bag, he started walking back to the main road, breezing by Lila, who turned her body away from the captain to avoid being spotted.

Holding the red bag tightly to his chest, Nash walked a few doors down the road before slipping into the entryway of the Hotel Caraïbes, a very posh-looking establishment. Lila trailed behind, walking through the hotel's carved ebony entrance and stopping behind an enormous bird-of-paradise arrangement to quickly get her bearings. She searched the lobby, but couldn't see Nash anywhere. And what with his cheap nylon sailing shorts and long silver beard, he wasn't at all difficult to find.

Then Lila spotted him. He was on the other side of the lobby, sitting in an old-fashioned wood-and-glass pay-phone booth. His back was facing her as he spoke to someone on the phone. Lila cut across the lobby and entered the booth right next to him. She picked up the phone, keeping her head angled down to avoid being recognized. Then she quickly turned toward him. In a brief glance she saw that Nash had the red bag unzipped on his lap revealing several stacks of 500-euro banknotes. But it was what was on top of the money that took Lila's breath away. She recognized it instantly—a snub-nosed .38 revolver with a cherrywood grip. The exact gun that would be discovered next to a pool of Jack Warren's blood on the night of his murder.

Shocked, Lila swiveled away from Nash and sank down in the booth's upholstered seat, still pressing the phone against her face as the dial tone droned in her ear. Captain Nash had the murder weapon. She had searched the yacht over and over again for this very gun. And here it was. Lila had just discovered a major piece of the puzzle, but where did it fit into the big picture?

Was Nash the killer?

She heard him open the booth door. Staying seated, she watched him walk through the lobby, still clutching his bag, and out into the street. The moment he was through the door, she sprang up out of the booth and hustled after him. But as she was leaving the hotel, she collided with a large group of chattering, backpacking French teenagers loitering at the front door. By the time she had pushed herself past the adolescent cloud of Parisian laughter and Gauloises smoke, she realized she'd lost Nash. She ran down the steps and into the middle of the street. Seeing nothing, she ripped off her straw hat and dark sunglasses hoping to get a clearer view, but it was no use. He was gone.

Cars puttered past, honking friendly warnings as she

searched the streets. Lila took a deep breath, trying to center herself, but it was no use. Seeing that gun (*the* gun that she'd seen, blood-smeared, in countless police photos from the night of the murder) made her realize she was closer than she'd ever been to actually finding out who killed Jack Warren.

Not knowing what else to do, she headed down the street and back to the marina. Now that she'd lost Nash, she had to return to the yacht as fast as she could in hopes of minimizing any damage her absence had already caused.

By the time she climbed on board, she'd been AWOL for only ninety minutes. If she was very lucky, Edna Slaughter wouldn't have taken note of her absence. But Lila knew that was almost too much to wish for. It seemed that nothing got past Edna.

She kept her head down as she rushed by Mudge and Pedro scrubbing the deck and then booked it back into Josie's room, the whole time praying that she wouldn't run into Sam or Edna. The moment she turned into the heiress's room, she became a whirling dervish of activity. She slammed the door behind her, threw the Fendi bikini in the hamper, folded up the sarong, and returned the hat and sunglasses to the closet. She reached under the bed, retrieved her underwear and her uniform, and was dressed in an instant. Just as she was buttoning the final button on her shirt, the door flew open and the chief stewardess stormed in.

Without any hesitation, Lila bent over Josie's bed and began fluffing pillows.

"Where on earth have you been?" the chief stewardess asked.

"What do you mean?" Lila answered, playing the innocent. She tried to conceal how out of breath she was with a giant, lazy yawn. "I've been busy servicing all the suites." She smoothed and tucked down the sheets, wanting to show Edna Slaughter that she'd just walked in on her stewardess tending to her daily rounds.

Nothing made Edna Slaughter more ill at ease than a thwarted opportunity to do some serious scolding. "Fine," she said, backing out of the room. "But don't think you can slack off the entire day. There's still plenty to do."

"Of course, ma'am," Lila said with a subservient nod.

Even though she tried to keep her eye out for Captain Nash's return to *The Rising Tide*, Lila didn't see him for the rest of the day. But an unexpected event diverted her attention from the gun-toting captain—the return of Daniel Poe.

Lila was up on the third deck when she saw him. It was half-past eight and she was getting the poolside area ready for cocktail hour. The low, red sun had just slipped below the horizon, turning the sky a dusty lavender color, which gave the night a surreal feeling. An adjacent superyacht was blasting cacophonous hip-hop as a couple of girls wearing only gold bikini bottoms danced, while two men sprayed them with Methuselahs of champagne. But her attention was diverted from the bacchanal when, a few docks down at the marina, she saw Jack, Seth, Paul, Clarence, and Thiago hop off the speedboat they'd chartered to go diving.

Everything looked normal until she noticed that Paul and Thiago were carrying a limp figure between them. It wasn't until they got closer to the yacht that Lila realized it was a barely conscious Daniel Poe, whose pathetically dangling feet the two men were dragging across the ground.

Once they huffed and puffed their way up the gangway to the main deck, the two men let go of Poe, leaving the enfant terrible of the art world to crumble to the floor a few feet away from Lila. He lay there with his skinny legs and arms splayed out around him. Lila could smell the days of unwashed excess on his skin as he mumbled something unintelligible to the men above him.

"Who knew a bag of bones could be so fucking heavy," Paul said as he stretched out his back.

The women, who'd come back from their rendezvous with Lady Kitty just fifteen minutes earlier, gave one another solemn, amazed looks.

"I can't believe it," Elise said.

"I know," Josie responded, her eyes wide with astonishment as she pressed her hands against her cheeks.

"What?" asked Jack. "What's the big deal?"

Josie said, "Lady Kitty literally just predicted this would happen. She told us that someone who our family had treated unfairly would return into our lives within two days. And here he is." She walked over to Poe, who reached up toward Josie and began to inappropriately run his hand up her long, tanned leg until she kicked him away.

Jack shook his head. "First off, this fuckup was not treated unfairly by our family. And secondly, that psychic stuff is bullshit."

"But where on earth did you find him, and why in heaven's name did you bring him back here?" Charity asked, not at all attempting to mask her displeasure about Poe's return. It was clear to Lila that Charity was still anxious over the fact that she had been the one responsible for spreading the news about Jack tossing Poe's golden phallus overboard.

Charity's silver-haired and rather dramatically sunburned husband answered. "The boys and I went to quite a lively bar after we were done diving. And who should we see there but Daniel Poe. Apparently, he'd made friends with the crown prince of Benin, who brought him over to St. Barts on his yacht a couple days ago."

"But what is he doing *here*?" Elise asked. Her voice sounded slurred, whether from pills or alcohol or both Lila didn't know.

"You're not mad at him anymore, Daddy?" Josie asked.

She'd been calling him "Daddy" since the whole Asher affair exploded in her face. It never failed to turn Lila's stomach.

Jack waited a few seconds before responding to his daughter. "Not in the least," he said finally.

Lila didn't believe him for a second. Jack Warren was the type of guy who could hold on to even the tiniest of grudges for decades. So, why would he let the man who literally shat all over his boat back on board? Then again, Jack had been skewered by the press since word got out that he threw Poe's sculpture into the ocean. Over the last few days, many opinion columnists had been busy calling Jack a cultural vandal and an enemy of the avant-garde. Had he brought Poe back to rehabilitate his image? Except Lila knew that Jack didn't care what the press wrote about him. It had to be something else.

"Anyway," Jack said, stepping away from Poe, who was still on the ground. "It wasn't my idea. It was his," he said, pointing at Liss. "That pain in my ass over there wants me to make nicey-nice to this drunken reprobate. He's saying it's good for my reputation."

"All I want, Jack," Liss said with a sigh, "is for you to look like less of a goddamn loose cannon. I don't think that's so difficult to comprehend, is it?"

Jack gave Liss a terrible little smile that turned into a shark-eyed stare and sneer. He was baring his teeth at his enemy. Most importantly, Daniel Poe was back on board, and back on Lila's suspect list.

"I'm not so sure this is the way to rehab my image, Seth," Jack said, shaking his head at Daniel Poe, who had started mumbling something incomprehensible. "And I don't know if it's the best thing for Daniel's image either. I mean even you should know that any half-decent artist is much more beloved once they're dead."

CHAPTER 20

WHILE DANIEL POE spent the following morning in his plush guest room, recovering from days and days of untold excess, his patron, Jack Warren, was on a treasure hunt. It seemed that the now-legendary story of Jack throwing Poe's multimillion-dollar statue overboard had not only caused a major sensation in the art world, it had also resulted in a bunch of modern-day buccaneers scouring the Caribbean Sea in search of the golden phallus.

But to Jack, what was his to throw away was his to take back. He was hell-bent on getting to it first.

Working with Captain Nash, First Officer Ben, and some very advanced navigation software, Jack calculated the sculpture's approximate location—about 225 to 236 nautical miles southeast of the Exuma Cays. He then got on the phone with a couple of professional deep-sea treasure-hunting outfits and contracted them to bring the statue up from the depths. He boasted to his guests while slurping down his breakfast miso soup that he expected it to be back in his possession sometime within the next twenty-four hours.

"The plan was to head back to Miami anyway, to restock supplies," he said. "So we might as well swing by the Cays to grab the statue. We should still be on schedule to land in Miami by tomorrow evening." All the guests were seated around the table for breakfast with the exception of Liss, which was unusual. Lila had his Tater Tots warming in a chafing dish and his Heinz ketchup artfully concealed in a tiny ceramic terrine, but she wasn't preoccupied about his absence. She was too busy thinking about Ava, who would board the yacht once they landed in Miami. Just the very idea of it filled her with excitement and dread—excitement that she'd see her sister again and dread for what lay in store.

"Then in four days it'll be your birthday, Daddy," Josie said in a treacly, babyish voice.

"The big five-oh," Paul said, holding up his crystal water goblet to toast his host. "It looks good on you, buddy."

"Sure does," Elise Warren said bitterly as she sipped on a spicy Bloody Mary while her breakfast of orange slices and steamed egg whites grew cold on the gold-rimmed china plate set before her. "In a few years, people won't think I'm your wife. They'll think I'm your mother."

An awkward silence fell over the table. Elise's overwhelming unhappiness often had that effect.

Never one to fear Elise's rage or sorrow, Jack said, "What my wife doesn't seem to understand is the only way to stay young is to have a purpose in your life." He addressed this bon mot to his companions around the table, specifically avoiding eye contact with Elise, who was absolutely glaring at him. Lila was continually amazed by the fact that Jack almost never looked at nor directly addressed his wife. It must've made Elise Warren feel like a ghost in her own life.

"Now, now," Clarence Baines cautioned in a fatherly tone. "No squabbling on such a beautiful day."

"Yes," Thiago said, trailing his fingers down the willowy and tanned limb of his young wife. "We must enjoy ourselves."

"Of course," Elise said irritably. "I'm having the time of my life." She downed the rest of her Bloody Mary and tapped the edge of the glass with her nail, which Sam and Lila knew meant that she needed another.

Suddenly the serenity of the morning was shattered by the sound of heavy footsteps and labored breathing coming from the hallway. Everyone turned toward the door to see Seth Liss burst into the room.

He was visibly enraged. A vein in his forehead was throbbing and his nostrils were flared. Everyone was expecting Liss to attack Jack, but it was Clarence Baines he was after. He ripped the Bluetooth earpiece from his head and whipped it at Baines, causing the senator to jump back in surprise, spilling his grapefruit juice everywhere.

"You fucking imbecile," Liss screamed. "Do you know what you've done?"

Charity Baines jumped up from her chair and stood protectively in front of her confused and cowering husband.

"Now, wait just one second," she said to Liss in a southern accent that was as sweet and cool as a mint julep. Liss didn't take his eyes off Clarence. He looked like a bull about to attack.

"Seth, control yourself," Jack said calmly. "Now tell me what this is all about."

"I just got off the phone with a reporter from the *Wall Street Journal* asking me about our plans to move Warren Software's manufacturing out of China and back to American soil. Seems our friend here," Liss said, pointing an accusatory finger at Baines, "has a new campaign commercial featuring you promising to make our products one hundred percent made in the USA."

Jack stayed silent and still.

"Tell me this isn't true, Jack."

"I can't do that."

"But it'll torpedo our margins. Just a whiff of this hits Wall Street and our stock price will plummet."

"Sometimes you've got to break a few eggs to make an omelet," Jack said.

"Hear, hear!" Baines cheered.

Liss's eyes nearly popped out of his head. "An omelet? Have you gone fucking crazy? We'll lose *billions*. How could you do this without consulting me?"

"I don't need to consult you. It's my goddamn company. This was an executive decision. What kind of leader am I if my politics and my business don't align?"

"You'd be like every other businessman who'd ever lived on planet Earth," Paul said. "Listen, Jack. I've got to side with Liss on this one. This isn't the kind of decision you can just make on your own."

"Big fucking surprise, Paul. Seems like you and Liss and Thiago over here don't like the way I'm running things. Well, that's fine by me. For too long I've gone against what I know is right. But not anymore. Trust me. It's all going to change. Starting with this. All of Warren Software's manufacturing will be moved to U.S. soil at the start of the next fiscal year."

"Fellas," Baines said, "I know this isn't going to be easy. But Jack's a leader, a maverick. And he's doing what's right for his country."

"Jack," Liss said. He clearly was trying to restrain his rage. "I know Baines has made some promises to you, but let me tell you one thing. He doesn't care about our country. He doesn't care about China eating up our manufacturing jobs."

Baines interrupted, "Now, wait one goddamn second there . . ."

But Liss continued, totally ignoring the protesting senator. "All he cares about is getting reelected. And he's using you to do it. He's taking your money and manipulating you into making decisions that are detrimental to the company you've built from the ground up."

"I must demand that you apologize to me!" Baines said, outraged.

Jack sipped his green tea, with a peaceful smile on his face, an island of calm in a raging sea. "Seth, Seth. You know me," he said in a measured and belittling tone. "You think Baines here is like, what? Some sort of Svengali that can bend me to *his* will? He isn't taking advantage of me. *Nobody* takes advantage of me. You think you can question my decisions? Well, let me tell you something, my friend. I'm twenty moves ahead of you right now. You can protest as much as you want. You don't see the big picture, but that's fine. That's not your job. You can stay down in the muck shoveling the shit every day. Leave the big-picture thinking to me."

"You're going to destroy this company!" Liss shouted.

"I thought you'd be delighted. Now you can add one more thing to your so-called Project King Charles memo that you've been sending to everyone in the company."

Liss looked stunned.

"What, you didn't think I'd find out about it? The level to which you continually underestimate me just proves how incompetent you are," Jack said.

"Jesus, Jack," Thiago said. "You can't do this. It isn't just about you."

"Ah, Thiago, my old friend. You and I both know that you can't lecture me about doing what's right. Both of you," Jack said, looking from Paul to Thiago, "were entertaining Liss's plan to take my company away from me."

Jack stood up, grabbing Charity's half-empty mimosa and

holding the glass up in the air. "So, here's to my so-called friends. May I return your loyalty in kind."

Seth rushed out of the room, yelling as he left, "I won't let you do this, Jack. Mark my words."

Lila, who had been trying to stay as invisible as possible this entire time, watched Jack, amazed to see how centered and how contented he looked. No one was on his side, and he didn't give a fuck, nor did he feel like he had to explain himself to anybody. That wasn't the state of mind of a normal man. Then she remembered what Ben had said, that Jack was a control freak who was happiest when everyone around him was in chaos. Well, Lila thought as she cleaned up the spills and clutter quickly accumulated during all the shouting and accusations, mission accomplished.

After breakfast, everyone once again scattered to their various corners. Elise Warren retreated to the gym, where she contorted her lithe body on the Pilates machine that, with its metal springs and leather, resembled a medieval torture device. When Lila walked by the gym to peek in, she was surprised to see how steady Elise looked doing her exercises, despite her breakfast of vodka and tomato juice. Josie was out by the pool with a copy of Franz Fanon's *The Wretched of the Earth* shielding her face from the hot Caribbean sun. She was constantly flopping from her back to her stomach, as if she couldn't get comfortable. Stuck out at sea with a bunch of adults and a freshly broken heart, Josie seemed as if she wanted to crawl out of her skin. Sam served her a steady stream of piña coladas, which she sucked down noisily.

Liss was, of course, in damage-control mode. Lila thought up countless excuses to go to his room: to pick up his laundry, to make his bed, to deliver his lunch . . . She needed to know what he was thinking. Was Jack pushing him so hard that he would resort to violence? The only reason Liss's rage had briefly settled was that Project King Charles was progressing. But now that a corporate coup d'état was impossible, would Warren Software's ambitious CFO decide to grab power the old-fashioned way?

He certainly seemed angry enough, but more than anything, he looked miserable. Sitting, stooped-shouldered, at his desk, surrounded by piles of empty chocolate soda cans, Liss spent his hours screaming into the phone in English or calmly speaking into the phone in Mandarin. It was obvious he was trying to comfort the Chinese businessmen who were nervous about losing a fortune if Warren Software took its manufacturing elsewhere.

Clarence sought shelter from the storm that he'd created by hanging out on the aft deck by a deep-sea fishing pole, distractedly watching the line drag through the water as he and his wife tucked into oversize gin and tonics.

Lila was refreshing their drinks, adjusting the pillows on the chairs, and setting out snacks for them so that she could eavesdrop on their conversation.

"It's too late now," Clarence said to his wife, who looked incredibly worried. "I've put all my eggs in the Jack Warren basket, for better or for worse. The man has brought in tens of millions of dollars. Without him I could never get reelected."

"But I'm worried that you won't be able to get reelected *with* him. I think he's spiraling out of control, my love. And I don't want you to get sucked into some kind of corporate scandal. Meanwhile, here we are, in the middle of the ocean, when we should be back home on the campaign trail."

"I know, angel. But I needed Jack to believe I'm in his corner. Otherwise he'll never pony up the cash we need. And if he withdraws support for my initiative to move his company's manufacturing back home, then my campaign would never recover."

"True."

"If we pull this off, thousands of jobs will come back to our state. And all this will be worth it."

"Lady Kitty told me that you were going to win, honey."

"That's the first time I heard that charlatan say something I can get behind. Now," Clarence said, looking around and then beckoning Lila over, "sweetheart. Me and the Mrs. need more G-and-Ts, plus can you wrestle up a couple nice shrimp cocktails for us? Might as well enjoy ourselves while we can."

As Lila was in the galley getting everything Clarence requested, Sam walked in and threw down her silver serving tray in a huff. "Everyone can go fuck themselves," she said. Her Floridian accent was always stronger when she was angry.

"What's the matter, Sam?" Lila asked.

Sam's gaze was fixed down at the tray and her mouth was set in a tight little grimace.

"It's just . . ." Sam said, gathering a deep breath. "Fuck Jack." Tears sprang to her eyes. "If I wanted to be treated like trash, I could've just stayed in my damn swamp-rat trailer park. I've done something with my life. I'm here, after all, aren't I? But that man can cut me down so quick. Make me feel smaller than I ever felt."

Lila could tell that Chef Vatel was listening in on their conversation, so she grabbed Sam by the arm and dragged her into the walk-in refrigerator. Both women stood there shivering among the tins of caviar and the fillets of black cod.

"Now tell me exactly what happened," Lila said, putting a sisterly hand on Sam's shoulder.

"I won't be treated like a whore," Sam cried, her teeth chattering from the cold.

"Who called you a whore?"

Sam quickly explained. When Jack wasn't busy antagonizing every man, woman, and child he encountered, he had been in his room working around the clock on something. "I don't know what it is," she said. "All I know is he sits at his computer typing like crazy basically for the entire night. Like, I don't think he sleeps. It's bananas. Whenever I, you know, visit him, that's what he's doing. I come into his room, he types. I undress, he's *still typing.* Then he gets up, bends me over the bed, fucks me, comes, zips up his pants, and before I'm dressed and cleaned up, he'll be back at his fucking desk. It's so humiliating."

"Wow," Lila said, but her mind wasn't on Sam's sorrow—it was on this new piece of information. What on earth was Jack working on?

"So today, I decide to try to talk to him. Like, I'm not a sex doll, right? I'm an actual human being. So I ask him what he's typing all the time. He tells me I won't understand. Nice, right? Like I'm too dumb to figure out what the great Jack Warren is working on. But I press him. I tell him I want to know. He says I'm spoiling the mood. So I stop pushing him. Things progress. I'm down on my knees in front of him doing you know what . . ." Sam gave Lila a knowing look, to which Lila nodded in response. "Then he says to me, and you won't believe this . . . he says . . . Christ, I don't even think I can say it . . . he said, 'You know the best thing about having my dick in your mouth? You can't ask any questions.' Can you believe it? He's lucky I didn't bite the thing off."

Lila didn't say anything. All she could think of was, This is the man my sister loves? This is the man who is about to ruin her life? The more she heard about Jack, the more she believed he deserved to die. Who *wouldn't* want to kill that son of a bitch?

But, as she promised Teddy, she couldn't let her feelings get in the way of her investigation. She needed to stay clearheaded. And what she really needed, more than anything, was to get onto Jack's computer.

Lucky for her, Lila's chance to gain unfettered access to Jack's room came a few hours later, when, on the voyage back to Miami, Jack got the call he'd been waiting for: the golden phallus had finally been recovered. One of the teams of deep-sea explorers he'd contracted to locate Poe's discarded work of art had just hauled it onto their ship and were about an hour away from *The Rising Tide*. Soon the two ships would meet in the middle of the Caribbean Sea, and Jack could get his treasure back. Lila decided that while Jack was overseeing the transfer and settling up the small king's ransom he'd promised to the divers, she'd be in his room, making a complete copy of his hard drive.

CHAPTER 21

LILA WALKED INTO the shaded elegance of Jack's stateroom and quickly headed toward the giant mahogany desk in the corner. She knew this was a risky move, but it was her only chance. She had to get a copy of Jack's hard drive, and she had to get it now.

Just seconds ago, she'd slipped away from the guests and crew who had gathered together on the main deck to watch as a giant crane from a rusty old ship transferred Poe's golden phallus to *The Rising Tide*. She'd only have a precious couple of minutes before this tender homecoming party disbanded. So she had to be fast.

She grabbed Jack's laptop from the middle drawer of the desk. Her heart pounding, she inserted her thumb drive and began downloading. It would only take a minute—but, it turned out, that wasn't long enough.

To Lila's horror, the door to Jack's room opened without any chance for her to hide. She flipped around so that her body was concealing the laptop. But she knew it was hopeless. Any chance of saving her sister was falling to pieces before her eyes . . .

And then Sam walked in.

Seeing Lila must have shocked Sam, because she let out a bloodcurdling scream that would have sent *someone* running in their direction if everyone else on the yacht hadn't been watching the statue transfer at that very moment.

"Holy fuck!" Sam panted as she shut the door behind her. "You scared the shit out of me!"

"What are you doing here?" Lila asked. She knew perfectly well what Sam was doing, or about to do, in Jack's room, but she was buying time until the downloading had been completed.

"I came to see Jack," Sam said with no hint of embarrassment in her voice. "Did you come for the same thing?" she added, eyeing Lila suspiciously.

"Of course not. Sam, you know I would never do that to you. No, Slaughterhouse asked me to come put Jack's laptop away. She said she forgot to put it back where it belonged," Lila explained as she deftly removed the drive and turned to reveal the open laptop sitting on Jack's desk. "See?" she said as she slid the laptop back into the drawer.

Sam was clearly too busy worrying that Lila was also sleeping with Jack to give a thought to the fact that she'd just caught Lila with his computer. Talk about a close call.

"Dinner's soon, huh?" Lila said as she turned to leave. "Guess I'll see you up there?"

"Yeah, see you later," Sam replied.

Just as Lila was shutting Jack's door behind her, she saw Sam begin to remove her clothes.

LILA HAD TO wait until all the day's duties were done to examine what, exactly, she'd copied from Jack's computer. Once she and Sam had retired to their cabin and Sam's breathing fell into the even rhythm of sleep, Lila was able to dig in.

For the first hour or so going through Jack's data, she found nothing. But she knew to keep digging. After all Sam said that Jack was constantly working on something. It had to be buried in the files somewhere. As Lila clicked around the travel itineraries and updates from Kingston S. Duxbury about his new catamaran, she started to worry that she'd come to a dead end.

But then, Lila found a curious file labeled *Nautilus*. Maybe, she hoped, this was it. But the moment she opened it up and saw screen after screen of Java source code, her heart sank. It might as well have been Greek. If this was what Jack had been tirelessly working on night after night, she didn't have the tools to decipher it. She went online to see if she could translate it herself, but after an hour of moving from the code to the encoder, she hadn't made it past the first line.

She couldn't shake that feeling that this was important, that somewhere in this code lay a clue that could help her solve the case. If Sam was right, and Jack had been devoting all his spare time to working on this piece of source code, it was essential that she at least have some idea of what it was.

What she needed was a brilliant mind, someone who could shed some light on what this endless stream of code actually meant. She knew plenty of hackers from her days as a detective, but they weren't right for this. Jack Warren was the most revolutionary intelligence working in tech today. Whoever could decipher this code needed to be able to match wits with him. What Lila needed was someone of unquestionable genius, and someone she could trust absolutely.

The problem was, she only knew one trustworthy genius: Teddy Hawkins.

If only she could ask Teddy, then all her problems would be solved. Wait, she thought. Teddy! Why not?

She wasn't even taking the idea half-seriously when she put his name into a search engine and discovered that, in 2008, Teddy was running a small tech consulting firm in Miami, where *The Rising Tide* was set to dock in just a few short hours. But the more she turned the idea around in her mind, the more she thought it was the perfect solution to her problem. All she needed to do was find some excuse to get off the boat, and then she'd stop by his office.

Lila knew that future Teddy wouldn't just say this was a risky and dangerous idea. He'd say it was bat shit insane. She'd met Teddy in the past once before, and future Teddy had insisted that she never let it happen again. But it hadn't hindered her investigation back then and it certainly hadn't changed the present day, so why would it be different this time?

As she clicked through the indecipherable code she tried to think of any possible way to tackle this without Teddy. But no better idea came to her.

Lila decided that she wouldn't tell Teddy who she was, and she certainly wouldn't tell him where the code had come from. If she kept their encounter short and vague, what harm could she possibly do? She knew it was a plan that was a little more fraught with danger than she would've liked, but so was traveling back in time.

AT ONE O'CLOCK the next day, Lila knocked on young Teddy Hawkins's office door. There were butterflies in her stomach, and the hand that clutched the thumb drive was slightly damp with perspiration. At least it had been easy to get there. She hadn't even had to sneak off the boat. It was September 8, the day Ava was set to board the yacht, and just two days away from Jack's birthday, leaving countless things to prepare before they set sail again later that evening. Which meant Edna Slaughter was running around on the verge of a nervous breakdown, shouting more orders than a deranged drill sergeant.

Lila had come up with a perfect excuse to leave the boat by volunteering to go to the Bal Harbour Shops to pick up a few things Elise had ordered. Even in the middle of the ocean, it seemed that Elise Warren could find multiple ways to spend obscene amounts of money. But before heading to the mall, Lila was swinging by Teddy's office.

When the taxi dropped her off at the location she'd written down, she assumed there'd been a mistake.

"Wait here," she told the driver as she slowly walked up to a run-down Cuban sandwich shop near the corner of Biscayne Boulevard and NE Twenty-ninth Street. It was the type of mom-and-pop operation where the old signs above the door and in the window were crudely hand-painted. Then Lila noticed, around the back of the sandwich shop, there was a blue door with a laser-engraved plaque that read ARGONAUT ENTERPRISES. After waving the taxi driver away, she went back to the door, pushed the bell, and was immediately buzzed in.

Lila climbed up a steep flight of stairs, covered in stained, gray industrial carpet, toward Teddy's office. She almost couldn't believe that Teddy Hawkins, the aesthete, the billionaire genius whom she knew so well, had started out in a shit hole like this.

Before she reached the top of the stairs, the door opened— and Teddy stood there looking at her. Lila was surprised to feel her heart leap, her pulse quicken, and an irrepressible smile break out at the sight of him. Only days ago, she'd been in his presence. But now here he was, ten years younger, standing in his dingy office with a puzzled look on his face. He had a boyish roundness to his cheeks and a brightness to his eyes that a decade's worth of struggles and disappointments had long since worn away.

"Nicky Collins," she said, reaching out to shake his hand. The feel of his skin on hers was like drinking a sip of water after a long thirst. Only at that very moment did Lila realize the toll that being undercover had taken on her; the accumulated strain that weeks of isolation and deception had caused. It was so nice, she thought, just to be with somebody she *knew*. Even if he didn't technically know her—yet.

"So," TEDDY SAID, keeping his eyes on the floor. "What brings you here today?" Young Teddy is shy, Lila realized with surprise.

"I've come across a strange file," she said, trying to contain her excitement at being in his presence again. She felt like she could finally exhale, that for the first time in weeks she wasn't completely on edge.

"What is it?" Teddy prompted.

"Actually," Lila admitted, "I was hoping *you* could tell *me*. I think it's code, but I'm not sure for what. I don't speak computer, so I need you to be my translator. And I'm happy to pay you handsomely for any insight you can give me." She tossed the thumb drive over to Teddy, who caught it. And then she pulled a ten-grand stack of hundred-dollar bills and threw it on the desk, too. The money arced into the air and landed with a satisfying thud. Teddy's eyes widened at the money, and he sat back in his chair with a stunned look on his face. Lila tried not to dwell on the strangeness of paying Teddy with money that his future self had given her.

She glanced around at the small, humble office, which was incredibly well organized. Always an obsessive reader, Teddy had a stack of books ranging in subject matter from Le Corbusier to Zen Buddhism. A postcard was taped to the wall over his spare and modern Eames desk. Lila recognized it.

"You like de Kooning?" she asked, pointing to the postcard, which showed an abstract painting made up of a jumble of wide and wild brushstrokes in peachy reds, sky blues, smeared whites, and jade greens.

"I love him. He's my favorite painter by far," Teddy said. He seemed pleased that she recognized the artist, but still confused about what this strange woman was doing in his office.

Lila couldn't help grinning. She knew something that at this very moment in time, Teddy could never imagine. Ten years from now he would own the very painting that was on that postcard taped to an otherwise bare wall. It would become the crown jewel of his art collection: a grand, seven-foot-wide Abstract Expressionist masterpiece that he purchased for $85 million. After he bought it at auction, he would confess to Lila that owning that painting was the realization of one of his lifelong dreams.

"Well," he said, plugging the device into his computer. "How'd you find me, exactly?"

Lila had known he would have lots of questions and had also known she wouldn't be able to answer any of them honestly. "Let's just say we've got a good friend in common."

"Who?" Teddy asked.

She crossed her arms over her chest and looked him directly in the eyes. "Listen, it's complicated and I don't have time to go into it. All I can tell you is that everything is aboveboard. So please, can you just take a look at this file and tell me what I've got here?"

After a moment of contemplative silence, Teddy nodded. "I'll be honest. You've got me pretty intrigued."

"The file is called 'Nautilus.'"

Lila stood behind Teddy as he clicked it open and scrolled through the text for a minute or two.

"Do you know what it is?"

"Just a minute," he said impatiently. Whatever was there on the screen seemed very interesting to Teddy. More time passed, and he was still hunched over his desk, mesmerized. Lila looked at her watch, horrified at the time. She should've been back at the boat by now, and she still had to drop by Neiman Marcus to pick up Elise's packages, then rush back to begin tackling her long list of chores in preparation for Jack's fiftieth birthday celebration.

"Listen," she said, after about almost ten minutes of silence had passed. "I don't mean to rush you, but I've got to go soon. Is there any way you can tell me what this is right now?"

Teddy pushed himself away from his desk and looked up at Lila, blinking himself back into the nondigital world. She couldn't help smiling at him once again.

"At first it seemed rather simple. This is the source code for all of Warren Software's applications translated into machine language. It's cool to see because this code is completely guarded—nobody outside the programmers at Warren has access to it. I feel like I'm in the land of Oz and someone let me peek behind the curtain."

"Okay," Lila said, trying to make sure she understood clearly. "So, these are instructions for how the software works?"

"Kind of. But not really. This is the program, but translated so that the computer can understand it. That's what machine language means. But there's something here that I've never seen before." He scrolled down and pointed to a bit of gibberish on the screen. Lila had no idea what she was looking at. "Right there," Teddy said. "That's very unusual. How'd you get this, anyway?"

Lila stayed silent.

"Fine. Not one for answering questions. I get it. I get it," Teddy said. He returned his attention to the computer screen. "At its most basic, this looks like a pretty standard software update."

"An update?"

"You know. Those annoying messages you get telling you to update your software? Well, that's what this is. Once this update is put out into the world, everyone who has any of Warren Software's programs on their computers will get a message telling them to install this newer version. But, still . . ." He kept clicking through the file, reading through the strange symbols on the screen. "I just don't quite know what I'm looking at. What I need to do is actually run this update on my computer, then I'll have a better idea about what this mysterious bit of code does. Do you have a couple minutes?"

Lila said she did. Teddy even suggested she go grab a Cubano downstairs while he installed the update. "I know it doesn't look like much, but they really are the best sandwiches in the city. Can you get me one, too?" he asked as he slid the top hundred-dollar bill off the stack that Lila gave him. "Hopefully they accept big bills," he added with a smile, handing her the money.

Five minutes later, Lila was back with two steaming sandwiches. Teddy told her that he was almost ready. They both sat hunched over the sandwiches that were balanced on their legs, Teddy at his desk chair and Lila on a rickety chair she pulled up next to him.

"Okay. I've got it all loaded in. Now I just have to run the update . . . here," he said as he pushed the return button on his keyboard.

Almost instantly the screen went pitch-black.

"What the . . ." Teddy said, tapping at his keys, but the computer was unresponsive.

Suddenly white vertical lines took over the screen, then the lines went horizontal. The computer began to whir noisily. "Fuck me!" Teddy said, banging on the keys. Then he tried to turn the computer off, but it was frozen.

"What?" Lila said, her mouth full of sandwich.

"Something is very, very wrong."

All the horizontal lines began to move into a kind of whirlpool, growing tighter and tighter, smaller and smaller, until they formed into something resembling a seashell in the center of the screen. Then, with a flicker, the seashell disappeared and the computer went black. The whirring stopped, leaving Teddy and Lila staring at a blank screen.

"What just happened?" Lila asked.

Teddy put the sandwich on his desk and jumped up out of his chair. He tried to turn his computer on, then off, then on again. But nothing happened. He held several keys down at once for more than a few seconds. Still unresponsive. Then he sat back in his chair, stunned.

"I'll tell you what just happened," he said. "Total data erasure."

"What?"

"Whatever that was just completely obliterated my hard drive." Lila looked at him, a bit confused. "To put it in simple terms, whatever was on that thumb drive of yours just murdered my computer."

"Oh my God! I'm sorry!" Lila exclaimed as she realized what that might mean for a man like Teddy. He probably had his whole life on that machine.

"Oh, no!" he said. "I'm fine. I've got all my stuff backed up in a million different ways. Trust me, I've learned that lesson the hard way. But now it makes sense. The code I didn't recognize must be what's responsible for frying the computer."

"Why would anyone want that?" Lila wondered aloud.

"I don't know. All I do know is this is an incredibly damaging bit of code you've got there," he said as he removed the thumb drive from his destroyed computer. "This could single-handedly wipe out all the data of everyone who has Warren software on their computers, which is, basically, everybody. So, let's do humanity a favor and . . ."

Without saying another word, Teddy put the thumb drive on the floor and stomped on it with the heel of his shoe until it was destroyed.

"Hey!" Lila said in protest.

"Sorry about that," Teddy said, with absolutely zero trace of regret in his voice. "But I really don't know you, and I don't want a stranger walking out of my door with something so dangerous in her pocket. Not worth the risk. But feel free to take back your money."

"No," Lila said. "It's fine. I didn't need it anyway. Keep the money. Use it to buy yourself a new computer."

"With this much, I can buy a lot more than that," Teddy replied.

Lila got up to go, but before she left, she turned back for one more look at her friend. "And, Teddy," she said before closing the door behind her, "see you very soon."

Just as she was about to rush down the stairs, Teddy called out after her. "Hey!"

She turned back to him. "What?"

He stood there awkwardly, not saying anything, shifting his weight from one foot to the other, as if he'd called after her without knowing what he planned to say.

"Teddy, I'm in a real rush," Lila said impatiently.

"Of course. Of course. It's only just . . . I was wondering if . . ."

His words were sputtering out of his mouth slowly, tripping him up. He paused. Then he took in a big, fortifying breath. "It's just, it's not every day that a beautiful woman walks into my office carrying a mysterious computer code like someone out of a spy movie. I think I've just had my mind blown. But not by that code, even though it's the most astounding technology I've ever seen. What's really mind-blowing is you. And I know I'd never forgive myself if I let you go without at least asking when I can see you again."

Lila felt her heart skip a beat as she looked at Teddy.

"We'll see each other again, I promise," Lila said.

"But how? I don't have any way to contact you."

"Trust me," Lila said. Then, on impulse, she ran up to him and kissed him lightly on the cheek. Before he could react, she turned down the stairs, and walked out of the building, leaving him standing there in a mild state of shock.

With a growing number of questions swirling around her mind, Lila hopped into a cab, heading first to the mall and then to the yacht. But all she could think about for the duration of the car ride was Teddy.

CHAPTER 22

Burdened with many oversize bags from Neiman Marcus and Saks Fifth Avenue, Lila trudged toward *The Rising Tide*. When she looked up, her breath caught in her throat.

A local TV reporter was, at that very moment, shooting the segment about the yacht that Lila had watched over and over again for ten years, because of Ava's brief appearance.

This meant that her sister was finally on board. Lila's feet flew under her as she began to run to the ship. But as she tried to board, she was waylaid by flurry of activity. Several women, all carrying large floral centerpieces, were walking up the gangway in front of Lila as the rest of the boat was swarmed with a cameraman, a TV producer, and the reporter, as well as the marina workers refueling the boat and deliverymen restocking its supplies.

As she pushed her way onto the main deck, Lila kept her eyes on the balcony where Ava made her appearance on the video. Lila heard the rapid click of a camera's shutter and turned to see a photographer taking hundreds of pictures of all the buzz. Then she noticed the TV camera was focused on her.

"Hi. I'm Christianne Gomez from 7News. We're here to do a piece on this *spectacular* yacht," the reporter said as she went to shake Lila's hand, which was impossible to do because of all the bags Lila was carrying. Instead, she awkwardly shook one of Lila's bent elbows. "Do you mind if I ask you some quick questions?"

Before Lila could answer, she heard Edna Slaughter call out from across the deck, "No, no. No, no! That's not necessary." Edna swiftly crossed the floor, with a tight smile on her face. Lila could tell that she was overwhelmed by the presence of so many strangers on the boat, and irritated that she had to pretend to be pleasant in front of the reporter.

"Yes, hello, Ms. Gomez. This here is Nicky Collins, one of the stewardesses," Edna said. "And she's running so very behind that I can't spare her right now. We've just got *soooo* much to do before the big soiree." Edna grabbed Lila's arm and squeezed it painfully. "Now, dear Nicky," Edna said, "please bring those bags up to the master suite. And then Chef Vatel needs you in the galley."

With a small nod of her head, Lila happily walked away from the reporter and her questions. She knew that at any moment Ava would make an appearance, and she didn't want to miss it.

And then she saw her—her arm, to be exact, reaching out toward the railing. Just seeing her sister's disembodied wrist was enough to make Lila let the heavy bags fall from her hands as she stood looking at the sister she hadn't seen for a decade.

Lila hurried to stand where Ava couldn't see her. Though her long dark hair was chopped into a bleached pixie cut, and yes, she was ten years older than her past self, it wouldn't be enough. These two sisters knew each other as well as they knew themselves. Lila understood that Ava would see beyond any disguise in an instant. It was crucial that Lila never interact with her.

Suddenly Ava turned, and Lila's heart broke. Her sister's beautiful face was looking sadly out to the ocean; she seemed lost in thought, unaware of her surroundings. Lila could tell from her swollen red eyes that she'd been crying.

Both sisters were natural-born tomboys, much happier in a T-shirt and jeans than a dress, but standing there on the yacht, Ava looked like she'd stepped out of the pages of *Vogue*. A blow dryer had straightened out any of the natural waves in her blond hair. Her face was artfully made up, her full lips painted, a sparkle of pink dusted across her cheekbones, and her eyes were rounded and highlighted dramatically with eye shadows and liners, though her tears were threatening to ruin it all.

Just as Lila had seen in the TV news video, Ava wore a floor-length, spaghetti-strap dress with a low back, which showed off her lean, tan body. A long gold chain sat at the nape of her swanlike neck and fell all the way to the middle of her back. Lila had never seen her sister look more beautiful, more fragile, and more miserable than at this very moment. More than anything, she wanted to run to her sister, grab her hand, and drag her as far away as their legs could carry them—away from this yacht, from Jack Warren, and from the dark world that surrounded him. But there were rules that Lila had promised to follow. For her sake and for her sister's, she knew she had to let the tragic events awaiting them unfold.

She was still staring up at the balcony where her sister was standing, when she saw Ben heading in her direction. She instantly straightened up and smiled at him, but his stone-faced expression went unchanged. It was almost as if he was looking right through her.

It had been a couple of days since he'd found her with the packages of cocaine, and during the entire time, Lila had been in a state of constant worry, terrified that he would rat her out. But nothing had come of it. She wasn't sure whether that little bit of good fortune was thanks to Captain Nash saving her ass or Ben keeping his mouth shut. From the look on Ben's face, it was safe to say he was still pretty angry.

"Hi, Ben," she chirped as she gathered up the shopping bags around her.

"Hey," he said coldly.

"Let me ask you a question," Lila said. "Have you ever seen that woman before?" She pointed to Ava, who just then turned around and stepped off the balcony. But not before Ben had gotten a good look at her.

"Nope. Can't say I have."

"Do you know who she is?"

"Not really. But I could make an educated guess," Ben said. "From the look of her, and the room she's stuck in, which is far away from the other cabins, I'd venture to say that she's Jack's flavor of the month."

"Flavor of the month?" Lila felt her stomach turn.

"Don't play dumb," Ben said with an exhausted shake of his head. "It insults both of us. Though I will say: even though I've seen Jack do a lot of cruel shit, bringing his mistress on board when his wife and kid are here is a new low, even for him."

"You can say that again," Lila said.

"Not like you can judge," Ben snapped.

"Please, Ben. It's not what you think. It's so much more complicated. I'm . . ." Lila trailed off.

"You're what?" Ben asked.

"I'm . . ." Shut up, she said to herself, forcing herself to stop talking. If she couldn't tell Ben the truth (and he wouldn't believe her even if she could), what was the point of continuing to lie to him? If he was going to make trouble for her, he would've done it already. But there was a wounded look in his eyes underneath the terse annoyance on the surface. She felt a pang of regret for getting them both in this situation.

"I'm sorry. That's it. I'm sorry that you feel misled. That's never what I wanted. But *you* kissed *me*," Lila said.

"You kissed me back," he said.

Lila's mind flashed to that moment in the hallway—the feel of his mouth on hers, the way he pressed her up against the door, the overwhelming, burning attraction she'd felt. Her desire suddenly reignited by the memory, she stood looking at him dumbly, not knowing what else to say.

"Fine," Ben said, dismissing her. "See you around."

"Yeah, see you," Lila said, though Ben was already out of earshot.

Before she could dwell any longer on the mess she'd made, her attention was pulled away by the sound of two people arguing. She walked toward the voices, climbing up to the second level, then along the side deck, closer to the balcony where she'd seen Ava.

"I want to go!" Lila heard her sister wail.

She heard the sound of Jack's voice, but he was quieter, more restrained than usual, so she couldn't clearly make out what he was saying. Lila thought she'd have better luck if she listened to the argument from outside her sister's door. She put Elise's shopping bags down and dashed inside the yacht, up the spiral staircase one level to where her sister was stashed. Then she tiptoed down the hallway toward her sister's voice.

"Why are they here?" she heard her sister cry through the door. "I thought it was just going to be us?"

Lila grew frustrated. Even though she was closer, all she could hear of Jack's side of the conversation were some incomprehensible mumbles. Then it was quiet for a moment until, suddenly, something smashed against a wall, violently ending the brief silence. Her sister let out a spine-chilling scream.

The door swung open, and Jack stormed out. He was so angry that he didn't even seem to notice or care that Lila was standing right at the door. She could hear his slightly labored breathing, and his always carefully arranged hair was now disheveled.

Jack rushed down the hall, passing Thiago and Esperanza, who were strolling arm in arm toward Lila. The sound of Ava's frantic weeping could be heard well beyond the closed cabin door.

As soon as Thiago and Esperanza went past, Lila heard Thiago whisper to his wife, "If that man keeps this up, he'll soon end up dead."

Lila's heart almost stopped. Did Thiago simply mean that any man who brought his mistress on a yacht with his wife and his daughter was playing fast and loose? Or was there more to it than that?

She watched the couple walk by without acknowledging her. She knew she'd have to pay closer attention to Thiago Campos. But not at that very moment. Right now the sound of her sister crying made it impossible to leave. Hearing Ava's misery caused a small blossom of hatred to bloom in the pit of Lila's stomach. She detested Jack Warren for making her gentle and loving sister so inconsolable.

But more than anything, she was furious with herself. She'd had ten years of preparation, two weeks with full access to everyone aboard Jack's yacht, and she prided herself on being a good detective. Yet, despite having every advantage—despite *traveling back in time*—she knew even less than she'd known when she started. At least before she traveled back to 2008, she'd thought she knew who the murderer was. But now all of her assuredness was gone. She'd become so lost in the case that everyone seemed like a suspect.

Her sister's wailing died down, and there was silence. The hallway was empty, so Lila pressed her ear against Ava's door. She heard her sister's footsteps and then the sound of water as the shower was turned on.

She sighed. She couldn't afford to loiter at that spot any longer. There was too much to be done. So she gathered up Elise's purchases and headed for the master suite. But a fist of rage squeezed at Lila's heart as she walked away from Ava, devastated that she had so little to show for all her effort.

Lila knocked on the door to the master suite and, hearing nothing, quietly entered. The blinds were closed and the lights were off, making it difficult to see. She flipped the light switch on and nearly jumped out of her skin when she saw Elise sitting at her vanity in front of a large mirror.

"Mrs. Warren, I—I'm so sorry. I didn't know you were here," Lila stammered.

Elise had her head in her hand and a half-full martini glass at her elbow. The sickly-sweet smell of alcohol coming out of Elise's pores mixed in the air with her Hermès perfume. Elise didn't move or speak.

The countertop of her vanity was littered with plastic pill bottles, silver and gold makeup compacts, and expensive creams and elixirs in frosted-glass bottles promising to stave off old age. And it all seemed to be working on Elise, who sat there dripping with elegant misery in a boned silk bustier with a matching slip, her hair pinned up, her makeup perfectly applied. A strapless Valentino was laid out for her on the bed.

"Do you need any assistance with your dress, ma'am?" Lila asked cautiously.

"No need. I'll be dining in my room tonight. Be sure to let Edna know." Her voice was raw and weary.

"Yes, ma'am," Lila said with a small nod. Then she quickly emptied the shopping bags of their many treasures: the Stella McCartney blouse, the Balmain dress, the Chloé purse. She unwrapped each item that was carefully encased in tissue and set it in the closet, next to all the other items that had been purchased in hopes of somehow numbing this woman's profound pain.

Once again, Lila felt the briefest flicker of pity toward Elise Warren. After all, if Jack could reduce Lila's very own, desperately adored sister to a screaming, glass-shattering mess, then maybe Elise's twisted soul was Jack's doing.

"Have you seen her?" Elise asked, lifting her head from her hand and taking a big sip of her martini.

"Seen who, ma'am?" Lila asked as she lifted a pair of red patent-leather Louis Vuitton heels out of their shoe box.

Elise glared at Lila in the mirror. "You *know* who. My husband's mistress."

"Oh," Lila said as she turned her back toward Elise and placed the shoes in her walk-in closet.

"Don't bother saying anything, you dumb little mouse. I know she's here. I saw her myself."

"There *is* a young lady who has joined the guests on the yacht, ma'am, but that's all I know."

"What you know couldn't fill a thimble," Elise said as she secured a pair of diamond-and-amethyst earrings to her ears. Lila noticed a slight tremor in her hands as she opened a small gold-and-opal pillbox and put two round blue pills on her tongue. "What I don't know is why my husband needs to rub my nose in his shit all the time. Of course, the real question is why am I still here waiting to eat it up? Perhaps I'll just go rub some of my shit in *his* face."

Elise stood up from her seat at her vanity, but she was very shaky. Her knees buckled, causing her to lose her balance. She grabbed on to the wall so as not to fall to the floor. Lila rushed to steady her, but Elise swatted her away. "Don't *touch* me," she hissed as she collapsed into the chair. "On second thought, perhaps I will go down, just a little later." She picked up a tube of lipstick and began to reapply the bright red color to her mouth. "Now make yourself useful and get me another drink."

Fifteen minutes later, Lila returned with a fresh martini. But Elise Warren had already left, presumably in the Valentino dress that was no longer spread out on the bed. Lila stood by the cluttered vanity, a silver tray in her hand, watching the martini perspire and wondering what she should do. There was no point in tracking Elise down on this giant boat. By then the drink would be too warm, plus she'd probably forgotten she asked for one anyway.

Lila let out a beleaguered sigh, grabbed the drink, and took a large gulp. The sensation of the ice-cold alcohol sliding down her throat was intensely pleasurable. Just as she was about to take another sip, Ben walked out of Elise's bathroom.

A small yelp of surprise popped out of Lila's mouth when she saw him.

"What are you doing here?" they said simultaneously. Lila, caught drinking in the master suite, and Ben, caught doing God knows what in the master bathroom. Both were understandably edgy.

"I was just bringing Mrs. Warren a drink," Lila said quickly, stumbling a bit on her words.

"But you decided to drink it yourself?" Ben asked, with a curious smile on his face.

"She wasn't here. And so I just thought, 'To hell with it.'"

Lila paused, shaking off the humiliation she felt, as if she'd been caught in the act of committing a crime, and frowned. "Wait, what are you doing here?"

Without missing a beat, Ben said, "I was looking for you. Sam said you were on your way here."

Lila was confused. "But I didn't see Sam."

Before she could say another word, Ben moved quickly toward her, until he stood a few inches away. Then he reached out and gripped her waist. "I wanted to tell you I was sorry. May I?" he asked, nodding to the drink Lila held between them.

She shrugged. "Sure." He picked up the martini, took a small sip, and handed it back to Lila, who finished it off. Then he set the empty glass and the silver tray on Elise's vanity, causing a clatter as a couple of lipsticks fell to the floor.

"Sorry for what?" Lila asked.

"What?" Ben was distracted.

"You said you were sorry."

"Right, of course. I wanted to apologize for judging you. For pushing you away."

Lila knew what was happening: she'd caught Ben red-handed, doing something illicit, and now he was trying to sweet-talk his way out of it. But she wouldn't call him on anything. He'd caught her transporting drugs and using a false identity. She knew it was better to have him on her side than against her.

"I'm sorry, too," she said. Although the only thing she was sorry for was getting caught.

Ben swept his fingers lightly down her cheek and over her lips. "Christ, you're so gorgeous," he murmured, as if Lila's beauty caused him physical pain. He leaned in and kissed her softly on the mouth. Lila closed her eyes, seeing flashes of white light dance around the darkness. She grabbed him, pulling him close, kissing him deeply.

But then she shook herself out of this momentary madness, realizing she was still in Elise Warren's room. "Wait, we can't be here. What if she comes back?" Lila whispered.

"She won't," Ben said. "Trust me." He grabbed Lila around the waist, picking her up so that her feet were dangling inches above the floor, and carried her a couple of feet until her back was up against the door. With a resolute click, Lila heard the sound of Ben throwing the lock. She knew what was next.

And she was okay with it. She needed to make sure that Ben wouldn't use the information he had against her. And with every kiss, he was asking the same thing of her. They were negotiating a silent treaty of mutually assured destruction.

She was, in fact, more than okay with it, she realized as she wrapped one leg around his hips. Ben quickly unzipped his pants, and when Lila felt his hand push her underwear to the side, she made no effort to stop him. There was no denying it. She *wanted* him, with an all-consuming ferocity. And as she felt him move inside of her, she clung to him, pressing her body into his with an unrelenting hunger, wanting only to feel him go even deeper so that she would feel nothing else but him.

She needed, for just a small stretch of time, to escape the pain of the day, to erase the sounds of her sister's tears, to turn off the steady stream of questions without answers. She needed, with every pulse of pure pleasure she felt as Ben fucked her against the door, to feel a moment of release before returning to the sorrow.

CHAPTER 23

"HAPPY BIRTHDAY, DADDY."

Josie threw her arms around Jack's neck and held him close for a few seconds longer than the billionaire wanted. Lila watched him uncomfortably wriggle his way out of his daughter's overzealous embrace. "Thank you, dear," he said, not looking her in the eye.

September 10, 2008, the day Lila had been waiting for, was finally upon her. It was Jack Warren's fiftieth birthday—the day of his death. The guests were in the middle of breakfast, and despite the joyous occasion, tensions never seemed higher. But Lila could barely breathe as she walked around the dining room, pouring juice and serving eggs. Everything came down to this one day, and everyone around the table was still a suspect.

The most suspicious one of all, Elise Warren, was sitting at the opposite end of the table from Jack. She spoke to no one and barely moved. A small bowl of nonfat yogurt sat untouched in front of her. Her face looked as miserable as a face that had been frozen and plumped by Botox and Restylane injections could look. Lila didn't know if Elise had confronted Jack about Ava's presence aboard the ship, but the ugliness of the whole thing, unspoken or not, sat there like a giant turd between them.

"Happy birthday, and cheers to you, Jack," Paul Mason said. Even though his voice sounded light, his face was unsmiling. After the news of Jack's decision to move all of his company's manufacturing back to the USA broke, the company's stock had plummeted 18 percent in one day of trading. That left Warren Software without the necessary capital to buy Peregrine. The deal that Jack had promised to his old friend Paul was dead in the water, which meant that Paul Mason wasn't going to get the tens of millions of dollars' worth of banking fees he'd been anticipating. He was like a dog who'd been doing tricks for treats. Now that the treats were gone, he wasn't going to be a good boy anymore. That was evident.

Right before breakfast, Lila had heard him on the phone, asking his secretary to book a private plane back to New York for the following day. "I've wasted enough time bending over for the wrong fella," he had said, loud enough for anyone to hear.

"Jack," Seth Liss said, standing up, his large belly encased in a garish Hawaiian shirt, white sunscreen making his face look ghoulish, "I wish you all the best on this momentous occasion." Seth had a wide smile across his face. Jack looked at him warily.

"What are you smiling about?" Jack said.

"Can't I celebrate my good friend's birthday? I'm here with a bunch of fine folks in a beautiful setting. How can I not smile?" Everyone around the table regarded Seth with confusion. He'd spent the entire trip in a foul mood, but now he seemed cheerful. Lila wondered if this was the killer taking delight in toasting his soon-to-be-vanquished enemy.

"Happy birthday, Jack," Senator Clarence Baines said. He stood up, and so did his wife, Charity, who was wearing a stars-

and-stripes shift dress. They both lifted their juice glasses to Jack. Even though they were on a boat in the middle of the sea, neither Clarence nor Charity's hair moved in the ample ocean breeze. "We toast you, Jack. It's patriots such as yourself that make America the exceptional nation it is. Charity here and I are honored to be your guests on such a special occasion. We want to thank you for your kindness and your generosity. When people ask me why I've spent my life fighting like a dog, standing up for my beliefs every day on the Senate floor, I tell them that I'm fighting for my country's future. I'm fighting so that men like you, Jack, can have all the freedom you need to achieve your dreams. If men like you fail, we all fail."

Clarence's voice was full of emotion and power. He was clearly more moved by his own words than anyone else was around the table. Jack looked at him with dull eyes and a slack face. Now that the kibosh had been put on the Peregrine acquisition, the senator was no longer of any use to Jack. But Clarence still needed Jack's money and his connections to wealthy donors, so the balance of power between them had been seriously disrupted. And they both knew it.

Clarence, not sensing that people had stopped listening, continued. "History has shown us that if you have a government that supports risk takers and celebrates achievement, and says go out there and do whatever you can, that is what makes us prosperous—"

Thiago jumped up in the middle of Clarence's speech. "Yes," he said, talking over him. "Yes. Thank you, Senator, for your inspiring words."

"You can say that again," Daniel Poe scoffed. Lila thought he rolled his eyes, but it was difficult to be sure because of the mirrored sunglasses he was wearing. He stood in his usual spot away from the table by the guardrail, where he was enjoying a typical breakfast of hand-rolled cigarettes and a beer shandy to wash down the orange Adderall capsules he kept popping.

The senator, not used to being so rudely interrupted, slumped back in his chair. His wife gave him a consoling pat on his arm.

"Jack, you and I met when we were just boys, both outsiders in a place where being an insider was the only way to succeed." A nostalgic look fell over Thiago's face as he recalled the past. "You were a tough kid back then. As tough as you are now. But then you had brains and nothing else. And I was a foreigner, made to feel like an outcast because of who my father was." A flicker of disgust danced across Thiago's face, which he quickly replaced with a smile. "But look at us now, here, today. Harvard begs us for endowments. Our old classmates envy us, dropping our names to elevate themselves. We have won, Jack, you and I. We have won. So, cheers to you. And happy birthday!"

Everyone around the table held up their glasses to Jack, who sat there glumly.

"*Have* I won, Thiago?" Jack said as his eyes swept around the table at all the faces looking at him.

"What do you mean?" Thiago asked as he sat back down in his chair.

"It's just, on days like today, a man takes stock of his life. And I've got to say, I don't like what I see. If I've won the war, then why do I always feel like I'm fighting? I have to battle with my shareholders and my board. My own CFO is my rival," Jack said, pointing to Liss, who gave him a curt nod. "My wife can't stand me. And then I got this in the mail yesterday when we were docked in Miami." He whipped a manila envelope down the table, where it hit Josie on the cheek.

"Ow, Dad!" she exclaimed, rubbing the thin red mark on

her face. The moment she looked at the envelope, the color drained from her face. "This is Asher's handwriting," she said.

"Sure is," Jack said, his voice bitter. Lila knew what was coming. The hundreds of pictures and hours of videos that Asher had taken of Josie were finally coming to light.

"What is it?" Josie asked tentatively.

"Like you don't know," Jack said.

"I *don't* know, Daddy. Tell me." Josie's eyes were wide with fear.

"Well, my dear daughter, your beloved knight in shining armor Asher sent me a thumb drive with a few choice images of you two together. And let me say, I'd give anything to erase those pictures from my mind. My own daughter, posed like a whore." A glistening of tears came to Jack's eyes but he quickly blinked them back. He was not a man who'd let anyone see him cry.

"No!" Josie screamed, covering her face with her hands.

"There was a video, too. I only saw one second of it. The whole thing is sickening."

Josie let out a loud, soul-wrenching groan.

"He hinted that there's a lot more where that came from," Jack said.

"I'm sorry, Daddy. I'm so sorry."

"Some kind of birthday present, huh? Getting tied up? Is that what you learned at all the expensive private schools and summer camps we sent you to? Is this how you repay us for giving you everything?"

"Jack, please," Elise said. "We can discuss this privately."

"Why? What's the point?" Jack asked. "Soon enough the whole world will see every inch of my little baby girl. Why should I hide it from our closest friends?"

"What does he want, Jack?" Paul Mason said, in a tone that

was all business. At this point Josie was loudly weeping, her head on the table, her hands pressed against her ears.

"A million bucks," Jack said.

Clarence Baines gasped at the sum. "Outrageous! That's extortion, Jack. Plain and simple. We should notify the police at once."

Lila saw Daniel Poe smiling grandly in the corner, loving every second of this debased scene. Lucky for him, no one else seemed to take note of his obvious glee.

"You know what I think? I think this little bitch is in on it," Jack spat, jabbing his finger in Josie's direction. "I think the two of them are extorting the old man for a million dollars. But I won't give a goddamn penny." He leaped up from his chair, lunging toward Josie. "You hear me! You tell Asher that he won't get anything from me. You think I care if the world sees you for the whore you are?"

Josie began to convulse with tears. Her mother rushed to her side, wrapping her arms around her daughter. "How dare you, Jack?" Elise said slowly, the hatred in her voice undeniable. She spoke every word through clenched teeth. "You have no right to pass judgment on her or on anyone." She guided her daughter up out of the chair. "Let's go, honey. Mommy will take care of this."

"Want to know how Mommy takes care of things?" Jack called out after them as he sat back down at the head of the table. "With a sedative and a Scotch. So, good luck counting on her!"

After Josie and Elise left, the others sat in a stunned silence.

Lila stood by the door observing everyone. She had suspected Josie of being the killer, but then crossed her off her list once she returned to the yacht after her arrest. But now things had changed dramatically yet again. Josie had been humiliated and abandoned—this time by her father, who had no compunction about calling his only child a no-good whore.

"See," Jack said to Thiago, an artificial calm overtaking his voice. "I wouldn't say I've won anything. And you know what?" He got up and threw his napkin down onto his half-eaten breakfast. "I'm done fighting."

Once everyone was gone, Lila and Sam cleaned up the detritus from yet another fraught meal.

"Is it just me or are these the most dysfunctional people that've ever existed?" Sam wondered as she carefully stacked the gilded china plates on top of each other. "I mean, I thought my family was screwed up. But compared to the Warrens, my mom with a drinking problem and my brother with PTSD are like a total cakewalk."

"Listen," Lila said. "Have you seen the new woman who came on the boat in Miami?"

"The crazy one?" Sam said in a hushed tone as she raised her eyebrows into curious half circles. "Edna told me to ignore her. But it's strange, right? She's just, like, been in her room without any food or anything? And I think I've heard her crying."

"So have I," Lila said. She'd passed by the door obsessively all day yesterday, many times hearing her sister weeping or sniffling. She was even more worried when she didn't hear anything. And she felt guilty for not being able to help Ava, for what happened yesterday afternoon with Ben, and for feeling totally lost in a case that had slipped out of her grasp . . . if she ever had a hold on it in the first place.

"I did see Jack go in and out of the room a bunch of times while I was vacuuming the hallway, so I guess she's his latest concubine. Good luck to her," Sam said sarcastically.

"Does that mean you and Jack are done?"

"Are you kidding? He won't leave me alone. Once men get a taste of me, it's over." Sam suggestively shook her hips as she pushed the dining room chairs back under the table. "It's a blessing and a curse. But that witch Edna is always up my ass, so it's been impossible to slip away. Besides, last night his bed was empty. He was probably breaking in his newest acquisition."

That meant Jack must have spent the night in Ava's bed. The thought of it absolutely sickened Lila. How could her sister fall for such a toxic asshole? And how could Ava expect the affair to end in anything but disaster?

By the time Sam and Lila were done cleaning up breakfast, it was ten o'clock. Lila didn't have much time. Despite the horrific mood of everyone on the boat—except for Daniel Poe, who seemed to be reveling in the Grand Guignol theatrics of the Warren family—Jack's birthday dinner was still happening. It was just eight hours away. And seven hours after that, four shots would ring out as someone shot Jack Warren.

However, after Jack's death, no one on the yacht would be able to confirm the exact time that Jack was murdered, or the precise location of the boat. Apparently Paul found the blood on the deck sometime around 1:00 A.M. He asked Nash to radio for help shortly thereafter. That meant Lila had about an hour-long window during which the murder might happen. But she had the advantage of knowing exactly where the murder would take place.

She'd assumed she would've been further along in solving the case by now. But never in her wildest dreams did she think that *so* many people could have *so* many reasons to want Jack Warren dead. Since she still wasn't sure who was going to kill Jack, and she'd be unable to tail all her suspects throughout the night, she needed to put a fail-safe plan in place. If it came down to it, she needed to watch the actual murder happen. So she headed to the exact spot where Jack would soon die, to make sure she'd be able to see his murder unfold when the time came.

As she walked up the exterior staircase to the rear of the second level, she saw Ben coming down. Despite her totally focused state of mind and her ever-shrinking window of time to catch a killer, she couldn't help feeling the pulse of desire deep within her. Just laying eyes on Ben made her mind flash to yesterday's encounter—his hands on her body, his weight against her, the memory of how good he felt inside her came crashing into her mind.

"Hey," he said, grabbing her around the waist and pulling her toward him. She let him do it. "I haven't been able to stop thinking about you since yesterday." He kissed her lightly on the lips as his hand gently traced the contours of her breast. Just as the other hand began to slide down her body, over her ass, and then up her inner thigh, they heard the sound of footsteps coming down the stairs and quickly pulled away from each other.

It was Edna, of course. It was always Edna.

The chief stewardess looked at the two of them and seemed to know instantly what they had been up to. "Nicky," she said sternly, "there's much to do before dinner tonight. And I won't warn you again."

"Ever get tired of being such a battle-ax, Edna?" Ben said, giving Lila a playful hip check. Lila didn't understand how Ben got away with giving Edna a hard time. It seemed like everyone else on the yacht feared her.

"That's right, Mr. Reynolds. Some of us have to actually work for a living. It must be quite confusing for you," Edna said as she pushed by Ben and Lila, her back stiff and her chin jutting haughtily out.

"I work for a living," he said with an exasperated tone. "I mean, no one can do what I do, just ask Nicky, here." Then he slipped his hand under Lila's skirt and up between her legs. She jumped away from his touch. As far as Lila was concerned, the moment was over.

"Nicky. No dillydallying," Edna yelled over her shoulder as she walked down the stairway.

Once the chief stewardess was out of sight, Ben grabbed Lila. "She's gone," he whispered into her ear. But Lila wriggled out of his embrace impatiently.

"Not now," she said. "I've got to go." Without looking back, she dashed up the stairs, took a left at the side deck, and arrived at the very spot where Jack Warren soon would die.

She surveyed the area, as she had done thousands of times since she'd boarded *The Rising Tide*. It was a tricky spot. She looked at the sight lines. It would be impossible to lie in wait for the murderer on the deck; there was nowhere to stake out the place without being spotted. Her only possible vantage point was up in the captain's bridge. From there she'd be able to finally find out who killed Jack Warren.

Standing in the very spot that would soon be covered in Jack's blood, Lila went over her plan for that night yet again, staring absently at the Caribbean Sea. For all its beauty, she thought, the ocean was a brutal, dangerous place, filled with creatures preying upon one another just underneath that serene surface. And it was the same for all the people on this boat. Under the resplendent veneer, they were all ravenous sharks, ready to devour anyone foolish enough to get too close.

CHAPTER 24

JACK'S PARTY WAS a complete success, though soon enough, no one would remember it in the shadow of his death. The scandals, betrayals, and subterfuge that had poisoned the mood over breakfast seemed to float away on the salty Caribbean winds as everyone sat down to dinner. The food came out course after perfect course. Even Lila had to marvel at the exquisiteness of the meal she was serving. Chef Vatel had really outdone himself. But only he would later have any recollection of what was served.

He'd planned the menu for months, refining each dish until it was flawless: a single oyster, fried perfectly, resting atop a circle of brioche; Patería de Sousa's legendary foie gras brightened with a splash of aged balsamic vinegar; sea-urchin pasta with a dollop of Russian caviar; risotto with white truffles flown in from Italy; Japanese *wagyu* beef cheeks slowly braised for hours in a hearty Barolo, all perfectly paired with priceless glasses of wine.

Even the table was a work of art. Candles encased in hand-blown hurricane lamps cast a sumptuous amber glow. The flower arrangements dotting the table were gorgeous, anarchic compositions that looked as if they'd been ripped out of an eighteenth-century Dutch still-life. Branches of wild honey-suckle were intertwined with orchids the deep yellow of egg yolks. The papery skins of the red poppies interspersed through-out the bouquets caught the candlelight, creating a fiery flicker on the edges of the night.

But all Lila could think about were the seconds counting down to Jack Warren's murder. She watched Jack carefully. He looked like he was the happiest man on the planet. Little did he know, with each exquisite bite, how quickly he was moving toward his own death.

His guests were also enjoying themselves. Quick to laugh, quick to groan with pleasure over the food, the wine, the ocean rolling beneath them. The only rival to the beauty of the sea was the magnificence of everyone's clothes. The women were all breathtaking in ornate gowns and perfectly coiffed hair. Josie was wearing a clingy, iridescent silver gown with her hair slicked back into a high ponytail and a thin string of diamonds hanging from each ear. There was something very powerful in her countenance that night as she breezed around the deck with a glass of champagne in hand. It was as if that morning's tears and humiliation had only left her stronger and bolder. Perhaps she found power in having nothing left to lose.

Wearing a cream-colored, one-shoulder silk sheath that hugged her thin, toned body, Elise Warren looked like a goddess. Her delicate wrists were wrapped with white-gold-and-diamond bracelets and her dark brown hair was elegantly drawn back into a chignon at the nape of her swanlike neck. Gone was the speech slurred with pills and alcohol, gone was the snarl and the snap of her biting words and withering glares. Now she was like an ice queen, dolled up in white and diamonds, impervious and grand.

Charity Baines wore a strapless, floor-length Valentino gown in eye-popping Republican red. Her hair was teased into a stiff golden helmet that swept high up off her chemically frozen forehead. The diamonds in her Bulgari necklace sparkled magnificently in the candlelight.

Thiago and Esperanza were legendary among the international glitterati for their outstanding fashion sense, and they didn't disappoint tonight. He wore a black velvet tuxedo, white V-neck T-shirt, and black Wayfarer sunglasses, despite the darkness of the night. Esperanza was the yin to Thiago's yang, wearing a stark white, raw silk gown that was so ethereal it seemed like something an angel would wear. A thin gold chain around her neck was all that held the dress up. Every time the wind blew, the thin fabric pressed against Esperanza's body, blowing back her long, black hair. She looked angelic, pure, effortlessly beautiful.

Jack wore a custom-made Armani tuxedo, looking every inch the successful billionaire he was. Senator Baines wore the same silk pocket square he'd worn to George W. Bush's 2004 inaugural ball, one of the most treasured nights of his life. And his hair was a sculptural masterpiece as unmoving as the Lincoln Memorial. Even Seth Liss, the man who seemed to wear his slovenliness with unwarranted pride, looked half decent. Sure, the cut of his suit wasn't what anyone would dream of calling fashionable, but for him it was quite grand.

But it was Daniel Poe who really stole the show. When he walked out, clean-shaven, wearing a perfectly tailored, slim-fit black tuxedo with a crisp white shirt and a long skinny tie the deep color of eggplant, everyone turned to look. Lila heard someone gasp. Paul Mason, ever the Brooks Brothers poster boy, broke into spontaneous applause.

Sam and Lila had been given strapless, black cocktail dresses and black stiletto heels to wear while working the party. Lila wasn't thrilled with the attire. Tonight was the night she'd be hunting down a killer, and doing it in a tight dress and high heels wasn't going to be easy.

Just as Lila had expected, her sister was not invited to the birthday party. But what Lila really didn't understand was why Ava was there in the first place. So far, it seemed like she hadn't even left her room. Was she there just as his hidden concubine? It struck Lila as wildly risky for a man as calculating as Jack. None of it made sense to Lila, but she'd been in the detective game long enough to know that the truth of a case always lay within the questions that seemed to have no answers. If she could unwrap the mystery of why her sister was actually on board, maybe she'd find out the truth about who killed Jack Warren.

Once the last course was served, the casual chatter that had enlivened the meal slowly petered out. Everyone seemed to be taking their cues from Jack, and he was being very quiet. But his silence wasn't seething, hard-hearted, or angry like it usually was. In fact, Lila thought, he seemed almost peaceful, which was not a word she'd ever associate with Jack Warren. He sat at the head of the table, a contented smile on his face, taking slow, appreciative bites of his caramelized white chocolate birthday torte.

After the delicate dessert plates were cleared away, Jack Warren said, "I know how busy you all are. And I'd like to thank you for taking the time to spend this very special day with me." He leaned to Sam and whispered, "Let's serve the champagne now, please."

Sam nodded and went over to the sideboard, where there were four bottles of champagne chilling in silver buckets.

While Lila and Sam poured the honey-colored bubbly in freshly set crystal flutes, Jack spoke. "At the height of World War One, a German submarine sank a Swedish freighter that was transporting goods to the imperial court of Czar Nicholas the Second of Russia. For over eight decades that ship, with all its glorious bounty, rotted at the bottom of the sea. When the ship was found, two thousand bottles of champagne in pristine condition were recovered. The sea had aged them perfectly. This is the most prized bottle of champagne in the world, and we have four of these shipwrecked beauties with us now. Everyone, please, enjoy."

As he lifted up his glass, everyone followed his lead. After taking a long, meditative sip of the champagne, Jack continued. "Great men are often at war with themselves. And I think as much can be said of me. I have no regrets for how I've lived my own life. My only regret is that sometimes this war within me had casualties. Many casualties. Elise, my wife." He said her name softly, turning to face her. She put down her flute of champagne and matched the intensity of his gaze with her own. "There is no other creature on the planet as fierce and as vibrant as you. When I first met you, you were electric. And now, looking at you, you're more beautiful today than you've ever been. To you." He lifted up his glass of champagne and took a small sip. Then he turned to his daughter. "Josie, your free spirit, your hunger for life, and your tireless search for what is real have brought so much energy into my life and into your mother's life. I want you to always keep that part of you alive, no matter what. It's your magic."

"I love you, Daddy," Josie said as a couple of tears fell down her cheeks.

"I love you, too," Jack said with total sincerity. Lila couldn't fathom what was behind this transformation. And neither could anyone else.

"Cheers to you, Jack!" Clarence said.

After all the champagne bottles had been emptied and the party conversation seemed to run dry, Jack began to pace the main deck, like a tiger storming around his cage. He wanted some fresh entertainment, so he picked up his phone to call the captain. "Nash, listen, we're down on the main deck having a little birthday party for yours truly. What do you say that you throw the boat on cruise control and you and your crew come and join us. We've got the makings of a real party down here." He paused. "Okay. Great. See you down here soon."

The crew joined the gathering with alarming speed, and kicked things into high gear. It didn't take long before the so-phisticated soiree was transformed into an all-out debauched bacchanal. And once the drugs came out and the wine cellar was raided, people started to really let loose. Daniel Poe immediately disappeared with Nash, Mudge, Pedro, and Josie into the main deck's bathroom. Thiago blasted samba music while Esperanza began to dance with a very excited, yet clumsy Seth Liss. Paul Mason joined Captain Nash and the rest of the degenerates in the bathroom while Sam disappeared somewhere belowdecks. Everyone, it seemed, was getting into the spirit of things.

Except for Lila. As the party got more out of control, it became increasingly difficult to keep an eye on all the suspects. But, she remembered, she just had to make sure she knew where Jack was at all times. As long as he was in her sights, she was okay. And at that moment, everything was fine. Jack and Paul were smoking Montecristos with their eyes glued to Es-peranza's ass, which was undulating to the music as she yelled for her dancing partner, Liss, to "feel the rhythm in your hips."

Then Lila saw Ben. He was headed across the deck toward her, carrying two drinks, with a smile on his face and a little salsa shake to his hips. "Finally, everyone gets to have a little fun," he said as he put a drink in her hand. She just nodded, distracted. There was no chance in hell she was going to join in. This was the night she'd spent a decade obsessing over, and she couldn't afford to slip up for a *party*. She needed to be in control. First, she wanted to check in on Ava, to see if she was still holed away in her fortress of a guest suite.

"Hey, Nicky, loosen up. It's a party after all," Ben said. Lila gave him a weak smile. He slid his hand across her bare shoulders and then down her arm. He leaned toward her to whisper into her ear. Before he could speak, though, a huge ruckus erupted from across the room as Daniel, Nash, Mudge, and Pedro burst onto the main deck with red noses and wild eyes. Daniel was dancing crazily, a chaos of spasmodic limbs in a fury of movement, while the others howled with laughter. It was pretty clear that they'd just sucked back an impossible amount of cocaine.

With a lit Roman candle in his hand, Pedro leaned over the railing while Mudge held on to his feet. The firework flared and then shot out of his hand, whizzing up into the starry sky, where it loudly exploded in a shower of silver rain. Daniel and Nash cheered wildly. Daniel handed Pedro another ignited firework.

As she turned her attention from the sky to the spot where Jack had just been standing, Lila's heart dropped. "Shit!" she said. He was gone. She frantically scanned the main deck. There was no sign of him except for his cigar, slowly burning in the heavy crystal ashtray.

"What?" Ben said. "Nicky, what's wrong?"

"It's nothing," she lied, putting her drink down. "But I've got to go."

"No," he said, wrapping his arms around her and pulling her close. "You've got to stay. And then maybe later we can—"

"Please, Ben. No!" She responded so emphatically that he immediately let her go. She rushed away from him without looking back. Her heart was racing. She had no idea where on this vast and many-roomed yacht Jack Warren had gone.

Her first stop was the scene of his murder. She ran up to the second level of the yacht, praying with every quick step of her feet that he was still alive. A wave of relief washed over her as she arrived and saw there was no blood and no gun. Jack's murder was still in the future.

Moving as quickly as she could, she ran inside the boat, headed toward Ava's cabin. She'd go see if her sister was still safe and sound. A firecracker exploded in the sky, making Lila almost jump out of her skin. She could hear the music and the cheering of the party twenty feet below her. As she got to the hallway, she noticed that the door to Ava's room, which had been closed since her sister's arrival, was now ajar.

Keeping her back to the hallway wall, she slid down to the room, stopping once her shoulder was flush with the doorjamb. She peeked inside. The door to the balcony was wide open, the bed linens had been ripped off the bed, clothes were all over the floor. And the room was empty.

"Ava?" Lila said, trying to mask her voice so her sister couldn't recognize it. There was no answer. "Ava?" Still silence, so Lila carefully entered. She checked the balcony, the closets, and the en suite bathroom (which smelled just like her sister—a mix of sandalwood soap and Nivea lotion). She even checked under the bed. Ava was gone.

"Fuck!" Lila cursed. Jack and Ava were nowhere to be seen, and the murder could occur at any moment.

Lila rushed to Jack's room. It was empty. She ran to the scene of the crime, but there was nothing. She spent ten minutes frantically searching the endless hallways and rooms of the yacht. Her heart was pounding so fast she thought it might burst in her chest. Finally, she heard voices coming from the master suite. She ran toward the sound. Frantic to find Ava or Jack, Lila didn't bother knocking on Elise's door. She just burst right in.

"Holy shit," Lila exclaimed, when she found the soon-to-be-widowed Elise Warren naked and straddling Ben Reynolds, the man who had just been trying to coax Lila into just this very position.

Ben gave Lila a wide-eyed look, but Elise, not caring if the help caught her in flagrante delicto, continued to rock and groan upon her lover. Ben said nothing as Elise moved his hands from her hips up to her breasts.

"Don't stop," she groaned as Lila dashed out of the room.

A sense of dread flooded Lila as she ran back to the main deck. She didn't care about the fact that Ben, at that very moment, was having sex with Elise even though he'd had sex with her the day before. She'd known deep down that Ben was sleeping with Elise when she saw him coming out of her bathroom. What mattered was that her primary murder suspect was currently in her room riding the first officer to her own *petite mort,* while her husband was nowhere to be seen, seconds, minutes, hours away from his own death.

Lila tried to steady herself. It was 12:16 A.M., two hours before the police were notified. There was a chance that Elise could still murder her husband, but Lila's gut told her that she had it wrong. A woman being happily fucked at that moment wouldn't turn around, put clothes on, and grab a gun. It didn't make sense.

Another firecracker exploded, momentarily turning the night sky an electric pink. She shot off toward the captain's bridge so she could be in position to observe the murder.

Taking the stairs two at a time, she climbed to the top deck of the boat and went to open the door. It was locked. She pounded on it over and over again, but there was no answer.

"Goddamnit!" She felt her whole plan crumble around her. The panic of the moment gripped her, but she knew what she needed to do. She had to somehow get the keys to the captain's bridge from Nash.

She rushed back down to the main deck. Nash and Poe, two of her other suspects, were facing each other across the bottle-strewn dinner table. She jumped back when she saw that Poe had a gun pointed to his head. His bulging eyes were staring at Nash. Jack wasn't there, and Clarence, Charity, and Paul were nowhere to be seen. Thiago and Esperanza were slowly swaying in a corner on the other side of the deck, seemingly oblivious to the mayhem surrounding them.

"Do it!" Nash chanted in his now-slurred Boston accent. "Do it. Do it."

Poe let out a wild scream as he pulled the trigger. A firework exploded in the sky, making Poe yell even louder. But the gun just clicked; the chamber was empty. Poe's hand shook violently as he put the gun down on the table. Lila saw that the weapon was the snub-nosed .38 with the cherrywood grip that she'd seen Nash get in St. Barts—the gun that would soon be drenched in Jack Warren's blood. The murder weapon.

Poe slid the pistol over to Nash. "Your turn now," he said. His face was a ghostly white, and his pupils were so dilated that you could barely see his ice-blue irises.

Nash picked up the gun and put it to his temple. Another firework exploded. Pedro and Mudge, who was no longer wearing pants, howled like wolves at the momentarily electric-pink night sky. Nash and Poe continued to stare intensely at each other.

It was like being in a fever dream, and Lila needed it all to stop. She needed to gain control of this night. She didn't know where Jack was, where Ava was, and she couldn't risk someone killing Jack when she wasn't there to witness it. Even though she knew this broke Teddy's number one rule, Lila decided she needed that gun, for now, just until she could regain control of this future crime scene. So, without pausing to second-guess herself, she snuck up behind Nash and snatched the gun from his trembling hand.

Both men turned to look at her, wide-eyed and amazed.

She turned the gun on them both. "Nash, I need the keys to the bridge."

"Look," Poe said, pointing a finger at Lila. "I told you an angel would come. If you test God, he sends an angel. A beautiful angel has descended from on high to tell us we won't die tonight."

"Keys! I need the keys." Lila felt hot tears come to her eyes. She was running out of time.

"Does that mean that I am chosen?" Nash asked, standing up. His eyes were wide and his face was filled with a beatific radiance. "Does that mean I've been touched by God?"

Lila stepped away, still gripping the gun. "What the fuck is going on here?" she asked no one in particular.

Nash fell to his knees and began to weep as Poe began reciting biblical passages. "*For as the heavens are higher than the earth, so are my ways higher than your ways and my thoughts than your thoughts.*'"

"Don't worry about them," Pedro called out to Lila as he crouched over a pile of unlit fireworks. "They're both tripping their asses off. Took three tabs each. Give them a few hours, they'll come around . . . I hope."

She leaned over Nash's body, searching his pockets for the

keys, but there was nothing. All he did was roll around the floor and girlishly giggle. She wasn't going to get the keys and she was desperately running out of time. She stepped away from the two men as they began to writhe around the main deck in the grip of major hallucinations. Could either of them commit murder in a state like this? Lila knew it was more than possible. LSD could make people do crazy things. But she couldn't wait around listening to them blather on about communing with the divine. She needed to find Jack Warren. She needed to find her sister.

With the gun in her hand, she bolted from the deck and ran up the stairs, back to the crime scene. The whole time she was rushing, hoping it wasn't too late, she heard Teddy's voice in her head telling her not to take the gun. *You're messing with fate. You're interfering with the past,* she heard him say. But she tried to push his nagging voice out of her mind. His cautionary words weren't what mattered now. All that mattered was the throb of panic in her veins as she came to the horrific realization that everything had slipped out of her control. She felt like she was drowning, and the gun was the closest thing to grab on to.

Gripping the rail of the staircase with one hand and the gun in the other, Lila rushed to the second deck, leaping up the stairs three at a time. Just as she neared the top, feet away from her destination, she saw them: Jack covered in blood and Ava standing there, with her back to Lila.

A soul-shattering scream ripped out of Lila's mouth as her worst fears came true in an instant. Her sister was the killer. Startled by the sound, Ava whipped her head around. Lila saw that her face and torso were covered in blood. Just as the two sisters locked eyes, Jack staggered away from Ava, lost his balance, and plummeted a hunded and fifty feet into the sea.

CHAPTER 25

IN ALL THE ten years she'd spent thinking obsessively about this very moment, nothing could have prepared Lila for what she saw. It was so surreal, so unexpected, that she couldn't process it. Her sister was the killer. She felt like she was having an out-of-body experience, floating above herself and her beloved sister. She'd gone back in time to prove her sister's innocence, only to find out Ava killed Jack after all.

Another firecracker exploded, waking Lila from her trance. She looked at Ava, who hadn't moved. She was standing stock-still, staring at Lila with a mix of terror and confusion on her face.

"How could you!" Lila roared at Ava. "How could you do this?" Lila's voice caught in her throat as tears flooded her eyes.

But Ava didn't say anything. She was staring at Lila like she was some sort of ghost. Lila had the urge to slap her sister hard across the face—to wake her up, to punish her, to make Ava feel some of the pain she was feeling. She'd never felt more angry and more betrayed.

Suddenly, as if waking from a dream, her sister blinked quickly. "What is happening?" she stuttered, looking frantically around. "Lila? Is that you?" Ava went to reach for her sister as if to check that she was real, then she saw the gun. She pulled back her hand.

"Who are you?" she asked Lila, her round eyes bulging with fear. "What are you doing here? Where's Jack?" Ava's eyes darted around, her chest heaving in terror.

Has she lost her mind? Lila thought. Had she been drugged?

"Jack is dead," Lila said, her voice cracking.

Ava looked down at herself. When she saw that her hands and dress were soaked in blood, she began to scream over and over again—short, bloodcurdling screams that Lila knew she'd never be able to erase from her mind.

A firecracker zoomed into the sky and exploded. A waterfall of purples and silvers arced against the black canvas of sky. Lila saw the light from the sky reflect off something on the ground by her sister's feet. A knife. Jack hadn't been shot. He'd been stabbed. By Lila's sister. It was all too much to bear.

Then Ava dropped to her knees. She held out her bloody hands, staring at them in horror. Her whole body was shaking. She took the knife in her hand. Lila rushed to her sister. But before she could reach her, Ava grabbed the knife and tossed it overboard. Lila knelt down, placing the gun on the ground, and threw her arms around her sister's bare shoulders.

Ava's skin felt ice cold.

"I don't understand. I don't understand," Ava said. Lila could hear her sister's teeth chattering in her ear as she held on to her.

"Tell me what happened?" Lila asked.

"I don't know."

"But you were standing right here. You must remember. You have to remember!"

But Ava just blankly shook her head. Lila had never seen her sister like this. What had happened to her? She was more confused than ever.

She took her sister's hands. "It'll be okay," Lila whispered, though she knew the very opposite was true. From now on, nothing was going to be okay.

Suddenly Ava lunged away from her sister and reached for the gun. Before Lila knew what was happening, she looked up to see her sister standing over her, with the snub-nosed .38 pressed against her own temple.

Lila spoke slowly. She tried to sound calm even though she felt as if her whole world had just collapsed. "Ava, put the gun down."

Her sister didn't say anything. Tears were streaming down her face. Her eyes were like those of a trapped animal.

"Ava, give me the gun." Lila carefully stepped closer, but her sister only pressed the gun harder into her temple. Then Lila's instincts took over. Without thinking, she dove toward Ava, grabbing the gun. As they wrestled, one shot was fired, then another. Then, as Lila knocked her sister down while trying to rip the gun from her hand, Ava squeezed the trigger, and a deafening shot fired into the air as both women crashed to the ground. As Lila tried to tear the gun out of Ava's fingers, one more bullet was discharged.

Four bullet casings were strewn on the ground. Just like the police files said. But nothing had happened the way Lila imagined.

Her sister, flat on her back, began to violently sob. A faint cloud of gunpowder smoke floated away on a tropical breeze.

It wouldn't be long until Paul would climb the stairs and see the bloody aftermath of Jack's murder. Lila waited for Ava to get up. But her sister remained lifeless and weeping, curled up in her lover's blood.

"Ava?" Lila whispered. She didn't understand why her sister wasn't moving. She had to start running now or Paul would discover her. But she just lay there, helpless.

And then Lila realized, Ava wasn't going to escape, not on her own.

Lila scrambled to her feet, grabbing Ava's hands and hoisting her up. She needed to get her sister out of there, and fast. She knew there wasn't much time, and Ava had no chance of fleeing the ship without Lila's help. She had to save her. There was no other choice.

Ava looked at Lila with dead eyes, like there was nothing left inside of her anymore: no light, no joy, no fear, no conscience. Nothing. Lila had never felt so sick in her life.

Taking her sister's hand, she dragged her down the side deck, pulling her step-by-step to the first level as Ava limply stumbled behind her. Then, staying out of sight, she brought her down to the lower deck, praying the whole time that no one would see them—both of them covered in blood, fleeing a murder scene.

Lila threw Ava into the crew bathroom, stripped off her ruined dress, and pushed her under a hot shower.

"I'll be back in a second," Lila said, but Ava didn't respond. She just stood there, naked and comatose, as water streamed over her.

Lila ran to her cabin and grabbed the passport and license Teddy had made for her in what felt like another lifetime. She also grabbed the thumb drive full of naked pictures and videos of Josie Warren, and jeans, a hooded sweatshirt, and a pair of sneakers, shoving it all into her duffle bag. Then she sprinted down to the lifeboat in the engine room and grabbed Teddy's remaining $10,000 stacks and her gun.

She ran down the hallway and into the bathroom, locking the door behind her. Ava was still standing there, but her hands were pressed against her face, and her naked shoulders were shuddering with every sob.

Lila turned the water off and wrapped a dry towel around her sister. Putting the clothes on Ava felt like dressing a sad, helpless child. Lila had no idea what had happened to her sister. It was like something had broken inside of her.

Taking her sister's hand in hers once more, she brought her to the internal dock at the yacht's stern. They walked by the two-person submarine, the Jet Skis, and all of Jack Warren's other high-priced playthings. Then she saw the boat that she knew Ava had used to escape, the fifteen-foot inflatable boat that police would find tomorrow morning floating off the coast of Cuba. Little did Lila know when she first heard that news that she would be the one to orchestrate Ava's escape.

Lila ran to the control panel on the west wall of the internal dock and pulled a lever to open the transom. With a large mechanical gust of air, the back of the yacht began to lower down, which made it possible for the inflatable boat to be quickly driven out into the sea, like a minnow escaping from a whale's mouth.

As the transom door was lowering, Lila rushed back to her sister's side. Ava was slumped in the driver's seat, her hands limply resting against the steering wheel, her head hanging down on her chest.

"Ava," Lila said, bending over so her face was just inches from her sister's. "Listen to me." Her sister didn't move, so she shook her shoulders. "Listen to me!"

Lila threw the tote bag into the passenger seat. "I'm giving you fifty grand in cash, plus a passport and a driver's license. This . . ." Lila said, holding the thumb drive, "this is something you can use only if you're desperate for money. Okay? Are you listening to me?"

Ava nodded, keeping her gaze down.

Lila turned the boat on and the twin engines powerfully

rumbled, churning up the water beneath it. Lila pointed to the compass in the yacht's control panel. "Head southwest until you hit land. You want to get to Cuba. It's about a hundred miles away. Go fast, but not too fast, and you'll be there in under three hours."

Ava slowly raised her head and looked Lila in the eye. She took her sister's hand and squeezed it. "Why are you helping me?" Ava asked.

There was nothing to say. "I don't know," she whispered. She bit down on her lower lip, desperately trying not to cry. Her sister had broken her heart.

Finally, the transom door was fully lowered. "Okay," Lila said, still clutching Ava's hand. "You've got to go."

"I can't do this."

"You have no choice." But Ava didn't move. "Go!" Lila screamed. "Go!"

And suddenly Ava throttled the engine and the speedboat lurched forward. She quickly eased out of the bowels of the yacht, cutting through the water like a knife. Then in a moment, she was out of sight.

All that was left was a ripple of wake being pulled back into the ocean's ceaseless current.

CHAPTER 26

THE NEXT FEW minutes were a blur. Lila stared out into the empty ocean feeling gutted. Everything she had thought she knew was all wrong. It seemed impossible to believe, but Ava was Jack Warren's killer. She stabbed him and then threw the bloody murder weapon overboard. Lila had *seen* it. And then, what did Lila do? She helped her sister, a murderer, escape.

Ava wasn't who Lila thought she was, but even worse, Lila had become a stranger to herself. She'd spent her life fighting for justice and making sure the bad guys paid for what they did. Now *she* was the bad guy. She'd betrayed her most profound beliefs, and she'd done it almost without thought.

It was a truth so horrifying all she could do was bury it deep down within herself. She stood up and returned to the lower deck.

IT WAS A little after 2:00 A.M. when Paul Mason discovered the bloody scene. He searched each and every room in the yacht, shouting frantically, until he realized that Jack was missing. He roused Captain Nash, who was lying in a fetal position on the main deck, still in the waning grip of his acid trip. Nash immediately radioed the coast guard that Jack Warren was dead.

It had been less than an hour since Ava had taken off. Lila thought of her sister speeding her way toward Cuba.

By the time the coast guard boarded the yacht, Lila had showered, careful to scrub every last bit of blood off her body. She had taken her and her sister's blood-soaked clothes, stuffed them into a bag along with a few bottles of liquor to weigh it down, and tossed the whole thing into the sea. She had really wanted to get rid of the gun, which had her sister's fingerprints all over it, but Paul had found it lying in Jack's blood before Lila had a chance to dispose of it.

She tried to console herself by remembering that the gun had also been handled by Nash and Poe, but Lila knew that the cops would focus on the fingerprints of the woman who fled the scene of the crime. After years on the force, Lila understood how the minds of the police operated. If a case looked cut-and-dried, no cop in his right mind would try to make it more complicated. Jack's mistress murdered him, then fled on a boat, case closed.

Unfortunately, for the first time ever, Lila couldn't disagree with this assessment.

At least not in her mind. Out loud, she had to play dumb. And it was nothing short of agonizing. When the coast guard came to question her, she pretended she'd been sound asleep in her cabin. They brought her up to the dining room, where an impromptu interrogation room had been created. A stone-faced cop sat at the table with a camcorder on a tripod pointed at Lila and a notebook set out in front of him.

She knew what to say. She'd seen nothing, heard nothing, knew nothing. Several helicopters surrounded the yacht, spotlights trained on the water. They were searching for the body. But Lila knew they'd never find it.

After thirty minutes of questioning, they quickly wrapped up her interrogation, and Lila was free to go. She returned to her room, seeing two forensic specialists hurrying to put a sealed tarp over the crime scene, only too aware that the seawater and salty ocean air could corrupt the evidence in a matter of minutes.

Then she watched Elise and Josie, clutching each other, walk with Seth Liss, Paul Mason, and Charity and Clarence Baines up to the helipad. It was clear that Elise and Josie had been crying. Their faces were red and puffy. Paul, Charity, and Clarence were stone-faced behind them. They all got into the helicopter and flew away.

The yacht shuddered and stopped. Then it began to turn around. Lila climbed up to the bridge, where Nash and Ben were standing behind the large control panel.

"Where are we headed?" Lila asked.

"Back to Miami," Nash said, staring straight ahead, "as fast as we can. I want the fuck off this damn boat."

Lila left the room, and just as she was about to go down the stairs, Ben grabbed her shoulder. She was so on edge she almost screamed from surprise at his touch.

"Christ, you startled me," she said, turning toward him.

"Oh, Nicky," he said, wrapping his arms around her. "The whole thing is so awful."

He crushed her body against his, and as her face was pressed to his chest, Lila let out a gigantic sob. It was the first relief she'd had in hours, and once the panic and fear dropped away, anguish stepped in to take its place. So she cried as Ben held her, cried for her sister, for herself, for this whole fucked-up case.

"I know, I know," Ben whispered, trying to console her. "I didn't mean to hurt you, Nicky. Elise means nothing to me."

Lila's crying stopped instantly and she extricated herself from

Ben's arms, amazed that he would think her tears were for him. "This isn't about you, Ben," she said. And then she turned and walked away. And somewhere in her broken heart she had a tiny pocket of gratitude in knowing that despite screwing up this entire case, she at least hadn't fallen for that joker.

"Nicky!" he called out, but she didn't bother turning around. What was the point? All she needed now was to get back to 2019 and, finally, try to move on with her life.

And it wasn't long before she was able to do just that.

As Sam and Lila were packing up, the boat sailed toward the marina. Lila saw that Sam was wrapping her sweaters around the framed pencil drawing by Picasso of a woman's one-eyed face, which usually hung in the master suite.

When Sam saw Lila shoot her a surprised look, she became defensive. "Let me tell you something, Nicky. You should do exactly the same thing. I mean, you don't think we're still getting paid, do you?"

Lila just shrugged. Of course she hadn't even thought about it. The fact that what Sam was stuffing into her suitcase would probably fetch around two hundred grand wasn't something that bothered Lila either. Let Sam grab what she could. After all, she hadn't been sleeping with Jack out of love. She'd made investments, and like any good businessman, she was now collecting her profit.

More power to her.

When the yacht pulled up to the Miami harbor in the early hours of that gentle September morning, a much greater level of fanfare awaited them than they'd received during the yacht's sendoff. But this time the reporters and the bystanders were there for darker reasons. One of the world's richest men had been murdered, and they wanted to gawk at the spectacle.

Thiago and Esperanza were the first to disembark. It looked as if Thiago hadn't slept all night. The usually dapper bon vivant appeared stricken, almost held up by his tiny wife, who had her arm wrapped around his waist. Lila and Sam watched from the main deck as the couple was swarmed by reporters and TV cameras. They kept their heads down and pushed their way past the throng, then climbed into a black Cadillac Escalade with darkly tinted windows.

Daniel Poe, the only remaining guest on the yacht, stood nervously next to his golden phallus sculpture, guarding it like a mother bear guards her cubs. He was waiting for workers from his gallery to arrive so that they could properly box it up and ship it back to his studio. "It'll double in price after what happened," Lila heard Poe say to some unknown person on the other end of his cell phone. "Let's put it up for auction as soon as humanly possible. Let's put a call into Christie's right now. Got it?" His bloodshot eyes glowed as red as a devil's.

Poe's greed didn't bother Lila. Actually, nothing seemed to matter to her. All she felt was numbness. Jack was dead and her sister was the one with blood on her hands. Lila knew she should be beating herself up for helping Ava escape the scene of the crime, but Ava was family. And Lila had never really had a choice. Still, she wasn't excited at the prospect of facing Teddy. She knew that he would never understand.

Lila and Sam walked down the gangway onto the dock of the marina, where the blinding glare and flash of cameras and the deafening roar of reporters awaited them. They held on to each other's hand, weaving their way through the pulsing scrum of people clamoring to get someone, anyone, to say something about the murder that had the world's attention. But the two women kept their heads down and their mouths shut.

Once they reached the street, Sam turned to Lila. "Well, I won't say, 'Let's do that again.' But I can say it's been nice knowing you."

"Same here." The two women stood there, briefly frozen in an awkward good-bye. "Where're you going now?" Lila asked.

Sam looked around, as if she was making her plans up at that very second. "Can't say I know. I think I'll find a half-decent hotel for a couple nights. Try to fence this drawing. And then I'll come back here and try to get on another charter or something. You know, back to life as usual. What about you?"

"I've got to go meet an old friend," Lila said with a bit of a smile. She was looking forward to seeing Teddy again, but she worried he'd be less than pleased with her. She had demanded he send her back in time, but the mission had been futile—one gigantic, heartbreaking failure.

The two women hugged and then parted ways. Lila flagged a cab and headed north, with two hours to spare until she was due to get transported back to 2019.

CHAPTER 27

THE TAXI DROPPED Lila off at the North Miami storage facility with plenty of time to spare, which, she thought as she walked toward the bleak, industrial building, was both a good thing and a bad thing. The first time she'd entered that meager box of a room to return to the present, she'd been frantic, seconds away from missing the deadline for returning to her real life, in grave danger of being forever stuck in the past. She was glad she didn't have to go through that again. But there was a downside. Now, with a full two hours before her scheduled journey to the present, all she had was time to think. And think. And think.

She unlocked the door to the storage unit with the key she'd kept around her neck and sank down to the hard cement floor, her back pressing against the rough cinder blocks. She took a giant inhale, bringing the room's stale air deep within her lungs, and closed her eyes. She could still feel the phantom rocking of the gentle Caribbean Sea beneath her. A sense of dread began to build steadily, threatening to consume her.

Her mission had been a failure, and now she'd have to explain it all to Teddy.

The silence, the solitude, and the stress of the moment combined to produce a surprisingly sedative effect. She felt tired on the cellular level as she began to crash from the previous night's traumas. Every hair, every pore, every inch of her needed rest. And she gave in to it. After enduring so much panic and heartbreak, she could no longer fight the physical and emotional exhaustion. Her eyelids dropped heavily over her eyes as she lay down against the cool concrete floor and fell asleep.

Lila awoke in a panic as a high-pitched screeching sound pierced her eardrums. She looked at her watch: 4:16 P.M. She quickly scrambled into the hazmat suit she'd discarded when she arrived and stood in the center of the room. This was it, her ride back to 2019. She'd been here before, but that never made it any less terrifying than the first time.

She pressed her hands against her ears, trying to block out the horrible whirring noise that kept growing in volume. Suddenly the world around her began to blur. Straight lines bent and wavered as known objects broke apart into tiny molecules and scattered around the room. Everything pulsated with an atomic energy. It was as if the world she thought was real was only a reflection in a puddle that someone had just stepped in.

Then silence. Darkness.

Her own body began to lose its form as it melded into the shattered world surrounding her. She felt like she was on the brink of total obliteration. Then came that terrible, sickening feeling of endless falling as she was plunged into the quantum vacuum of dark matter, where she stayed, floating, melting, drifting, in a hidden dimension where space and time had ceased to exist.

Then finally, sound. Light.

As if she were being birthed back into the world, Lila saw the dark void retreat and was thrust into the physical realm.

The light blinded her. Her body felt solid, once again subject to gravity and the familiar world of Newtonian physics. Blinking her eyes open, she gasped for air as her lungs remembered to expand and contract.

Her fingers gripped the armrests of the seat in Teddy's time-traveling contraption. She had made it.

Then just as quickly came the forgetting. She looked around, confused, panicked. A blankness settled over her mind until the door to the time machine began to lower. Standing there was Teddy Hawkins, waiting for her with a relieved smile on his face. He rushed up the stairs toward Lila, and forced to hunch over in the tight confines of the cockpit, he put his hand on hers.

"Welcome home," he said. Just as they had done before, the memories came rushing back. The warmth in Teddy's voice made Lila's heart swell even as the dread sitting in her stomach sharply twisted within her.

Teddy helped her out of the time machine and escorted her to a large laboratory adjacent to the control room. Lila could feel his curious eyes on her, trying to read how the mission had gone from her body language. But she couldn't look him in the eye.

"Sit here and relax," he said as he eased her into a reclining chair. "Conrad is going to check your vitals. I'll lay out some clothes for you. Wash up, change, and meet me upstairs. Then we'll catch up."

Lila slowly nodded, keeping her eyes down.

"Love the hair, by the way. Very Jean Seberg. Very Parisian chic."

Lila self-consciously pulled at her blond pixie cut. It would serve as a reminder of her failure and her sister's guilt. She wanted her old hair back, but more than anything she wanted her illusions back. The truth was too painful. She closed her eyes and lay back in the chair.

"That's right, Lila. Just rest," Teddy said.

"It's good to hear you say my name." She slightly opened her eyes, watching Teddy watch her.

He nodded. "See you in a moment, Lady Day."

Then Conrad came into the room to perform a battery of tests. He took her pulse, several vials of her blood, and ran her through an MRI, EEG, and a CT scan. When all his probing was completed, he brought her into the guest room upstairs that she had come to think of her own room. She saw a pair of her jeans and one of her tank tops laid out on the bed.

"Take your time," Conrad said. "Mr. Hawkins will be waiting for you in the main room."

No matter how shitty she felt, the cavernous bathroom with its claw-foot tub overlooking Biscayne Bay remained one of Lila's favorite spots. She took a long, hot shower in a slate-tiled stall that was actually bigger than the tiny cabin she had shared with Sam for those weeks at sea.

As she prepared herself to face Teddy, she went over in her mind what she'd tell him, working out ways to try to make the mission sound like anything other than a total disaster. But every time, no matter how vociferously she fought on her own behalf, Teddy won each of her imagined arguments. She felt sick.

Clean and dressed, Lila walked barefoot down the stairs to join Teddy and curled herself into the chair next to his. The two of them looked out at the peaceful turquoise water.

Teddy was the one who broke the silence. "It didn't go well, did it?"

"No," Lila said softly. Once she was faced with the conversation she'd been dreading, she realized that she didn't want to defend herself. She was too tired. "You were right."

"About what?"

"About my sister. About me. I went into it not seeing anything clearly."

"I warned you."

"I know."

"So you're saying that your sister shot Jack Warren?" Teddy asked.

"Not exactly," Lila said hesitantly. It was so much more complicated than that.

"What do you mean?" Teddy turned toward her, looking at her for the first time since they started talking.

Then Lila rushed into an explanation. She told Teddy about how the snub-nosed .38 at the scene of the crime actually belonged to Captain Nash. She told him about the hundred grand in drugs that she brought on board. About the LSD-fueled game of Russian roulette. About taking the gun from Nash.

"You took the murder weapon, but Ava still managed to kill Jack?" Teddy asked.

"Yes," Lila whispered.

"Do you have any idea how many rules you've broken? How much possible damage you could've inflicted on the very fabric of the world? What if Jack hadn't died?"

"It wouldn't have been the end of the world, would it? At least my sister could have had a life."

"That's not the point!" he said. She'd never seen him so angry. "You can't play God, Lila! There's no way to calculate how your actions could've impacted the world." Teddy got up and walked over to the bar in the corner. He grabbed two crystal tumblers and filled them three-quarters full with bourbon. He handed one to Lila.

"Please don't tell me that Ava saw you," he said.

Lila stayed silent.

"Should I take that as a yes?"

Lila nodded.

"Did she recognize you?"

"I think so, she said my name. But she was so out of it, Jack. Something was wrong with her that night."

"Something other than the fact that she'd just committed *murder*?"

"It was more than that." Lila was instantly transported back to the yacht, seeing the flash of recognition as her sister's eyes took her in. She remembered Ava, frightened, shivering, covered in her lover's blood.

"This whole thing was too risky. I knew it from the start. I blame myself for letting you go."

"It's my fault, Teddy. Let me own that, okay?" She picked up the glass of bourbon and took a big gulp, relishing its comforting burn. "There's something else I have to tell you."

Teddy rubbed his eyes with the heels of his hands and let out a big, exasperated sigh. "From the look on your face, I think I'd better sit down for this."

Lila gathered up her courage. "When I was in the past"— she paused for another sip of bourbon—"I visited you."

"You *what*?" Teddy was aghast.

"Jack was working on a computer code that I couldn't decipher. I thought it might be a clue, but I needed help."

"So you came to see *me*? Lila . . . I . . ." Teddy fell into a flabbergasted state of silence. He didn't know what to say. "Of course!" he exclaimed a moment later, slamming his fist down onto the table. "I remember. You stopped by my office and showed me that beautiful piece of code. Then it annihilated my hard drive. I can't tell you how many times I thought about that gorgeous woman over the years. And now to find out that *you* are the mysterious woman that disappeared from my life . . . astonishing. You're astonishing."

Lila knew he didn't mean this as a compliment. "I didn't know who else to turn to!"

"You shouldn't have turned to anyone! Don't you realize? That encounter could've permanently altered the course of my life. What if that meant I didn't build a time machine?"

"But you did. From what I can see, nothing changed."

"That is *not* the point, Lila, and you know it."

"Isn't it?" Lila asked. "But I know you're right. Anyway, that source code was just one more dead end in an endless string of them."

Teddy sat back into the chair and stretched out his long legs. He closed his eyes. "I can't do this with you anymore. You don't get it."

"Teddy, please."

"No, Lila. You've got to listen to me. You've got to listen to *someone*. Have you ever heard the saying that life can be a double-edged sword?"

"My mom used to say that all the time," Lila said.

"So you know what it means. Every strength can also be a weakness and vice versa. Well, that's what I see in you. You're so insightful as a detective, so devoted, that you can go blind to the world around you. And your single-mindedness stops you from seeing all the damage you're doing. But that's not the worst part. The worst part is that I don't think you value your own life. And that makes you too dangerous, because it means you don't value anything."

"That's not true!" But even as Lila spoke these words, she feared Teddy was right. There was a strain of recklessness in her, one that she'd always known and felt, that scared everyone in her life. It even scared her sometimes. And now it had finally scared off Teddy, the one person she finally trusted.

Lila turned to face Teddy, but he kept his eyes on the window, looking out to the ocean. She could see the muscles in his jaw clench. All she felt was hopeless. Teddy was too good a man to burden with her baggage. She should let him live his life. It'd be better off without her around.

"Fine," Lila said. "I'll go."

"That would be best," Teddy said in a small, sad voice that made Lila's already pummeled heart wince in pain.

As she headed to the door, Lila turned back around, figuring she might as well deliver the rest of the bad news. "I haven't even told you the worst part, Teddy." He didn't say anything. She forced herself to continue. "I'm the one who helped my sister escape. I'm the one who got her into that boat to make a getaway. I gave her the passport. I even gave her my money."

"You mean *my* money."

"Right," Lila whispered.

"So, let me get this straight. I gave you money to help you prove your sister was innocent. And you gave that money to her when you found out she was a murderer?"

"I'll pay you back . . ."

"Stop!" Teddy yelled, his eyes closed. "Lila, for once in your life, know when enough is enough. It's over. Now, please, just go."

CHAPTER 28

A WEEK PASSED, maybe two. Possibly three. Lila couldn't be sure. Things began to blur.

Her final conversation with Teddy had unleashed a tsunami of regret and loss, which had knocked her down, pulled her under, and left her stranded in some dark, unknown place. She felt empty and numb. Without a case to obsess about or Teddy to ground her, she felt lost. There was nothing calling her out into the world, so she stayed holed up in her apartment with the blinds drawn and a bottle of Wild Turkey always within reach.

She didn't fight the self-pity she felt engulfing her. Her mother was gone; her sister was a murderer on the run; and the one true friend she'd grown to love had just told her that she was too dangerous to be around. Lila thought she'd bottomed out before, but she now knew that she'd been mistaken. Here, right now, was the bottom, and Lila wondered if she'd ever be able to crawl out from this emotional muck.

As the days slowly crawled by, she started to digest what had happened on *The Rising Tide,* working through the details of the case and finally accepting the new, harsh reality that her sister had killed Jack. She felt foolish and betrayed. But the most acute feeling was loss. In one terrible moment the illusion that had kept her going—that her sister was innocent—had vanished. With her faith in Ava dashed, Lila now saw her undying belief in Ava's innocence for what it was: a crutch. And she was shocked to see that she could barely stand on her own two feet without it.

Everything she thought she knew about herself had been wrong. Everything she once believed to be real was only a shadow of her hopes and dreams. Her sister, Ava, wasn't an innocent victim. She was a murderer. And Lila wasn't some brilliant detective. She'd been average at worst, and lucky at best. In fact, Lila now considered that maybe she wasn't even as honorable as the rotten and corrupt cops she'd spent her career detesting. At least *they* were honest with themselves and with everyone else about who they were. They didn't delude themselves into thinking they were working to save the world, like Lila did.

The person she once believed she was—a good cop, a moral person, a caring friend—had wound up being just a bunch of false hopes, and Lila felt deeply ashamed.

And then there was Teddy.

Meeting him had saved her life. That was one thing she still knew to be true. His faith in her allowed her to, once again, have faith in herself. But she'd played fast and loose with his trust and had lost it. Now he would never give her another chance to go back in time. And without that—without the mental challenge of solving those cold cases—what would she do?

Inside her head an unrelenting voice cataloged her failures: not seeing her sister for who she was, pushing harder than she should have, forever falling for the wrong guys, alienating anyone who ever cared for her, and on and on and on. To pull herself away from the self-flagellation, she turned on the TV, flipping mindlessly from channel to channel.

The television comforted her. She stayed on the couch for

hours, guzzling Wild Turkey as her brain was soothed by the TV's undemanding companionship. As she was flipping channels, an image caught her eye—a grand sailboat racing along a choppy sea underneath the Golden Gate Bridge.

Lila paused at the sight. The boat looked just like the one that Ben and Jack designed with that master builder, Kingston S. Duxbury, in the Caribbean. It had that telltale sail, which looked like an airplane wing. The wing sat stiffly atop a giant, space-age catamaran that hydroplaned along the water. It was a mesmerizing boat. Lila watched, her head firmly pressed against the sofa cushion, intrigued, but not enough to sit up.

A blond reporter standing in Golden Gate Park walked toward the camera in that slow, purposeful pace they must teach people in journalism school. Spreading her arms out in front of her, she said, "Crowds have gathered with eager anticipation to witness the final leg of this year's America's Cup, held in beautiful San Francisco. Our country's hopes are pinned on one man, Ben Reynolds, the skipper and helmsman of the American team." Lila couldn't believe her ears.

The camera then panned to Ben. That was enough to make Lila sit up. "What the fuck?" she said, her face creased from hours of being squashed against the pillow, her voice slightly slurred by whiskey. Ben looked almost exactly as he had in 2008, which for Lila was a mere two weeks ago, not the eleven years that had actually passed. His face was a bit narrower and the lines in his tanned skin were carved deeper. A few strands of gray hair could be seen in the riot of his dark curls.

Astounded, Lila watched as Ben brought the reporter onto the boat. But her heart nearly stopped when she saw another familiar face from *The Rising Tide*: Asher Lydon. Startled, she jumped to her feet. "Holy fuck," she said as she turned up the volume to a near-deafening level, anxious not to miss anything. Asher was only on camera for a fleeting second, but it was undeniably him—the corn-silk-blond hair that he had kept boyishly long despite being a decade older, the affable smile, those model-perfect features.

Asher and Ben, together? Lila couldn't believe what she was seeing. How was any of it possible? How did Ben achieve his dream of being skipper on his own multimillion-dollar boat in the America's Cup despite the death of his only patron? And how was Asher, who was a sworn enemy of the Warren clan, sailing on a boat that had meant more to Jack Warren than practically anything in his life?

Nothing seemed to make sense. Then she wondered if she'd been wrong all along. It suddenly dawned on her. What if Ben murdered Jack? Her spinning mind quickly sifted through all the facts. That night, she'd found Ben naked in bed with Elise. Less than an hour later, Jack was dead. How could he have done it? Wouldn't Lila have seen Ben up there with Ava and Jack? And could he have managed to extricate himself from Elise fast enough to get to Jack? It didn't scan.

Still, something kept tugging at her. Seeing Ben and Asher together was enough to make Lila believe that there was more to the story. She kept her eyes on the TV, watching as Ben's handsome face and easy smile worked their charms on the blond TV reporter. Then it came to her. "Of course!" she exclaimed out loud to an empty room. What if Ben and Asher had been working together? What if Ben smuggled Asher back on the boat without anyone realizing it? They both knew the yacht well enough to keep Asher hidden. Then, while Ben made sure Elise was distracted, Asher could've stabbed Jack and then gone back into hiding, leaving Ava stunned and standing on the deck by a pool of blood while Jack fell into the water, dead.

There were plenty of reasons why either man would want Jack dead. He'd been a controlling, cruel, and abusive boss to both of them. And after Asher's plans to get to the Warren fortune through

Josie backfired twice, he could have decided to take matters into his own hands. Perhaps Ben, knowing he was close to losing his plum position as helmsman on Jack's racing yacht, knew he had to get rid of Jack before Jack got rid of him. Had he been sleeping with Elise to make sure that she'd put him in charge of the America's Cup boat once he and Asher had murdered her husband?

The voice in Lila's head that had been beating herself up just minutes ago was now frantically trying to answer all these questions. But more than anything, she was thrilled that there was a flicker of possibility, no matter how small, that Ava might be innocent.

Feeling invigorated, Lila grabbed her laptop and searched Ben's name. Slowly, by visiting a few different sites, she began piecing it all together. It seemed that upon Jack Warren's death, Elise had given the racing yacht to Ben, just as Lila had suspected. Then, she read in an interview with *Sailing World* magazine, Ben declared that every day he worked to honor "the amazing legacy of all that Jack Warren did to innovate this most regal and gentlemanly of sports, yacht racing, and make it what it is today." If he was really honoring Jack's legacy, why did he include Asher on the team, the very man who seduced and abandoned Jack's only daughter?

She'd seen enough. She booked a nonstop flight from Miami to San Francisco for the next morning. She'd be in the Bay Area by ten, giving her plenty of time to watch the final race of the America's Cup.

Teddy had told her it was over. But she couldn't let it go, not now, not when there was a fresh lead. A thought popped into her mind: What if this was just one more way to hold on to Ava's innocence? What if she was only grasping at straws, seeing a pattern where there wasn't one?

But she pushed these ideas out of her mind. As long as she had a doubt, it wasn't over. Not yet.

CHAPTER 29

BY THE TIME Lila arrived at San Francisco Bay, securing a spot under the shadow of the Golden Gate Bridge by the finish line was close to impossible. She had to squeeze past the thousands of people who were already packing the walkways. The crowd was humming as people talked excitedly about the race, leaning over the railings to get closer to the action on the water, waving small American flags, jockeying for a good vantage point to watch the last leg of this high-stakes contest. Everyone wanted to be the first to see who would claim the America's Cup, this oldest trophy in sporting history.

With a pair of binoculars hanging around her neck, Lila pushed her way to an ideal spot by the finish line. It was a spectacular day, sunny and clear, which was a rarity for summertime in San Francisco. While she waited for the yachts to come into view, she scanned the scene . . . for what, she didn't know.

After an hour or so pressed up against the railing, searching both the crowds and the vast expanse of deep blue water, she heard someone in the crowd exclaim, "Here they come!" She trained her binoculars on the horizon, where, sure enough, two exquisite yachts suddenly came into view. Both had solid carbon sails that stretched up over two hundred feet into the sky. The Team USA boat had a red sail and a blue-and-white twin-hulled catamaran racer. About forty feet of meshlike fabric was stretched between the two hulls, and a dozen or so sailors, all wearing helmets and sunglasses, rushed from one side of the boat to the other. Even with her binoculars, Lila couldn't identify Ben or Asher in the group scurrying frantically around the boat.

Team USA's closest competitor was Team New Zealand, which was just a couple dozen feet behind. The crowd began to cheer. Then the chant "USA! USA!" began to build and build. The throng of people standing behind Lila began to surge forward, pushing her, somewhat painfully, into the railing. She jabbed a couple of people with her elbows, trying to take up as much room as possible.

Lila watched both boats soar through the water. But they weren't like any boats she'd ever seen. They were more like magical flying machines. Team USA miraculously glided through the air at fifty miles per hour as its catamaran hovered an incredible five feet above water with only three small hydrofoils, which looked like upside-down shark's fins, skimming along the surface of San Francisco Bay. Lila now understood why Ben was so excited by what the shipbuilder was cooking up that day he took her to visit Kingston S. Duxbury.

Team USA turned around a giant orange cone in the middle of the bay and then headed straight toward the now-frenzied crowd. The New Zealand boat lost some speed on the same turn and fell farther behind. It was clear to everyone that Team USA had won the America's Cup. As this good news slowly dawned on all the spectators, the cheering of the crowd grew even louder. Everyone had their smartphones out, to record the moment of victory.

As the catamaran got closer, Lila was finally able to see Ben through her binoculars, at the helm of the large, red steering wheel. Despite his colorful helmet and his dark sunglasses, she knew it was him from the toothy smile overtaking his face. Victory was his.

The moment the boat crossed the finish line, the entire team began to whoop and wail, jumping up and down, throwing their arms wildly around one another. When they all stripped off their helmets, Lila was able to see both Asher and Ben more clearly. They embraced each other, and then, with their arms resting on each other's shoulders, they turned to the joyous crowd of spectators celebrating their monumental triumph.

Lila watched them carefully through the binoculars. She saw them searching the vicinity, clearly looking for something. Then they seemed to spot it. Both men looked directly at something, or someone. Her eyes pressed into the binoculars, Lila followed their gazes and found what they were looking at—Kingston S. Duxbury, the West Indian shipbuilder Lila had met in the Turks and Caicos. He was conspicuous in his powder-blue shirt and Panama hat. Then Lila noticed Kingston turn to shake a man's hand. From where Kingston was standing, Lila couldn't see who was next to him. All she could make out was that the stranger had a Team USA baseball hat pulled low over his face. The two men held each other's hands and laughed, in what Lila thought looked like pure delight. Kingston bent slightly back, allowing Lila to see the other man's face. He was wearing oversize aviator sunglasses and had a large, bushy beard. But there was something there . . .

Lila shifted her focus back to the boat, where Ben and Asher were jumping around triumphantly. She saw Ben give a thumbs-up. Then Asher joined him. Again, they were both looking at a fixed point in the crowd. She whipped her gaze back to Kingston, only to see that he and the bearded man were returning the gesture in kind. She kept watching Kingston, wondering if he had played a role in Ben and Asher's bloody deeds. But something distracted her. The man with the beard had thrown his arm around Kingston—and there was something about it that itched at Lila's brain.

She thought of the pictures she'd seen in Kingston's shop, the framed photos of him posing triumphantly in front of his boats. And in every picture, a man had his arm flung around Kingston's shoulders. That man was Jack Warren.

She moved her binoculars away from Kingston to look for the bearded man, but he had left Kingston's side and disappeared into the crowd. Lila scanned the vast throng of people. She had lost him.

But then she spotted him once more. He was moving through the crowd, pushing to get out to the street while the crowd surged in the opposite direction, hoping to get a better look at the boats. His head was mostly turned away from Lila, so she couldn't see his face. But, in one moment, she saw his profile. And with one glance at that long, aquiline nose, she was shocked by recognition. The man in the baseball hat was Jack Warren.

He was alive—wearing a hat, beard, and glasses, hoping to remain unnoticed in the city that he'd once ruled.

Adrenaline flooded Lila's body as her focus became razor sharp. If Jack slipped out of her grasp, she was certain that she'd never locate him again. This was her one and only chance.

She took off like a shot, only to hit a brick wall of celebrating spectators. She ducked around them. A chorus of "Hey!" and "Watch it!" was left in her frantic, clawing wake. But Lila didn't hear them. She could only think of one thing, and that was finding Jack Warren, and getting an explanation for what the hell was going on.

She finally pushed her way through the massive crowd, but by the time she broke free, she'd lost sight of Jack. Her heart pounding in her chest, she ran around the perimeter of the crowd, searching for him.

Suddenly, in her peripheral vision, she saw him—climbing up a steep flight of stairs that cut up a verdant hillside. He was about two hundred feet ahead of her. Then he stopped and turned once more to the water. He gazed out over the cheering crowds and watched as the Team USA boat made its way to the dock. She could tell he was relishing this victory. And in that moment, Lila hated him more than ever.

She sprinted after him, wishing she had a gun or handcuffs. But all she had was her wits and her strength. By the time she got to the long stairway, Jack was almost at the top. Lila raced to catch him, but he was too far away. Her only advantage was that he didn't realize she was after him. And that was an advantage she'd now have to give up.

As a last resort, she decided to call his name. It was risky. She knew it would definitely spook him and alert him to her presence, but it might slow him down for the split second she needed to gain on him. "Jack Warren!" she screamed as she pushed herself to climb the stairs faster.

Jack stopped dead in his tracks and turned around. She saw him look at her with total confusion. Then, suddenly, the shock of recognition came across his face.

"Remember me?" Lila shouted.

He took off, running faster than before. Her lungs began to burn in her chest. But she was gaining on him, taking the stairs two at a time. He was slower than her, now a man in his sixties struggling to escape, but not so slow that he didn't reach the top before her, disappearing out of sight.

The instant Lila reached the final step, she had to make a split-second decision whether to go left or right. But before she could pick one or the other, she heard a loud crack, followed by a hissing whistle through the air. The stone step inches away from her shattered. She heard the terrified scream of a female bystander.

Jack Warren was shooting at her.

Lila reacted immediately, having no time to think. She threw her body to the ground just as another bullet ricocheted off the metal handrail. The shots were coming from behind a cement wall about twenty feet away. Looking around for some kind of shelter, she saw there was nothing but open green space. But then she spotted, about five feet away, a steel garbage bin. She kept flush to the ground, moving toward the bin in an army crawl. Another crack came from behind the wall. The last bullet was so close that she could pratically feel the sound.

She stopped dead for an instant, waiting for the searing pain of a gunshot wound to register. But she hadn't been hit. Before Jack fired another shot, she ducked behind the steel bin, gulping down air as she tried to catch her breath. Police sirens sounded, getting closer.

She waited a few seconds, then, with her pulse racing, leaped up and began running for the wall. No shots were fired. Jack, probably spooked by the sirens, had left his post, getting a head start on her once again. Then she spotted him, sprinting along the dirt path to a busy street just a hundred feet away.

Lila sprang over the hip-level wall and kept racing after him. He looked back at her, causing him to lose his footing. He tripped forward and hurtled down to the ground, sending his gun flying across the grass. He scrambled up and kept charging ahead.

She was getting closer.

Then he hit the pavement. It was a major city street, with four lanes of busy traffic. Jack dashed out into the middle of the street, waving his hands. Lila realized he was trying to flag down a car so he could jump into it and make a final getaway. But his plan went horribly wrong. The car that he lunged in front of was slow to brake. Lila watched as the vehicle's wheels screeched and the driver swerved, in an attempt to avoid hitting anything, but ended up spinning out of control, sideswiping Jack as it did a three-sixty in the middle of the road. Jack went flying through the air and fell to the pavement with a heavy thud.

Lila ran toward his splayed-out body as people began to jump out of their cars, rushing to the ailing man's side. In the panic and horror of that moment, as she rushed toward Jack, all Lila could hear was her own voice saying over and over again, "Don't you dare die. Don't you dare die."

If she was going to get the justice she so badly needed, Jack Warren had to be very much alive.

Lucky for her, he was.

CHAPTER 30

IT WASN'T UNTIL Teddy joined Lila at the St. Francis Memorial Hospital and smoothed things over with the local police that Lila was finally able to see Jack Warren.

"You got banned from interrogating the man you caught? You must've really showed them the classic Lila charm, huh?" Teddy said to her with a tired smile. They were both exhausted. It had been a full twenty-four hours since that car had sent Jack sailing through the air, but in that brief time, Lila felt as if her whole world had changed. The despair and doubt she felt had been eradicated. And she had been vindicated. She finally knew she was right about her sister and, most importantly, she had the best proof imaginable to show that Ava had been falsely accused of murder. She had Jack Warren, alive, breathing, and in handcuffs.

Finally, she could clear her sister's name.

She had only phoned Teddy with the news once she finally convinced the cops on the scene that this bleeding man on the pavement was indeed Jack Warren, the billionaire who the whole world believed was murdered eleven years ago. Teddy, in total shock, had hopped on his private plane within the hour, desperate to be with Lila as fast as he could. "I can't believe it," was all he could manage to say on the phone. "I just can't believe it."

He arrived in San Francisco before midnight, joining Lila outside Jack's hospital room, which was flanked by two police officers. Both Lila and Teddy looked down at the scrum of journalists gathering in the parking lot outside. Each was jockeying to get the scoop on the story of the year: Jack Warren had been resurrected from the dead.

Teddy reached for her hand. "Lila, listen," he said softly. "I know you may not want to hear it, but I feel terrible about what I said to you the last time we spoke. I had no right. You would do anything to protect the people you care about. And that's what you did for Ava. I should've been more understanding. I was wrong."

Lila kept her eyes on the news cameras. She squeezed his hand. "I was wrong, too." Lila paused and turned to look at Teddy. She brushed his dark blond hair out of his face with her fingertips, only realizing at that very moment how happy she was that he was once again by her side. "I know I pushed too hard."

"True. But if you hadn't, you'd never have been able to prove Ava's innocence. I should know by now to listen to you."

"I don't know. This whole case has been so complicated and confusing that at the end, I didn't think I could even listen to myself. I stopped trusting myself." She felt a palpable feeling of sadness about the whole thing. "But now all the confusion will be put to rest, once we get in there to talk to Jack."

Traveling in time couldn't erase the decade that her sister had spent on the run. It made Lila hate Jack even more than she already did. His actions had cost Ava so much. Now she wanted him to lose everything.

"Well, you got him, Lila. No one else could have done it but you."

Lila started to say something, but fell silent for a few seconds. "But, about visiting you in the past—"

Teddy held up his hand to stop her. His face was stern. "I was going to mention that, too. Yes, that was dumb. With everything I told you, you should've known better." Then his face broke into a devilish smile. "But with great risks come great rewards."

Lila gave him a confused look. He continued, "Spending time with that nasty bit of software that you brought into my office was one of the most important moments of my life. Reading source code that Jack Warren wrote was like taking a master class in the power of technology. I learned more in that afternoon than in all my years at MIT. Without it, I wouldn't be where I am today."

"Wait," she said. "Are you telling me that you owe all your success to my bullheadedness?"

"I wouldn't go that far. From now on you still have to stick to my rules."

"I promise to try," Lila offered.

"I guess that's the best I'm ever going to get," he said with a smile.

Though she felt better that she'd patched things up with Teddy, Lila's mind was focused on getting answers out of Jack. With Teddy looking on, she kept pacing up and down the hallways, desperate to talk to him, needing an explanation as to how—and why—he'd done what he'd done. But thanks to Teddy's charm, and a few hundred bucks slipped to one of the sleepy police guards—one bribe Lila was glad to see accepted—they were finally able to stand face-to-face with Jack Warren.

When they walked into his room, they were both taken aback by how small and withered he looked in his hospital bed. The man whom Lila considered the scourge of her sister's life was just an old man now. He was propped up at a weird angle, as if the nurse had struggled to get him upright and just kind of left him where he was. His wrists were handcuffed to the bed. His neck was in a brace and a morphine IV was dripping painkillers slowly into his veins. The doctors had told Lila that Jack would make a full recovery. There were some broken ribs and a sprained neck, but the injuries weren't too bad. Lila had been relieved. At least he'd be fit to stand trial.

Neither Lila nor Teddy said anything for a minute or so. Jack was just lying there, blinking at them. But he kept staring at Lila. She returned his gaze defiantly.

"I know you," Jack finally said. His voice was raw sounding, and syrupy slow from the heavy narcotics.

"You sure do. I'm the one you shot at yesterday." Lila walked closer to him, leaning over his body. "I'm also Ava Day's sister. Do you remember Ava?"

Jack closed his eyes and nodded. "Of course. Of course I do."

"Do you also happen to remember that you framed her for your murder? Or did the car knock that straight out of your head?"

"Mistakes were made. I'll be the first to admit that. I am not a perfect man."

"Are you kidding me?" Lila said with an outraged laugh. "You call framing my sister and ruining our family a *mistake*?"

"Lila," Teddy said in a warning tone. She knew she had to fight to stay as professional as possible. Otherwise her rage would stop her from getting the answers she so desperately needed.

"I don't expect you to understand." Jack stared out of the hospital window, which overlooked a brick wall. "I don't expect anyone to understand. But I know that history will absolve me."

Teddy and Lila exchanged glances.

Jack continued, "What I did, I did for my country. And every great patriot has to make sacrifices. Ava was a small sacrifice. Giving up my life was a much greater one."

He wasn't making sense. Lila continued her questioning: "If history will absolve you, you must first explain yourself."

Jack turned toward Lila and gave her a conspiratorial smirk. "Ah, see! You understand me. Many times," he said, lowering his voice, "great men are terribly misunderstood by their contemporaries."

"Yes," Lila said, turning to Teddy with a shrug of her shoulders. Then Jack began to nod off as the morphine worked its magic. Teddy leaned over Jack, lightly tapping him on the cheek to bring him back to coherence.

"You were telling us that you are a great patriot," Lila said. "But you haven't told us why."

"I was?" Jack said. He was confused, looking around the room as if he were seeing it for the first time.

"Maybe we should wait," Teddy said. "He's totally out of it."

Lila shook her head. She knew this was the ideal time to get the old man talking. When the morphine drip was turned off, he might not be as chatty.

She sat herself down on Jack's bed, causing him to wince in pain as he held his hand against his ribs. Jack Warren trained his widened eyes on Lila. "The tree of liberty must be refreshed from time to time with the blood of patriots and tyrants," he rasped.

"And which one are you?" she asked.

"I told you, I'm a patriot."

"But you still haven't told me why."

"Because I made the ultimate sacrifice that any freedom fighter can make. I died for my country."

"You seem pretty alive to me," Lila said. "Banged up good, but still breathing."

Jack shook his head and a dry, wheezing cough overcame him. He picked up a cup of water, which dribbled over him as his shaky hand brought it to his lips. "It seemed like a decent bargain at first," Jack said. "I didn't have any money and his family had more than they needed."

Lila didn't understand what he was talking about, but then it clicked. "The Campos family," she said. She translated for Teddy: "When Jack was just starting Warren Software, his college buddy Thiago convinced his dad, who was a Brazilian general, to pony up the seed money."

Teddy nodded, signaling that he understood.

"Yes. Thiago Campos," Jack answered. His eyes were closed, as if he had been transported back in time. "I needed investors for my company, but I was young . . . untested. Thiago said that his father was willing to give me what I needed. I knew about his family. I mean, everyone did. That's why Thiago was so unpopular at Harvard. All those liberal twits didn't want to be seen with the son of a right-wing general. But I didn't care."

"Why would you?" Lila said.

"Exactly!" Jack exclaimed. "But let me tell you, now I know that the Campos clan deserved their terrible reputation. I should've seen it coming, but I was too anxious to build my own company. There was no way I was going to turn down that money."

A nurse walked in and put an anemic-looking tray of food down in front of Jack. Lila delighted in watching this erstwhile gourmet who feasted on caviar and oysters be given a cold grilled cheese sandwich.

Jack continued, "It was fine for a decade or so, but then everything fell apart. It was 1988. Warren Software was growing beyond my wildest dreams. I was a newlywed. And Elise had just found out she was pregnant. That same year *Time* magazine named me Man of the Year. I brought the personal computer to the world. It was around this time I heard from Thiago again. It had been over a decade. I figured he was calling to congratulate me on the whole *Time* magazine thing, but he sounded strange, saying he was in town and could I meet him that night. He said it was a matter of life or death. So I met him. Of course I did. He was acting totally nuts. Said his country was on the brink of a coup, that his father had been arrested and thrown in jail. It was crazy stuff. But you know how unstable third-world countries can be."

"Sure do," Lila said, willing to say anything to keep Jack talking.

"Where was I?" Jack asked.

"A coup in Brazil," Teddy offered from his seat by the window. He gave Lila an encouraging wink.

"Oh, right. Right. Well, Thiago asks me for a favor. And, looking back on it, this is where I made the one crucial error. This is the thing I wish I never did. By that time Warren Software was the default operating system in every personal computer on the planet. Thiago wanted to know if I could somehow hack into the computers of his father's rivals. Then he could find out what information they might have on his dad. And I said absolutely not. But Thiago begged me. He had once been a good friend and I owed a lot of the success of the company to the Campos family. Plus, Thiago said these men were terrible thugs. And could kill his father. So I did it."

"Sometimes you have to do bad to do good," Lila said.

"Hacking into the system was remarkably easy. But of course it was for me. I designed it." Even in these terrible circumstances, Jack was still vain about his talents. He continued, "I gave Thiago the information he needed, and he went away. But it didn't last. He came back again, and this time his request was much worse. So I refused. I told him I wasn't afraid of him or his father. Thiago said it was way bigger than that. These were dangerous men that would ruin me in a second. They'd ruin me, and they'd murder my family. So I did what they asked. I didn't think there was any other choice. Starting in 1995, I did whatever they wanted. Using a back door in the software, I was able to hack into the operating systems of the CIA, the FBI, British Petroleum, GE, you name it."

"Do you know what they did with the information?" Lila asked, amazed at what Jack was saying.

"Never. I didn't want to know anything." He began to whimper slightly. "And then September eleventh happened. I remember it so clearly. That was the morning I knew I had to change everything. If I kept helping foreigners access secrets of my government, I was no better than the men who flew the planes into the World Trade Center."

"So you faked your own death?" Lila asked, still not seeing how the pieces fit together.

"That wasn't my first plan, let me tell you. I tried everything to sever my ties with those Brazilian scumbags. But nothing worked. That's when I started palling around with Senator Baines. I had him sic the CIA on those South American bastards, but that only made them angrier. They started having me followed. Then I started spending more time on yachts." He paused. "At least out there in the middle of the ocean, you know when you're being tailed."

Lila couldn't believe what she was hearing. For years she'd thought Jack had been killed by a jealous wife. The truth was a million times more complex.

"Campos's thugs threatened to kill me if I refused to cooperate. They threatened my daughter and my wife. That's when I knew I had to really give it all up to be free of them. Including the company that I spent my life creating."

Lila and Teddy sat there, stunned. "The source code," Lila whispered, figuring out the final piece. Jack realized that if his software had a weak spot that allowed hackers to access every user's private data, he'd need to destroy every hard drive that was vulnerable.

"I had it all planned. I was going to take myself out and destroy Warren Software, leaving that prick Seth Liss to clean up the carnage. I wrote a source code for a software update that should have destroyed the hundreds of millions of PCs with my operating system. But that didn't make its way through the system as I had intended. My declaration that all manufacturing would be returned back to American soil knocked some of the stuffing out of the company's share price, just as I had wanted, but it eventually rebounded. And our acquisition of Peregrine, which was a lousy-piece-of-shit company that I thought might spell the end for Warren, also fell through. Seth, unfortunately, turned out to be less of an idiot than I had thought. He kept the company alive even after I was gone. All I managed to do was take care of myself, and my family. And now I haven't even done that." He laid his head back and closed his eyes.

"But how did you do it?" Lila said, not feeling an ounce of pity for this pathetic man. "How'd you fake your own death?"

A glimmer came to Jack's eye. "That part was easier than I'd expected. Unlike my plans for destroying Warren Software, my own death was seamless. Once I decided that I had to die to be free, I started siphoning off money into a Swiss bank account with the help of my personal banker, Urs Hunziker. By September 2008, I had a billion dollars socked away under my new identity. But if I was going to die, I wanted it to be a spectacular event. The stuff the world would talk about forever. I wanted it to be legendary."

Lila looked at Teddy with disbelief. She couldn't stand Jack's grandiosity, even in defeat.

"Walk me through what happened that night."

"I had pints of my own blood drawn over the last couple months, which I brought on board with me, of course. I brought my mistress on board and drugged her heavily for days, keeping her isolated. I knew she'd be the perfect patsy."

At Jack's mention of Ava, Lila felt rage build inside her. She struggled to keep calm as he continued. "I threw a giant party that night to make sure that people on the ship were both inebriated and away from where I would stage my murder. I sedated my mistress, then brought her to the deck with me. When she awoke she found me covered in blood and her holding a knife. It wasn't a bad plan."

At least Lila now understood why Ava had been so out of it that night.

"But how'd you survive the water?" Lila asked, remembering the image of a bloodied Jack plunging a hundred and fifty feet into the dark ocean waters.

"Yes," he said with a smile. He seemed to be basking in his cleverness. "That *was* complicated. For that, I needed the help of a couple good men."

"Accomplices," Lila said.

"Call them what you will. Even great men need a helping hand or two."

"Asher and Ben," Lila said. But it still didn't make sense. "But those two men weren't your friends. One made you a cuckold. While the other seduced your only daughter and tried to extort money from you."

"Yes, you're right, but only about Asher. Ben *was* my friend. Is still my friend, even though it'll mean jail time for him now. His affair with Elise was all my idea. Call it an insurance policy against a costly divorce. I thought it would temper her judgment about my own extracurricular activities. This, of course, was before I'd cooked up my plan to make a new life for myself. But Ben proved himself so competent, so loyal, that I knew he was the only one I could trust with a secret this big."

"And what about Asher?" Lila asked, amazed.

"Sadly, he did take things too far with Josie. But I thought it was important for my daughter to know that people weren't what they seemed. My little lamb needed to learn some difficult lessons, because she wouldn't have me looking out for her in the future. Still, Asher acted in a way that left me greatly disappointed in him, in both of them."

Now that she was looking at events with Jack's twisted logic, they began to make sense. He used the last weeks of his life on the boat to teach all of the people in his life lessons that he thought were important—about loyalty, honor, and forgiveness.

Jack continued, "Asher met me underwater with a submarine, and I went into hiding. The whole thing was very cloak-and-dagger. And went off without a hitch. I have to say I enjoyed it. And those men didn't suffer too much. I made them rich and, today, I made them world champions."

"But what about Ava?" Lila asked. "Did she mean nothing to you?"

"Ava," Jack said, dragging out every syllable. "She was beautiful. That I do remember. Beautiful and willing. But not much more. She seemed trusting, vulnerable, just what I needed. It was nothing personal. She was just collateral damage."

Upon hearing this, Teddy looked at Lila nervously. True, Lila wanted to leap upon the old man and make him hurt. But she knew that wasn't the best way to exact revenge. He already felt like a victim, and Lila wasn't going to help him actually be one.

Jack continued, "The truth is I'm glad it is all over now. I'm tired of hiding. It's a hard thing watching the world go on without you, like you don't matter at all. Nothing in the entire world has made me feel worse than that."

CHAPTER 31

AN INTERNATIONAL MEDIA storm erupted when the news broke that Jack Warren had faked his own death. The story only became bigger when it was revealed that he did so in order to extricate himself from a software spying deal gone wrong. Once the shadowy group of Brazilian kleptocrats at the heart of the scandal were forced out of the darkness, the story became only more explosive. But despite Jack Warren's predictions, he was never, ever labeled a patriot. Not once. None of the *New York Times* editorials, the Fox News segments, the mentions of him in a State of the Union speech, the congressional investigations, and the dozens of books written about the scandal called Jack Warren a hero to his most beloved country. History, it seemed, was still not on his side.

Nor was it on the side of anyone connected to Jack Warren. The fallout was massive. Warren Software's stock price went into free fall, basically bankrupting the company overnight. What Seth Liss hadn't lost in the market would surely go to lawyer's fees for all the class-action lawsuits and government inquiries he was facing for the foreseeable future.

Thiago Campos and his lovely wife, Esperanza, had all

their American assets seized and were extradited back to Brazil, where Thiago and his father would stand trial for spying and treason. After a quick divorce and a return to her maiden name, Esperanza recovered from the shame and shock of the whole affair on her family's estate in Bali, where she dove into kundalini yoga and began toying with the idea of starting her own line of handbags.

Clarence Baines was forced to resign, though he stuck by his story that he was one of the few forces of good in Jack Warren's troubled life. Hoping to return to public office, he self-published a memoir called *The Confessions of a Conservative*, detailing his innocence in the Warren scandal and his plan for creating a new American utopia based on the political principles of Barry Goldwater. It was unanimously declared to be one of the most delusional pieces of writing the world had ever known. After leaving her husband, Charity went on to marry a politically ambitious man who owned a small but profitable chain of barbecue restaurants in southern Florida. She helped him successfully run for the Florida State Senate in the 2022 elections, happy to be, once again, a politician's wife.

Ben Reynolds and Asher Lydon were convicted on several counts of conspiracy and insurance fraud. Officials from the America's Cup officially expunged their names from all records. But Jack Warren's design innovations forever changed the sport of sailing, though no one would admit it out loud.

Daniel Poe dined out on his Jack Warren stories for the rest of his drug-fueled days. The golden phallus went to auction again, this time resulting in a bidding war. It finally sold for $35 million to a buyer who asked to remain anonymous.

Elise Herrera (formerly Stadtlander formerly Warren) leveraged the shocking revelation about Jack to land yet another wealthy husband. British betting firms were giving five-to-one odds that he wouldn't make it to the year 2025. Edna, her faithful servant, remained by her side.

Sam Bennett, ever the opportunist, sold the story of her steamy affair with Jack Warren on *The Rising Tide* to a national tabloid for three hundred grand. In 2021, she starred in Season 28 of the moribund reality TV show *The Bachelorette*, where twenty waxed and gelled bachelors competed for her affections. Her engagement, marriage, and quickie divorce failed to grab the attention of Hollywood as she'd hoped. So she hawked her engagement ring to pay for some small cosmetic procedures she needed before returning to TV to work on her self-diagnosed "love addiction" on yet another reality-TV show, this one set in a rehab facility on a farm in Idaho.

Josie Warren, aside from becoming obsessed with a scintillating email correspondence with the freshly jailed Asher Lydon, gained years and years of material to discuss with the three different therapists continually in her employ.

Lila watched all of this unfold from a distance. What happened to Jack, Elise, Josie, Ben, or anyone else from *The Rising Tide* didn't really matter to her. What mattered was when Ava would finally come out of hiding.

After the news broke about Jack, Lila woke up each morning thinking that *this* would be the day that Ava came back home. After all, there was nothing left to fear. Every corner of the globe knew that she was innocent. But days passed. Then weeks. Nothing.

Ava was still gone. And as the weeks went by, Lila began to worry that her sister would never come back to her.

Luckily, Teddy was there. Always Teddy. For the first time in her life, Lila began to understand what it really felt like to count on someone, to know that he'd always be by her side. Since the afternoon when Jack almost gunned her down, she'd seen Teddy every day. She couldn't think of anyone on the planet whom she liked better. The fact that they alone shared the secret about her involvement in the Jack Warren case—not counting Conrad and Jack Warren himself, of course—only continued to solidify the bond that existed between them. It felt like the beginning of a new life, a life that wasn't as lonely as the one she'd been living for so long.

IT WAS A perfect day in Miami, and everyone in South Beach was outside enjoying the beautiful weather. Lila was home with her windows thrown wide open. The gentle breeze and the cheerful voices from the people walking along the strip gently floated in, along with the smell of the salty sea air. She was running late. Teddy was on his way to pick her up for their now-customary afternoon lunch. She threw on a sundress and pinned up the bleach blond pixie cut she'd been anxiously growing out for the last six weeks since she traveled from the past.

Then she heard a knock on the door. Without turning around, she shouted, "Come on in, Teddy. Door's open." Then she scrambled into her bedroom, searching for her shoes.

"Found them!" she exclaimed as she dragged a pair of red espadrilles from beneath the bed. But the moment she stood up, the shoes fell back down to the floor.

"Ava?"

Standing there in front of Lila, a duffel bag flung over her shoulder, was her long-lost sister. "Is it really you?" Lila cried as she ran toward the beautiful, fragile woman whom she'd missed every day for a decade. She wrapped her up in her arms and drank in her scent.

"It's me," Ava whispered, holding her sister tight.

"Thank God you're back." Lila buried her face into Ava's neck. "Thank God."

They stood holding each other, sometimes crying, sometimes laughing, for what felt like hours.

When Ava pulled away, Lila felt her eyes on her, studying her closely. "Your hair?" Ava said. She paused, looking at her sister as she ran her hand through Lila's still short, white-blond hair. "So, I wasn't crazy," Ava said. "It *was* you?" she said. "Everything was such a fog that night, that terrible night, but your face was the one thing I remembered clearly. You saved me, didn't you?"

Lila didn't know what to say. She couldn't lie to her sister, but she also couldn't tell her a secret she'd promised Teddy she'd never spill.

"Okay. You don't have to answer. But . . . how is it possible?"

"I've seen so many impossible things since you've been gone. But you returning is the best one of them all," Lila said with a smile.

"It feels so good to finally be home," Ava said as she squeezed her sister until Lila thought she'd break. Lila saw that underneath the joy, there was so much sadness still in her sister's eyes. Lila grabbed her hands in hers and kissed her sister's tear-soaked cheeks.

"Lila, I need to say something to you." Ava closed her eyes and let out an anguished sigh. She looked at the ground. "I'm so sorry I wasn't here for you and Mom. And when I found out she died . . ." The words caught in Ava's throat, and she fell silent for a moment. "When I heard she died, all I wanted was to come home, to call you, to be there for you. But I was too scared. I didn't want to go to jail for the rest of my life. But there hasn't been one day that I haven't thought about you, and missed you, and wished I was right here with you."

"Look at me," Lila said. But her sister's eyes were still focused on the ground. "Ava, look at me."

Ava slowly lifted her head. The two sisters' eyes met. "That's all in the past, okay?"

"Can you ever forgive me?"

Lila threw her arms around her sister, who began to sob. "Ava," she whispered. "Of course. We're back together now. That's all that matters. Mom understood. We both always knew you were innocent. It was never a question in our minds."

She felt Ava hold her closer as their grief and sorrow began the long, slow journey to forgiveness and love. Lila knew it would take time. But she had her sister back, and it was better than she had ever dreamed.

"Knock. Knock." Lila looked up to see Teddy standing in the doorway with Conrad hovering close behind him. Her already radiant smile grew even brighter.

"Ava," she said to her sister, taking her hand firmly in her own, "I'd like to introduce you to someone very special."

"Conrad," Teddy said as he reached out to shake Ava's hand for the first time, "I'm delighted to say it'll be three people for lunch today."

"Splendid, sir," Conrad said with a bow. "Just splendid."

NEW FROM LIV SPECTOR

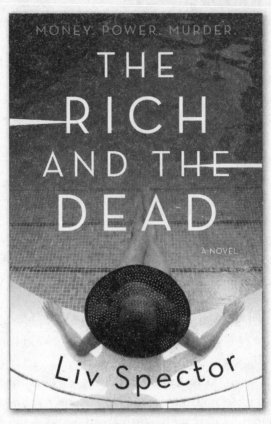

THE RICH AND THE DEAD
A Novel
Available in Paperback and eBook

Welcome to Star Island, where Miami's wealthiest residents lead private lives behind the tall gates of their sprawling mansions. It's a blissful escape from the hot and dirty city—or it was, until New Year's Day 2015, when twelve of the most powerful people in the world were found murdered in the basement of a Star Island mansion. The massacre shocked the nation and destroyed the life of investigator Lila Day. Her hunt for the Star Island killer consumed her. But the case went unsolved, resulting in her dismissal from the Miami PD. Now, three years later, life hands Lila an unexpected second chance: reclusive billionaire Teddy Hawkins approaches Lila and asks her to solve the case. But how do you investigate a crime when all the leads have long ago gone cold?